THE Forest ON THE Hill

Richard Girling

THE VIKING PRESS   NEW YORK

To
LES MANLEY
Devonian

Many people helped, but I have to thank Jo Cox, of the University
of Exeter, for her invaluable advice on local and ecclesiastical history;
Ilsington farmer and local historian Dick Wills for so generously
giving access to his own notes and documents; and the Master and
Fellows of Corpus Christi, Cambridge, for their kindness and
hospitality during Lent Term, 1980.

Copyright © 1981 by Richard Girling
All rights reserved
Published in 1982 by The Viking Press
625 Madison Avenue, New York, N.Y. 10022
Originally published in Great Britain under the title *Ielfstan's Place*.

LIBRARY OF CONGRESS CATALOGING IN PUBLICATION DATA
Girling, Richard.
The forest on the hill.
1. Devon—History—Fiction. I. Title.
PR6057.I68F6   1982   823'.914   81-69973
ISBN 0-670-39187-5   AACR2

Printed in the United States of America
Set in Garamond

CONTENTS

Okehampton

Exeter

Chagford

Moreton-
hampstead

R. Bovey

Manaton

R. Teign

Bovey
Tracey

Haytor ▲

ILSINGTON

Teignmouth

Widecombe in the
Moor

Kingsteignton

Princetown

Ashburton

Buckfastleigh

Torquay

R. Dart

Totnes

Brixham

Dartmouth

Kingsbridge

Scale in miles

0 1 2 3 4 5

ENGLISH
CHANNEL

Author's Note

The real history of Ilsington will be written one day: a faithful account of real people and their real deeds that will exceed in drama, colour and unlikelihood anything I have been able to imagine. For although Ilsington is a real place (a rambling, half-wild parish under the peak of Hay Tor, 16 miles from Exeter on the south-eastern border of Dartmoor), this is not its "real" history. Nor, in the strictest sense, is it even a "reconstruction" of that history. It is too frankly fictional for that. And yet: the history of Ilsington, an ordinary English village, is the very substance of it.

The Forest on the Hill tells its story not as an unbroken saga of names, events and dates, but through a collection of stories, or vignettes, each one (in ambition, at least) the reflection of an age. They begin with the innocent barbarisms of the Palaeolithic hunters, many thousands of years before anyone thought even to identify the place with a name; end with the fractured innocence of the First World War. In the intervening centuries Ilsington, like any other blameless rural parish, falls victim to invasion, epidemic and civil war; and to the brutal disinterest of metropolitan governments. Yet, despite all, it survives with its spirit intact. The jump between chapters is sometimes a handful of years, sometimes several hundred, as the pace of history dictates. By inventing characters and writing stories about them I have of course abdicated all pretension of "accuracy"–though the background historical detail is as true as I can make it. If the result anywhere rings untrue, or seems unfaithful or uncaring of its subject, then I hope this will be taken as a failure of accomplishment rather than of design.

Richard Girling 1981.

WILD HORSES

The tundra grass lay smashed and sour where the animal had lain. Already the bed was cold, although the body that had warmed it was still only a tree's length distant. Slowly, a creature of great bulk was dragging towards the lower terrace, its heavy movements made clumsy by the dead weight of a wounded foot. On its back, long red hairs glistened coldly, clogged with dew; on its hind leg, where the tendons had been cut, the wool was tarred with old blood.

It was early. The sun's rays were still flat and pale, but already the life was draining from the animal. At each wrench of the limb, his head pecked a little lower and the body twisted more acutely across the path. As the strides shortened to half-strides, and the half-strides shrank to nothing, he plucked for comfort at a bush, nudging his shoulders into the damp fronds and greening his tusks on the leaves. Distantly inside him, a warning sounded. As sharply as he was able, he raised his head and spread his ears. Far below, on the rim of the marsh, there had been a movement.

On the plain, it was the day of the mares. At the end of their journey north to the summer ground, their bodies were heavy with new life. Within a circle of stallions and maiden females, they had settled on the dry earth to wait. From the flat mud-pan that cradled the tail of the estuary, the country was theirs to command: no movement could escape the eyes of the sentinels, nor scent evade their nostrils. Yet their composure was as brittle as horn. The first whimpers of unease had stirred small eddies of alarm on the fringes of the group, quickening inward when the mammoth turned the hill. As the reek met them fully on the wind, sharpened by the taint of wolf, a young stallion rose up and screamed a warning that choked in a tumult of hooves. Exposed in the wake of the herd, the pregnant mares,

I

too, struggled to their feet and threshed themselves to run.

The mammoth watched as the horses swept along the riverbank, then sank back dully into his bush. Further away than he could see, the mud-spurts had turned dangerously to spray. As the leading animals felt the first tug of the deepening marsh, the stampede piled up and flooded back on itself, torn by the conflict of perils. In a mist of hot breath they turned to face the empty plain behind them. By the time the sun had risen above the high terrace, their eyes were calm again; their flanks no longer heaved and they were on solid ground, bending to their food. At the heart of the group, the mares had settled at last to sleep.

A soft rain gathered in the roof shadows and beat down gently on the rock. When the man stretched out his hand to catch it, the silver droplets broke across his palm, ice-cold and heavy. Beneath his fingers on the cave floor, the water was beginning to stand in points, building the tiny limestone nipples that could draw blood from careless feet. He caught another drip and extinguished it between finger and thumb; then carried the moisture to his lips and returned again to the hard studs on the floor. The question was still there in his eyes when the woman touched him on the shoulder.

The people were ready. They stood at the lower entrance to the cave, waiting for him. This great vault in the rock was where he had led them, many winters ago, when the first headman had died for want of food. Here they had found the wintering bears and had speared them as they slept, thankful for the flesh and the fur. But now the new year's bears had been awakened by the warmer weather and could not be approached even by the bravest hunter. The bones of the last kill lay blackening in the fire that still filled the cave with its spicy tentacles of juniper. A new season had come. The same sun that had fed the bears would also feed the people. The softened earth would more easily give up its roots; and soon the bushes would yield their seed-filled fruits. But still the people needed meat.

A wisp of breeze cooled the skin and fluffed the men's furs as they turned towards the high ground that lay between the cave and the river. The headman numbered them: a man for each finger on both hands, a boy for each thumb; and himself, an old man. He had lived many years, and the weight of leadership was heavy. But the people were young and needed his wisdom as they needed food. He must not deny them. Before the sun had touched the top of the sky, he had found the track of the mammoth.

A furrow of churned earth on the bed of a dried cataract showed where it had fallen and split its foot against the rocks. The blood had soaked into the silt, leaving a ragged stain from which a broken trail led upward over the hill. Where it passed over hard ground or rocks the blood was still sticky, and the men dabbed their fingers and carried it to their tongues. In their bellies the appetite stirred and they willed the old man to hurry.

At the mammoth's sleeping-place he prodded the warm dung and shaded his eyes to the sun. The animal was close: before their shadows grew long, they would be upon it. But instead of following the trail directly, the headman led his people behind the hill, away from the river. They would cross the ridge higher in the valley, so that they would be ahead of the weakened animal, and downwind. Then they would take it by stealth.

But when they did break the skyline the men found themselves further upriver than they had wanted. There was no mammoth; not even the mark of a mammoth. Only a herd of horses, peacefully grazing. The young men grinned and jabbed their fingers, but the headman signalled his tiredness and pulled his fur about him to sit. His legs hadn't the speed for horses.

Within the herd, the first foals had come. On soft wet legs they struggled to meet the demands of life. By nightfall, any animal not strong enough to move with the herd would be meat for a cat, or for the hyenas that skimmed the plain for placentas. Again the lookouts were restless. They lashed their flanks with dark muddy tails, and seldom lowered their heads. On the air came something too faint to recognise. But something, all the same, that was foreign. A threat.

When at last the men revealed themselves, making wild mouth-noises as they ran from cover, the herd broke inwards upon itself. The animals barged and wheeled in a thickening swirl of dust. Some were trying to run from the men: others fought back to escape the marsh. A pale stallion, the colour of wet sand, punched the air with his forelegs and was at once swept aside by the pressure of the pack. Beneath him as he squirmed, a gritty, sticky foal was silently crushed. And then the tide was flowing again, nose to tail and flank to flank, back along the bank downriver. Only one full-bellied mare, staggering with her burden, was too heavy to rise before the hunters had closed their cordon.

For a moment she stood her ground, hooves splayed wide and forward, as if she were pulling against some unseen powerful force. Her head plunged angrily, and a foreleg nagged at the mud. The nagging quickly became a pounding, and she snapped at them with her teeth. But still the men came on. Overlaying a sweet, strange smell, they bore with them the terror scents of bear and cat. Knowing her peril, the mare shuffled her hind legs and stammered anxiously back, a small step at a time, until she felt her hooves beginning to cut into the moistening ground at the marsh's edge.

She was racked by the weight of the foal, yet fear multiplied her strength. Like a cat she gathered herself: one last effort, to pummel the air at her challengers' heads. Down she splashed, then up a second time, to fall with a jolt that brought a sudden movement from inside: a flutter, like a bird, then a tearing and a fork of pain. Before even the first stone had struck her shoulder, the choice had been made. Her rump, palely encrusted with dried earth and dung, darkened in the storm of water flying from her hooves. And then she was wallowing, belly deep, in the marsh. Up she went again, hooves flailing; then up again, until exhaustion stilled her to a tremble, beyond hope. Behind her, the water slapped and sucked as the men thrashed into the shallows with their spears and flints and sharpened bones.

It was a flint axe that calmed her, splitting against the bone and flooding her eyes. The pain soaked out of her, and she stretched her neck quietly along the water, as if to sleep. Once, only once, she looked back at the froth of yellow and pink that billowed into the water from her belly. Beneath her tail, like new buds, the front hooves of the foal hung limp and wet, the birth arrested by the shaft that had fastened it through the mother.

The mare felt nothing as the men began to drag at her hooves. On the firm ground, in the crimson dew where another mare had dropped her foal, a boy picked up a strand of something, sniffed it, and tried it in his teeth.

4

On the ridge, the headman drew himself up. The men were looking to him, and he clapped his hands and chattered. They had hunted with skill. Soon, he knew, they would be able to find food on their own, without him. He had shown them the magic. Now they must return with the meat to the women in the red cave. For himself, hunger was nothing to be feared. He would journey alone to the far rocks, to see what food lay in the new lands beyond. Here, in other summers, the men had drunk the blood of ox and reindeer. At nightfall he would turn his face to the river again. He would sleep at the hunting cave in the green country, and at sunrise he would return to his people.

The climb was long and steep. The length of his shadow told the headman also that it was slow. Behind his legs, where the muscles gathered in small hard bunches, there was the pain of a whole winter's march; and his chest cried out in its craving for breath. At a stream he drank and rested, and suffered the disobedience of his body. From some bitter depth within him, he spat up the morning's bear-meat, clutching his fingers to his belly as the spasm racked him. He sensed the weakness in himself, and felt the thinness of his limbs. In his head, he numbered his summers. One each for the fingers and thumbs of his hands; one each for the fingers and thumbs of his woman and their son; and one each for the fingers of the one-armed man.

From the river, the far rocks had seemed small, a bony ridge like the brows of an ox. When the headman reached them, they looked down on him like a mammoth at a cat. From the high summit he could see the broadening of the river, and the red-stone ridge that hid the people's cave. Behind him, where the sky was pale as ice, he saw nothing that he knew. No animals moved, and there were no food plants; only thin sharp grass and rock. The headman looked to the green country where the hunting cave lay, and he understood that night would be there before him. For an instant, he hungered for the home cave, and for the warmth of the woman. But then he opened his fur and looked down at himself, and he knew that the woman no longer stirred him. His body was cold, like a fallen deer, and there was sleep in his heart. As he stretched along the rock shelf, careless of the wind, he carried a picture of warm stone and summer terraces long ago.

From the pinnacle across the valley, the mammoth caught the last slight movement of the man. And then he slept.

CIRCLE OF LIGHT

The bee boy was wrong in his head. In the cold months he lay in his hut like a wintering mouse, not caring to poke his nose out of doors. In spring, when the queens stirred from their hibernation in search of new nesting places, he too stirred, throwing off his lethargy like larval skin. All sumer long he brimmed with a hunter's energy and seemed to need no rest. No bee was safe from him. No sooner had the first workers begun to sip than he was down on his haunches to pry. Some nests were inside old trees that had been carved out by fire or by time, but most were underground, in burrows or mouseholes. By flitting with the bees, from bush to flower, and flower to nest, he came to know them all. The people saw strong magic in him and were afraid. They saw that he could endure the stabs of a cloud of bees and suffer no pain. They saw him pick up bees and pluck their barbs with his fingers. When the pollen was heaviest, and the insects were dusted all over with yellow, he would suck the sweetness from their bodies and bite into the downy shell, where the body juices were too bitter even for the birds. The bee boy wore a deerskin coat. Inside it, against his skin, he brought living bees which, in the dark of his hut, he kept in upturned clay beakers. Throughout the season, he broke into the nests and stole honey for the village. Yet he was no savage. As the years mellowed him, the wild white eyes showed more of their inner gentleness and he came to know his bees as a chieftain knows his people; he learned to lure them into nesting holes that he had hollowed out for them with an antler, and he covered them with broken slabs that he could lift to take the honey. The bees, too, found an understanding, and swarmed across his arms and face in peace. The bee boy could speak no words; neither could he hunt deer, nor build nor sow. Yet the people feared the spirit in him, and brought him gifts.

To the chieftain and to the priests, the bee boy was a demon. They, too, feared the devil in him, but they knew that they must drive it out. The gods demanded it. So it happened that on the day the sun stood longest in the sky, the chieftain went alone to the tall stone on the hill, where his father lay, and set down an offering of meat. All day and all night he rested by the stone; and in the morning, with his spirit refreshed, he returned to the village. He cut short the hubbub as the people came out to greet him, and bade them remain by their huts. At the hip of his woollen coat he wore an axe and the copper dagger that some traders had brought from far away over the sea. His hand rested on the hilt as he walked alone out beyond the houses, downhill across the stream bank and beyond the people's view on to the lower terrace.

The shadows of the tribe grew hard and sharp as they waited; and then the bee boy called. On this day at last he had felt an impulse too strong to be contained. It was the first cry of his adult life, wordless and brutal. Some people took it for the bell of a stag; others for the scream of a wounded hound. Only a few men, who had known battle, were sure that it was the voice of a man. Alarmed, they drew their axes and made a line, shoulder to shoulder as if for war, waiting for their chieftain's command. But no call came. Some ragged black birds, put to flight by the commotion, flapped out of the bushes in a line for the village, veering sharply away as they saw the people. In the far distance an animal nipped the silence with a single sharp bark; then nothing moved, no one spoke. Tiny birds of fear fluttered in the stomachs of the chieftain's sons. They caught each other's glances, each waiting for another to show a sign. It was the priests who stepped out of line first; and then all the people ran down the hill in a fearful, babbling herd.

The chieftain lay on his back with his head propped against a mossy pillow of rock. A hut's length from his feet was a small dark hole in the ground and a stone slab, newly-upturned, where the earth-grubs still hurried from the light. Around the hole dashed a small number of black bees, angry and eager to fight. The rest of the colony, coiled and bunched with the temper of a single animal, seethed in a horde around the body, jostling for positions like dogs at a banquet. The man's fingers lay quietly throbbing at his side, while the outline of his head was obliterated by the density of the swarm. The bees held themselves high on their legs, steepening their abdomens to pump the venom deep. Then, mischief done, they would grow anxious for their own lives, fighting back against the weight of the swarm, exhausting themselves in the struggle to escape the snares of clothing and hair, and twisting in frantic attempts to loosen their barbs from the skin. Some

8

were already dead, hanging as slack as berries. As the fury abated, a parting in the throng showed one of the chieftain's eyes, open and staring. Inside his mouth a bee was trapped and crushed against his palate by the swelling of the tongue.

Crouched by his side, the bee boy rocked on his haunches, watching through his fingers with loud crying eyes as the man grew purple and choked. When the people came, he rose with a whimper and ran fast into the trees, not stopping until he knew he was lost. In the people's minds, strands of fear and confusion made knots in their comprehension. A devil was loose. Only the old nurse, silently within herself, held a secret understanding. The bee boy was wrong in his head. And the chieftain was dead.

The nurse had never had children of her own, nor even a man. But she had given all her devotion and care to the chieftain's family, his five sons and a daughter. The boys had all left her now. One of them, the eldest, had died in her arms as a child: taken, the priests had said, by a demon. In the night he had grown hot and spiteful, and for two days he had trembled like grass. Then on the third night he had screamed with the demon's own voice and the life had flown out of him. With fear and ceremony they had burned his body on the hill, and had scattered him wide. But his magic had lingered on. Within two summers a second brother had gone. One day early, while the sun was still young in the sky, he had walked out of the village with his axe in his belt and had passed beyond the high rocks towards the pools. The marks of his feet had shown clear for many days in the drying mud, but they had been the only sign. No man ever saw him again.

Now the chieftain's three living sons were nearly men. One had already taken himself a wife and, in their bodies at least, the others were ready to do likewise. Their fecundity had been robustly celebrated, in ways that had earned them beatings from their father: if they wanted women at this time in their lives, then it was not the nurse that they craved. Secretly she grieved her loss, but she had made herself take comfort in the companionship of the daughter, a tiny dark girl six years old. Between the two of them they had forged a union made doubly strong by its natural impermanence. In time the girl, too, would grow away from her; and the nurse's day would be done. They were much alike, the child and the woman, in body as much as in spirit. Both were tall, slight and delicate, marked out by their frailty among a people of short stature and bullish strength.

The girl was greatly affected by the death of her father. She squatted in the furthest corner of the house with her head pressed into her robe, and would take no food. The nurse brought her meat and fruit, and cracked nuts with her teeth, but nothing would move her. Honey and milk were thrown like offal at the fire, and she would not stir her feet. Only at the hour of her father's burying, when the priests had decreed that she must remain concealed within the hut, did she rise up and deliberately show herself. The procession had gathered, flickering, by the stream at the foot of the stone avenue. Ahead of it, uphill, stood the tall stone and the circle of light. In the trees, the night birds were beginning to call, even though the sun still lived on in the sky. In her spine, the nurse felt the touch of ice. She knew she should bring the girl inside, by physical compulsion if necessary, but she too felt the need to watch. Together they sat on a stone, their arms about each other's bodies, and waited. No word passed between them; but the shared guilt brought them enduringly closer.

Nearby in the village, two of the long-legged hunting dogs snapped over the remains of a deer that had been cast aside on the morning of the chieftain's death. The stump of an arrow, grimed with blood and dust, still jutted from beneath the animal's jaw like a broken tusk. Winged insects with bright bodies busied themselves in the dogs' jaw-marks, and there was a bad smell. With the discreet wisdom of the evenly-matched, the dogs sparred and snarled in ritual contest before settling at opposite ends of the meal, each to take his share. They locked their teeth into the flesh and growled fiercely, as if to quell a living enemy, spreading their forepaws and wrenching with long angry sweeps of their heads. Behind them, circling at a distance, the smaller, younger dogs lolled their tongues and awaited their turn.

From the hill came a low rhythmic chanting as the funeral procession began to move, two by two, from the flat boulder along the stone avenue towards the circle, where fires already burned. Again the nurse felt the touch of ice, and pressed her cheek against the small dark head nestling on her shoulder. In shape at least, the bee boy had not returned. But the people were afraid, and the priests had spoken of bad magic. There had been talk of a new circle, and the chief of the priests had been to the hilltop with his measuring thong. They feared cruel spirits had escaped from the dark crowded tombs of the field people whose lands they had taken.

The nurse had told no one of her doubts, but the demons did not disturb her. Too often she had crossed their path, accidentally at first and then, as she had grown bolder, by design. And yet no ill had befallen her. Perhaps she was a charmed spirit; perhaps she was a demon herself; perhaps there were no demons at all. She did not know, but still she felt unthreatened by their magic. It was the priests themselves who frightened her. From wandering metal traders she had learned of a circle far beyond the furthest hill where, it was said, a young brother and sister had been put to death to appease the spirits that had taken their father. Their bodies had been burned, and the priests had scattered the ashes like seed across the sanctum. Now the priests of the nurse's own village had demons to appease. She tightened her grip, and the girl responded with a shiver.

On the ridge-top, where it commanded the hills and valleys all around, the granite circle thickened and filled as the procession funnelled between the stones. Fires flickered and flashed as bodies moved across them, and the light glinted once on something metal. The men's throbbing chant gave way to the call of a single, bird-like voice, high-pitched and shrill; then the chorus throbbed again and stopped. In the silence, broken only by coughing in the smoke, they raised red clay cups to their lips and drank long cold draughts of the sacred barley beer. When the procession moved again, to the burying place, the priests walked at the head, followed by four shuffling men whose progress was made awkward by the weight of a shared burden. Behind them came the chieftain's sons; and behind them, the people. The men's lips were still, but from a place near the back of the column, where a stumbling figure was supported between two others, the wailing voice of a woman called upon the spirits in her grief. The nurse raised the child's face and asked the question with her eyes, but again the girl shook her head. No, she would not go into the house.

Dark streaks were beginning to draw across the sky as the people laid their chieftain to rest. He was doubled over with his chin almost to his knees, lashed together with thongs like the trussed carcass of a stag. A small coffin of thick stone flags had been sunk into the soil, in a pit scratched out with antlers and flints. Into this tiny chamber the body was tucked as neat as a wintering mouse. The cold hard stone was lined with the chieftain's buttoned woollen robes, and he was given the pick of his earthly possessions as comforts to his spirit. Beside him were laid his bow, his arrows and a stone wrist-guard; then a decorated ceremonial beaker, and his copper hunting dagger, crumpled at the tip where he had once tried to dismember a calf. The rich dimpled metal was too soft to cut with, and he had later worn it purely for ornament, ostentatiously, as a symbol of his kingship.

In recent days there had remained only one thing on earth which had been more precious to him than this copper dagger. He had admired his two elder sons and had mourned their deaths; but he had been able to find little pleasure in the three who survived. They did not measure with their brothers. They lacked strength, both in their bodies and in character, and they had disappointed him. Neither, lately, had he cherished his wife, but had cast her aside when she failed any longer to please him. The full depth of his love he had shown only to the youngest child, the gentle one, his daughter.

The girl, too, had felt the special bond which daughters share with their fathers. When her mind was ready to acknowledge it, the grief, too, would be of a special kind. But for the moment her eyes had the numbed detachment of a wounded doe: pained but not understanding. She felt the gap in her life but had yet to see the enormity of it. Her head held no picture of tomorrow. Around her the shadows congealed into night as the last rocks were placed on her father's mound. The people showed black against the sky, their outlines smudged by the faint wraiths of smoke that stood up from the glowing carpets of embers. At their backs, a wafer of moon lit the silver rim of a cloud and caught the white faces of two field people who had moved to the foot of the hill to watch. The girl saw them start like deer and bound backwards into the field-scrub. Her limbs had grown cold and stiffened against the rock. This time, when the nurse raised her eyes, she nodded quickly and allowed herself to be lifted. The feeling had drained from one leg and a foot, and the woman had to support her for a moment before she could bear her own weight and walk to the hut.

Behind them the chant grew suddenly louder as the priests led the people back into the circle of light; and then it stopped. The sounds of night seemed to swell, as if to fill the silence. Somewhere underfoot, a gargle of running water spoke out like a chorus of arguing voices. Unseen, high above, a rush of dark wings drummed the air and faded into the forest. The nurse had quickened when the chanting rose, but she turned and froze as it stopped. The people stood silent as stones in the circle of light. Only the pale robes of the priests were moving, slowly downhill towards the houses. Fear hollowed the nurse's belly and thinned her breathing. Already, then, the time had come. She had begged herself that it might be otherwise, but how could it be? There could be no other way; no escape from the decree of the spirits. They could not run, for they hadn't the strength. And even if they did flee, to enter the wild country could bring them only another kind of death.

Inside the hut she petted the girl and rubbed comfort into her limbs. Fear passed between them. When the two priests entered, they found the girl clasped tight in her nurse's embrace, cheek pressed to cheek and arms entwined as if they would never part.

There was no pause. In the light of the moon, which beamed through the opening with the power of day, the chief priest stepped forward with his arms outstretched towards the princess. Between his hands hung something thin and dark, like a knotted thong. His head was bowed almost to his chest so that his eyes, which he kept fixed upon her face, slanted narrowly upwards from beneath the heavy ridge of his brow. He moved slowly, dragging his feet until the hem of his woollen robe brushed the girl's bare foot. Then he raised his head and spoke in a ringing, well-rehearsed voice, loud enough to be heard from the hill.

To the new queen he offered the gift of some shiny blue beads and the blessings of her people.

JULIUS SABINUS

The fire had been dead for many months, maybe even for years, though the grass still kept a distance from the poisoned black slabs of its embers. No ash stirred; not even when a soldier chopped into it with a boot. His leather heel cut a sooty black imprint that oozed a pearly glaze of water. The firepit lay amid a low circle of stone that had once been the wall of a house. Within the circle, everything was brittle, dead and wet. Outside, the grass was dry and softer than a senator's bed. The fatty bounce of the turf, stiffened by a wiry mattress of tiny purple flowers, was a welcome salve for feet long punished by rock.

The hut tribe, keepers of the fire, had gone – beaten from the slopes by long centuries of relentless rains. It might have been a year since they left; or a thousand. In all his lifetime of travel, the centurion Julius Sabinus had never seen a place more desolate than this. His mind roamed back over the days before the invasion, prompting a thin, sour smile of reluctant amusement. When they had been ordered to sail here from Gaul, the legions had stood on the very brink of mutiny. They had looked out across the stormy sleeve of water, and they had balked like horses at a ditch. Only the oratory of Aulus Plautius had recaptured their hearts as Romans; and he would never be able to carry them again. Julius Sabinus well knew that if any soothsayer among the men had seen a clear picture of the land ahead, then not even Juppiter and Mars together could have moved them.

He stared up at the grey boulders squatting on the hilltop, each one as massive as an Emperor's bath-house. He looked at the tumble of broken rocks in the valleys; and at the jumbled walls, crusted with lichen. A wilderness. And yet, somewhere within its raw cold clutch, the stone must hold a vein of wealth. The ball of clinker at his feet was spongy and tinged with red; and the same rich colour was burned into

14

the earth around a small but well-worn pit. In the corner of the ruin stood a large flat-topped stone, chipped and smoothed by hammering: an anvil.

Julius Sabinus wrapped his kilt about his knees and sat, leaning back on his hands to take the weight from his feet. There were no blisters, for twenty years in the Imperial Service had thickened the skin to a horny yellow rind. The pain was deeper, in the bones themselves. He knew that age had begun to dismantle him, and that the landing from Gaul had taken more out of him than a man of his years could hope to restore.

The campaign had begun well enough. After beaching at Rutupiae in 43, they had easily smashed the armies of Caractacus and Togodumnus, and had marched on westward with their appetites sharpened for rich and mighty conquests. But after only a few leagues they had been brought up against a further impediment: a teeming river guarded on the further bank by another clamorous army of war-painted Britons, whose tempestuous squalling had reminded Julius Sabinus of a colony of seabirds. Without respite until nightfall they had bawled across the flood in their meaningless foreign tongue. But then, while the estuary was blanketed in sleep, a troop of Gaulish swimmers had cut silently through the water and paunched the Britons' chariot horses with their javelins. Bearing the rank of *Primipilus*, the most senior of his legion's sixty centurions, Julius Sabinus had swum behind the young Gauls at the head of the main force. There had been no Silver Eagle to rally the legionaries in the dark, so he had drawn them forward by yelling out the Oath to the Emperor, fighting the weight of his armour as he kicked against the current in midstream. Afterwards, with the battle won, he had found a ribbon of pain, knotted at the back beneath his belt and streaking down behind his leg.

Now, after four more years of marching, he understood that the pain would never leave him. Perched on the anvil, he swivelled his buttocks to relieve the pressure, though he knew it would be only a matter of moments before it gripped him again. The sweat of the day's march had chilled him bitterly. Far away to the south, the sea looked flat and untroubled; but the power of the wind told him that the waves would be steep and bruising. He needed to blink hard to steady his focus, for his eyes were rimmed with fluid. Every morning when he awoke, he had to bathe his eyelids in water before he could unmesh the lashes, and each day he smeared on a poppy ointment which the legion's eye-doctor had given him. But he wasted no hope on it. Throughout the army, the eye disease had an unshakeable hold. The men accepted it, and had grown accustomed to pursuing their enemies through a rheumy, yellow-grey fog.

On the hill above Julius Sabinus's head, approaching the rocky spur itself, the *Legatus Legionis* of the Second Augusta, the future emperor Vespasian, was also cupping his eyes against the metal glare of the sea. On the ridge, the gale plumed his cloak along the skyline like the tail feathers of a bird. Nodding at his elbow, the legion's Prefect of Craftsmen was pointing at this stone and that, and running his finger in imaginary lines along the contours of the valleys. Behind him came two mining surveyors, darting hither and thither like hunting dogs. Along the terrace below them, the legionaries lay drinking from cupped hands at an iron-tinged stream. They were the First Century of the First Cohort, supposedly the hundred best fighting men in the legion. The main body of the Second Augusta, nine full cohorts and the remaining five centuries of the First, was camped on a promontory overlooking a riverbank eleven leagues to the east. Here were six thousand battle-toughened soldiers, the pick of the Empire, being driven day to day like pack animals along a trail with no end. Julius Sabinus stabbed angrily at the red bloom in the firepit. What tributes might they reap from this battle without a foe? Iron, cattle and corn; slaves, animal-hides and dogs? Yes: among all things British, Rome's first and highest passion was the dog!

There was no disloyalty in Julius Sabinus; only the bridling impatience of a fighting man who found himself neither at peace nor at war. He was a passionate believer who yearned to be a hero for his Emperor, not a dog merchant. This mobilised inertia, in which they moved on to possess one undefended wilderness after another, was an affront to his dignity as *Primipilus* – a rank which had not been won by herding animals. From brow to foot, his skin showed the shiny white pits of honours painfully gained. He might be an old bull now, with a head of iron grey and a belly that tightened against his cuirass; but old bulls were often the most dangerous. The evidence of his own decline had whittled his temper; and if his agility or endurance were in any way impaired, then there was still no man in the legion who would dare to charge him with it.

The first seeds of his disgruntlement had been sown almost at the beginning of the campaign, not many days after the injury to his back. Following a short march, through which Julius Sabinus had limped with bellicose determination at full campaign speed, the army had come upon a second great river, lying open and undefended. Julius Sabinus had expected that they would forge across at once, to catch and eliminate the remnant of their enemy; but instead they had been ordered to lay down their weapons and pitch camp. Vespasian had announced that the Emperor Claudius himself intended to lead them across this new frontier in a procession of symbolic triumph, and they would have to wait there for him to come up with them. Immune from all possibility of attack, he had arrived at last to accept a hero's welcome, godlike in his modesty, with a full detachment of guards and an elephant train. And then, when this carnival had set a victorious first foot upon the opposite riverbank, the entire Imperial caravan had turned about and sailed off to enjoy its triumph in Rome. Julius Sabinus had flogged a legionary who complained aloud of the Emperor's vanity; but he had muted his arm and taken care not to cut the man too deeply.

In the four years that followed, the Second Augusta had swept far to the west, through the rich chalklands of the southern coast to the dead wilderness of Dumnonia. Two powerful tribes had been humbled, and twenty forts had been taken, one after another along the low spine of chalk. Among these hills Julius Sabinus had seen strange and troublesome things. Long avenues of upright stones, each many times bigger than a man, stretched for league after league and led the soldiers into huge open temples where vast boulders had been mounted in faultless circles of arches. Julius Sabinus was powerfully disturbed by the unquiet stillness of these empty places, for it seemed to him that the building was far beyond the skill and strength of the barbarians themselves. His need for spiritual reassurance had led him to erect an altar by the wayside, and to dedicate it to his own gods: to Juppiter Optimus Maximus and Victorious Victory; to Diana and Apollo; to Mars and Minerva; and to the Genius of the Land of Britain. He had offered the gods a taste of meat; had sweetened the fire with incense; and had scattered the good white wine before falling to his prayers. For several days, while the scent of the incense still clung to his clothing, he had felt newly awakened and secure. But then one morning, leading his men through a wide shallow valley, he had suddenly been assaulted by a vision of such stark barbarian power that his faith had buckled again, and snapped. Two leagues distant, rearing above a grey shimmering plain, had appeared a giant white horse, more vast and more terrible even than any creature of fable or legend. In a single stride, Julius Sabinus had thought, it might vault a mountain or straddle a sea. It was the most awesome icon he had ever seen: carved into the chalk to oppress the spirit of all it gazed upon. The legion had swung away sharply to the south, and increased its speed of march until it was safe behind a further wall of hills.

Even after four years, Julius Sabinus had found no understanding of such images; nor of the stone temples, which even the native people themselves were careful to avoid. Rather than stone, they seemed to worship a particular kind of tree, a forest giant with a massive, squat trunk and dense canopy of round-toothed leaves. Julius Sabinus had become aware of shadowy moonlit ceremonies, moving among groves of these trees; and he knew that they were especially venerated when they supported another, more mysterious, plant which twined around their limbs and would sometimes yield pearly white berries. Wherever these sacred fruits were found, they would be cut by white-robed elders with golden sickles. And white bulls, too, would bare their throats to the blades, and warm the silver-cold soil with their gush.

Julius Sabinus himself was no innocent stranger in the matter of blood sacrifice, for the Mithraic cult was common throughout the Empire; but there was a coldness in the British rituals, and a menace which no amount of mess-tent banter could exorcise. To improve their harvests, the chalk hill tribes would tie a man inside a wicker basket of human shape and chant while they burned him on a great pyramid of fire. And they would foretell the future by carving the heart from a living victim and reading their signs from the contortion of his limbs. Whenever he heard tales of such gods as these, Julius Sabinus was chilled.

In great measure it had been this very raw fear which had provoked his hatred of the hill tribes, for there had been little in their military performance to inspire such dread. It was true that they had been irksome in their habit of swarming down from the heights in sudden harrying attacks, drawing pinpricks of blood on the Roman flanks before galloping back to their sanctuaries in the hills. But, whenever they had been pursued to a fortress, their riotous ill-discipline had been swiftly punished by the legion's own tight battle drills. If the Romans had been to any real degree discountenanced militarily, then it had been by the obvious futility of the resistance. The Second Augusta had been like a horned bull tormented by a wasp, seething in its anxiety to deliver one final lash of the tail.

It had happened on a clear day in the middle of the year. The legion had descended from the chalk ridge in search of a passage across a river; and there, not more than a league ahead of them, they had seen the unmistakable outline of a massively buttressed earthwork, thronged with people. Here, to judge by the bulk of it, was an important objective: the home fortress of their tormentors; the wasps'

18

nest. The cohorts had made their first approach from the west, but had immediately encountered a surprise. The fortress gate on this flank had been as narrow as a cattle pen, and so heavily defended that no attacker could hope to pass through it unscathed.

At once Vespasian had halted his advance and called his officers to counsel – an act of generalship which in itself might have been sufficient to win the day. While the Romans rested, the tribesmen loosed wild hails of slingshot which died childishly short of their mark, pattering across the chalk in harmless little avalanches of pebbles. Against such enemies as these, the fortress was Vespasian's to take as he pleased. But in this campaign he well understood that his legion was not to be consoled by tactical mastery alone.

The assault began outside the eastern entrance, after Julius Sabinus's men had fired some thatched huts to make a smokescreen. Julius Sabinus himself, eyes smarting in the smoke, had led the second wave, stooping painfully low to avoid the storm of machine arrows whirring over his head from the rear. Ahead of him his cohort standard bearer waddled awkwardly in his bearskin; and from his left, where the smoke was thickest, came the legion's Silver Eagle. The Eagle-bearer's lionskin, with the man's eyes staring fixedly between the gaping yellow fangs, was already stippled with blood. Even before the main attacking force had crossed the inner rampart, every slinger had been knocked from the tower and stabbed. The resistance had been crushed; but not yet the life. When there were no more tribesmen standing alive, then the soldiers hurled their javelins at the women and the children. When there were no more women and children, then they hacked the bodies of the dead until the smoke-stunned air was sweetly fouled by the scent of their butchered flesh. In a ditch, Julius Sabinus had found the smashed relics of some meagre homes, where slave families had lived surrounded by the stink of their own household waste. Their bodies lay one upon another on a bed of broken jars. One woman there, young, with a swollen belly, had been taken captive, and knelt with her wrists lashed behind her back. On the rampart above, a young legionary with a broken nose called down to her, and smiled, before crushing her head with a stone.

As always in battle, Julius Sabinus's sword had done the work of two, sending ripples of shock through his arm as it rang against the bones. There had been no pity in him for any enemy of the Empire. And yet, as the soldiers had wiped their eyes and taken off their helmets to rest, there had crystallised in his mind a new feeling that had been less than triumph – a feeling that more had died there among the chalk hills than a simple barbarians' village. Was this surrender to base instincts, this fear-driven defeat in victory, truly the glory that Claudius had demanded of them? Seated at his anvil, tormented anew by the stabbing in his back, he leaned forward and split a slab of clinker with his sword, opening a gash that showed red through the puckered skin of mud. His legionaries were sprawled in insolent attitudes of boredom, each man detached from his fellows in a private cell of brooding. None spoke with any other, nor showed any curiosity in the country. For the first time, Julius Sabinus looked at his cohort and saw a picture not of ebullience and enterprise, but of listlessness and failure. In the slope of their shoulders and the casual viciousness of their hatreds, he had begun to recognise the measure of their decline. And more than this: he realised with a sullen shock that their torpor was nothing less than a mirror of his own.

The *Primipilus* shook his head like a dog and made himself a soldier again. Vespasian and his assistants were coming down the slope towards him, and the Prefect of Craftsmen was pointing with a finger, sketching a plan on the terrace where the legionaries lay. So this was where they would make camp. At least there was one benefit to be had from this barren land: turf enough to enclose a whole city with ramparts, and only a few leafless bushes to be cleared. But the relief was minimal. This was the very poorest part of Britain: it had no firm government, so no coinage; and no pride among its people, who had raised not a squeak of protest against the legion's march. At least the chalk tribes, by their resistance, had shown an energy that might be turned to the Empire's advantage. Julius Sabinus shrugged bitterly. If only he could have retired a year earlier: then might he have enjoyed a climax worthy of his twenty years' service. And there would have been some real meaning to the hero's welcome which his townspeople would give him. He would still have his tribute, of course, though the gloss would be dimmed by anti-climax. And perhaps he would be elected a magistrate: a *quaestor* maybe, to collect taxes and fines, a man of position and authority . . . . Yet, for another season at least, such fancies would be idle. The army had not finished with him yet, and the way ahead stretched long and hard. He stood up and looked westward, in the direction of march, and found nothing to please him. The scarred brown desert offered little food for his belly, and none for his pride.

Attentive to his duty as Vespasian approached, Julius Sabinus stamped the life back into his legs and stood his men to their ranks. Even as he shouted the order, he was making a soldier's assessment of the camping ground. It did not matter whether the legion stayed here for a night, or for a month, or for a year. The encampment would be the same fortified township, wrapped within a solid rampart of turfs. It would be precisely rectangular, with leather tents pitched along straight roadways that would cut the site from gate to gate. To-morrow, Julius Sabinus supposed, the rest of the legion would be brought up to dig itself in. He licked a finger to chart the direction of the wind, and noted the course of the stream. The latrines, he decided, should be dug well away down the hill.

But Vespasian surprised them all. He had made up his mind: the way west was not worthy of Romans. They would turn back for the ore beneath the eastern hills.

As evening fell on their return to Isca, and the legionaries' boots slapped eagerly through the rain, Julius Sabinus caught a soldier smiling. The punishment, dealt back-handed with his centurion's vine-stick, was vicious and intentionally painful. The men were becoming flabby. Tomorrow they would have javelin practice, and a route march with full equipment.

THE PROPHET

The woman counted her heartbeats. Seven, and then a flash of lightning. Another seven, another flash. At each flash, the grey wall-stones blazed white and fixed in her mind a picture of the room.

It was a storm of unforgettable violence, and yet there was peace. Neither ox nor dog was disturbed from its sleep; neither did any child awake. Only the woman arose, feeling the rhythm of her body drawn up into the rhythm of the sky. She was conscious of no particular thought, only an awe which lay deeper within her than any mortal fear of danger. The flashes became longer, the shadows shorter, until the sky hardened into a single brilliance and the house flared as if consumed by a star. She felt no more heartbeats. Within the circular house-wall, the shoulders of the granite were dissolved in the glare, leaving a host of winged black shadows. A black wooden loom, with dangling weights of clay, threw long sharp claws across the body of her husband. The embers of the fire seemed suddenly cold, and dull as iron in the light. Outside, the rain and the wind had died to a murmur, and the night birds fell silent in the hush.

The angel came without a sound: he cast no shadow, nor stirred any dust. He was like a flame, a body of light, as if hewn from the air itself. From his shoulders flowed a weightless mist of animal skins, and in his hand was a white wooden stave, joined in the image of a cross. The woman was blinded and afraid: she covered her eyes and put a hand to the swelling in her belly, to guard the new life forming there. Slowly the angel raised his stave and struck it three times, hard upon the floor. The sound came to the woman from afar: hollow, like the beating of a drum. His voice was as loud and wild as the thunder; soft and gentle as a fawn. Even from her distance across the room, the woman felt his breath as a warm shiver in her ear. It passed through her

22

with a shudder, half coals and half ice, and made an ecstasy in her loins.

His words flowed over her then, and soothed her in the heat of her passion. "Do not be afraid. I bring you a gift, a treasure beyond wealth."

He lowered his stave and touched the cross to her belly. "From your body shall spring forth a holy child, wonderful in his power. He shall hear the command of Christ and shall forsake all comforts of the earth. Neither fruit nor flesh shall he know, and through this saint shall a firmament of souls be lifted up to heaven."

Again he bade her, for he saw that she was weeping: "Do not be afraid. From your bosom he shall be raised to a glory above men. Yet even as you are given up to your enemies, he shall be your saviour. In prayer you shall call upon him as your own true saint, that he may show you God's victory and bring you to peace. And this peace shall be for ever, among mountains cool and green."

As the light faded into night, and the vision slipped from her eyes, a bolt of thunder tore through the oak grove and blackened the ground. It brought down a curtain of mistletoe, and the mightiest of the trees.

The boy grew sturdy and was given up to his teachers. He had the strength of a man at the plough, even though he weakened his limbs by fasting. Neither his body nor his mind knew idleness, and he refused all comfort save that of prayer. Before the end of his tenth year, he had exhausted the wisdom of his masters, yet he bore their infirmities with grace, as he had borne his bodily hunger, and did not chastise them for their failings. When his beard grew, he was sent on a journey to a land of bright green mountains, across a mighty river to the north. After many days' travelling he came to a monastery near a great sea. The monastery was named Menevia. Its abbot was Dewi: called by some men David. For this was to be his soul-friend, his confessor and his master.

Along the way he walked barefoot upon the sharpest stones, so that the flesh was rent from the bones; and he would not bathe his wounds in the streams where he drank, so that his blood became food for insects and worms. In his arms he carried only a rock, to weigh the more heavily upon his feet; and he would not rest or sleep. For meat he had only the green plants of the wayside, which so poisoned his stomach that even the pure water turned to venom on his lips. His hair loosened from his head, and his skin glistened with a cold grey dew. At the gates of Menevia he fell immediately upon his knees and pressed his cheek against the wood. A thin spine of sunlight pricked the cloud and dressed him all over in gold. His head grew warm and sang with the promise of sanctity, so that he was moved to weep tears of joy, and to make a cross with his arms to receive the hands that would bear him up. Yet no man came. Within the gates the monks continued to work silently at their yokes and to answer the calls to prayer. There was no greeting for the traveller. No bread. No wine. No blessing. The brothers turned away their heads and would not look at him. For ten days and nights the young man lay declining in a fever, with neither food nor drink, and only fitful sleep. Death summoned him, and he turned his cheek to receive its kiss. He did not understand the reason for his abandonment, but he had come to welcome it and rejoice. He knew now that he had suffered for his faith, and would die a martyr and a saint.

On the morning of the eleventh day a very old monk, with spare grey hair and mottled skin, came out and opened the gate. He offered neither word nor helping hand, but only beckoned. The young man's legs staggered like a colt's, for the flesh was like liquid and would not answer his commands. Three times within the gates he stumbled, as the surge of blood rose scorching in his veins. Three times he crawled and scrambled to come up with him again, for the old man would not wait. At last, beyond one plain door and then another, the monk stood aside to let him pass. In a small bare cell, cold with dripping stone, he stood before the subject of his prayers. Ashamed and afraid, he wrapped his arms about himself to quieten the shivering.

"You have passed the test."

There was no smile on Dewi's face, nor pleasure in his voice. But the young man understood him and fell at once to his knees. He needed no rebuke, for all the folly and wickedness of his conceit were there revealed to him. With his brow touching the stone, he made confession to his master and was forgiven.

At Menevia there were many tests. To enter its gates was to shed the former life and be born anew. The postulant came naked, with no chattel to call his own, not even a book of learning; and naked he remained. His garb was stitched from the coarsest material, made raw from skins. His day was a redemptive rite of work and prayer, with little time for sleep. Idleness here was a sin: idleness of body and idleness of mind, the begetter of all sins.

One winter's evening, after a day's labour which had bruised his shoulders at the plough, the young man spoke of his pleasure in sitting at last to rest. He had exceeded his duty in the field, ploughing far beyond his allotted strip, and he was justly tired; thirsty, too, and hungry. Set out before him was his ration of herbs and salted bread; yet, as he leaned forward to eat, the abbot touched his hand and bade him rise.

"No. Not for you."

He had expressed pleasure in idleness, and this was a sin. In place of his meal, he must wait outside to pray for his own improvement, standing up to his knees in the hard cold waters of the spring. The chill of the immersion pained his legs like the slow tightening of iron bands. The thick material of his robe tugged and filled in the current, grinding an even sharper edge to the icy stabs of the wind. His whole body quivered, so that the prayer sprang from his lips in a babble. The words of it were mechanical and distant from his mind, for once again the serpent had caught him. It filled him with self-pity, and showed him a picture of himself as a victim, blamelessly persecuted.

When the meal was over, Dewi himself came out and watched quietly over the young man's suffering. He stood in deep shadow, so still that the small night animals ran through the grass even to his feet. Only when the last of the monks had gone to their prayers did he reveal himself in the moonlight and speak.

"Go now. Join your brothers at nocturns."

And immediately he took the postulant's place in the stony water. The young man looked back from the chapel door and wondered, in his shame, how it could be that his master had understood him so clearly. In penance he shunned the mattress and stood awake all night in his cell. As the darkness paled, just before the early bell, he caught the fleeting glimpse of a watching eye, pausing silently before his door and passing quickly on.

Within the monastery, Menevia gave shelter to widows and fatherless children. In his second year there, the young man came to be deeply troubled by one of these women. He did not know her name, but he had seen that she watched him and that she seemed to know his movements. As he went about the monastery he would find her standing, quietly alone, as if she were waiting. As summer ripened, he found that her image moved with him inside his head. She was a tall woman, almost as tall as the young man himself, and she walked with long swinging strides as strong as any man. Yet there was frailty too: palpable frailty in the thin smooth arms, and an inner frailty that showed in the biting of her lip. Her voice, among the other women, was as raucous as a crow's, but to the young man she never spoke a word. Only watched. He saw that her long dark hair seemed quite black until it was caught by the sun, when it would light up with an aura of rich flashing bronze.

On a night at the beginning of the harvest, his sleep was upset by a vision of this woman. In the dream he saw the shape of her body through her robe, where it swelled out and filled the rough material. The hem was raised up so that he could see the white of her knee; and her lips were softly parted to reveal the moist pink tip of her tongue, held lightly between her teeth. She was above him, looking down with unfaltering dark brown eyes. The young monk came half awake and touched himself where she had aroused him. At once the guilt spilled over him, starting him from his bed and bringing him fearfully to prayer. He did not confess the sin to Dewi, neither dare he sleep. For three nights he stood awake in his cell: urging himself, holding his mind to the subject of his prayer and the reaffirmation of his vows. Poverty. Obedience. Chastity.

On the fourth morning as he worked in the field, the tiredness jabbed into his eyes with sharp dry needles. For half the day he continued to deny himself rest, driving himself, refusing to sit until he felt himself beginning to fall; and then at last he closed his eyes, awash amid the warm afternoon sunshine, the gently wafting breeze and the low choir of insects. Instantly he slept. From far away came the relentless lapping of the ocean, moving to a rhythm. Slowly the laping came closer, the rhythm more irresistible. It filled his head until his whole body seemed consumed by its motion, faster and faster, on the flood of the tide.

He awoke. The scent of crushed grass, the flush of the sun on his skin, and the ocean's rhythm in his loins. Green stems loomed over him, and shiny yellow blooms, so close before his eyes that they seemed to explode like suns. Beyond the unfocused mass of colour, filling the sky, knelt the woman. Her eyes, though fixed upon his own, seemed far away; and her mouth, though wide as a singer's, was empty of words. Her hand beneath his robe was moving to his rhythm, the rhythm of the sea.

26

For a moment he rode upon the crests, waiting for the warm rising sea to open and break over him, unafraid to drown. And then, as he hung at the very brink of the fall, so all his fears were reawakened. The petals of the flowers hardened in his eye, and the woman shrank against the sky. As he struck out through the lake of green, he heard her furiously sobbing and calling the name of a man long dead.

On his belly before the abbot, the young man beat his head on the ground and poured out his confession in a garbled torrent of remorse. He would tear out his hair, would swallow hot embers, would flay the skin from his own back; for his contrition reached far beyond the one immediately sinful act, and encompassed the entire range of his mortal imperfections. He no longer saw any possibility of absolution and was in terrible fear for the wardship of his soul. Even as he prostrated himself, he was more than ever conscious of the unfathomable distance that lay between himself and Dewi: not only in years, but in wisdom and purity. It was a distance which a man of his own spiritual frailness could never hope to span. He shrank against the ground, cowering like a dog from the whip. The holy man's skin was parched tight against his skull, which seemed to pulse and throb with all its wisdom. His thin lips were pressed forward into a small sad knot; his eyes clenched darkly in their hollows. The two men were as distant as earth and the stars. And yet a man such as Dewi could bridge the heavens in a moment. He replied gently, with the tips of his fingers pressed one hand against the other in front of his face.

"You have been tempted, as all men are tempted. But you held fast against that temptation, as few men do. In knowing the temptation of a woman there is no sin, but only a lesson. Your surrender was to idleness, and for this alone you must seek redemption."

The penance was a hard one, but temptation was plucked off at the root. The young man's age, in this summer of flowers, was seventeen years.

As the angel had foretold, so it came to pass. The young man, in his maturity, took the word into the land and by his example led many men to God. In his home country, in the village below the high rocks, his mother had grown old. His father had died from a bursting in his stomach, leaving her to dwindle into poverty. With no man, neither husband nor son, to attend it, the great house had fallen into ruin. The room that had been a church tumbled in upon itself, so that not a stick remained standing in its allotted place. For a while longer, worship went on outside, before a simple stone cross on the flat ground between the houses. But news came to them of a new people approaching from the east: a race of heathen men with foreign tongues and warlike habit. All Christian believers in their path were to be put to the sword, and their churches to the torch. From all around the old woman, the families were fleeing in their hundreds: landward to the west, and across the sea to the distant country called Armorica.

At last she was sure, as she stood alone before the cross, that the angel in the bright vision of her youth had spoken truly. She prayed, and prayed again, that it might be so. Now truly, as the angel had avowed, was she given up to her enemies. Now truly, as he had avowed, did she call upon her son as her own true saint, to show her God's victory and bring her to peace.

Peace for ever, as the angel had foretold, among mountains cool and green. Perfect peace.

On the morning when at last he stood before her, she knew him for a holy man before even she knew him for her son. He was tall, thin to the bone, and solemn. His eyes were shrouded by the high peaks of his brow, and a cascade of fine white hair sprang in long sparse tufts from the toothless hollows of his cheeks. He carried nothing save a plain white stave of some knotty wood, which he held loosely in his fingers. He tapped with it as he walked, but never suffered it to bear the weight of his body. At the instant she saw him, the old woman was touched by his aura: even in the silence of his standing there, she felt a deep mystical power that compelled obedience. He chilled her as the angel had chilled her. Yet even as she had been willing him to come, night and day in her prayers, still she did not know him until he spoke.

"Mother."

The cavernous eyes and thin pale lips at last found a place in her memory. Sharper than any remembered vision, they recalled the face of her husband, worn out, gaunt and old beyond his years, as he had seemed to her on the day before his death. She fell to her knees and pressed her lips to his feet, mopping the tears with her hair. He blessed her, then gently raised her to embrace.

"Mother. My mother. I have come to take you."

"I have prayed that you would." She was weeping. "To a land of peace, together for ever among green mountains."

He frowned at this, for she had never told him the story of the visiting angel. "To Armorica, mother. To a monastery."

"Across the sea?"

"Across the sea."

To reach the water was a long day's walk, during the course of which they encountered many other people moving in the same direction. Their ship, which was drawn up for them on a flat of mud-grimed sand, was fully thirty paces long, and broad enough for four people to sit together at each plank. It was built of heavy oak and pine, and driven by a great square sail of red-dyed cloth. Save for some heavy stones, placed along the keel to square its balance, the only cargo was mortal. Most of the people were monks, but there were a small number of postulants, some widows, and two young families, whose small children clung tightly to their mothers. None had brought any goods or chattels, and all fell down before the old woman's son with a great display of penitence. Many begged him to hear their confessions before they sailed. The old woman herself had wondered if she should make her confession to him, but could find no words to ask. From her place high in the stern, she could look across the people's heads to the prow, where the cowled figure stood as lightly as an angel. Only once, as they struck out into the tide, did she look back along the line of the estuary, and fancy that she could see on a far-off hilltop the twin peaks of rock from which the ravens flew.

It was early in the year, and cold. A shiny dusting of frost lay along the topmost spar of the mast and stiffened the sail. The old woman's feet had already begun to pinch with the chill, and her fingers were numb where she gripped the wet oaken planking. The sky above the ship was empty and pale but, in the far distance, a thin skein of cloud was spun out along the horizon, making her believe for an instant that she was facing a low strip of land. Immediately ahead, where the tide ran free of the bay, the busily chopping waves were foam-capped and steep. But already, in the calm water, the sickness had taken hold of her, crushing her breath as the contractions gripped. The voyage was so little under way that the sound of her suffering came back to her as an echo from the dusty red cliffs.

As the country faded behind them, the swells began to lengthen and deepen. The tiny splashes as they broached the waves became heavy slaps, and the slaps became hammer blows as the wind reared up and the gathering cloud came smoking against them in long black fingers. At each crest the ship staggered and froze, held motionless by the opposing forces of wind and tide, before plunging down and staggering again. A wail went up from the children, and from among the women came the choking sobs of sickness, embittered by fear. The old woman herself could contain her terror only by thinking ahead to the new country that lay beyond the tempest. Again and again she repeated the angel's promise. Peace for ever, among mountains cool and green. She summoned a vision of Armorica, rich lands ripe with corn, where British bishops would shepherd their monasteries to a new age of golden prosperity, and her son would be hailed their saviour. She forced her eyes to remain open against the lash of the salt, and watched him through the spray. He had not drawn back from his station at the prow, even though it plunged wilder than a stallion, but held on as steadfast as faith, his body following the liquid motion of the sea, as if he were locked in some private communion with its rhythms.

All around them now, the sky was a whirl of black. The men had to furl the sail and fight to hold the ship on the oars as they cascaded through a flying wilderness of foam. On the crests, the old woman felt herself winging higher than the terns, that skimmed and screamed about her head. On the giddying descents, she was sure the prow must cleave on down and race headlong into the furthest depths. She wondered if he would bring the vessel about, and turn the helm for shelter. But even as she thought of it, she knew that he would not.

The waves increased their violence until the oars could no longer keep their hold. The ship was stunned from its course so that it veered and rushed along a trough, beam on to the breakers. In the pit of the ocean, the old woman looked up in silent awe as a green hillside bore down on her from high above the mast. The ship rolled under the cataract and was swamped. Beneath the waves, the mast parted like a trodden twig and the ballast-rocks smashed great yawning holes in the sides. As the vessel came slowly upright, bursting from the sea like a log from a waterfall, the old woman saw that all the people had gone, save only herself and her son. Still he did not flinch as the ship flew rudderless before the storm, settling ever lower as it went, until only the stern and the prow still stood above the foam. The great mass of water within the hull held it steady for an instant, as the saint turned at last to face his mother.

Slowly he raised his arms, straight out from his shoulders until they were level with the horizon. All around them, above and beyond for as far as the old woman could see, there rose towering mountains, cool and green.

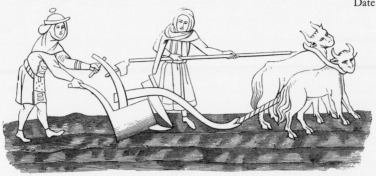

IELFSTAN'S PLACE

The dogs were barking even before cock-crow, dancing on rangy legs and fogging the air with yawns, almost as if they knew what day it was. All over the village the first needles of light were pricking beneath the curtains and doors, making pale golden spirals in the dust. In the yards of hovels, ragged men came out to untether their animals. Knowing exactly what day it was, they spat and coughed and threw insults at their wives.

Up at the hall, Ielfstan and his guests lay in vaporous disorder, smitten by the mead. Some had arranged their limbs along the benches; others sprawled with their arms across the tables. A few had abandoned themselves to the floor, where they slept on a cold pearly sheet of mutton fat. In the shadows at the foot of the wall, dark shapes lurked and darted, testing their boldness. One after another they would ripple across the floor, to steal a crumb of meat and run with it back to the nest. Morning, too, stole up on the men and took them disarmed like an enemy by stealth. Knives and swords lay far beyond reach, littered among the drinking bowls in tacky amber pools. The broadest of the blades stood solid in the table, its jewelled hilt misted with chicken grease. Caught in a slant of sun, it cut a dark shadowy bar across the neck of its master, whose head lay turned away from it on the boards. Before the wine had silenced him, when the blue pointed drinking glass had at last rolled empty from his fingers, he had been saluting his sword in song. "To a Wondrous Creature, Shaped in Strife." A chequered draughts board and twenty-four horse-tooth draughtsmen lay strewn with the scabbard around his feet.

Among all the revellers, only one had not slept where he fell. Ielfstan's chieftain, Morcar the thegn, had removed himself early to a bower and had arisen refreshed and clean-headed with the dawn. Now

31

he fanned the door like a bellows, both to rouse the sleepers and to cleanse the air of their reek. Irritably, when no one stirred, he dealt the empty iron kettle a rap with his heel, spinning it on a heavy arc so that it squealed on its chain and laid a dusting of embers in a line across the floor. Up by the hook in the rafters, the sparrows hopped and trilled; yet still not a head was raised from the table. Morcar blew out his breath and beckoned to the serving women.

"Scream," he said. "Scream, I say!" He stung their behinds with the flat of his sword, yelling in time with the blows. "Vikings! Pirates! The murderers are coming!"

Sorely hurt, the women screeched like sows, quite shrill enough to penetrate the warriors' stupor. Blind hands paddled through the mire, fumbling for their knives. Glass pealed and a bench spilled backwards, pitching two young lordlings into the swill. Morcar hooked his thumbs into his belt-thong and hugely enjoyed the joke.

"Up, brave boys, and at them! The hunt is ready! The hounds await!"

Ielfstan, who was both Morcar's tenant and his host, tripped on his garters and sprawled on his knees at the master's feet.

"Oh, what a lord! With a lake of mead in his belly, such as Grendel[1] himself might have drowned in, he rises as fresh as the dew. Had any other man drunk thus, I'd be counting the cost of his *wergeld*[2]!" He put on a show of mirth that hurt his head, and placed himself first in the race for the latrines.

Outside in the compound the hounds were boxing each other with their paws, choking on their leashes and wrestling with their handlers. Other peasants were busy with the horses, smoothing the saddle cloths and blowing warmth into their nostrils to soothe them. Animals and men packed every part of the yard and blurred their own outlines with their breath. Morcar squared himself in the doorway, hands on hips, and glared into the turmoil – combatively, as if he would challenge any man to meet him eye to eye. He was not a large man. His back was slightly humped, and his legs were bowed and of unequal length so that his gait was as graceless as a pig's. Yet his ceorls knew him as a bloody and slaughterous warrior, whose constantly itching sword-arm struck fear into all who encountered him. At times of idleness, when among those who were not his equals, his warrior's temper could lead him to acts of merciless cruelty.

Now it happened that among the houndsmen this morning was

---

[1] The lake-dwelling monster in *Beowulf*.   [2] The sum payable to the kinsmen of a dead man by the one who had slain him. In the case of a thegn, this would have amounted to 1200 shillings.

one ceorl who neither recognised Morcar, nor knew of his deeds. This man was Eadric, a new smallholder who had come only lately to the village with his bride. He was a young man of uncommon strength, broad and tall, as well-formed as Morcar was ugly. Being still young and impatient, it was not in his nature to give ground willingly, and he would admit fear of none. Instinctively he looked with disfavour upon the bow-legged little chieftain with the fine white beard, and nudged a neighbour with the point of his arm.

"Who is this old fool who wears his breeches to his ankles?"

"Hush! It is Morcar, our master's own Lord!"

"Why does he swagger thus, with his belly so full of piss?"

"Hush!"

"A piss-belly, I tell you, and drunk with a surfeit! Look, did you ever see such drunkards? Last night, while they stuffed their bellies and sang, I came to piss in their mead butt. Now they're all of them drunk with peasant's piss. It's true!"

The listener recognised the falsehood, but let it pass.

Among the huntsmen, Ielfstan himself was the last to horse. He fiddled with the brooch that fastened his cape, then dismounted again to ease his garter-thongs. The fleas had been busy, and the swell of his calf beneath the leggings was raw from the scratching. When at last he was ready to ride forward, he found that his way had been closed by an outbreak of scuffling among the ceorls. There were two of them against one, kicking up the dust in a sudden clearing of space. A huge young man with bullish chest and limbs was caught between two older men, who were fighting to pinion his arms. It was not an equal contest. Ielfstan watched in disbelief as the young man swung his hands in front of him, clapping his assailants together with a violence that robbed them of all further determination to fight. Then the man stooped, gripped each of the elders by one ankle, and threw them insolently on to their backs. Only then, as the victor plunged on through the crowd, did Ielfstan realise that, far from assaulting him, they had been trying to hold him back, to restrain him from some further act of mischief. The man had a red beard, as thick as a thorn bush, and wore a rough green shirt over bare legs. Ielfstan feared for the peace as he plunged on, shouldering between the horses to raise a finger and shout up at the thegn himself.

"My plough-ox is struck dead, master. What shall I do?"

Morcar paused for an instant before urging his horse to the gallop, taking a steady look at the young man as if to imprint the face upon his memory.

"What should you do?" he smiled. "Eat the beast before it rots."

Eadric's ox had been dead for two nights. Early in the morning on the first of the week's ploughing days, he had found it stretched on its side with its neck thrust out, as if it were reaching for grass. Its flesh was still warm beneath the skin, but a slow crimson ooze, gathering to a bright dark gel on its muzzle, forbade any hope of life. Even to Eadric, who people said knew little of animals save how to drive them, the disaster was unmistakable.

In truth the ox had been already fleshless, full of worms and half broken by overwork when he had first received it. An old smallholder, whose wife had borne him no sons, had died at the furrow behind his plough. According to the rule, his property had fallen to the manor and Ielfstan had given the order to Ulf, his reeve, to find a new tenant. No local-born man had come forward, so the land had been granted to the fortune-seeker Eadric, a wanderer who had failed to win a holding in the village of his birth. Ielfstan had welcomed him with the customary gifts: a small wooden house with tools and cooking vessels, two oxen for the plough, a cow for milking, six white-faced sheep for wool and mutton, and seven acres ready-sown with barley for bread and beer. Eadric did not know how to read the age and condition of an animal. He had driven all his beasts into the yard of his new house, and as he gazed at them it had seemed to him that he had become rich beyond his dreams.

Not all the villagers had thought it right that a stranger had been granted land; yet not one among them had envied Eadric his lot. Ale had poisoned the previous tenant, and by neglect he had poisoned the holding. The house and animals had declined beyond hope of repair; and the soil was a prisoner of the weeds. All the drunkard's property was held to be tainted, as if it were sown with ill luck and would yield only despair. More rationally, the people had seen how it had broken the spirit of one man working alone, and they held out little hope for the success of another. Because of their unease, and the resentment they felt at the admission of a stranger, they had been slow to offer Eadric their friendship. And the newcomer himself, though clearly enraptured by his fortune, did not always reward their interest. Nevertheless, when he did first provoke trouble with his neighbours, it was his good humour that was at fault, rather than any show of ill temper.

It was Eadric's habit as he worked to sing. He sang to the plough, and sang to the pigs, and sang to the jays in the wood. One day he sang to his milk cow, and so alarmed it that it bucked through a thorn hedge and gouged a strip of barley with its hooves. This was an offence. Neither his bewildered innocence nor his great strength could preserve him from the wrath of the others, and he was badly bloodied in the fight. Afterwards the reeve had come to see him, and he did not laugh either.

"Foolish churl! Next time they will catch your cow and cut its throat."

"What! For straying through a fence, they would kill my only cow?"

"It is the law."

Yet for all his mischief, and for all that he was disrespectful of his elders, Eadric was a strong and ready worker. His labour was spread thinly across the land, but he did as much as one man could. Despite their complaints, the villagers did not dislike him. They called him Eadric the Innocent.

For a year he had lived without a care, freely enjoying the fruits of his master's land. In return he had to pledge only that for two days in each week, and for three days in the corn harvest, he would work for Ielfstan in his fields. And throughout the year, in the tradition of the manor, he would have the care of a hunting dog. But now everything had changed. With the honeymoon year all behind him, the new smallholder was no different from the old; no different from Thurbrand his neighbour; no different from every other one of the anxious grey ceorls in the field. Henceforward, every year until he died, he would have to pay all the dues his lord demanded: ten pence at Michaelmas; twenty-three sesters of barley and two hens at Martinmas; and a lamb at Easter. Neither was this the end of the debt. The three acres that Eadric ploughed for Ielfstan would have to be sown with seed from his own crop, and it would be his duty to give bread to the master's swineherd.

At the very beginning, a year past, the older men had shaken their heads and warned that by his own hands alone he would not meet his dues. Now, with the ox stretched cooling in the grass, he knew the truth of it. Madselin his wife, a thin girl already grieved by her failure to bear children, had stepped out from the house to join him in his sorrow. With only one ox, Eadric could not draw a plough. He could

35

till neither his own soil nor his master's, and he would forfeit his rights as a tenant. He drew Madselin into his arms, nestling his beard in her hair.

"Wife! Don't you cry now. I shall find us another ox, a better one than this old croaker's been!"

"But we have no money. And nothing left to barter with!"

"Trust me. I shall find another ox!"

In the days that followed, Eadric's humour sharpened and soured. To the warrior thegn, departed on his hunt, he gave a new name: Morcar the Piss. And to Ielfstan's reeve – a clumsy, crimson-faced official with an ugly limp – he gave the title Flea. "For he hops from bed to bed, and fattens himself on better men's blood."

It was before this Flea that Eadric was made to lay out the story of his ill fortune; and yet he could not sufficiently lower himself to make a plea. The reeve was malformed, short in stature and physically weak. That he should stoop before such a figure was more than Eadric's pride could withstand. His petition for redress, though desperate and heartfelt, owed nothing to humility and everything to rage.

"That ox was broken and wormy. It was a cheat! Ielfstan owes me another in its place."

"It was no cheat. It lived and worked a year. Time enough to earn you the price of another."

"It was sick. You owe it to me!"

"I owe you nothing! Stupid, squanderous ceorl!"

"Then may you be cursed! May your water be poisoned, and your piss turn to blood!"

That night Eadric added ground madder root to the reeve's best beer tub. Afterwards he stood alone on the high part of the fallow ground and spoke urgently to himself. The wind had switched, sending silver-rimmed mare's tails chasing before the moon. He stared up at the black turrets of rock, high above him on the hill. Within sight of that pinnacle stood a hundred good oxen. A thousand!

Morcar, Ielfstan and the huntsmen were away two days. On the night before they returned, after he had dyed the reeve's beer red, Eadric bade Madselin a sudden farewell and slipped away through the ash wood. He killed a sheep to leave her for food and barter, but took for himself only a flat barley loaf, some fatty ribs of mutton, and his knife. Two days, he promised her. Perhaps three, but certainly no more than four. She watched him, and did not cry until he had gone. If only four days, then why waste a sheep? And why run off so quickly, with his hands still crimson from the butchering?

Early next morning, Ulf the Flea came stumping on his unequal legs, florid and excited. This unhappy man had been the choice of the people themselves to serve over them as Ielfstan's reeve; yet there had been little honour in it. The reeve's time was so much dedicated to the administration of public affairs that he had little opportunity to give proper attention to his own. It was not a job that even the richest peasant would hanker for, and Ulf had been acclaimed more out of spite than affection. This morning, Madselin could see at once, he was taut with anger.

"Your husband is not in the field! Where is he?"

"You can see he is not here. He is on a journey!"

Her eyes were dark with exhaustion, and she twisted her hands as she spoke, flinging a hail of mud-brown dough flakes from her fingers. Over the months she had caught Eadric's habit of looking down at Ulf as a figure to be ridiculed: a tiny man puffed up by authority, determined to command men's fear if he could not command their love. Ulf for his part had been abashed by the frankness of Eadric's contempt. With a confidence fed by his enormous advantages in strength and size, the young man had refused Ulf's instructions and ignored his advice. The reeve had at once recognised a force of character more powerful than his own, and had never dared push his authority to the full: his dignity was too precious to be put at risk. Instead he had accepted the smaller humiliation of permitting Eadric to retain his pride and to bungle his husbandry in any way he chose. The newcomer's punishment, and with it Ulf's satisfaction, would be the unavoidable consequence of his own obstinate mismanagement.

Protected by her husband, Madselin too had added her grain of scorn. One day Ulf had offered her the gift of a chicken – in return, he had said, for her friendship – and she had immediately realised the power she might hold over him. She had laughed, and told him he must ask Eadric about the hen, so that he had reddened and withdrawn the offer in shame. But it was only now, with Eadric gone, that she understood the full force of his resentment.

"On what journey?" Ulf's voice broke at the top of its pitch like a boy's. "He creeps at night to poison my ale, and now he runs like a dog!" He took a pace forward, scratching himself beneath his woad-dyed shirt, and stretched to his fullest height.

Madselin made a laughing noise. "Ha! The dew's still wet on the ground, and already the reeve has tasted his beer! Piss-bucket! You think my husband would run from a hog's bladder like you?"

In truth Ulf knew that he would not, and the mockery stung. Wilder than ever he raged, and wanted to hurt her.

"*Then where has he gone?* Answer me that! And for how many days? Tell me now! The *master* will want to know." He dwelt on the word, and watched the fear sink in. She did not understand all he meant by the threat, but there could be no mistaking his determination to wound. Her own anger grew uncertain, and tremulous.

"It is not your business to know where he has gone! It is all because you cheated us with the ox! In two days he will return and shake you by the ears!"

"Two days! No, sweet fool, he has *gone*! Can't you see? He will not return. And if he does come, he shall not remain!" Madselin listened, stunned by her own mute complicity, for she could not disbelieve him.

Yet Eadric did come. And before him he drove two fine oxen with deep strong chests, and coats as smooth as cream.

On the southern sea, the great dragon fleet rode at anchor and took the measure of the wind. The longships were a picture for the poets: slender sea-hawks straining at their thongs. Unleashed, they would obey none but their master, Sweyn Forkbeard, King of all Denmark. Sharp and eager, they were the iron tip of his furthest-flung spear.

Sweyn had been weaned on blood. He was the grandson of Gorm the Old, first King of Denmark, and son of Harald Blue-tooth, whom Sweyn himself had turned against in war. His queen was Sigfrid the Haughty, once the betrothed of bold Olaf Trygveson, King of Norway. Against this Olaf, at Sigfrid's own bidding, Sweyn Forkbeard had once let loose his birds of war. For half a year now the bones of Trygveson had washed beneath the Baltic deeps; and Sweyn Forkbeard was master of the sea.

For the dragon fleet, spring was the season of plunder. The sea-hawks soared on the easterlies and cast long shadows of fear wherever men lived close to the sea. With winter behind them, the talons were newly sharp and hungry. The sailors were proud Vikings again as the first vessels shipped oars and reefed their sails, waiting for the fleet to take its station. And then they were away on the breeze. The great sails crackled like fire, and the oars struck foam against the tide.

Eadric and Madselin rejoiced in their profit. Not only did they have fresh young oxen to put to the plough, but their neighbour Thurbrand had taken the survivor from the old pair in exchange for three good ewes. It was a fine spring. The earth turned light and dry beneath the plough, and the sowing was early. Into the soil went madder and woad for the dyers; rye, wheat and barley for the granaries; and vines for Ielfstan's sharp white wine. Eadric's sheep, being new to him at the beginning of his year, would make no new lambs until the following spring; but he could still tally his stock and find much to smile over. He knelt and worked out the sum, scratching the figures as pictures on the floor. First he drew a cow.

"One milking cow," he said. "The same as Ielfstan gave us." Then two oxen – but powerful workers with a long life ahead of them, in place of the broken plodders that Ielfstan had given. And now, too, they had eight sheep instead of six. In truth they had fretted a little over their price for the old plough-beast. The value of a good ox was six sheep, but Thurbrand would offer no more than three, and even these came shorn of their wool. Yet the bartered ox itself was slow and very nearly used up, so Eadric had taken a draught of ale on it and called the matter square.

He drew some more. Beneath the cow he made marks for the cheese and the buttermilk which they got from the old woman cheese-maker in return for their milk. Then he reckoned the crops from the field and the vegetables from the garden. With the new year's corn harvest, and the wool, he showed how easily they would earn their ten pence for the Michaelmas rent; and the barley for Ielfstan at Martinmas was already rooted in the field. Eadric scuffed his foot through one of the sheep. In the market it would earn five pence: enough to buy the lamb they would owe at Easter and the two hens for Martinmas, and still leave a penny for profit. Next spring, too, they would have a dozen new lambs. Eadric rested on his haunches and scratched a deep thick line like a box around his working. The drawing was fat with sheep at its base, narrowing to the pinnacle of the milk cow. From a distance, with her long dark lashes half closed in front of her eyes, Madselin saw a hilltop fort with turrets and terraces: a castle of hope.

Eadric stood up and rested his arm about her shoulders. "See," he said. "Every year we shall have more than the last!"

She laughed. "Before we are grey, we shall be rich as thegns!"

For four days Eadric furrowed the common plough-land. His oxen, richly coloured like honey and cream, were the envy of all who saw them. In size and weight they were as alike as bees, so that they drew a clean straight furrow and needed Eadric to guide them only when they turned at the head of the furlong. The plough-share cut as keenly as a Viking's prow, leaving a pluming white wake of seabirds, clashing like thegns over their plunder.

On the fifth day, as his duty demanded, Eadric worked his plough on Ielfstan's field. On the sixth day, Ulf came. In the first slant of morning, before the sun had risen above the rock, he stood in the doorway and called into the darkness.

"It is Ielfstan who commands you! Come out!"

Eadric was only just awake, and not yet fastened into his shirt. His mood was still dark with sleep, and there was a threat implicit in the way he drew himself up, stretching his body as if to remind the reeve of their physical inequalities. His shoulders were bulked by the tight folding of the arms, and a long bunch of muscle flickered above the knee.

"Well, Flea. What brings you out so bright and early? You have a three-legged ox to wish upon me?" It was a sour jest, made without humour, and in the expectation that the reeve would be unnerved. Yet Ulf laughed aloud, as if it were the funniest remark he had heard since Michaelmas, and showed no inclination to retreat.

"I repeat. You must come at once. Ielfstan is waiting."

"Ielfstan! For me? Why?" Eadric unfolded his arms and braced his hands against his hips, rocking awkwardly on his heels. He could see that the reeve was as sharp as a rooster, quite without fear; and it puzzled him, for this was not the Ulf he knew.

"Why?" said the reeve. "Perhaps he is in the mood to reward you for your fine ploughing."

Eadric's oxen were tethered to stripped oaken posts in a corner of the small compound, where they had been picking over a limp, bad-smelling mound of stalks and leaves. Ulf indicated them with the crook of one finger, and at once the young man understood.

"Those beasts are properly mine," he said angrily. "I bought them!"

"My dear Eadric! Of course you bought them! Your wealth is famous to us all!" Ulf wiped a hand across his lips, like an appreciative diner, and made a hungry yellow grin. "It is true we are jealous, but nobody says you stole them. Such fine beasts! And such a ploughman! You turn your daily acre more quickly than any man alive. How strong you must be!" He spread his fingers and slapped Eadric lightly on the arm, where the flesh was as hard as a tree.

"But *are* you so strong? Could you, say, pick a stone from a boiling kettle? Could you pluck an iron from the fire and carry it? How quickly would your flesh mend?"

In the silence, Madselin appeared from the shadow of the wall, to take her husband's hand and press her fingernails hard into his palm. In the cool bath of light, her face washed pale as clay. The black hair bunched raggedly in a clump where she had sawn it with a blade, curtaining her brow in shade. Her eyes were deeply hollowed and trapped in a web of thin sharp creases, which gave the face a sorrow beyond its years. She was opening and closing her mouth, stupidly, like a cow. Stone from the kettle! Iron from the flames? These were the common instruments of ordeal, by which an accused man might be tested. By the healing or the festering of his wounds, he would be judged innocent or guilty!

It was Eadric who restored himself first; his voice flat and colourless, as if it were a matter of small concern. "The ordeal? Why do you speak of such a thing, when you admit my innocence? This is no moment for a jest!"

"You are right!" Ulf beckoned with his arm. From behind him, through the stockade, came a guard of six sturdy smallholders, each man armed with a spear. Among them were neighbours that Eadric knew, the most prosperous land-holders in the manor, and yet they would look at him only with the coldness of strangers. Their fingers on the spear-shafts gripped and ungripped, ready – perhaps even eager – to strike. For Ulf over Eadric, they held the power of life and death.

"Now!" said Ulf. "Do not mistake me. I did not say that you were innocent, only that you did not steal." He spoke rapidly, no longer with amusement, in the voice he might have used for bargaining at market. "Eadric! Did you tell your neighbours that you would travel outside the hundred to buy animals?"

Eadric looked at Madselin, then back again to Ulf. In neither face –

terror in the one, blankness in the other — did he find any sign to help him. "No," he said. "I told only Madselin. It is of no account!"

"It is an offence!" Ulf held up a finger in front of his face. "When you returned, did you tell your neighbours where you had been? And, before the fifth day, did you turn out the animals on the common pasture?"

"You saw me! You did not tell me that I should! You know I did not!"

"It is an offence!" Ulf put up a second finger, to keep a count.

"An offence! It is nothing! The beasts are mine! I gave money for them!"

"If you are guilty, you will forfeit the oxen."

"This is *wrong*."

"It is the law."

Eadric passed from Ielfstan's hall to stand in court before the Man of the Hundred. He did not deny his guilt, and was not put to the ordeal. As punishment, above the loss of his oxen, he was commanded to pay a fine: five pence to the Court of the Hundred, and five pence to the manor. The Man of the Hundred did not inquire of him whether the beasts had been honestly gained; nor did he ask who had been witnesses at the sale. For it was the law that stolen beasts must be returned to their master who had lost them. The Man of the Hundred was old and wise, and particular in his reading of the law. Eadric's oxen, he said, being properly purchased but illegally brought into the manor, must lawfully pass to Ielfstan his lord.

Like Ulf the Flea, the Man of the Hundred was of small stature with legs of irregular length. He had a gruff voice, small darting eyes and a fine white beard. His name was Morcar the Piss.

It happened that the thegn Morcar had a distant kinsman, a seafarer whose name was Pallig. On the same morning that Eadric met his ruin, this Pallig was standing high in the prow of his ship, cupping his eyes to the horizon. In a light swell at the turning of the tide, the small English fleet tugged and snapped at anchor in the rivermouth, lashed together ship against ship in the Viking fashion. Somnolently, one after another, the decks rose and fell like the ribs of a sleeping animal.

This was Pallig's estate: the endless grey acres, furrowed by the wind. He was a merchant, a thegn of great wealth, with a town house and two manors to show as profit from his trade. From England he sailed with slaves and fine woollen cloth; from foreign shores he brought pottery, glass of many colours, and wine. By his enterprise he had made his name familiar even to the idle King Ethelred, who had rewarded him with a position of great trust – commander of the English fleet, defending the southern sea.

It was in pursuance of this duty that Pallig now scanned the waves. The vessels in his command were broader and heavier than the Viking longships, but as stout as the oak from which they had grown. It required forty men, dragging every sinew against the oars, to pull each one through the water. But in war at least, thought Pallig, their ponderousness was of small importance. When both sides were willing to fight, hand to hand across the boards like men, then each would wait upon the other. No warrior worthy of the name would employ his speed in flight.

The morning was awash with noise. Every fibre of the fleet was alive to the sea. Strake rubbed on strake, chuffing their hollow drumbeats against the clapping of the waves. The deck-planks croaked, and the wet sealskin ropework twisted and cracked like flails. Above it all, rising in urgency, came the rush of floodwater as the tide began to run beneath their keels. The sun rose high and burned away the mist in vapid coils. On the decks the men floated mysteriously – busy legless bodies in hanging swirls of steam. Aloft on his perch, Pallig loosened the drying leather braids to ease the discomfort of his leggings. When he turned again to the sea, he caught the first far pinprick of white: no more than a flash, so quick and so slight that he could not be sure that he had seen it. And then it came again; and then another, so that he was certain there could be no mistake. He called up his captains. Within minutes, it seemed, the full square sails of the longships were cramming the horizon.

Pallig's commands were carried along the line until all words were lost in an uproar of ropes and oars. In the hubbub behind him, two men plunged together over the stern of a ship. He heard their screams as the marksmen's arrows pinned them in the water – and the sharp chorus of shouts as a third man made safely to the shore and hid among the trees. Pallig's eye turned only briefly from the sea-hawks. Three cowards among so many: that was better than he had expected. With the lashings all set free and the anchors drawn clear of the mud, the Englishmen turned to meet the invader. The oarsmen bent their backs

43

and the warriors stood up straight to order, bows and javelins to hand, eighty to a vessel. A tremor ran through them as the wind thundered in the sails and the decks keeled to leeward; but they braced their feet and held stoutly to their ranks.

Behind them the land fell away to a low grey smudge. Ahead of them the water narrowed to a strand. They could hear the riffle of the Vikings' sails, and the orders shouted in strange tongues to the crews. From the prow of the command ship, where he stood as solid as a figurehead, Pallig could plainly see the gilt shield and scarlet cape of the Viking leader. Only a furlong separated them when the steersmen hauled on their oars and wrenched their prows to the west.

Between the two commanders, Pallig and the Viking, a signal had passed: two upraised fists, and two swords to the western horizon. Together they set their course and forged their tyrannous squadron: partners in plunder, thegns of the sea.

All their poverty was laid out with sad clarity in the dust on the floor. Two more sheep had been sold to pay Eadric's penance, leaving only five. If he sold them all, even at the highest price, he would still not have enough to buy even a single ox. He had tried to persuade Madselin that they could settle their dues with the barley already growing. But she had shaken her head and he, too, had known that the calculation was a cheat. Without oxen they could not live.

This was not a day on which he was pledged to work for Ielfstan at the manor, so he went instead to the common ploughland, to kick out his temper on the mockingly-perfect furrows of his strip. Unseen above him, a small bird hung like a star and poured out a liquid cadence of song: a tiny waterfall in the sky. Other birds were on the field – plump, grey and busy, packing their crops with barley shoots. Eadric skimmed a stone, showering the flock across the bank into the next field-strip, where a pair of oxen were nodding at their work. Behind the plough walked Thurbrand, the smallholder who had bartered his sheep for Eadric's old brown ox. Eadric still wondered what the man had wanted with the animal. It did no work, but only stood chewing every day on the pasture.

At once he stopped and stared. For a moment, while the idea

flowered in his mind, he watched the older man turning his plough at the headland. Then he cupped his hands and called out to him to wait, and ran along the field-bank to slap him excitedly on the shoulder.

"Thurbrand! You are my friend. You must help us!"

The old farmer spat a yellow gobbet into the mud and fixed his young neighbour with impatient, wind-reddened eyes. "Help you? How could I help you?"

"Have you not heard how those mongrels robbed us?"

"Robbed you! I heard only that you were in trouble with the courts." He made to shake out the reins, but Eadric gripped him fiercely by an elbow.

"They take my oxen and steal two of my sheep! This you call *trouble*? They would have us starve!" He lowered his voice and loosened the pressure on Thurbrand's arm. "But we shall not starve! Let nobody say Eadric is beaten. Still there is a way!"

Thurbrand sighed and let the leathers fall slack to the ground, shaking his head like a reluctantly indulgent father. "A way?"

"A way that you could help! Until I have money to buy new animals of my own, you could lend me your plough team. On the days when you are not using them yourself."

Thurbrand did not try to conceal his scorn. "*This* is your way? Fool! When I am not ploughing, the beasts must feed and rest. What you ask is not possible. You know this."

It was true. Eadric did know it, and the rebuttal was nothing less than he had expected. Yet he was not disheartened, for his real demand was yet to be revealed. He worked his eyes in a sly affectation of injury. "Then at least give me back my old ox! So that I should have to find only one beast more."

Again Thurbrand laughed, screwing a finger to his head in an open gesture of contempt. "*Give* you the ox? Madman! I paid three good sheep for it, as we agreed. There were witnesses!" But still Eadric was proceeding in accordance with his scheme.

"Very well then," he said. "As you are so much determined upon fairness, I shall give you back your sheep."

Thurbrand pursed his lips and seemed to be trying to hide a smile. He tugged at his beard for a moment, then looked up sharply and, for the first time, met Eadric eye to eye. "Three sheep?" he said. "No, that is not my price."

There was a long silence. "*Not* your price?" Eadric's mind balked at the unexpected hurdle, lost for an argument. "*Not your price?*"

Thurbrand turned up his palms and shrugged. "How could it be?

45

To buy at a price, and to sell again for the same! Is this the way of a trader? No! The ox is any man's to buy, for twenty pence or four fat sheep."

"*Four* sheep?" Eadric struck the palm of one hand as hard as he could with the fist of the other — and yet, to his own surprise, the temper was slow to rise. Instead of anger, he felt only the shabby hollowness of defeat. He spoke almost involuntarily, as a reflex, and not through any true spirit of belligerence. "Four sheep? How can that lame old ox be worth four sheep?"

"You said yourself it was worth six. My price is cheap." Thurbrand shook out the reins and the oxen began fretfully to take up the slack.

Eadric saw then all that had been done to him, and felt shame at his failure to prevent it. "So you *knew* what would happen to me? You knew I would be taken to Morcar and stripped of my beasts! Yet you said nothing to caution me. And you took my last ox! Why? Why did you cheat us?"

Thurbrand whipped up the team and smiled. "My price," he said, "is four sheep."

There was no need for Eadric to scratch any new reckoning on the floor. He could carry it in his head and show it on his fingers. For Ielfstan, in partial settlement of his dues, he had one lamb and two hens. For himself and his wife there remained one ox, one sheep and one cow.

"It was a hard bargain," he said to her. "But at least now we have an ox. We *have* to have an ox."

Within Madselin all hope had died. "One ox. One sheep. One cow." Her voice tolled the litany and her fingers numbered each accusation in turn. "One ox. One sheep. One cow." The three fingers bunched into a fist. "Idiot! You have ruined all chance!" Her white knuckles beat down around his head and shoulders until his skin was splashed with purple and her own fingers were too painful to continue. Eadric had begun to raise a hand, but he dropped it again and stood quietly until she had finished.

He had acknowledged his guilt and would accept her anger. There was pride even in remorse, and he wanted her to know that he was strong enough to endure it. She could abandon herself if she wished, but – even without her encouragement, if she were determined to withhold it – he would not accept defeat. Leaving her to lie dry-eyed and snivelling on the pallet, he went outside to the milk cow. Distractedly for a moment he gentled its bone-filled head. From the wet flare of its nostrils, his fingers brushed swiftly along the muzzle to linger at the velvet slopes behind the ears; then, more urgently, he traced the line of the shoulders, and the hard stiff folds in the hollow of the chest. He slapped its rump and stepped back a pace to examine the quarters, stroking his jaw all the time like a buyer at a market. Then, with sudden determination, he seized the animal's tethering rope and ushered it briskly backwards until its heels were knocking heavily against the beam of the plough. It was not an easy affair, to tether a startled milk cow alongside an habitually disgruntled ox; but after several moments' fretting and lashing – and enough noise to attract a considerable gathering of onlookers – he did manage to establish the pair in some kind of fragile accord.

The success lasted for some three or four paces, while the ox and the cow drew obediently forward and nodded in unison like a team. It was precisely as Eadric was raising his eyes to give thanks to heaven that the cow lost its composure. Angered, and unendurably confused by the imposition of these alien constraints, it lowered its head and did its best to run, becoming more and more frantic, bucking and kicking like a young bull, as it encountered the resistance of its companion. Hopelessly unbalanced, the plough scythed in an arc around the ox, dug into the turf bank and spun on to its back. Eadric, still clinging to the traces, was hurled like a hog into the mud.

"Hey Eadric!" called a man's voice from among the crowd. "If you churn that cow hard enough, d'ye get butter straight from the tits?"

Inflamed by the laughter he thrashed all the harder, driving in with his shoulder against the cow's rump in a last, despairing effort to straighten it. But still it would not be subdued, and now the ox, too, was beginning to catch the panic and spoil for a fight. Their horns clashed and locked like rutting bucks, threatening grievous injury to themselves, and utter destruction to the plough. Their master swore through his helmet of mud. Very well, then, he would put *himself* in harness alongside the ox and be driven by Madselin like a beast. Or he would carve a breast-plough and turn the soil by hand, working all day and all night until the job was done. He threw down his stick and wrestled with the cow to untangle it.

The animal stood for a moment, whisking its tail; and then, with

47

no warning beyond a single, mildly irritable toss of the head, it bolted. Finding the homeward path blocked by the crowd, it mounted the turf bank, cut a swath across the corner of a barley strip and set off at a gallop towards Thurbrand's house. Eadric waved a hand dismissively, content to let it run; until the thought occurred to him that it might not exhaust itself in time to stop at Thurbrand's boundary. A pit opened in his belly as he recalled Ulf's warning. If his beast broke through a neighbour's fence, then the man might kill it and return to him only the flesh and the bones. It was the law.

He set off after it at a run, tottering clumsily on the heavy plates of mud that had attached beneath his soles. The hooted advice of his neighbours was not necessary to convince him that the pursuit was hopeless: it was immediately plain that he could not overtake the animal until it stopped, and that in consequence he could do nothing more useful than watch wretchedly from a distance. As it came to the fence, the cow belled and lowered its horns, seemingly determined upon one final, explosively destructive gesture of protest. Only at the very last, as the disaster had begun to seem altogether unavoidable, did the animal throw up its head and ease away to graze. Afterwards, when he had soothed his way up to it, Eadric patted it softly on the muzzle and murmured his thanks.

"Enjoy your grass," he said. "You have done me a service!" It had shown him the idea that must alter his fortune.

Neither Thurbrand nor any of his family heard the commotion during the night, but in the morning there was devastation. Five stakes lay uprooted where a clean wide hole had been opened in the stockade, and all the animals – save only the house cow – were scattered across the manor. Every plant in the garden had been laid waste, either trampled or eaten. Outside, the sheep were strung like beads across the fallow field towards the common. The pigs and one of the oxen had got in among the rye, and the hens were picking in the wheat. Of the second ox there was no sign at all.

Thurbrand restrained his anger in the emergency and sent out each of his family to an appointed task: his wife to tether the house cow and gather the chickens; his sons to drive in the pigs and the sheep; himself to catch the oxen. There was no time yet for recrimination. In the uneasy balance of a smallholder's affairs, the loss of an animal, or the spoiling of a crop, could push a family across the thin divide between hunger and starvation. But Thurbrand did not wait for all the sheep to be herded before he recalled his sons, Godric and Aelfric, to the stockade.

"Leave them now. We can fetch them later. One ox is still missing, and it is plain that we have an enemy!" For question and answer had come together in Thurbrand's mind, certain beyond all doubt. Again there were tasks: the younger son Godric to run with a message to the reeve; himself and Aelfric to go together and test his suspicion on a man they had once called the Innocent. From a distance of a furlong or more, they could see the gap in Eadric's stockade, exactly similar to the one in their own. The same heap of five palings lay uprooted on the ground, dusted with fresh earth. Thurbrand approached slowly, crouching like a stalking cat. He was no coward, but then neither was he a fool: Eadric was the strongest man in the entire hundred, whom none but a bull would challenge incautiously. Aelfric, walking behind him, shared his father's taut unease. Separately they had each begun to doubt the wisdom of their boldness; yet each of them feared the scorn of the other almost more than he feared the wrath of Eadric. There could be no question of retreat.

They entered the stockade through the gap, stepping quickly across the fallen stakes. One of the timbers was split along the grain, adding the sweet scent of raw wood to the mustiness of the turned-over soil, but the others were quite whole and unmarked. In the compound there was no evidence of uproar to compare with the chaos in Thurbrand's own yard. Everything was in perfect order save only for the body of the ox, lying amid a cloud of blue gauzy flies, stiff-legged in the dust where its throat had been cut.

Eadric himself showed neither surprise nor obvious concern at their sudden appearance, but smiled broadly and waved a hand at the carcass.

"Thurbrand my friend! And Aelfric his son! You are welcome, though I fear you catch me awkwardly."

His smile faded as he switched his gaze to the ox, then brightened again. "But perhaps I am lucky and you have a moment to spare? Could you help me haul that dead beast there, out of my garden before it begins to stink?" Across the front of his shirt spread a brown, fern-leaf splash of blood.

Thurbrand looked at the huge young man smiling at them, then at the body of his ox. He pointed with trembling finger. "That is my ox!"

"*Your* ox?" Eadric widened his eyes. "*Your* ox? How could that be? You of all people! Who could believe such carelessness? You, who are the very example of prudence!"

"Carelessness?" said Thurbrand, trying not to seem discomposed. "How have I been careless, save only to sleep too soundly in my own bed? You have killed my ox! You stole it from my yard and killed it!"

"Certainly I killed this ox. Why do you fret so?"

"You do not deny it?"

"Of course I killed it. In the night it broke through my fence there, as you can see, and I killed it. That is my right. It is the law."

While Eadric spoke, Thurbrand was further disturbed by the sudden passing of a ghost in the doorway behind him – a livid face hanging by an invisible thread, with death-dark eyes and empty jaws. It hovered for an instant, as if it might at any moment abandon its haunt and fly out into the yard. But the pull of the dark was too strong. With a single, baleful, blink of the eyes it shrank from the sunlight and was gone. Thurbrand turned to his son, and saw mirrored in his face the same stunned bewilderment that he knew now must be fixed on his own. He curled his fingers and sharpened his resolve.

"Eadric! You plot to ruin me, but you shall not succeed. Ulf is coming, and the court shall have you again. You will be stripped of everything! All that you possess!"

Yet Eadric only smiled, with a birdlike cocking of his head. "My friend, don't take on so! I killed the ox because it is the law. But don't despair. I, Eadric, am your neighbour and friend."

He stepped into the full sunlight and held out his arms. "Look. Now *I* have one ox, that I bought from you with the sheep." He raised the first finger of his left hand to number it. "And *you* have one ox." He raised the first finger of his right. "It is simple. I shall lend you my ox to help plough your land. You will lend me your ox to help plough mine!"

He twined the two fingers to make a pact. "There, it is done. We are brothers."

From the top of the hill the river appeared flat and still, a dull strand of pewter winding through the deep wooded valley. From time to time it crooked out of sight behind the trees and reappeared threading long bright tails through scatterings of rock. But from this great height even the turmoil was made to appear tranquil: the rapids seemed a motionless pavement of white. It was a clear sunny day, hot enough to prickle beneath the shirt; yet the glare was entirely shut out as the horsemen turned aside from the ridge and began to move down the woody underworld towards the riverbank. All the sounds and smells were of earth and water. The soil beneath the hooves turned loose and black, giving off a foetid, musty smell like autumn ploughing. Slippery grey roots made a precarious staircase of the one-horse track, which cut a faint broken zigzag along the valley side. For much of its length the path gushed with water. A heavy dew smeared the moss-green boulders and dripped into rivulets that spindled and danced to the river, throwing out showers of brilliant jewels wherever they caught a fleck of sunlight. Most of the trees were of great age, wearing thin grey beards of moss and lichen: sometimes the bark would crumble at a touch and open a dead sooty heart, as black as fire. Many of the younger stems, stretched thin in the race for light, had fallen to the winter gales and made awkward barriers across the way. The men had to lie along the horses' backs, and weave a slow careful path through the mantle of ferns.

In the valley bottom, the tussling waters made a thunder that shook the riverbank. Not even the jays, drowned far overhead in the leaf-canopy, could cut such a din. By the rapids, the air was a chill smoke of spray, a perpetual autumn that offered cool refreshment, tantalising in its allure on a hot steamy day. The fugitive had submitted eagerly to its appeal. He rested where an eddy had washed out a cavity in the bank, burying his toes in the soothing wet sand. In the slack pool around his feet, the surface was alive with long spindly insects that seemed to have the trick of walking on water. He watched, idly fascinated, and wondered what could be the reason for their tireless industry.

It was only when Morcar snapped a branch with his foot that the man turned at last and saw how the trap had been closed behind him. The horsemen sat in a line above the lowest elbow of the path, staring down at him with expressions of amused contempt. Morcar alone had climbed down across the crook of the path, sword in hand like an assassin. The thegn held himself just beyond the fugitive's reach, and angled the blade at his throat.

"Stand fast, outlaw! We are too many for you!"

The man bent his head to examine the sword from both sides, as if to confirm that it was real; then he looked behind him at the heavy whirl of iron-tinged water. Eadric knew now that he had no choice beyond death or submission.

Slowly he raised his hands from his sides and gave himself up.

Pallig gazed down from the ridge above the estuary and was glad that there was no enemy to be faced. Sailing upriver on the flood, the sea-hawks had strayed far from the channel. Even as Pallig and the Viking had stood scanning the country from their decks, the tide had slipped away and abandoned them like hogs in a wallow, so that the fighting men had been made to wade ashore through a rotting pulp of deep green mud. Behind Pallig now, where in the morning had stood a large and wealthy village, gentle coils of smoke built pale columns on a dark foundation of ash. Below him the longships were heavier for the weight of plunder – gold and silver for the journey; meat and women to be enjoyed before the tide.

They sailed early next day, rising clear on the flood then furling their sails to race from the estuary with the ebb. The steersmen called for assistance at their paddles as the current sucked them between the sand bar and the cliff-stack, through the fierce narrow channel into the sea. When they settled into slack water again they turned their prows to the east, into the face of the wind, and began to draw steadily on the oars. They did not pull landward until the low line of cliff, with its flaky red pillars and tide-washed caves, had levelled to a sandy fringe that darkened and gave way to mud. This estuary was broader than the first, and the channel was deep and easy. Yet Pallig was afraid. They were coming to bear arms against the chief town of the region, which the Romans had called Isca. In the time of Pallig's father, King Athelstan had enclosed it within a mighty fortress of walls; and even now, in the reign of the feeble King Ethelred, the citizens would fight furiously in defence of their homes. It was his contempt for this King, who had gained his crown by the treachery at Corfe[1], and whose defence against the Danes had been lamed by surrender and betrayal, that had brought Pallig to his dangerous allegiance with Forkbeard. The Danish king had vowed to hunt Ethelred like a wolf, and to leave his own son,

---

[1] King Edward's murder in 978

Canute, as heir to the English throne. Wherever he looked, in all the land, Pallig could see nothing to halt such an invader; and yet he was afraid. This was still his own country. If the battle were lost, then he would stand revealed as a traitor; and no Viking would preserve him from the vengeance of his kinsmen.

From along the tideline came a flurry of black and white wings. Pallig listened to their piping as the flock settled, and watched broodingly as their sharp red bills speared deep into the mud. A short distance to the north, Eadric, too, was watching birds. High above him, looping in the scented air, a pair of glossy black ravens were looking for a meal. Lying back, he imagined their foul breath on his face, and the pale horny beaks stabbing into his eyes. All around him, on a hillside that fell steeply away from a narrow ridge road, armed men stood and sat in various attitudes of preparation – or unreadiness – for battle. Some he recognised as thegns by their likeness to Morcar: they carried swords and helmets, and wore heavy ring-mail shirts beneath their long coloured capes. Others were rough-shirted peasants or smallholders like himself: some carrying shields and iron-tipped spears, others with pointed sticks. Eadric was no more exhausted than any other of these villagers who had been driven forward by masters on horseback. But he was truly the only one among them who had been roped to a tree.

It had amused Morcar to bring his prisoner to the battle. "It would be a waste to kill you here," he had said, as they faced each other by the riverside. "The ravens will never find you. If we push you into war, at least you might finish a Viking or two before you die."

Eadric had offered his captors no struggle. He had been stung so badly by the shame of his failure that he would not look the thegn directly in the eye. Back at the manor, when his crime had been uncovered, he had flown from Ulf and the tithing men like a common coward. And then, like a fool, he had been caught by men who were not even looking for him, leaving Madselin abandoned with neither friend nor provision to sustain her. Ielfstan's men would have taken all she had.

In the morning, after a long night of dark deliberation, he was roused by the din of a man shouting. "To your feet, men! To your weapons arise!" At first he could see nothing beyond the other sleepers who had risen in front of him. But slowly he forced himself up, bracing his feet and pushing his rope-linked arms painfully up the young beech stem behind his back. Along the ridgeway came a monstrous shape, of smoking breath and nodding heads, which seemed hardly to move in the swirls of mist but only swelled and grew as it floated there. Eadric shook his head and creased his eyes. On horseback rode a tall robed thegn, plumped out with sheepskin and armour. Hooked upon his arm stood a pale speckled falcon, bobbing in a hood.

The thegn was Kola, the King's High Reeve and commander of the levies. In front of Eadric's tree, where the press of men was heaviest, he reined in his horse and dismounted.

"Men of England!" he was calling, while he fanned the air with his arms. "Brave men of England! The invader is within our sight! He comes against us to rob and kill. It is time for us to face him now, to fly at his breast with iron!" He fumbled at his wrist, and the great hunting bird rose high in a jangle of bells.

"Lords and men! Our animals have served us well in bringing us here. But if the battle should go badly with us, then they could serve us equally in flight!" He let go his own horse's leathers and slapped its rump to scuttle it along the road. "There will be no flight! Think only of your courage! Set free your animals and march with me to victory!"

Above the murmur, Morcar's laugh yapped sharp as a puppy. "Men of England! Men of courage! What foolery is this? Just look at the churls!" Yet he let go his horse and chopped through the rope that bound Eadric to the tree. "There," he said. "Both my beasts are loose. One to flight and one to fight!"

Kola brought the men up to the ridgeway and bade them form their line. Those with shields were put to the front, to form a hedge with their spears. Behind them, without order or particular purpose, stood the rabble with their sticks. Eadric was held fast in the crowd, hemmed in with a small knot of spear-men, while Morcar himself stood with the other sword-bearers in front of the throng at Kola's side.

The Danes had drawn up in the valley. Eadric could see the pale glint of their helmets and the dark bristle of javelins. They looked fewer in number than the defending force, but heavier by far in weight of arms. It was no peasants' rabble that rode with the sea-hawks – this was an army. As Eadric watched, a figure detached itself from the enemy line and walked slowly up the hill towards the road. The man wore neither helmet nor breast-armour, and carried neither sword nor spear: indeed Eadric soon saw that he was no soldier at all, but more a peasant or smallholder such as himself. When the man came within shouting distance, he stopped and raised his arms in a submission of peace. He was a farmer from the banks of the Isca river, he said, made to come forward and treat for the Danes as their messenger.

"Noble thegns! These bold seamen have sent me to speak. They

54

say it would be better to defend yourselves with silver and gold than with your sticks and bones! Better to pay a tribute than to die! Disband your men and give the seamen the gold they ask. They will accept your truce and return to sea in peace."

Kola stepped forward and unsheathed his blade. "Hear this then, brave farmer! Tell the seafarers that swords alone await them! If they've a taste for English metal, then this shall be our tribute!"

"I will tell them."

At the front of the Danish line, where he stood with the Viking commander, Pallig gazed up at the massed body of defenders, his countrymen, and felt a terror in his heart more awful than any he had known as commander of the fleet. When the formation tightened and began to advance, he crouched with his head between his knees and pretended to be sick. After it had passed, he swallowed his self-loathing, turned away from the battle and ran along the valley path towards the west.

Yet all his fears were idle. The hilltop army, of old men and fools, did not hold the Vikings long. Not every defender submitted without a struggle, but bravery and hope were dull weapons against a shirt of mail. Their blunt wooden jabs were turned aside and answered with iron thrusts that opened their bellies and heads. In place of armour the Viking blades met only flesh, scything as they pleased like reapers at a harvest. Eadric was half stunned by the shaft of a javelin, that stood quivering in the breast of a neighbour – a peasant whose field-strips lay close to his own at Ielfstan's Place. For a moment the battle noise seemed to fall away into the distance, as if he were alone with the one man dying. There came a froth from the opening in the chest, and a catch in the throat, like a harness flapping in the wind. Eadric bent low and forced a path between the bodies, crouching to take shelter from the hot pink rain.

When they had let go their spears, the Vikings came on with their axes, reaping bodies and limbs until not a man was left who would challenge them. The pressure of comrades around Eadric's shoulders increased as the mob pushed back, then eased again as they fell. One man came hard against him, crushed to his chest like a lover: blond-haired, hardly more than a boy, whose skin still showed pink beneath his fluff of beard. Eadric felt the warm brush of the body as it slipped slowly away, inch by inch, to drown; felt the steaming wet heat as the head tipped open, without a sound, and emptied itself against his legs.

At first he was one among a herd, nudging and jostling downhill away from the ridge, racing for cover. But one by one his comrades fell out, to rest and look back, as they realised that they were not being pursued. Soon Eadric was alone, walking quite slowly with his back to the sunrise, in the direction he thought must lead him to the manor. For the first time that morning he thought of Madselin; and he understood, with a mild shock of gratification, how easily the common defeat might be turned into a kind of personal victory. He was a free man again, with neither rope nor sword to threaten him; free to slip in through the ash wood, as cunning as a lizard, and steal her away. Yet his pleasure was not immoderate. For where would they go? And how should they save themselves from starving?

The morning had fallen silent. Behind Eadric the ridge was blue with smoke; but he could see nothing moving there, only the high slinking ravens. Ahead of him, to the east, another ridge, thickly wooded, rose almost as high as the battle hill itself. It was so steep in parts that he had to fall to his hands and knees, grasping at branches and roots to pull himself upward. Once, in a deep stony furrow that tumbled along the line of a winter stream, he caught a quick flash of movement: a low, reddish, dog-like body, pointed snout and upright ears, a flowing white-tipped tail. He watched it weave out of sight among the heavy grey trunks, and caught the sharp animal smell imprinted on the air. From the top of the hill, the ground fell away even more steeply ahead of him. The trees ended at the fork of a river, where two thunderous streams made a force on their flight to the sea. The country beyond stretched low and undulating to the north west; higher still and rocky towards the south. Eadric guessed that his journey to the battle-ground had taken him closer to the sea than Ielfstan's Place; that he should follow the further of the two streams as it curved northward around the bluff.

It was colour that alerted him, not movement: a paleness in the shadow and a bright slash of red. Resting with his back against a boulder, an old man lay shaking with fever; his eyes tight closed, his hands lying empty at his sides. The fine white beard was wet with saliva; his long green cloak clotted with blood. Eadric felt a freezing clutch of anxiety, and turned to scan fearfully through the trees.

"Morcar!"

So the thegn, too, had come to earth like a fox. He was grievously wounded. A spear had been thrust clean through his right thigh and deep into his left, so that he had been pinioned like a roasting goat. To free himself he had snapped the shaft between his legs and hobbled forward one step at a time, spreading his thighs to keep the stumps from grating in the holes. But it was clear to Eadric that the thegn would not be travelling further; not this day or ever. He seemed too enfeebled even to notice the young man's presence, and did not turn at the sound of his voice.

Again Eadric craned into the bushes behind him, and as far as he could into the wood on either side. But there was nothing; neither movement nor sound. "Morcar! Are you alone?"

The thegn had become elderly: thin, and white as death. His eyelids showed blue in their crescent hollows, and his lips were grey and waxy. Too weary to show surprise, he opened his eyes and smiled rigidly against the pain.

"The outlaw! Free again, like a running beast!"

His head rolled involuntarily on the rock and he lowered his eyes as if he would fade again into sleep – or sink into death, for his time could not be long in coming. There was not enough blood left in him to keep a man alive. Yet still he stirred his head and willed himself to remain awake, knotting the veins in his neck and shouting plaintively in a whisper.

"I am alone! My legs! You must help me!"

Eadric laughed as he knelt to listen. "Help you? Help the man who ruined me? What foolishness is this?"

Morcar's fingers fluttered like a birdwing against the broken spear-butt; then he lay back and yawned as if Eadric were of no more concern to him than any ordinary peasant to his thegn. Inside the bloodstained cloak was a purse still heavy with coins, and a wooden cup hanging from a belt – fine trophies both, yet Eadric was disappointed to find only a dagger for a weapon. The great sword had been lost in the field.

"Help you? Perhaps I will. But first you must help me!" Without gentleness, he stripped away the cloak and breast-armour, and unfastened the cup, dagger and purse. He did not know how to count the coins, but he was certain it must be a great deal of money: enough, surely, to buy more animals and take Madselin to a new village far away where no one would know them. The chain-mail was too small for him to fasten, but he hung it about his shoulders and wrapped himself in the cape: no longer a peasant, but a proper lord of the battle.

"Now!" he said. "You are as poor as a peasant. Before you die like one, how shall I help you?"

Morcar struggled to point at the cup. "A drink . . . Leave me water!"

The sun was at its highest, cutting almost vertically through the trees as Eadric looked over the brink to the river, wondering if he dare risk the time it would take to gather water and bring it unspilled over so steep and uneven a climb. And the thought died instantly in his mind. Staring back at him, less than half a furlong distant, was the sea-captain Pallig.

Neither man spoke, but they weighed each other like cornered stags. Each of them was in his own way an imposter – a brave man flawed through failure; ready to kill to redeem himself. Eadric, in command of the high ground, stood firm while Pallig climbed towards him. Slowly he came, step by step, not lowering his eyes until he stood level with Eadric on the ridge. Neither man knew the other, and was himself glad not to be known; and yet each felt a deep unease. To Eadric, there was a strangeness in the sudden arrival of a thegn, alone and on foot, from a wild river valley that showed no discernible path. And Pallig, with his rich man's eye, was immediately chary of this huge, unkempt young man with the bare legs and ill-fitting blood-caked battle-dress.

"You have been in battle, my Lord? How does it go? Am I too late for the fight?"

"Too late you are!" said Eadric. "All is lost. The Vikings came upon us like hawks upon a mouse!"

Pallig held his distance, his suspicion sharpened by the rough peasant voice and awkwardness of manner. His eyes, combing the man for signs, dwelt on the hilt of the dagger in Eadric's belt, then darted to the inert figure against the boulder. He knew his kinsman at once; as he had known the dagger, for he had long ago brought it to Morcar himself, across the sea in his ship. He settled his hand around the jewelled handle of his own knife, idly closing the fingers as if through force of habit.

"Too late, then! Yet I must continue. I had men there among the levies. I must take care to discover their fate."

"You travel in vain. No man who remains there is alive. Those who live have all fled to the hills; and not all these will see another day. My own friend here lies at the brink of death."

"All the same, I shall go!" Pallig felt an irresistible surge of anger. It was the duty of a thegn to betray his cousin in politics if he thought it right. He mourned the injury that had been done to Morcar, but it had been in the service of a cause. For the health of England, which demanded an end to Ethelred and all his ways, the thing had to be done. But this robbery here, at the hands of a peasant, was no worthy way to mark his death.

"I shall go," he said again, and passed hurriedly into the forest – to steal back across the ridge, to watch, and to arm the shadows with his knife.

Eadric stood and listened until all was still, then turned again to kneel by Morcar. "I have no water," he said, and laughed. "Instead I shall bring you wine!" He stood up, and from behind the thegn's head came the sound of liquid rushing into the wooden cup. "Here," he said. "Warm golden wine. You shall have it after you have helped me one last time."

Morcar was almost spent. His voice came as the merest rustle of breath between his teeth, so that Eadric had to bring his ear right against his lips to hear him.

"You? How can I help you?"

"Tell me the way to Ielfstan's manor. Which way should I walk?"

Morcar sighed. His answer took a long time to come, but he delivered it clearly, and with a smile.

"To the north. Follow the river."

He smiled because Ielfstan's Place lay far away to the south-west, in a deep hidden cleft in another range of hills. Away to the north, the stream led into a desolate wilderness of treeless rocks and dust.

"My thanks," said Eadric. "Here then, take the wine." At once the old man smelled the bitterness, and felt the saltiness on his lips. He spat and turned away.

"Farewell to you, outlaw," he said.

"And farewell to you then, Morcar the Piss."

CHIVALRY

The falcon bated on the fist, taking great gulps of air with its wings and jabbing its black silk hood like the head of a serpent. From deep within his own furred cowl, the knight made soothing music with his tongue. He could feel the stab of the talons even through the stiffened ox-hide glove, and had to brace his fingers against the tugging of the jesses. The silvered Italian bells chimed a chord around the bird's feet as, for perhaps the hundredth time, it cast itself from the glove and spun head downwards from the leathers.

"What a boiling temper," said Sir Philip, "when the purpose of this hoodwinking is to keep you sober!"

But for the hundredth time he spread his free hand patiently to gentle the falcon back to its perch, and lightly caressed the hood until it was calm again. It was a young saker, still unflown, and with the fury of the wild still pumping in its breast. Sir Philip endured its misdemeanours with stubborn composure, for only by stealth would the conscious will of the man and the raw appetites of the bird be joined in common purpose. When the goose feathers whistled again, the tiercel held steadfastly to his master's fist and did not bate.

Trimmed and whipped to a smooth shank of ash wood, the goose plumes flew fast and far from their native wing. The archer stood submerged in the moonless ocean of the wood, listening for the quivery shock of the arrow meeting its mark. But after a flight that he knew at once was too long, there came only the faraway *chick* of metal into earth.

"Again, young Stephen!" said the knight. "I will *not* keep an esquire who fails me with the bow!"

But in truth his anger was an invention; for Stephen's failings were the common ones of youth and did not arise from any lack of application. The bow which Sir Philip had given him was stronger than any he had held before, and the yew sprang brutally in his hands. The flaxen string whipped against the leather bracer, hard enough to bruise his arm; and his cheek, too, was sorely inflamed, for he had fallen into the fashionable habit of drawing the bow to his ear instead of to the breast.

Sir Philip glared into the darkness. "The night may hide you from my eyes, yet I have a clear enough picture of your wanderings! The bow flutters like a lady's kerchief, and your aim's held longer than a maiden's honour. You are well named, Stephen, after the most unsteadfast king that ever England or Normandy knew!"

It was a sharp reproof, for there was no man on earth that Sir Philip had held more deeply in contempt than the late King Stephen. Indeed, he had joined arms with Robert of Gloucester in a pledge to unthrone the usurper in favour of King Henry's daughter Matilda; and, unlike the turncoat barons of the eastern counties, he had done it through honest conviction and not with any thought of plunder. England in those dark years had been divided against itself. Town against town, castle against castle, until at last the King (by grace of God, it had seemed to Sir Philip at the time), while stunned by slingshot at Lincoln, had been beaten into submission. Yet for Sir Philip there had been no glory in it, for the haughty Matilda had proved a degree too sour for dainty English stomachs. The common people had risen up to drive her out of London and her barons had been routed at Winchester, leaving the verminous Stephen to take up the crown again without fear of reprisal. Matilda had lingered in brief hope of a miracle, but had abandoned her cause and withdrawn to France in 1147.

"Now thank the Lord," said Sir Philip. "King Stephen is six years in his grave, and King Henry the Second is a true son of Matilda's. A fine man for the hunt, who would not relish the sight of such shooting as yours! If you would live to be a knight, take heed!"

The saker was disturbed by its master's agitation and bated again in a flurry. Sir Philip reproached himself for the lapse and quietened it with long gentle strokings of the breast. His words lost none of their sharpness, but he crooned them as gently as a lover's pledge.

"Wretched bird! Miserable boy! See how sorely I am vexed."

The bird fawned against him like an overfed dog, though it was kept purposely on the edge of hunger. The young esquire, too, was kept hungry for praise. The pangs would drive them both to keener endeavour, the bird and the boy alike.

"Now, fretsome pupil," he said, with carefully exaggerated

patience. "Let us sharpen your aim, for tomorrow we may depend on it." He fixed his eyes on the distant rush lights, which flared palely against the bark and raised lucid smoky ghosts among the trees. "Split the flame!"

Stephen's most intractable error was to let his eye rest on the arrowhead as he drew back, and thereby lose sight of the target. This now was Sir Philip's remedy: to make him shoot at rush lights in the dark.

"Think hard now! Have you nocked? Then draw slowly back . . . To your right pap, now, and no higher! Left arm straight! Eye on the target! Hold it steady . . . and loose!"

The string slapped, the feathers hummed, and the topmost light guttered as the arrow clipped the flame. The knight sucked a strand of fish meat from his teeth and the tiercel kicked up a mad harmony with his bells. For a boy drawing a man's bow, it was a tidy shot.

"May heaven protect us," said Sir Philip bitterly. "For such shooting never shall!"

Next morning the boy and the man were ready to die. It was not their intention to do so – indeed, all their efforts were concerned to prevent it – but they were ready all the same. It was a willingness (or at least, a possibility fully acknowledged) which had made the tournament such an object of distress for the Bishops of Rome. Lethal combats were prohibited by Papal decree, and their victims were not deemed fit for ecclesiastical burial.

Sir Philip was fussing with the girdle of his linen breeches. They were of the new kind, cut only to the knee, with the coloured stockings drawn up around them and suspended by cords from his breech-girdle. Stephen's first mistake that day had been to tie up his master's underwear too tightly: the cords had been drawn taut as bowstrings, so that the breeches had been pulled down over his hips as he tried to straighten. The boy's second mistake, more gross by far than the first, had been to laugh.

"What!" said the knight. "On the field of battle, you would have me drop my drawers like some beshitten cottage-pup? To offer my rump and be lanced like a hog on a spit? True, 'tis only my linen! But make such a fix with my mail and the field shall swill in my blood!"

The cottage they stood in had been built for the particular purpose of arming knights for the tournament. It was hardly a cottage at all: little better than a cell of mud-daubed hurdles. The saker stood on a pole in the middle of the floor – unhooded and beady, cocking its head. Facing it from a pole of its own, puffed up in its feathers like an enormous chick, was Stephen's lanner falcon – a bird only slightly smaller than the saker itself, which Sir Philip had given him in place of his fierce little hobby.

"A hobby for a boy," Sir Philip had said. "But a lanner for an esquire."

In the heavy shadow of the arming-lodge, both the falcons might easily have been taken for their aristocratic cousin the peregrine. In full light the lanner was paler in its body, and the saker paler still. The esquire looked up and met the hard yellow glare of his bird. Its thin dark moustache and predatory gaze lent it the character of a law baron passing sentence. Stephen feared it judged him ill.

Sir Philip drew his shirt over his head and smoothed it around his breeches. "Let us pray," said Stephen, "that by God's mercy at the end of the day it shall be soiled with nothing more grievous than sweat!"

The knight stopped abruptly and eyed him with cold disfavour. "It would behove you," he said, "to take better care in what you pray! For honour, yes. For mercy, never! Better that my blood should be spilled honourably in defeat than that I should sweat humbly in surrender! Pray you for *honour,* boy, for *chivalry*! 'Tis courage we seek, and out of courage strength, not any maidenly virtue!"

Stephen was sixteen: still tall beyond his strength, but wanting for nothing in bravery. From such a youth would a true man grow, for he was careless of all wounds save those to his pride.

"Do you take me then for a milk-skinned coward? Shall I be damned, Sir? I'll ride in your place and to hell with your maidenly virtue! My prayers are well meant, Sir. The Church teaches . . ."

"Church! Would you be a man or a monk? *God is in my sword*!" But Sir Philip was not displeased. He had schooled the boy for battle: had knocked him down until his teeth cracked, then had knocked him down again. And not once had Stephen let him see a tear.

The esquire helped his knight with the thick quilted jerkin and laced it; then knelt at his feet with the *chausses* of mail. The kneeling was in homage to more than a man; it was to an ideal, to *valour*. It was an image of his own future that he worshipped, a celebrant at the altar of his own ambition. Carefully he fitted the *chausses* over Sir Philip's stockings, lacing them at the back from foot to thigh, and testing the tension before he tied the thongs at the breech-girdle. Afterwards he smoothed the chain with his fingers, as caressingly as if it were cloth of silk. He had rubbed it, link by link, until it gleamed.

The hauberk, too, had been burnished times beyond number. If its strength in battle would improve with Stephen's care, then it might have repelled a thunderbolt. Sir Philip raised his arms and leaned forward to roll it over his head. It was tight to the wrists and neck, with fitted gloves and a hood, and hung well below the tops of the *chausses* to complete the covering of his thighs. The skirt was divided front and back so that it would lie snugly across the saddle in two flaps, which Stephen tied down one to each thigh. Sir Philip circled his arms and raised his knees to test the fit; then, satisfied, took up his weapons.

"Are you ready, my Lord?"

"Ready."

They went to their horses – the man to his charger, the boy to his palfrey. At the saddle-bow Sir Philip carried the leathern arming-coife that would protect his face and head from chafing beneath the steel, and the helm with the nose-guard that he would put on over the mail. It was to be a combat of two parties: the knights who had travelled from the south and west of the tournament ground would do battle with those who had come from the north and east. They made up twenty lances to each station, with each man paying a fee according to his rank: twenty marks for an earl, but only two marks for a landless knight errant. It was little wonder that tournaments did not find favour among kings, for the barons made sport of their battles, and battles of their sport. Beneath heraldic pennons they settled their feuds and made ready for war. The ghosts of Stephen and Matilda could bear witness to the dangers.

Sir Philip in these affairs was something of a mercenary. He lived by the fortunes of organised combat, taking captive after captive for the profit of their ransoms. His purse, while he skirmished, rested with Stephen, who kept it fastened to the breech-girdle beneath his tunic. It was the esquire's duty to attend closely to the tournament and keep his master always in sight. It was not an uncommon thing for armed robbers to run out from the trees and fall upon any knight made feeble by the affray. If any such brigands should threaten Sir Philip, then it would be Stephen's business to deal them a sharp retort with his bow.

The battlefield here was a tufted plain, hedged about with yellow-flowering bushes and dusty thorn trees. A row of mottled grey standing stones ran along one flank of the open space, sank out of sight beyond a gentle dip in the plain and reappeared at a distance in an unbroken chain to the horizon. It was with their backs to these stones that Sir Philip's party assembled and made ready. Among the clustered pennons, Stephen could easily pick out the device of his master: a black clenched fist on a field of primrose yellow. At his knee, the same brave totem glared out from the centre of his shield.

Honour. Chivalry. To be a man among men. The clods flew high among the larks as the horses were driven to their business. One by one the shields arose and one by one the pennons dipped, while to Stephen's ears the hooves rang hollow in the silence like a pounding of hearts. Sir Philip had singled out an earl with a bold green eagle on his shield, and crouched low against his horse's neck to take him. Slowly, slowly, the clenched fist aimed its strike, the ground between them shrinking at the rate of two horses galloping. Yet to Sir Philip it was like falling through a dream. He had time to notice a pair of buzzards soaring in lazy circles above the shallow valley; time to notice a knight on a grey horse bearing off at an angle, away from the point of combat; time to notice that the mail had discovered a parting in his breeches and was chafing his skin. Time to think: that an earl's ransom would make a handsome picking for a knight. But his blow never landed. The eagle swung away to the left and took issue with a horned black bull. Sir Philip heard the drum-like *clop* of lance against shield, ash wood against hide. And then he was through the line and turning. Behind him the charge had broken into a wheeling mêlée, in which it was no longer easy to determine which knights were the friends, and which the foes. Already one man was sprawled among the hooves, stripped of his helm, while his horse ran gratefully into the furze. Another animal lay twisting in a frenzy of broken bones, while two knights thrust and parried across its body. Other horses backed and turned in a slowly unwinding knot, and Sir Philip looked out for an opponent. He scanned the field for the earl with the eagle but found, too late, that he was himself the target of another. A knight bearing a boar's head on his arms was spurring into him at close quarters from the right, threatening to catch him squarely in the flank. Astonished at the man's impetuosity, and properly angry with himself for having been taken by surprise, he dragged hard on the leathers and spun round to meet him; but there was no time, he was only halfway round, and the knight was too close for him to raise his own horse to a gallop. The man's mouth was opening and closing as if he were shouting: proud promises, drowned by the drumming of the charger. Cursing blasphemously, Sir Philip threw himself flat along his animal's back, to the left side of the neck, raising a faint hope with his shield and prodding blindly with his lance. There was no weight in the blow, for his horse was driven back on its quarters, but the late and aimless thrust took the boar's head foolishly without a guard: there had been no thought in his head but attack. Sir Philip's body rang with shock as the man rode against the tip, and the lance went spinning from his grasp. But it remained unbroken; and, God be thanked, the knight dropped heavily into the dust.

This shallow victory stiffened Sir Philip in his resolve. He spoke coarsely to himself, and pounded his leg in a fury, as he trotted to the corner of the plain where Stephen would hang the beaten man's sword, helm and shield in a tree to signify the capture. All day long the tournament raged, galloping far across country away from the field and back again. As the numbers dwindled, so did the knights make alliances in their assaults: two against one; three against one; even, late in the afternoon, five against one. Sir Philip saw one dismounted baron, separated from his comrades, hemmed in by hostile swords. The man fought like a Galahad, scorning all invitations to surrender until the steel was hacked from his fingers and he had only the choice of to yield or to die.

Three shields now lodged in Stephen's tree, but still Sir Philip was hungry for the earl, for the bold eagle himself. He watched and he waited, until at last, as the trees hardened against the sun-shot sky, they came to face each other, the two of them alone across the empty plain. Three times they charged, and three times the lances clattered from their shields. Steam from their horses' flanks turned them into smoking devils, sombre gods of war, as they gathered themselves for the fourth run, lunging forward in a weary gallop that rose scarcely above a trot. Victory came suddenly. Sir Philip met a blow full on the boss of his shield, shattering the eagle's lance. In the fifth attack he could unhorse the earl and pin him to the ground.

"Your shield, Sir, please. And your sword and your helm!" It was a sweet moment: a chivalrous victory over an honourable foe, and with a rich ransom to swell his fortune.

Evening was so nearly upon them that Sir Philip expected at any moment that the tournament would be called to an end. He had fought to the limit of his strength, and his body was limp with exhaustion. Yet there remained in the field one man to stand against him: the knight on the quiet grey charger, whom he had seen ride away from the combat in the morning. The knight who bore the red dragon on his shield, as if he were brave King Arthur himself! Sir Philip scorned the man for having taken upon himself such an emblem; and despised him for his strategy. It was a common ploy among certain knights to circle the battlefield, holding themselves aloof as if they had come only as witnesses to the sport. Only late in the day, when some valorous knight had grown weary from the struggle, would they ride out and give challenge. It was not an offence to the chivalrous code, but neither could it be considered a mark of great courage. Sir Philip could see that the red dragon was one such as this.

He sat loosely at his saddle and waited for the man to take up his position. The sky had died to pale orange, and the chill had begun to bite beneath the armour. Sir Philip wheeled his arms to loosen the joints. The muscles were stiffening in the cold; the shoulders numb from the impacts of lance and shield. He became conscious, as he sat, of other discomforts: the deep ache in his legs from having ridden so long; the open lesion where the mail had rubbed his thigh; the blistered fingers. He glanced across his shoulder to where the thin shadow still waited with the palfrey beneath the trees. In the branches the four shields nested like rooks. Soon, very soon, there would be a fifth.

Each knight couched his lance and raised a hand to signal to the other. When the hands dropped, the two great horses would come huffing like bulls: the grey fresh and high-stepping, upright and eager; the other heavy-legged, barely lifting. Sir Philip fixed his attention on the other man's shield: a red dragon on a yellow ground. He made a target of it and angled his lance, kicking at the tired wet flanks to beg for the last pennyweight of effort. He would smite this pretender full in the breast, would cleave into splinters the boastful wooden shield and prong him like a hog. Suddenly, when there remained but twelve horses' lengths between them, the dragon knight reined back as if he had taken fright and would withdraw. Then in an instant, as Sir Philip hesitated, he dug in his spurs and gave the grey its head. The two lances struck as one. Sir Philip's shivered on the shield-boss and made wood for some peasant's fire. The other came lower. There was a sharpness and a heat in Sir Philip's leg: a moment of delicious warmth as he lifted from the saddle, to be overwhelmed by a crushing pang that throbbed out again and again. The pains were like bells: a first light chorus of silver, then the heavy tolling that drowned all else. Released from its burden, Sir Philip's horse trotted for a few paces more, then settled unconcernedly to graze.

The lance had found a way beneath the hem of Sir Philip's hauberk and had entered the flesh above the *chausses*. It had drilled through the meat until it broke beneath the hip, leaving a stump that he thought at first was his thigh bone. Hot blood churned into the *chausses* and broke out in rivulets between the links. He touched it with his fingers, like a blind man, out of curiosity. A pale crescent moon weaved its first silver threads into the tall grasses that barred the sky above his head. He detached his mind from the pain and believed for a moment that he was lying in a wood.

"Your shield, Sir, please. Your sword and helm. And the trophies that hang in your tree!" The knight's voice grated on him, and drew him back to the plain.

"I will not surrender."

"Yield, Sir. I beg you, yield!"

"I am no esquire to be made sport of. *I shall not yield*!"

"Then, Sir, you would rather die?"

For answer, Sir Philip raised himself; first to his knees, then stiffly to his feet. The wounded leg buckled and pulsed, but he made himself press his weight on it. Pain came coursing in long tongues that licked into every corner of his body. But, for chivalry, he could not own to his suffering. He had never been a maid and would never again be a boy: it was *courage* that had made him a man. A man among men . . . Would never yield . . . Never! He snatched the red dragon's bridle and threw back the horse's head. But the knight was nimble. He leaped from the saddle as it reared and balanced easily on his feet.

"Yield, Sir, I say! Yield, or to your sword!"

Maddened beyond reason, Sir Philip stepped inside the man's sword-arc and brought down his blade, two-handed, like an axe upon his cap. It was not the thrust of a swordsman, and the knight was unprepared for so vulgar a cut. It bit deep into the helm and made a gash across his brow, laid open to the bone.

"Yield now," said Sir Philip. "*God is in my sword*!" He was ebbing away. Like the passing of life itself, the hilt slipped slowly from his fingers as he fell.

The dragon knight cleared his eyes of blood and raised high his blade, downward pointing like a dagger.

"Your trophies, Sir! Or your life."

Being both active and entirely healthy, the dog was against the law. All the country hereabouts – the moors and the rivers, the rocks and the woods – was Royal Forest. The whole wide swathe of land, from coast to coast, was marked "safe mansion" for wild beasts. Neither deer nor boar, neither hare nor even wolf, could lawfully – or safely – be hunted here by any but the King's men. The law was served by a skulk of informers, who traded their whispers to the royal foresters and woodwards, who gilded their tales for the verderers and regarders, who presented the guilty to the forest Justices. Who assuredly would hang the cottar and his son if they were caught, for their offences were multiple: not only had they neglected to mutilate their lurcher (the law required them to remove three claws from each of his forepaws, to keep him from the game), but they carried with them each a full quiver of arrows and a bow – common ash wood instead of the best yew, but almost as deadly, and equally offensive to the law. They hooked and untangled their way through the densest thickets, far from any forest trail, stalking into the wind.

Away ahead of them in the forest deeps, the men could hear the does and their fawns piping to each other in gentle reassurance. The deer were a small group of roe, including at least two young bucks but headed by an old matriarch. Only seldom did the men catch the white flashes of their rumps between the stems, too distant and too obscured for an arrow. It would demand a long and stealthy crawl to come upon the animals in a glade where they might have time and space to shoot. Each would let fly a single shaft and only then, if they failed to kill, would they slip the leash from the dog. Once, much nearer than they had anticipated, a straying buck barked out in alarm and the woodland froze, hunters and hunted together. Up went the heads of the deer. Down, until the danger had passed, went the heads of the men. What had disturbed the animals? The men's own twig-snapping clumsiness? Or a forest officer passing by?

The cottar was not a sporting man: he needed the meat to feed his family, and took no pleasure in the chase. He held only the meanest scrap of land, and could subsist only by selling his labour (and his son's, and his wife's) to the wealthier villeins and to their Lord Beaumont. If there were no employment for them, then they must starve – or steal. Against the deer they had tried to use the law's own principle of hobbling by mutilation. Weeks earlier they had watched a pregnant doe to her lair in the ferns, and had stolen up on her at the very instant of birth, to snatch away the still-wet fawn; but not, then, to kill it. They had used a thin-bladed knife, sharpened against a riverstone, to cut through the tiny soft hooves until the blood had flown from the quick. The injury had been designed to prevent the animal's escape until it was handsomely fattened, when they would return to cut its throat. But weakened fawns do not long prosper in the wildwood. The doe had moved on with the herd, and the calf had made a meal for a mouth more savage than the cottar's. And now, to add to this disappointment, came new anxieties. Ahead of them the wood was thinning towards open country: between the trees already they could see the sunbathed slant of a bare hillside, and its heavy cap of rocks. The deer were going to break cover.

The poachers' fears were threefold: fear of failure in the chase, for there was no time left to find another source of meat. Fear of discovery, for the forest way followed the rim of the wood and they would emerge in full view of anyone passing along it. And fear of the Horned Devil. This last superstition they owed to two travelling men who had run into the village late the previous evening, their shocked faces as white as a lord's linen. While they had been marking a pathway of tussocks through the bog beneath the high rocks, they said, they had met with a spectre of such vileness that they had splashed away like startled pigs, quite heedless of the mire.

"A bone-white face it had, and eyes as dark as caverns! And horns! Such horns! Horns as big as trees!"

The bog where this devil lurked lay on the moor beneath the hill that stood in the path of the roes. The cottar and his son watched the sudden flowering of white tails as the animals frisked into the sun. It was the boy who let slip the dog.

A fat brown toad had been killed by the horse's hoof. Only the head had escaped the crushing, though the skin of the body had stretched and flattened to its new shape without being broken. When Stephen made a light pressure with his foot on the belly, the jaws were pushed open by something bulging up from within; something purplish and shiny that steamed in the late afternoon chill. Sir Philip raised himself on an elbow and watched.

"Behold! How strange a habit is this? To torture broken frogs?"

Stephen laughed. "Master, you charge me wrongly. It is a toad."

"Nay, don't bandy with me. Frog or toad, the habit is the same."

The boy turned the body with his toe. "Methought perhaps it should make a meal for the hunters. There is meat for them on the legs."

The saker and the lanner were tethered without their hoods, each to a rowan stem. The lanner stood quiet, sunk into its breast with hooded eyes, but the saker prowled like a wolf; first one way to the limit of its leathers, and then the other. Its head cocked and darted at each small sound or shadow. Once, at a sudden movement far below them at the margin of the wood, it bated and tried to fly.

"I despair of this hothead bird!" said Sir Philip. "No, leave the frog to rot. They are well enough fed. Let them be." But still Stephen went on with his game.

"You have a thirst for blood, boy?"

"Not the toad's, Sir, for I have worthier foes in mind. *Oh, for how much longer must I wait*? When shall I be a *knight*?"

Sir Philip used his hands to help move his wounded thigh, laying it flat upon a couch of heather. "Then there is nothing you have seen which blunts your hunger for knighthood?"

"No, Sir. Nothing."

What Stephen had most recently seen was the snatching back of his master from the very edge of death. Sir Philip had bled so freely on the tournament ground, and had swooned so deeply, that the dragon knight had believed him already slain and had sheathed his stroke. But for Stephen, who had come out to claim the body, the joy at discovering his master still alive had been entirely dispelled by the expectation that the end could not be much delayed. And yet the miracle had endured. With the lance-head withdrawn from the wound and the gash staunched with clean linen, Sir Philip had woken from his sleep and, day by day, had regained his strength. He remained sickly pale and lame but, after no more than twenty days at his mattress, he was strong enough to ride. With Stephen to support him along the way, he had chosen to complete his recovery at the family manor in Cornwall. For this first night of the journey there, after they had rested by the tor, they would circle down into Ilsington and seek shelter with his kinfolk the Beaumonts.

"Is this not the very likeness of the tale you told me?" said Stephen. "Of King Arthur being carried to Avalon for the healing of his wounds?"

Sir Philip laughed. "Nay, boy! I'll not say the notion doesn't take my fancy, but nay! No Arthur I! Nor is there any other to be called his equal. And think on this, too, that to this day King Arthur has never come back to us. You would not wish your master to vanish thus?"

"No indeed, Sir. Then did he die there?"

"There are some who say he lives on yet. At Bodmin in my father's time there once came a band of Frankish fathers bearing holy relics. And there came out to meet them a man with a wasted arm, begging to be healed. And this man told the priests that Arthur lived. When they laughed and scorned him, the man's neighbours rose up and beat them, as if they had denied the Holy Father himself."

"If he lives, then why does he not appear to us?"

"If he lies abed! Or if he lies cold in the earth with his faithless queen! It matters little. If it pleases God, and if England has need of him, *he shall return!*"

Sir Philip sat up and leaned against his hands. "Look at the country about you, how the valleys lie jugged in silence. This is the peace that Arthur won. Through the King's forest here, across this very hill, the heathen Saxons once swarmed like rats through a granary. It stains the honour of their people. At a great city in the north, King Arthur had beaten their army to its knees and herded them like sheep into a forest. For chivalry then he heard their pleas, and suffered them to issue forth on a pledge. They were to sail at once to their homeland and return with tribute, gold and silver, to their master. But they were treacherous. As soon as the tide swelled beneath their planks, they turned southward and around the shore to Totnes, whence they spread slaying and burning through Arthur's kingdom here, spilling a river of blood that ran all to the Severn Sea. But as they tilled, so did they reap. In the province of Somerset, at the Mount of Badon, the King's army came up with them again. Picture it! Arthur, like the spirit of thunder, striking bolt after bolt into the devil's own lair. With the name of Holy Mary on his lips, and his own sword Caliburn in his hand, he slew that day four hundred and seventy men. Whomsoever he touched, he slew at a single stroke. And never again, for as long as Arthur reigned, did Saxon foot set down upon his kingdom's shore."

At the root of the rowan tree, the saker leaped and beat against the jesses. On the narrow plain at the foot of the hill, where the valley soil laid the first thin flesh over the bones of the rock, a dozen or more deer trotted lightly from the cover and stood with their heads up, tasting the wind.

"Pray hood those birds before they rupture their pinions!" Sir Philip cupped his eyes towards the trees. "Ha! Roes! A quarry fit for maids and boys! But no matter, tomorrow perhaps you'll see some sport. A day's ride from here once I saw a boar driven into a thicket. He put out with his tusks and sent fifty hounds to their deaths before the spearsmen could ride close enough to stick him. Such a hog he was. Five good spear thrusts it took . . ."

He stopped and rolled on to his stomach so that he could push himself to his knees and stand.

"The falcons, quickly! The horses!"

The cottar cursed the boy for his madness. "Goat-head! Have you a hog's dinner for a skull? Would you bring down upon us every King's officer in the realm?"

The herd flew like swallows, bounding and bobbing, seeming to skim the ground rather than touch it. At their head the old doe made in a straight line towards the rocks, which afforded the only possibility of haven. But midway up the hill she recoiled as if from some new and greater horror, and flashed across the slope to the cottar's right, trailing the herd behind her in a frenzied dash for the bog. At their tails the dog came low and straight, flanking wide as he saw them turn, shortening the angle to head them off. No sound came from the flying feet; nor were there voices to betray their trespass. But still the cottar clung within the skirts of the wood.

The boy was enraged. "Let us be men! Let us not hug the shadows like wounded hens! We have stalked all day. Shall we now give up all hope of meat? Come, we have earned it!"

From behind him the man stepped forward as if to reward the insolence with a fist. But, even as the boy raised an arm to defend himself, he pushed past and moved to the very fringe of the cover, parting the brush to scan out like a harboured stag. It was too late to think of retreat: if nothing else, they must at least recover the dog.

"In truth, I despair of your ways! I pray for a witch, to spread potions in your brain and cast out this pottage of warts!" But he held back no longer, stooping from the hips as he started to run, to improve the thrust of his feet on the hill. "If I did not know it otherwise," he shouted, "I could believe you were sired by the hound itself."

"The devil take you!" laughed the boy as he ran easily ahead. And the devil very nearly did.

From ahead of them beyond a shallow brow they could hear the slapping of hooves in the mire and the first small yelpings of the dog, reedy and birdlike in its agitation. Beyond the crest, the ground opened to a vision of ripe confusion: an opportunity too rare to let pass. The herd were hock-deep in the bog, some of them already sunk to their hams and struggling. The dog bucked and floundered in wide plumes of spray, its instincts torn between fear of the yielding ground and the carnal appetite for blood. A young buck, sinking backwards, released a smoke-cloud of crimson into the water to show where the jaws had already left their mark. The predators closed in. Wordlessly, as if acting to some prearranged plan, the man and the boy raised their bows, each to kill with a single arrow. At once, even before the first animal had fallen, the boy nocked again and took steady aim at the lurcher's wounded buck.

"All of them!" he cried. "We'll carry two now and fetch the others at nightfall!" But the arrow remained unloosed.

"Run!" yelled the cottar. "For pity's sake, run!"

In the excitement of the chase it had slipped from their minds, but now here it was, right there in front of them: risen out of the hags, the Horned Devil, guardian of the mire! It floated close against the water in a low boat of mist, and fixed them with a glare of dark malevolence. Black eyes in a gaunt face, with huge antler tines forked against the sky. It seemed to hover, with no legs to support it, as if it were master of the air itself. For the boy and the man there was no thought beyond a brute instinct to survive. Over tussock and stone they plunged, bruising heels and buttocks as the hill dropped away and they slithered towards the security of the wood. Behind them the hooves drummed closer and closer; then faded until they had entirely disappeared; then came again, stronger, faster and closer. Long, long before the trees, they would be caught. The boy still carried his bow, with the arrow still nocked between his fingers. He stopped and turned, unable to bear the horror of being taken blindly from behind; and was at once seized with a new pang of terror. The devil had turned into a boy on a horse – a boy of around his own age, dressed like the Lord Beaumont himself in a fur-lined *pelisson*. A boy with a bow at his shoulder and a falcon at his fist.

Sir Philip followed the chase from the hill, whence he descended slowly and with caution, not caring to chance a fall on so slight an errand. He watched Stephen gallop from behind the bluff in direct pursuit of the poachers, then veer away to skirt the drop and come at them again, lower down on the terrace. The manoeuvre was not without promise. The young man rode hard and fast, with the bravery

74

of a knight, and marked his quarry with the shrewdness of a huntsman. But then the younger of the two fugitives turned to face him with a bow.

"Ride on," said Sir Philip softly, as if to the saker. "Ride on and strike him down!"

But Stephen had not prepared himself against the possibility of attack. There was a sudden, cold brutality in the arrow's threat which had no echo in his knightly imaginings. This was not the well-fought pageant of pennons and lances that his visions had armed him for; not a lordly celebration of valour and steel. This was a ragged boy making ready to kill him. With no etiquette to instruct him, he was cast back upon his native resources, as naked as a deer. He reined back the horse and pressed himself hard against its neck; while the cottar's son, seeing that the devil had become all too clearly mortal, recovered his mind sufficiently to let fly a shot. The arrow skimmed the esquire's shoulder, not touching, but close enough for him to feel the waft of it in his hair.

Two men now watched their apprentices at play, for the cottar had reached the sanctuary of the wood. On the upper terrace, motionless now astride his destrier, Sir Philip mouthed silent encouragement. "Ride on! Ride on and strike him down!"

But the peasant gave out his breath in a roar. "Run, boy! Don't stand to fight him! *Run!*"

Once more the contest had become a race. Stephen, who had closed his eyes in anticipation of the arrow, heard the running footsteps even before the cottar's shout. Beneath him the palfrey wheeled and skittered, tossing its head at the confusion of signals from the reins. The boy was pricked by the shame of his failure, but restored in courage by his enemy's retreat. Clumsily he fought to bring the animal's head round, to kick forward and renew the pursuit. But there was no time. Within a few strides the cottar's boy would be lost among the trees.

Stephen knew that he would have to use his bow, but he could not draw it with the lanner still clamped to his fist. With hasty fingers he peeled away the hood and launched the bird into the sky, praying for it to fly at the fugitive's head. But it had no idea of its quarry and offered only enough wingbeats to save itself from falling, sculling low across the ground to settle at a boulder, where it stood tilting its head and making a sceptical review of its surroundings. Stephen fought against a tightening clasp of panic, sweating coldly in the glare of the watching eyes. His knees pumped at the palfrey to align it, while his fingers fumbled with an arrow and he tried to brace his body against the spring of the yew. The string was drawn high to his ear; his eye fixed immovably on the arrowhead. It was, even by the standards of a boy, a woeful shot: the flax bit viciously into his forearm and the arrow buried its barb in the earth not twenty paces from the horse. The cottar's son never knew that he had been a target.

At the edge of the wood, the peasants' noisy intrusion put up a flock of small brown birds, which began to seethe and chatter in the canopy. At its boulder the lanner slanted its neck with renewed interest, settled its breast low against the talons, then sprang in a sudden whipcrack of feathers. High in an ash tree, spinning dark against the pale grey bark, it snared its jesses at a fork and hung upside down in a bate.

On the upper terrace, Sir Philip nudged his horse forward in a slow walk towards the village. He noted the fresh carcasses in the bog and wondered at the age of the old red stag, which time and the weather had stripped to the bone.

THE APPLE TREE

It was a marvel how soundly the tree slept: so cold and drawn in upon itself, as if it were dead. It was the boy's favourite tree: his own, given him by his father. He smoothed his fingers along the wrinkles of its skin, and nuzzled it with his cheek. It had yielded its first fruit in the year that he was born.

William loved everything about the garden, even in the winter when the vegetables dissolved in long green smears and melted into the earth. Only a few scrawny cabbages, tall and thin, with woody stalks like saplings, had withstood the bite of the frost. Their hard veiny leaves had repelled every attack by beak and claw, and the fire would need many armfuls of wood to boil them into soup. William knew every tree in the garden: the plums and the pears, the nuts, the apples and the medlars. He understood their every phase and mood; could feel in the air the first faint whispers of seasonal change that would bring new leaf, or the unfolding of blossom, or the sweet mellowing of fruit. But to his own tree he was more even than a friend: a brother. Since their first shared year of life, thirteen years ago, there had been two sisters borne to William's family, and every autumn the brimming basketfuls of fruit. Each apple was brushed with crimson where it faced the sun, and each grew exactly to the size of William's palm.

The household was a comfortable one, warmly wrapped against all the darkest miseries of serfdom. Roger Wilde, William's father, was an envied farmer whose industry – helped a little by inheritance – had placed him among the richest villeins at the Ilsington manor. His house was in the first rank next to the church, with a large and fruitful garden. His field strips made a full virgate of thirty acres, and he held more sheep than he knew how to number in words (though he could notch an exact tally of them on his sticks). For both house and land he owed

77

duty to the manor; but he held also an assart, a freeholding of three good acres, grubbed out and hard won from the scrub, that was his alone. This was where William's own house would be built when he came of age; and here, too, would he make his garden. There would be more trees: cherries, quince, and many, many apples. And throughout each of the seasons there would be vegetables, a living pottage of colours and scents. At its heart would be a dark stock of cabbage, with peas and the pale-flowering beans that would swell and ripen in their soft secret beds of milk-white down. William loved the mild greenness of them on his tongue; and the richer, more golden flavourings of onion and leek, made vivid by garlic and pot herbs. His garden would have them all.

Christmas was coming. For the peasants there was little work to be done beyond timber gathering for fences and houses, and carrying out the manure ready for the spring ploughing. It was a bitter season for the poorest among them, the landless cottars who had no crops of their own. The richer men like Roger Wilde could manage in the low season with their sons alone, and had no employment to offer; and at Christmas, for two weeks or longer, all work on the manor was set aside for celebrations of music and dancing, and a great feast of meats at the hall. For the cottars it was a festival of dark skulkings among the trees, of subtle desperations in quest of forbidden fur and feather. Like wolves in their master's woods, they killed and stole and ate.

On the Thursday evening in the week before the feast, Roger Wilde's family was settling to its meal. The house was dark and sombre, for the rush lights were kept dim and the fire made only a dull glow beneath the heavy iron soup-crock. There was no chimney, and on still days the smoke would hang thick as linen, so that William's eyes would stream and he would have to clutch his throat to prevent himself from coughing. On this particular winter's evening there was a current of breeze strong enough to suck the smoke in long billows through the yawning thatch. But still the flame was damped down low. A house in the village not long ago had taken fire from a spark, and the widow inside had been roasted with her sheep. Roger had not yet forgotten what he had seen among the ashes.

William came uneasily to the table, for he knew that Agnes his mother had some sorry news to bring; and he could see from the sharp cleft above his father's eyes, darkened by the thin strain of light, that his humour was already low. Roger had been taking corn liquor in the alehouse, a sport quite untypical of his usual sober habit, and had returned bearing the mark of thunder on his brow.

"I fear for the bread," Agnes said at last, breaking the loaf in a shower of dark sharp crumbs. "The baker has kept it too long in the oven, and it will want for flavour."

William coiled his fingers and tugged till the knuckles cracked. His father's eyes moved with the wreaths of smoke, fixed yet detached, as if held by an icon. He cared nothing for the bread.

"And the flour," said Agnes. "I am more than ever certain that the miller did not return as good as we gave. This poor stuff cannot be the fruit of our own land! We should present him at the Manor Court for a thief!"

Roger hunched his shoulders and turned up his palms. "I know John well. He is not a cheat. The flour is good enough. It does not matter."

There was gravity in his voice, though he spoke quietly and without anger; but still William felt a cold gnawing fear, for he knew that his mother had even sorrier tidings to follow. He listened while she pursued her customary litany of daily tribulations, wondering how long it could be before she would bring herself to the matter that was uppermost in both their minds. Roger himself seemed almost to be dozing while his wife threw herself into the familiar peasant's raillery against the manor house dovecote, whose birds they were forbidden to kill, even though they robbed them of their crops. But after that the confession could be deferred no longer.

"Husband, we have had a mishap with the bacon."

"A mishap? With the bacon for our dinner?"

"That, and the other. All the bacon."

"What is amiss with it?"

William twisted his neck and looked into the corner behind the fire, where, at the height of Agnes' fury, the thick strips of fat had been thrown into the straw; and where they still lay glistening among the fish skins, undisturbed even by the hens. The grease still clung to his own fingers, and he wrinkled his nose at the smell.

"It was not sufficiently salted. It has all gone bad. We cannot eat it."

Meat was an uncommon luxury at the table of a peasant, even in the houses of virgate-holders like the Wildes. Pig and salt alike had cost them dear. And yet Roger still would betray no sign of particular dismay.

"It would ill befit us," he said, "at this moment to concern our minds with bacon."

"Ill befit us!" To Agnes, the loss had seemed a disaster; but now her husband's apathy struck her as almost more shocking than the waste of meat itself. Her excitement was too high to ebb into mere indifference, and the fear turned easily to anger.

"Ill befit us! With the corn harvest so piteously bad that our bones poke through our skins, you tell me it ill befits us to mourn the loss of our meat! Should it behove us, then, to starve?"

Roger raised his head from his hands and gazed at her steadily, without rancour. "If all the corn in the granary were turned to sawdust, still we should not starve! There is not time left for anyone here to starve."

He looked at each of his family in turn. At Agnes and William, who seemed more than ever alike with their faces fallen into the same slack expressions of bewilderment. At the two girls, Cicely and Johanna: Cicely in her twelfth year and Johanna in her ninth, who rested their elbows on the bare trestle table and stared up at him with puzzled unconcern.

"Come now, wife. Put aside your anger. Let Cicely serve us our pottage and bread, and afterwards you shall listen to what I say. Then shall you tell me whether your bacon still vexes you, or whether you would not find more comfort in a prayer."

For a moment William wondered whether his father had been too long at the alehouse; but he was man enough to know that the strangeness in Roger's manner grew more from an excess of sobriety than from any lack of it. He watched the thick mush of beans and peas settling in his beechwood bowl; and touched the steaming surface with his spoon to draw it into a stipple of glittery points. Agnes had been right about the bread. It was hard and dry, so that it drew all the moisture from the mouth and was impossible to swallow. The family squashed it into their soup and sluiced the liquid through it into their mouths. Afterwards, William took some cheese, leaving a pattern of dark finger-stains on the damp white skin, and wetted his throat with a cup of beer. Then he waited.

"Well, husband," said Agnes. "Will you not now tell us how I have deserved your rebuke?"

"By the heavens, woman, you are not rebuked! Unless it is by the Almighty Himself!" He did not look at her, but settled his eyes on a parting in the thatch, where a long sliver of pale night sky was seething in the wind.

"My news is grave, but I beg you all to listen carefully and not to be afraid. This is what I must tell you. Early this afternoon there came into the alehouse a wandering carpenter, who had journeyed from the east. And this carpenter, being like all travellers, fell at once to laying out his story before the idlers there. But they soon found that his was no ordinary tale. Such was its import that even those pickle-heads could see the weight of it, and they ran at once to call Richard the reeve. And when Richard in his turn had listened, he brought in all the men from the fields and byres and made us listen to it too. It was as if the alehouse were the Manor Court itself.

"What the carpenter told us was this. There is moving across the country a great pestilence that kills everyone it touches, good and evil alike. In the city the dead are piled one upon another like autumn leaves, with no one left to bury them. A man from a ship has told our carpenter that every foreign land is laid waste by this very same sickness, and that men can do nothing to save themselves even though they flay their bodies for penance. He spoke of a great battle in a distant ocean, a war between the sea and the sun. The sun drew up the water into a cloud so vile with the corpses of fish that it befouls the world with its stench. It is this cloud that bears down upon us now, not a day's journey from the village."

William had forgotten his thirst as he listened, but continued to busy his hands and mouth with rapid little sips of beer. His sister Johanna put a crust of bread between her lips and held it there unbroken, while Cicely and Agnes, intending reassurance, smiled stiffly at each other as if in embarrassment.

"To be touched by the cloud is to be touched by fate itself. There comes first a fever, enough in itself to lay brave men low. And then come boils that grow on the body the size of apples, and give out great agony and stench. There is a coughing of blood and a black vileness that oozes from the body, so foul in its stink that not even a mother can bear to be near her suffering child. Death comes before the end of the second day. It finds the sufferer alone, with neither love nor blessing as consolation . . ."

Cheese and bread were hurled into the straw as Agnes sprang to her feet, grasping her daughters so tightly by their wrists that they cried out in pain. William, too, had begun to rise.

"Husband! Is the sickness already in your head? Why do we sit here waiting like beasts to be slaughtered? We must gather our things and run to a place of safety! Come, at once!"

But the slow sad shaking of Roger's head forbade all possibility of hope. "Let there be no deceiving," he said. "Even as we talked in the alehouse, the rector brought before us a travelling friar who had seen the sickness too. The cloud covers all the land from sea to sea and travels at the speed of the wind. There is no sanctuary. Nowhere it would not seek us out. Even the masons in the great city cathedral have been slain at their work. It is a judgement of God upon the vileness of all His people."

"Then there is *no escape*? Death must take all?"

"It spares neither rich nor poor. Neither old nor young. And yet, even so, we must not forsake our prayers. Wherever the plague strikes, there are a few who remain untouched, and a few who are touched yet live. There is a faith among the doctors that scented smoke can rob the cloud of its power. They burn sweet woods in their houses and walk abroad with spiced apples in their coats."

Never again, from that evening forward, was Roger Wilde's hearth kept dull by any mistrust of flame. The fire became their life's spirit. Green ash and juniper were stacked high on the iron to purify the air with their smoke; and Roger cut up the fine flock mattress, that had been a symbol of his wealth, and nailed the material to make a seal across the windows. The family breathed the vapour for as long as their lungs would endure, then would fall choking into the straw to pray. William shut his smarting eyes and muttered some words; but his true comfort lay elsewhere. It was outside, in the moon-bright air of the close, where he would kneel once again upon the frost-baked soil and press his lips to the bark. If one apple might preserve a rich man from the plague, then what harm could befall a boy who was brother to a tree?

By Sunday morning the miasma had still not reached the village; but there could be no doubt of its approach. More itinerant craftsmen had come crowding through with news of rampant death; and bands of refugees had been seen on the high ground, fleeing westward along the tradesmen's route. The moon still showed pale in the sky as the people made their way to Mass. Their understanding of the spiritual eternities reached no deeper than it had ever done; but at last it was more than habit alone which guided their steps to the church. There was, in all of them, a new craving for belief. From his place among the men, William craned above the women's heads to see again the painted horrors of the Last Judgement. Other eyes followed his own, anxiously to contemplate the scourges of Hell. The wall-picture was as familiar to them as light and dark; but the images burned their eyes with a new urgency. Horned and scaly devils rending the milk-white limbs of the damned; the flaying of skin, the plucking of bowels, the searing of the flesh. In front of William stood John Perkyn, his father's cousin, who had been summoned to appear at the Manor Court to answer a charge of land-stealing (it had been claimed by a neighbour that he had unlawfully moved a boundary stone). Two long fingers of muscle were working beneath the skin at the back of Perkyn's neck, and William himself felt a nervous tug in the stomach. Suppose the man were guilty, and the pestilence should carry him off before he had atoned? There would be nothing then to keep him from the furnace. And yet: suppose the plague should pass him by? Then his reward would be hell on earth: to be buried to the neck at the place of his crime, and his head to be left to the mercy of the plough.

Hunted as he was by these devils of fear, William was surprised by his own preoccupation with the mundane. He had remarked a similar strangeness in his father: an imperishable interest, amounting almost to an obsession, in the conduct and security of his holding. He had sealed the holes in the house roof; had carried out the soiled straw for ploughing into the field; had gathered timber, broken the garden soil, and endlessly counted his sheep. At the last tally, one animal had been marked missing. After Mass it would be William's job to seek it out and drive it home.

For the first time ever that William could remember, the hubbub in church was kept to a brief exchange of whispers. There was no ale-talk, no jests, no bargaining for hogs. And, for perhaps the only time in the entire span of William Doderidge's rectorship, the voices fell wholly silent at the commencement of the Mass. Doderidge was a better rector to his village than many of his kind, though it was more his poverty than his faith that had made him so. He was not sufficiently wealthy to live in the city and to appoint a curate to his tasks, so he had been obliged to make his home in the rectory and to conduct the Mass in person. He had held the living for six years and enjoyed the distinction, uncommon among the poorer clergy, of being able to construe the service-book Latin. This was an exotic achievement, far beyond the comprehension, or even the appreciation, of his congregation; and it distinguished him less in the popular mind than his exemplary fidelity to his wife. So far as any woman in the village knew, and the tongues left little unsaid, he had lain with none other. Yet neither pious Latin nor faith in matrimony could open a way into the people's hearts. In the fields, where he farmed alongside them at his glebe, they had found him a tireless champion of his own causes; and they had yielded their tithes each year with no good grace.

William nudged sideways along the row to improve his view. The rector was an ageing man with an uncommon face: wet-mouthed, with a tremulous lip and a chin that had receded entirely into the smooth folds of neck. The jowls hung from his cheeks in fatty drapes, whose weight pulled out his lower eyelids in wet pink crescents. Never had the face been rich in colour; but today it was as white as mutton fat. William listened hard to the mumbles of Latin, as if by their sound alone he might absorb the essence of their magic. He did not know their meaning, but he did not doubt their power. If they could turn common bread into the body of Christ, then how easily might they divert a cloud? William and Roger together murmured the *Ave* and *Pater Noster* as the rector and clerk sang their responses; but the words made no further impression on William's understanding. More than ever he was grateful for his apple tree.

Even in common English, Doderidge was not a compelling speaker. Oratory was the business of the wandering friars, and the rector had held himself to the minimum that the Bishop had pre-scribed: four sermons a year. But today the people were looking to him. He must speak. It had been his intention to follow the habit of the friars, in building his address from a modest preamble to a pinnacle of inspiration. But his nervous excitement had placed him far beyond the range of such subtle calculations.

"Lechers!" he shouted intemperately. "Drunkards! Irreverent unbelievers! Stealers of cattle! Thieves of land!"

In front of him William saw the agitation in John Perkyn's neck quicken almost to a spasm, and the skin flushed brightly pink in strange irregular patches. Yet it had not been in Doderidge's mind to single out individual malefactors. He meant to exclude none of them.

"Miserable sinners! You have lowered us to the very *brink* with your slatternly misconducts! Through all the length of the world, wherever there are tongues to wag, there is talk of England's victories. *Crécy! Calais!* The earth *cowers* before the storm of English arrows. Under our noble King Edward, are we not made *mighty*? Are we not the very *cockerel on the dunghill*?"

Doderidge's jowls swung like dewlaps, and spittle flew from his lips in a sun-flecked parabola to the floor. Sitting cross-legged in the straw, William surprised himself again by yawning: he did not feel in the least bit tired.

"Who shall possess the *earth*? You? The drunkards rolling in their lechery? The miller vying for his corn? The Kings disputing their Kingdoms? No! It is all wicked, idle vanity! God alone rules! And he who challenges God shall *find no victory*!" He embraced the entire congregation in a wide scooping movement of his hands.

"The Lord is among us, and we are marked with His wrath! We have broken His *patience*! We have made issue with His *word*! What shall prevent us now from dying in payment for our sins?"

High above him, the pewter sky slammed heavily shut and the church grew dark and cold as if the end were already at hand. William turned to see if the first wreaths of poison had yet begun to coil beneath the door; and sniffed as he looked, but still he found nothing unusual in the air.

The rector's energy was almost spent. "Be advised," he said, "that tomorrow the lord returns to the manor, and there will be a sitting of the Manor Court to decide upon our course. But hear you this, and mark it well! Know that the pestilence travels also on the lips of strangers. Admit no traveller to this place, lest he thank us with the kiss of death! Now may God go with you . . ."

Outside, the air was cleaner and less chill. Yet: in its winter garb of brown and muted greens, the country itself looked as remorseful as the people. They gathered in family groups, over-swollen by grandfathers and cousins. Throughout the whole village there were not more than five such clans altogether, close-tied and intermarried with a nearness of blood that was both unavoidable and yet unlawful by the canons of the church. William's corner was as silent as stone, each elder among them burdened by the certainty of his guilt.

Yet their restraint was not universally shared. Within his own family group, the miller John Wode was raising a commotion over a cousin of his, a cottar whose face bore more than the common ration of boils.

"He steals like a jackdaw! Look at his face now! How he bears the mark of the devil in repayment! He carries the pestilence! We should cast him out now, before he brings death to us all!"

From all around him came an uproar of argument: some voices taking the miller's part, some the cousin's. And as the other families clustered round to add their own opinions to the dispute, it began to seem that the unfortunate man would be made to bear the full weight of the village's ill humour. Only by inspiration at the last did he manage to save himself. As Wode and some others stepped forward to lay hands on him, he pressed a pustule on his chin and bade them

85

observe the ordinary colour of the discharge.

"Ah," said Roger Wilde, shepherding his wife and children homeward. "That John the miller! Do you know this riddle? What is the boldest thing in all the land? No? The answer is a miller's shirt, for it clasps a thief daily by the throat!"

"But, husband," said Agnes. "You scolded me when I said as much. You said to us that John was a good man, and true."

"Ah now, so I did!" It did not trouble him to be caught out by his wife, for he had wished no more than to raise a little cheer. Yet, even through the midday meal, Agnes remained much oppressed with notions of injustice.

"Is it not true," she said, "that if a man do die and William Doderidge do live, then he shall take himself a profit?"

"The heriot and the mortuary tax," said Roger. "You know the law as well as I. If a bound man dies, then his best beast shall pass to the manor . . ."

"Aye! And his second best beast to the Church!"

The rock reached up sharp and black, as if it would punch a hole in the sky. William was almost in its shadow, sunk to his waist in a rolling sea of dead brown ferns. His legs were etched with fine white scuffs, jewelled here and there by shuddering droplets of red. He stood like a deer taking scent, though it was no hunter that he feared. The sun was already well down, spreading a low faint splash across the thickening screen of grey. Even on the stillest of days, the wind here was strong enough to stream the hair. Today, when he reached up to the summit, William found he could draw breath only by turning his head away from the sea. The hair flicked and stung in his eyes, and the gale lashed through his wet clothing until his limbs were stammering with frost. Below him and all around, the grey clitter of rocks showed plain through the scrub, each offering the hunched illusion of a browsing sheep. How often had he crept within a dozen places of such a stone, happy in his heart that he had found the missing ewe? He nerved himself for a direct confrontation with the wind, and stood to his full height on the peak. On the steep side, towards the coast, nothing moved; only wind-blown ripples, chasing through the trees. There was not an animal to be seen, and no mark of one beyond the tiny beards of snagged grey wool that streamed out from the thistles. On the landward side, where the air stood motionless in the shadow of the rock, the hill began more gently, before plunging suddenly away to a river whose steep valley slopes smoked with a leafless tangle of grey winter branches. William closed his eyes and opened them again. The tree cloud was *moving,* rolling up the valley side towards him: not twigs at all, but mist. On a day of gales, of power enough to snap branches, there hung above the river an unmistakable pall of *mist*! The breath in his chest began to hammer, and the blood rang in his temples as he recognised the sign. He did not pause. Down across the rock, where normally he would have eased himself on hands and knees, he leaped and flew, careless of injury, to plunge half falling, half running, through a clawing mattress of brambles. It was not until the ground began to level out again, when he was almost on top of them, that he raised his head and saw the men.

Moving directly across his path, one behind another along the tradesmen's route, came a party of walkers, heading west. William caught the slow nodding of heads above the low scramblings of thorn. They were not any peasants that he recognised; but from the soiling of their tabards he knew them for tin miners. A band of five had struck out some distance ahead of the sixth, who was reeling from side to side in his gait as if he were the worse for ale or exhaustion. It was immediately in front of this last man, and behind his companions, that William broke through the thorn canopy on to the path. Fear of the miasma had overcome all his habitual wariness of strangers, and he made no attempt to conceal himself. But the miner offered him no threat: indeed, he flinched from the boy and threw out his hands as if he were himself afraid of attack. William saw that the man's fingers were heavily crusted with mud, and that his legs were bruised and cut in many places. Beneath a muddied leathern tabard he wore a tight-sleeved *côte-hardie,* torn to rags at the knee; and leggings which had unravelled to ensnare his feet. The head-dress, too, was out of the ordinary; for on top of the usual cloth helmet, which enclosed his head and neck and turned into a long grubby point over one ear, he wore a round-brimmed hat. Around his midriff was a broad girdle, from which hung a long-bladed knife: a murderous weapon, fit for a robber, though he made no movement to withdraw it. His hands remained rigidly outstretched – like a blind man's, feeling for William's face.

"Stay by me, boy!" The voice was hoarse and dry; the face florid, and streaked where the sweat had cut into the mud.

87

"No!" said William. "You must run, too! The cloud is upon us! Look!"

He followed his own finger towards the heights, where the stones still grazed among the bracken. The cloud was high, and fast-running as a mountain stream: whirling currents of iron-tinged spume, wind-lashed across the sky. A pair of ravens hung beyond the rock as if hooked to the wind, then keeled and dropped with their black cloaks outspread over some carrion on the ground. Of the miasma there was not a wisp; yet, even though the wind lay fully against it, William felt no sense of escape. It would come; it *was* coming.

"Stay by me!" The man's breath was sharp, and foul with animal decay; his sudden spasm of coughing a warm sour rain on William's face. His fingers, which he tried to close about the boy's neck, were cold and damp, and weak as a baby's.

"Stay!"

William wrenched away, churning with revulsion, and made a distance along the road. The man shuffled a pace after him and stopped. A word was shaping on his lips but he seemed to fall asleep before he could give voice to it. His eyes were already closed when his head struck the ground and he did not re-open them. Nothing about him moved; not a finger. Behind William, fifty paces beyond, where the pathway divided to the village, another miner had hung back to watch. He cupped his hands and shouted.

"Leave him, boy! Get away! If you know what's good, leave him!"

The darkening sky wore a tinge of saffron to warn of approaching death. William did not look again at the fallen man, but left him to fortune and fled. Dusk unfolded its mantle and rustled in the thorns: ahead of him and above, the forest guardians arose on throbbing wings and screamed their loud alarms. All his senses prickled with the certainty of pursuit. The village roofs clustered darkly like calves to the mother church, their smoke-lit eyes glowing dull with orange fire. A child cried, and from nearby as he ran to his tree came a commotion of hens. A man shouted, and a low-running animal came rippling into the underbrush. There was a smell, in the smoke, of apple wood.

THE PRAYER

Inside the church the birds were nesting again. They darted in and out through the chancel roof, stealing straws from the compost of old thatch that was sagging through the holes. The woman knelt. She listened for a moment to the heavy drip of water from the moss-grown walls, and smelled the bare-earth smells of plants and mud. She was not, by any standard, a handsome woman. The memories of pocks lay like rose petals on tallow cheeks, and her teeth were pulpy and grey, filling the breath with decay. Her peppery dun hair, white-streaked from the crown, hung wetly in strands even though the day was dry. It served to conceal her eyes behind two precisely congruent curtains of shadow, parting only sufficiently to reveal the bulbous swell of her nose, surprisingly blue-veined like an old man's and cushioned on an underlip of startlingly vivid pink. Her limbs were shapelessly, almost liquidly, plump, and so tentative in their movements that, to many eyes, she formed the image of a grossly swollen infant. Neither were any of these disfigurements improved by her costume. The plain woollen robe, in which she lived and slept, had holes even through the patches; and it smelled like the lair of a fox.

While her knees spooned up a mound of cold black mud, the woman was praying, as she had prayed every morning since her seventeenth birthday, for a husband. There were no words in this prayer, for she could speak only in the sad language of her eyes. Her tongue would occasionally thrust itself like a caged bird against her teeth, as if it were bursting to take wing on some epic flight of invention or entreaty. But almost always it would loll back again like a dying thing. On the few occasions that she did contrive to utter, the outburst was sudden and shocking: a watery, swallowing noise which she forced out with her tongue pressed tight against the palate. Only her father, when he took the time, could find any meaning in it.

But God could see. He looked inside her head and could understand the meaning of the pictures there. She was so certain of this fact – so certain, too, of the enduring quality of His love – that when the day came on which her prayer at last was answered, she could accept with simple, unaffected gratitude a visitation which more sophisticated minds might have regarded as a miracle. She felt it as a presence suddenly behind her: a small movement, a breath of warmer air. There was no other sign – no blinding light or choir of angels – yet she knew at once that she had received the gift. She made a half turn on her knees and flung herself forward on her elbows to smother the earth with kisses.

The young man who stood looking down at her was a stranger, well-clothed in an unpatched robe edged with animal skin. Her hair, as she crouched, was nestling in the fur. Slung across his shoulder – proudly, as if it were a trophy – the man carried the equipment of a journeyman stonemason; and he held in his hand a square piece of parchment with some straight black lines drawn on it. His dark hair and beard framed a face which, in the clarity of the eyes and softness of the mouth, would confirm the woman's expectation of moral power and spiritual gentleness; although, if she had been looking directly up at him instead of worshipping the ground at his feet, she would have seen that his lips for the moment were pursed forward in an expression combining the more ordinary qualities of amusement, inquiry and distaste.

Blindly she stretched her fingers to touch his foot, but found that he had stepped back so she could no longer reach it. Slowly then, with modest courage, she raised her head to look, arching her neck until the tip of the mane was brushing the curve of her spine. Oh praise be! Oh glory! The fine strong shoulders! The eyes! Up she sprang, kittenish in her joy, to wrap her arms around his shoulders, and to pour the worship of her breath full stinking into his face. She gave her thanks to God and, as the picture of gratitude took shape in her head, so did the word break perfectly formed from her lips.

"Husband!"

Richard Lynde had been commissioned by the master mason Robert Morton to assist at the rebuilding of Ilsington church. He had walked that morning from a farm in the Teign Valley, where he had spent the night on his journey from Exeter, and had entered the nave with the innocent intention of composing a well-sounding opinion on the condition of the walls. He was an energetic young man, with his ambition firmly fixed on a mastership of his own, and was not one to squander any opportunity of demonstrating his worth. For the moment, however, far from winning an advantage over his fellow journeymen, the only reward of his enterprise was to find himself trapped in the clutches of a madwoman. He was knocked off balance by the weight of her assault and had to fight to recover himself, twisting his head violently to escape the stench.

"Let me loose, woman. Let me loose I say!"

Utterly enraged when he could not immediately break her grip, he lunged with his fist and caught her a blow of such extraordinary force – in truth, far harder than his predicament required – that she was pitched on to her shoulders to roll over backwards with her toes striking the ground behind her head. Richard recoiled from what he had done, though not entirely through fear that he might have injured her. The plain fact was that he had never seen a woman so completely revealed before. There, to burn for ever in his memory, was a picture of pitted white fat and clogged dark hair, all scabbed and besmirched with mysterious soil and blood. And then her pleading eyes, and the smell. It revolted him, and he ran.

In the weeks that followed, Richard seemed to see the woman almost every day. She never approached him directly, but would entreat him silently from afar, like an abandoned child. On the first morning of his employment, when she came and stood close by the church, the master appeared angry and called away the journeymen to increase their distance. The reason he gave was the need to protect confidentiality among craftsmen, but it seemed to Richard – grateful though he was to be removed from her sight – that there was no harm the simpleton could do in the way of betrayal. She was, after all, unable to speak. He wondered if she might have made a similar assault on the person of the master himself, the devout and scholarly Robert Morton; and, disturbed as he was, he found it impossible not to smile. For this Morton was a man apart. It behove any guildsman to be a stern and particular master, a servant only to God and his craft; but Robert Morton had the sanctimony of a bishop. The lodge he built was a typically poor affair, made in the local style of poles and thatch; yet, had it been the city Guildhall itself, he could not have revered it more devoutly. Almost more than St. Michael's itself, it was hallowed ground, and holy in its purpose.

"From this lodge," he was fond of saying, "shall issue the best work that God can produce, using Robert Morton as his instrument."

For Richard, who had come only lately to the higher skills of set-square and compasses, it was a hurtful disappointment that his opinion of the work was not invited. Only the master, with the rector John Drake, was admitted to discuss the design with his patrons Sir Thomas and Lady Arundel – and it was a fact, which Richard was quite old enough to have understood, that any other arrangement would have been unusual almost to the point of uniqueness. Nevertheless, the supposed slight caused an injury to his pride which cast him low for many days, amounting even to weeks.

The work itself was of a common enough kind. The old church, which had stood for two hundred years, had been built to an ordinary cruciform plan of chancel, nave and transepts. It was small and earth-floored, with a roof that threatened at any moment to fall in and break the congregation's heads. Plainly it was no longer the kind of building which could be thought proper to a district so richly blessed with wool and tin. The dignity of the manor required it to burgeon both outward and up: outward into arcaded aisles and chancel chapels, all lavishly embattled and decorated; and upward into a tower. Morton's contract allowed three years for the work, and named a sum of money whose exact figure was not revealed to any mason outside the Morton family; for the master had brought with him not only his younger son John – a mason newly returned from his wander-years – but also his nephew and apprentice Stephen Wode, a boy aged fourteen. For skilled labour there were five local journeymen engaged on account of their reputations as willing workhorses (Richard felt this, too, as an affront); and there was a motley and ever-changing crew of villagers to lift the barrows, mix the mortar and lash the scaffolding.

From the very beginning, when the masons were doing no more than trim the poles for their lodge, there was always a crowd: sometimes no more than a chorus of urchins, whose favourite sport was to bait the apprentice with rude mimickings of his uncle; sometimes a coarse throng of men, women and boys, all in blatant truancy from the fields, who seemed to have taken upon themselves the function of an examining committee. They would mutter in low private voices, and afterwards call aloud to Robert Morton in a manner which astounded the masons for its almost offensive lack of respect.

"Hey master, why doan' 'e set that corner straight?"

"Hey master, why doan' 'e tak of th'coat an' show un th'way?" (This after Richard had been admonished for imperfectly squaring a block.)

For all that he had the ear of Sir Thomas Arundel (and a spiteful tongue to match it with), they would show no fear of the master mason. One thing alone could persuade them to break off their harassments. Whenever the woman simpleton approached too nearly for their peace of mind, they would fall back as if menaced by a devil.

But even this would afford little comfort to the masons; for with the mob dispersed they had only to endure the woman in their stead. She would stand as mute and immovable as a boundary post, just watching. Her eyes would pursue Richard wherever he went: up and down the scaffold, in and out of the lodge. If he passed out of sight through a doorway, then she would watch the void until he reappeared. All the men were unnerved by the intensity of this surveillance, and were in no way assuaged by the obvious fact of her imbecility. The strength of her preoccupation bespoke some peculiar malignant force from which they could find relief only in humour.

"Could you not keep this *wife* of yours at home, Master Richard?"

It all served to extend even further the distance which Richard felt from his fellow journeymen. He had seen from the very beginning that he was their superior, separated by his ability to measure and to translate the master's templates on to the stone. Yet at the same time he was able to feel no closer to Robert Morton himself, who kept within his family and lodged with the patrons at the manor. There was no particular encouragement for him, no promise that he would be helped towards his mastership. Whichever way he looked, beneath him or above, he could find no one to call a friend, and no one to admire. Only the woman, with her damnable haunting, had picked him out for any singular quality of his own.

It was not until the autumn of the first year, when the outer walls were already growing like a new skin around the nave, that she made an attempt to contact him more directly. He discovered her one evening in the lodge, hovering among the tracings and templates on the master's side of the partition; and stood facing her, idiotically tongue-tied like herself, across a gulf of silence. Watching her watching him. He knew that it was his duty to evict her; yet he feared it would not be possible to persuade her by words alone, and he rejected the thought of laying hands on her again. It would seem a pitiful admission of weakness, but he knew there was nothing he could do beyond running to the manor and warning Robert Morton of her trespass.

As it happened – and as he would have anticipated, had he been in any condition to think – his departure from the lodge was all the persuasion she needed. Faithfully she kept pace with him all the way to the manor, stopping when he stopped, hurrying when he hurried, as if they were joined by a measuring pole. When he appeared before the master, with the woman looming solid in the dusk behind him, Richard felt more than ever foolish in continuing to press his complaint. And yet, even as he was prepared to admit that he had not conducted the matter well, he was in no way ready for the stinging, uncontrolled savagery of Morton's rejoinder.

"Impudent whelp! I should whip you for it! Why must you encourage her so? Do you seek to *mock* me by it?"

Richard was aghast, uncomprehending. He wheedled and twisted his hands in an agony of uncertainty. "But I did not encourage her, master. It was as I said. She was in the lodge, in the very tracing room where not even the journeymen masons are allowed to go. I found her there."

"I heard you well enough! And I repeat! Do you seek to mock me by it? Do you pretend you did not know?"

"Know master?"

"That this woman is my daughter!"

For the remainder of that year the work went ahead at good speed. The new outside walls and porch were up to their full height and, at the west end, the tower was beginning to climb. At last Richard had begun to win some small reward for his diligence. Morton had invited him to carve the tracery in some of the new aisle windows, and – better yet – to oversee the setting of new half-columns against the outside of the nave. Later, after these had been matched with their opposite halves on the inside, they would bear the weight of the roof when the old walls were knocked away. Morton had even made it the subject of some friendly banter.

"Master Lynde," he said, "you must be sure to remain inside the church while those walls are taken down. Then, if your columns are not up to their work, it will be entirely on your own head!" He had wholly set aside the acrimony concerning his daughter and, in full and generous recognition of the young man's special worth, had shown himself ready not only to restore their relationship to its former condition but (so it seemed to Richard) positively to raise it to new levels of co-operation and understanding.

This new accord was further marked one day when it fell to Richard to represent the master at the quarry, to inspect a fresh shipment of stone and to arrange its transport to the village. The principal difficulty here was that between the church and the quarry, which was carved out of a terrace behind the great rock on the moor, there was no track wide enough to haul a cart. All the stone had to be brought down by pack horse, which was a long and exhausting piece of business for men and beasts alike. And there were other, more obdurate, obstacles too.

The hewers at the quarry had a separate lodge of their own, a damp and sombre cavern whose cold grey slabs seemed never to have been touched by the sun. Its dark, unwelcoming aspect corresponded precisely with the demeanour of the quarrymen themselves, whom without exception Richard found lewd, uncraftsmanlike and sullen in their manner. For the men at Ilsington, the gradual flowering of the church was a subject not only of great pride, but of humility too; and their labour as much an act of worship as a matter of commerce. But the hewers had no such joy or conviction in the higher purposes of their calling. Richard found it difficult to like them – and difficult not to be a little afraid. He was shocked by their casual profanity, and by the forthright disrespect with which they had received him; and ashamed by their ridicule when he tried to separate the good stones from the bad.

"Not well enough dressed for you? What, boy, d'ye want your corbels ready carved for 'e? Garn, be on your way, silly pup!"

And they turned their backs on him as if he were unworthy of their attention. But if Richard was nervous of the hewers, then this was nothing to set against his quite undiminished fear of giving offence to Robert Morton, or of lowering his opinion. Some of the stones they pressed on him were so lumpishly misshapen that the masons at their bankers would have been unable to square them without losing fully half of the material to waste; and this, he knew, would set his master roaring like a bear. So Richard duly disputed with the quarrymen, but he did so only because he dare not do otherwise. And he disgusted himself by managing the affair like a common servant.

"Either you will oblige me," he said, "*or I shall make a report on your conduct to my master, Robert Morton.*" And so it was Robert Morton that the men obeyed, more commanding even in his absence than Richard could make himself by personal appeal.

There were other indignities to follow. Richard had brought with him two labourers to attend to the loading and conduct of the horses – a wordless, mud-caked pair who seemed, by the glances they fired at each other from beneath their lowered bony brows, to be harbouring some hideous mutual grudge. Each squandered the greater part of his attention on the other – presumably through fear of sudden assault – and it soon became plain that they were quite unsuited to the business for which they had been employed. They were so thoroughly unable to grasp the need for balanced loads that some of the animals were cripplingly overburdened on one flank and could move only half side-ways like crabs. Richard repaired the imbalance as well as he could, but the sky was already darkening and the need to complete the journey in daylight was more pressing than the comfort of the horses. In the end, as they picked their way over the slippery, rock-stepped path, it seemed to him a miracle that disaster should take so long to strike.

By the unkindest of ironies, the accident did not happen until the track had levelled comfortingly in the floor of the valley, and the first rooftops of the village were already within sight. The victim was an animal at the very rear of the column which, without any sort of warning, suddenly craned forward over its front legs and collapsed. There had been no root or boulder to snare it: the barrier was simple, insurmountable, exhaustion. Richard flogged at its rutted, sudsy flanks idly with a rope, but with no real hope that it would be able to rise unassisted.

And then, afraid of seeming indecisive, he began to shout at the labourers: absurd instructions to pull and push. But they would only stand there, shaking their filthy heads, refusing even to walk back to him along the track. Richard's voice began to crack womanishly, out of control; but he knew, even as he screamed his wild, random, ridiculous threats, that they were right. Whatever they did, the horse would go no further.

He saved himself by transposing his fury to the animal, raging at it and bidding it to die, until he was able to calm himself. "Very well," he said then. "I shall wait here. You men take the other horses on to Master Morton and unload them. Then bring two of them back to gather up this load here. Now hurry!"

The stones had been trimmed already to a workable size but they were still of great weight, sufficient to call for the whole of Richard's strength to roll them from the panniers. He wondered as he worked, how severe would be the wrath of Robert Morton, and was mightily thankful that the labourers had preceded him to absorb the worst of it. In his heart he knew that this was the reason he had sent them in his stead, why he had chosen to sit here and play nursemaid to a horse. He tried as hard as he was able to put the thought from his mind, but it would not leave him. Until:

"What! Has the horse been hurt? You misuse it so cruelly!"

It was a woman's voice, angry; and Richard was startled suddenly to find another pair of hands wrenching at the stone alongside his own. She was dark-haired, young, perhaps even younger than himself; a stranger, but narrowing her eyes at him as if in expression of a powerful lifelong hatred. He stood up hurriedly, dusting his hands on his robe, and tried to look at her without meeting the fury in her eyes.

"Come now, Master Lynde!" she said sharply. "This is no time for you to be idling. Please remove these stones at once!"

He stooped, dumbstruck, though willing enough to resume his hauling; glad, even, for something to absorb his attention. He was sure he had never seen her: he would have remembered. Fiery emerald eyes with a disconcertingly – surely unforgettably – direct way of looking; a small nose as straight and as narrow as if it had been cut from a template; pink lips.

"Madam," he said. "I do not know you. How is it that you know my name?"

"Your name? I have heard speak of it. You *are* Master Lynde, are you not?" She turned away from him to comfort the horse: long thin fingers tracing light patterns across the cheeks, behind the ears, combing through the mane. "It is too unkind to treat a horse so! The stones are too heavy. You should use a cart."

"The path is too narrow for a cart. Where, I pray you, have you heard speak of my name?" He pulled clear the last stone and stood up again, looking down at the back of her head, noting the milky whiteness of the scalp through the raven blackness of her hair. "How do you know me?"

She turned, no longer angry, and froze him with a smile. "There! You see? It will be up on its feet again in no time, quite well again!"

"It is only a horse," he said sulkily. "It is a horse's purpose to be used."

"But not so cruelly that it falls to the ground and dies! A dead horse is no worker. Use it kindly and it will repay you better. Like a mason will, or a wife! Do you have a wife, Master Lynde?"

"No. I have no wife. But tell me how . . ."

"*My name is Margaret Morton.*"

He knew at once how stupid he must look, with his brow crumpled like a bedcloth and his tongue poking out between his teeth. Excitement, dismay and embarrassment, all in the same ridiculous facial extravagance. But *Margaret Morton*? He wished he could organise himself sufficiently to look at her again, but he was held back by a feeling – as absurd, he knew, as all the others – that it would be almost improper for him to see her.

"You are . . . his wife?"

He would never forget the way she laughed. "I am his daughter."

In contradiction of all that Richard had been expecting, Robert Morton dealt kindly with him and did not seem displeased with his enterprise at the quarry. "You did well to settle so fair a bargain," he said. "Those hewers are rascals who cheat. At the next meeting of the guild I shall make a petition against them."

Richard's consuming task at this time concerned the erection of the tower – or, rather, the erection of the scaffold surrounding it. This was a job which customarily would have been left to the village carpenter, but the man at Ilsington had shown himself to be of so little competence that Morton dare not trust him. He was a grey-skinned man, with a baby-smooth hairless head that obscured his age; but he could not have been less than forty and his skills would not have flattered an apprentice of fifteen. He was sufficiently clever with an axe to strip the sap-wood from raw poles, but beyond this he needed to be watched with no less vigilance than the common herd of labourers. Richard stood at the top as the first tier rose, and looked down importantly at the toiling heads. An earlier master of his had died from a fall on the scaffold, and he was mindful of the responsibility he had been given. He saw to it that the putlogs were driven deep into their sockets, and that the ropes lashing the uprights were twisted so tightly with wedges that they were as solid as the wood itself. As an insurance against the risk of falling stone, he made certain that none of the planks was less than six inches thick, fussily discarding any that did not fully satisfy his measure. It soured his name with certain of the workmen, and severely curtailed the rate of work, but he had the reassurance of knowing that nothing could come amiss with the scaffold for which he could personally be held accountable.

An advantage of being engaged on the tower was that it kept him at a more comfortable distance from the idiot woman who watched, though he could seldom keep himself entirely from her sight. Above everything he preferred the indoor work, in the new aisles where it was cool and still, and where he could bask in the gloaming of his own imagination. The vision of himself as master would be broken only by the brief clatter of a rudely awoken sparrow, or the rhythmic grind of the capstan winch as another stone bundled its way to the head of the scaffold. He liked to run his fingers over the stone boastings which he had set there ready for the master to carve into saints or heraldic beasts; and he would tilt his head with narrowed eyes and dream of the carving he could have made himself. He saw an angel, a seraph, with hawk wings and delicate hands and the face of Margaret Morton. He hoped it was not a blasphemy that this heavenly creature, in his vision, had piercing emerald eyes.

From time to time he had misled himself into the belief that he would ask Morton's consent to make this very statue. *Master, she would be the most serene of angels, like a prayer formed in stone.* But he knew he dare not do so, for – if nothing worse – it could too easily be taken as a sign of ingratitude or discontent. Already he had been raised up above the common journeymen, whose work at the bankers had not advanced beyond the squaring of quoins. Without supervision from the master he had been permitted to cut the arched heads for door and window openings, and to set the columns for the aisles. Morton had placed no greater trust even in his own son John, and Richard knew that he should accept it as a mark of confidence; and he knew, too, that this rate of advancement should be swift enough to satisfy. But then another voice within him would bridle at his own complacency. Through stone-cutting alone, it said, he would never become a master.

It was into this eternal inner conflict that Margaret Morton broke one shady afternoon, walking on cushioned feet to surprise him from behind, her voice swelling to hold back a mischievous tremor of laughter.

"Master Lynde! Your mistress waits so faithfully outside. Why do you not go to her?"

Richard's feet swayed perilously on the ladder, and the long plumb-line began to beat against the wall, softly like a heart. He engrossed himself with his level; muttered a remark to the mason whose head showed through the reveal, where they had been setting a table-stone on the sill; and fretted with his trowel at the mortar. But there was nothing he could do, nowhere he could turn, to escape his awareness of her eyes. He tried to whisper, as if to moderate the indecency of uttering such a thing in church. *"Mistress?"*

"The pretty one!" Her voice rang with the clarity of a bishop's, echoing unconstrainedly in the vaulting emptiness. "The talker! Your one true lover!"

"You would speak thus? *Of your own sister?*" He hissed through his teeth and made a damping movement, palm downwards with his hand, begging her, if not to silence then at least to reduce her voice to the level of his own. But still she continued gaily to declaim.

"Sister! Such a sister! She is an idiot, as anyone can see, and should not be let live. My father is too weak-willed." She paused to savour the effect, for Richard's face on hearing this was crumpled in alarm. "But I can see that you are fond of her too. How closely she follows you! How she must *excite* you with her flattery!"

At this Richard's companion, who had remained transfixed at the reveal like a saint in his niche, could suppress himself no longer. The laughter burst out of him in a long, vulgar ululation, joyful and triumphant: a fine tale to bring to the members of the lodge! Richard was not anxious for the interview to continue at all, and certainly not on a footing of increased intimacy, but for the sake of his own privacy he was compelled to descend the ladder.

"Madam, I beg you please! Do not speak of such things!"

She lowered her voice then, mockingly to a whisper, and cupped her mouth in the manner of a conspirator. "It is all right! She cannot hear us!" Again the words were pulsing with pent-up laughter. "Though she looked in mighty sore dudgeon when she saw where I was walking."

"Sore dudgeon? But why?" He dared to meet her, just fleetingly for a second, eye to eye, as if he might find there some explanation for her mischief.

"Why? It is simple! *Which sister would you choose?*" She laid the tips of her fingers against her lips in a pretence of stifled mirth, making what through Richard's eyes seemed a grotesque parody of prayer. He remembered the image of his carved angel, and the sacrilege of the emerald eyes.

"Master Lynde!" It was the mason at the window who called. "Come quick!" There had been an accident. A young boy, whose hands had been wet from mixing mortar, had let slip the handles from a barrowload of stone and crushed the bones in his feet.

The two sisters now both were a disturbance to him. The silent wraith, who clung to the coat-tails of his shadow; and the other, who danced across his consciousness like a moth, brushing with her wings but never settling. Her words fluttered and teased, but there was always in her levity a trace of something more purposeful than idle mockery. Wherever he walked, he carried a small thrill of fear. Not on account of the simpleton, who remained all too predictably discomfiting; but entirely because of her sister's habit of stepping out at him suddenly and without warning. Each corner as he turned it was a challenge to his nerve; yet the excitement he felt was not altogether unpleasurable. He occupied himself in composing verbal darts to throw back at her – questions as pointed as her own. But they remained – as they had to remain – unuttered, and he would fall back instead on a stonewall countenance of disdain. Only at night, while he slept at the lodge, did their relationship materially change: then, with his imagination left unguarded, he would awake to find there were more compelling urges to suppress.

The time came, late in the spring, when the tower was almost to its full height and only the battlements remained to be completed. On the morning that Richard was ushering the last small caravan of stone down the deepening groove from the quarry, Margaret walked out along the valley path to meet him. She did not pretend that their encounter was a matter of chance, but stood solemnly to wait for him beneath an oak, within sight of their very first meeting place. For the only time that he could remember since that day, her voice was firm and level, in low humour.

"The church is fully built," she said, "and your days here now will be few." He nodded. "And then there will be no more work for you? You are not to be engaged upon the woodcarving?" This was an insight of almost unnatural sharpness, as if she had been looking into his mind.

"Woodcarving! Oh yes, there is much woodcarving! Bench-ends as magnificent as any cathedral's, all delicately cut with crockets and fine tracery! And a rood of sumptuous ornament, with panels for the saints! Yes, there is much woodcarving! The master and your brother, with a woodcarver from the city, will divide the work between them. It is no business for a journeyman!" He broke off and stared up into the green haze of the oak, afraid that he had revealed too much of his final, stunning disappointment; that, in his implied complaint against her family, he would have offended her. But it was not so: she had begun to smile.

"You are not like the others," she said. "I have seen how you hold yourself apart. You have skills beyond any other journeyman in the lodge. Before many years, you shall be a master on your own." Again she had pricked the tenderest shoot in the whole field of his sensibilities. Such was the rawness of his feeling – and such, still, his fear of being scorned for it – that he could protect his ambition only by denial.

"*Master mason*! How can I be a master mason when I have no money to buy instruction?"

"Was not your father a mason? Did he not apprentice you and teach you?"

"My father is long dead."

"And Master Morton, though he trusts you, does not teach you well? No! I can see that he lends all his time to young Master Wode. Ah, what it is to be of kin!"

"What indeed!"

"It is a pity that you are not of a mason's family. With a father such as Master Morton, there could be no limit to your attainments."

Richard snapped out of what had become a drift towards reverie. *With a father such as Master Morton?* Now, surely, the moth had begun to flutter again, and she was returning, a creature of the wild, to her former, irresistible habit. He turned abruptly and addressed his attention to the pack-horses, trying to reconstruct the aloofness which, in her company, he had made his custom. But the smile had gone out of her eyes: she was not laughing at him now.

"I despair of you!" she said, reverting almost to anger. "I do not believe you have the *will* to be a master. The way is plain, but you will not take it. Even your mistress simpleton could tell you. *The answer stares you in the face!*"

The wind had risen to a tempest among the treetops: rolling and crashing, wave upon wave in a wild green sea. Margaret stood to face it, opening her lips as if to feed upon the gale. The long black hair was tossed like a stallion's mane, and her robe made a light pressure against her skin. In the outline of the wind as he looked back up the hill, Richard could see the small firm swell of breast and belly, the jut of her hips and the hollow junction of her legs. For an instant he saw a picture of thick white thighs, soiled and streaked in dark mysterious folds, and took away with him a feeling of delicious unease.

In the church, the carpenters had put up their cradle for the roof. Soon the plasterers would follow, and the glaziers and the plumbers, and the painters to dash their vivid scenes across the spandrels in the aisles. Richard shut his eyes and let his hands enjoy their own creations, up and along the window mouldings, where each cut was a master-work of rich simplicity: ogees and rounds, quirks and fillets, pride and sorrow mingled. For the journeyman it could be an ending; for the church, only a beginning. Whatever became of him, whether fortune carried him to a mastership or to a pauper's grave in the soaking earth outside, here was something which could never cease to be a part of him. For perhaps two hundred years, the village would bear the imprint of his hand.

He smelled the mortar and the dust, the fresh-hewn timber and the soil. Two hundred years! But what should he care for two hundred years, when he could see no future beyond the next two hundred days? He thought of Margaret Morton and Robert Morton – and of the future that lay in the master's gift. It was an audacious thought, an obsessional and a dangerous one. *With a father such as Master Morton*! Was this, then, the answer? Was this what Margaret had intended? Could he really *marry* her? When he had no fortune to his name beyond a beechwood mallet and a bolster? Would Morton be content to receive him like a piece of freestone, to carve into the likeness of a master mason for his daughter? *Would* he?

The wind had fallen with the dusk, leaving not so much as a sigh among the trees. The moon seemed drawn towards the earth, chilling with its silver touch, and brushing long black shadows into the under-places; shadows so deep that they seemed to have a physical form, as if Richard could reach out and grasp them. He rested his eyes on the spine of the hills, following the clean bare line through all its dips and rondures until it led him back again to the wood. Simple curves, yet breathtakingly intricate, like the tracery at his windows. Thus was the craftsman truly an instrument of God! Above his head, a cluster of new young leaves stood hard, black and motionless, cast in iron against the moon. Delicate, yet with a secret strength that would defy a storm. He thought of his own delicate gifts, preserved in stone for all history; then he let fall his hands, loosely at his sides, and stepped deliberately into the darkest, deepest pool of shadow. It did not swallow him. The light crept behind him into the dark, and the ground held firm beneath his feet. Tomorrow he would go to Robert Morton and ask!

The night was restless, full of anxieties. The cold did not come in a tide, riding on the wind as it had done throughout the winter, but soaked up silently through the earth to creep into the flesh and stun the sleepers' bones. It was a night for the hunter. Unseen in the field, a pair of blunt dark wings settled over a tiny fleeing body and bone-hard talons wrung the last small whimper from the grass. Richard heard the shrill commotion as he turned for the hundredth time in his fight for sleep. His mind refused to rest. Images of the simpleton, pursuing images of Margaret. Images of the master; images of failure and rebuff. No! It was too wretched, too unbearably painful; he could not accept so unbalanced a wager. Better to live with might-have-been than lose his dignity to a whim: a *feckless* whim, for Margaret was plain of face and ordinary, he was sure, in spirit.

But in the morning she was beautiful. With the sun weaving golden threads into the black halo of her hair; with fire trapped in her eyes like emeralds; with her dark dancing footsteps in the dew, she was beautiful. She was shaking her head in beautiful sorrow.

"Master Lynde, you shame me. I think you do not care for me at all. Why must you always turn away your head? Do I revolt you so?"

By the maidenly lowering of her gaze she kindled in him the chivalry of a knight: a hot suffusion of courage like a sunburst – or a draught of strong beer. It made a stag of him; sent him leaping and bounding as if there were no obstacle that could not be cleared at a stride: the carpenters' woodpile; the simpleton's outstretched arm; the churchyard wall; the back court of the manor house; the door. He rapped and stood back, wetting his lips. His lungs were heaving from the exertion of the run and he could reach back with his tongue and find the faintest salting of blood. He realised, as the footsteps sounded from within, that he had not prepared a speech; yet he could not be afraid while the stag still lived and ruled. He retained a kind of heightened calm, even to the dryness of his palms, and spoke with as little excitement as his panting would allow.

"Master? Oh master, forgive me! I have a question."

The master stood hunched into his shoulders like a kestrel on its pole, eyes glittering in the pale shadow of the porch, impaling the younger man with a stare of predatory intensity as if he were hungry for a meal. It restored in Richard's mind the memory of his last intrusion at the manor, when he had laid his complaint against the simpleton – a memory whose weight rolled crushingly upon his spirit like a boulder of despair. He danced a little from foot to foot, stirring a pebble with his toe, while the silence beat punishingly at his nerve.

"A question?" said Morton. "Concerning what?"

"Concerning your daughter, master!"

"*You want to marry her?*" His face showed the briefest flicker of amusement – too rapid even for Richard to catch – then at once resumed its previous stony thoughtfulness. For all the warmth he let dwell in his eye, he might have been judging the quality of a yard of stone, or of a balk of timber. It discountenanced Richard, as it had discountenanced all who had sought to treat with him in business. "Well, young man! *Do you?*"

"Then . . . *You knew?*" The stag was paunched.

"I had thought it possible that there might be something of the sort between you. I know how she dotes." Again the shadow of amusement.

"*She dotes?*"

Morton straddled his nose with thumb and forefinger to trace the long parallel pleats in his cheeks, still intent upon weighing the substance of his bargain. "You must think," he said, "that marriage to my daughter would bring you particular favours. That you would become my pupil."

"I had not thought." Richard's lips were tight; his hands white-knuckled at the falsehood.

"You cannot be such a fool! Of course, for my daughter's sake, I should want to make a mason of you. This must be your thinking. You cannot care for the girl?"

"Master, I do care!"

"Then you are a bigger fool yet! Howsoever, I am not the man to stand between a fool and the subject of his folly. I see your scheme, yet I cannot begrudge it. You will be a fine master one day." He clasped his hands and pumped the palms, making an oily sucking sound like pretended mocking laughter. "There! By the grace of God, you shall wed my daughter! You have my blessing. Let us shake hands upon it before you alter your mind."

The smile had returned to his face while he spoke, and this time he let it remain.

The shiny yellow flowers in the grass were like stars in the heavens: as bright, and as plentiful. Richard plucked a handful and sniffed, but found they held no perfume; only a sprinkling on his hand of dry yellow dust. Yet, on this golden morning, no fragrance could have seemed more perfect. The chill had lifted from the ground so that tiny wraiths of steam hung over the stone, and the leaves felt warm to his touch. He watched his shadow as he walked, admiring the litheness of the figure as it snaked across the grass. Richard Lynde, master mason, who would have a fine strong son for his apprentice! Together they would build cathedrals of such beauty that even Heaven itself would weep! He looked up at the tower of St. Michael's, with its fine embattled crown, and embraced it in his heart. No longer an ending. For both of them a beginning. Here, between the clean new walls that were the work of his own hand, he would be married.

The masons' lodge as he approached it was a hive of noise, pulsing with excitement, and it was clear that his arrival had been eagerly awaited. One of the journeymen, who was no particular friend of Richard's, ran out ahead of the others to greet him, and Richard spread his arms ready to receive his congratulation – not pausing to wonder how the news could have travelled so quickly ahead of him.

"Richard! Have you not heard? You must summon the master!"

The man's demeanour was mournfully agitated, full of foreboding; and at once Richard felt a cold clutch of fear. He looked around but could not see Margaret: something, he knew, was dreadfully wrong. "*Why*? What has happened?"

"A new mason has come into the lodge! Even into the master's tracing room! He says he is our new master, and tells us what to do."

Richard puffed out his cheeks and released them in a low whoop of nervous laughter. Then the emergency did not touch upon Margaret at all; nor upon his own future: the problem was Morton's alone! But then immediately it came again, the coiling of the serpent. A new man pretending to the mastership, supreme to Robert Morton? Of course it touched him! Touched him on the very pulse!

"Is this an old man or a young?"

"A young man."

"Where is he now?"

A third journeyman spoke up, a local man of dull wit who chipped all day at the banker. "He has gone off over the hill there. Down the steep way, towards Sigford."

"An impostor then! A jester! He has gone about his business."

The man's face stretched into a long slow smile, showing his tongue through the gaps in his teeth: half stupid, half knowing. "Mistress Morton is with him."

"*Mistress Morton?*"

"Gone with him! Down the hill, a while ago. Like I said."

Richard's whole body rang with the shock of it, right down into his wrists and hands like the jolt of a hammer on crystalline rock. It was a challenge to the new man in him: one more test which fate required him to pass; one more wave in his own history breaking over his head. He knew he must act; for the fear of being thought unmasterly now gripped him more powerfully than any other.

"You go to the master! I shall find this man and uncover the nature of his business." From her station by the boundary wall, the simpleton hobbled forward as he passed, and shaped her fingers to pluck at his sleeve; but he increased his speed without looking at her and would not let himself be touched.

The morning was awash with the music of leaves. The hill caught the full onslaught of the wind from the sea, so that the branches swished and lashed in a spring tide of raw virility. The path hung for a last golden moment on the brow of the hill, gilded with morning, then plunged abruptly into the forest night. Richard saw the sky above him as a distant stitching of blue, like pin holes in a garment. Here and there a thin shaft of sunlight would pick a way through the maze and make a prim splash of yellow on the underworld floor. In the deep, there was no sound at all. The green fathoms closed out the rushing of the breakers far above; even the birds were silent. It was a silence that Richard understood. The birds were keeping their distance because this was not the first disturbance of the morning. Someone else had walked the path not long before him.

At the very bottom of the wood, where the path turned gently to the east and began to rise again, Richard waited and listened. The rattle of a stream, in chattering debate with its ancient boulders; the liquid cry of a woman. The two sounds became one as he spun around to seek them; then unravelled again and became two. The water was lower down and behind him; the laughter faced him from above.

He found them not far from the path, in a small bed of golden light where the forest opened to the sky: Margaret and the man.

The hearing was arranged like a court in the lodge, before Robert Morton and a full assembly of the men. Outside the colour had drained from the sky, leaving a thin sediment of stony grey, and the damp had reached inside, so that Richard shivered in his sweat-blackened shirt and had to clasp his arms to quieten himself. His neck, chest and limbs ached from the fight and there was a spiritual numbness too, a feeling of separation from his own affairs as if he attended them only as a witness. He held his head high, with eyes to the fore, oblivious to the stares.

Robert Morton wore his finest robe, brushing the floor with a heavy sweep of fur, and a short cylindrical hat like an upturned beaker on his head. At his right hand, similarly though more flamboyantly attired, with long pointed shoes that curled like claws from beneath his hem, stood John his son: a crow come to pick at the kill.

But it was not to Richard that the elder Morton turned first in his wrath. It was to the stranger – a tall, pale-haired man who had kept himself at a distance from the others and who now was concentrating his face in a sour compression of anger, black enough to rival Morton's own. For a moment it seemed that he would outstare the master eye to eye, but he could not do it. The heat of Morton's passion – he having prayed for the guidance of the Almighty – was too terrible for mortal challenge. It was as if failure to flinch from his ire was in itself an act of unrighteousness.

He extended a finger to point. "Unworthy before God! Unworthy before your fellows! *Unworthy before your father!*"

An excited murmur rustled through the men like a breeze through corn: elbows nudging, glances passing between neighbours. At the very back of the lodge, behind Richard where he could not see, there was a sudden disturbance – a collision of bodies and a reluctant dragging of feet.

"Richard Lynde!" Morton turned towards him, slapping his hands flat on the surface of the bench and throwing up tiny white spirals of dust. "Master Lynde! I thought that I had understood you, and yet your conduct here has surpassed all reason. This young man had no business to enter the lodge as he did, and he shall be properly punished. So far from being its master, as through seemly conduct he might have been, he shall be made to wait for three years more, or until his manner *befits* a master mason! *But*, Master Lynde, his error does not excuse your own." He straightened from the bench and pointed again with dust-capped finger. "Look now!"

Richard saw that he was pointing at Margaret. "This woman I call my daughter *because she is married to my son*. This son here, who today has returned to snatch so clumsily at his birthright!"

Again the murmur ran around the room, and Richard's fingertips, which seemed peculiarly distant from him, began faintly to prickle for want of blood. He examined the bruise that swelled over the knuckle of his right hand, tracing its outline with a nail as if it were the only thing in the world that concerned him. On the wider issue of his own future, whose principles had once seemed so plain to him, he had entirely lost his hold. In front of him and behind, there were currents of movement; exclamations of laughter; a susurrus of whispers. His head swam with a vision of Margaret, monstrously unreal, brushing back her hair and smiling openly with affection. He fell into the web again, trapped by the emerald gaze – and followed it to where Robert Morton, his rancour set aside, was shyly smiling back.

The merciless torture of silence, and then the master was speaking to him again: loftily still, but more kindly. "But my natural daughter, about whom we remain agreed that you shall wed, forgives your misconducts and stands now at your side. May God bless and keep you both!"

The simpleton's lips reached forward to suck at the air, and the tongue ran around her mouth to gather and give shape to the sound. Her head lolled happily on her shoulder as she looked up at him; and Richard noticed, for the first time as she smiled, that her eyes were blue as violets.

"Husband!"

MANNA

Benet's grip on the shovel handle was weak, so that the force of the current threatened to pluck it from his grasp. Barely a sip of water remained on the blade when at last he managed to raise it to his lips, but he fastened to it like an infant to the dug, and dipped again. To spoon the water, even with the shovel, was an unusual refinement in his behaviour, but his head was in no condition to be lowered directly into the stream. He had as yet no notion of the time. Although the grass around him was still grey with dew, he had only the feeling that, somehow, it must be later than he had imagined. The idea that a gap had opened in his life – a gap which his memory could not bridge – was only part of a general sense of loss which, so far, he could not account for.

Having sipped, he slumped forward and let his brow rest on the cushion of his forearms. He could never understand why, when he had drunk so much, he should wake so thirstily; but he comprehended only too clearly the feeling in his head. No labour with the shovel could have cost him more effort than this opening of the eyes. They seemed to hang from the bone on long stalks of pain, rooted far back in a cavernous space that seemed greatly to exceed the known size of his skull. Flattened beneath him against the chill slab of grass, his belly was in no less of a ferment. Vomiting had helped for as long as there had remained anything to vomit; but now the dry retching offered up nothing but pain.

"Water," he said aloud. "Must have water."

He slithered forward again until his trunk hung down over the stream, gritting his teeth as the pressure intensified in his head. Instinctively he reached a hand beneath his hip to protect his purse from spilling; but he was immediately reassured. It was quite safe, there was no danger: it was already empty. He coddled it in his palm and was reminded of Squeaky Nicholas Parr and his flat empty scrotum: poor Nicholas, for whom old age had become merely a kind of wrinkled boyhood. Poor Nicholas, who in all his life had fathered nothing but a repetitious litany of cruel jokes.

"Poor Nicholas. Poor Benet Torr . . ."

Consciousness dawned in a sudden, unwelcome flood as Benet was reminded of Nicholas Parr's laughing face. Nicholas Parr, laughing at *him*. He struggled to sit upright and tugged frantically at the purse. There had been six shillings. He could remember showing it. *Six shillings*. Even with two thirds of the silver removed by debasement, six shillings was still a tidy pocketful: enough, in a plentiful year, to buy a whole quarter of grain at market. *Six shillings*. Could they have robbed an old man of so much? Old man! His memory lurched in concert with his stomach, and laid out his folly in a sullen pool of misery. At the Ilsington alehouse he had boasted of his age.

"Look at me! Feel my arms! Feel my legs! I'm as strong as any man half my age." The year was 1550, the third in the reign of the boy king Edward VI, and Benet Torr was as old as the century.

"An' what have ye to show for thy great age an' wisdom?" asked a labourer called Walter Babish. "Nought but a wooden shovel and a braggart's tongue!"

"I was a rich man once!"

"Rich man! All thy richness lies between thy legs, wi' thy brains! An' thy brain 'as lain a-slumber these thirty years . . ."

"Thirty years is afore thy time, Master Babish. I was a rich man, then. We all was. Tin by the ton we got from these ol' hills. We was bringin' it out so fast, the meltin' house could scarce keep speed wi' us. Stream tin, it was, o' th' finest! You young 'uns reckon ye know tin! Ye know nothin'! Your mine-tin is like to stream-tin as piss is like to mead. We 'ad thirteen parts to twenty o' purest tin, fetchin' fourpence a pound. Ton after ton . . ."

"Then how comes it you'm still a poor ol' tin-scratcher, waggin' thy shovel for two shillin's a week?"

"'Cos thass what God made 'un," said Silvester Mole. Silvester had been a friend of Benet's for as long as either of them could remember, back into their boyhoods. Silvester, too, had shovelled a fortune into other men's pockets; and Silvester, too, had felt the sting of envy. "If toil was to bring its just reward, then our Benet'd be as rich as any Ford or Pomeroy! Ban't I right, Benet? They grand families is jus' brung into th' world wi' more money an' more brains . . . . Though 'eaven knows, thinkin' upon't, there's some among th' Pomeroys that 'as no more brain than poor ol' Benet isself . . ."

It was kindly meant but careless. "You best mind your mouth, Silvester Mole!" said Benet furiously. "Pomeroys wi' small brain! I know where you'm leadin' wi' your slimy tongue. Doan' 'e think I doan'! Sir Thomas Pomeroy were a saint!" He stabbed the blade of his shovel hard into the dirt floor.

"Hush, Benet!" shrilled Nicholas Parr, rolling his eyes in an exaggeration of fear. "Contain thy anger! Ye'd not speak thus if th' Lord Protector could 'ear thee. An' it's no' safe t'say it 'ere! Even in an alehouse, not everyone knows ye speak it as a jest."

"IT IS NO JEST!"

Benet's admiration for Sir Thomas, of Berry Pomeroy near Totnes, had indeed been almost religious in intensity. A year earlier, with John Bury of Silverton, Sir Thomas had been his leader in the uprising against Cranmer's Book of Common Prayer, and Benet himself had been among the tinners who had tried to tunnel beneath the city walls and open the way for an occupation of Exeter. Silvester Mole, too, had felt a sly sympathy for the cause. The poverty of tinners at the time had been such that ownership of a blanket and a heap of straw had been the limit of most men's ambitions. There had been little affection for the employers and merchants who had demeaned them with petty prices; or for a government that had sought to impose its will from two-hundred-and-fifty miles distant. Yet Silvester had seen the futility of armed revolt . . .

"Hold thy girlish tongue," he told Nicholas Parr. "If thou were twice the man, thou'd yet be less than half o' Benet Torr! 'Twas for such milkish maidens as thysel' that 'e marched. 'E 'ad but as much 'ope o' victory as thou 'as thysel' o' sirin' a litter o' hogs. An' yet 'e went for'ard wi' 'is tool full cocked. Would that ye could do alike, eh Mistress Parr?"

"E'en Nick's *conscience* goes unpricked," said Walter Babish, commencing one of his favourite themes of banter. But Benet himself would not be amused.

"I 'ave no need o' friends such as thee, Silvester Mole. 'Twas no fool's errand that us marched upon! Us 'ad artillery an' arms, an' near on ten thousan' men. Had us but th' comradeship o' faint 'earts such as thysel', then us'd have carried th' day. Now, for thy faintheartedness, ye're obliged to hear the Supper o' th' Lord in th' heathen tongue, an' 'ave thy whelps go unbaptised to th' grave.[1] No' that this'll be any penalty to Master Parr . . ."

"Nor to thysel' neither," said Parr spitefully, "wi' thy wife so long dead!"

"Aye, an' m'two sons likewise, by th' grace o' God!"

"So what's to be gained?" said Silvester Mole, growing weary. "Why must ye hear th' Mass in Latin, an' no' in th' King's good English?"

"Latin is th' tongue o' th' Lord," he said, stiffening a finger in caution. "English is th' language o' th' Devil!"

"And o' thysel', Benet Torr."

And so now he was drunk and penniless. He had opened his purse in the face of their taunts, and had floated his false ambitions on a bitter sea of ale. Six shillings, he had said, was a sum of no consequence to any true tinner. He could dowse for metal with hazel twigs, and he knew a field near Widecombe where a sleeping cow would cover its own weight in ore. All he had to do was take his shovel and dig. They would see. *Six Shillings!* Why did they not take another jug of ale and cease their nonsense? Did they not believe him? As it happened, they didn't; but this was not to stop them from drinking him into penury.

"Cranmer must burn! *They shall all o' them burn!*"

He beat his leg with the flat of the shovel as he walked, bringing up a deep red flush on the bare skin of his calf. There were few tinners left anywhere on the moor – even among the oldest men such as himself – whose shovels were not now shod with iron. But Benet would suffer no change. Not many years earlier, a labourer at the harvest had hoisted a stook above his head to shelter from the rain. A bolt of lightning had caught the iron tines of his pitchfork and struck him

[1] A preface to the order of baptism advised that it would be "most convenient" for the ceremony to take place only on Sundays and other holy days. With the high incidence of death in the first few days of life, this had given rise to the fear that infants would have to be buried unbaptised.

dead – and any man who failed to learn the lesson of *that*, in Benet's view, was worse than a fool. Divine interventions of all kinds crowded his thoughts as he shuffled slowly up the hill towards the rock. Beyond the tor, a distant lake of purple was seeping like blackberry juice upward into a wheaten sky. It darkened even as he watched, the liquid streaks conjoining first into slow gaseous swirls, then into solid black towers whose smouldering force seemed to mock the common frailty of the rocks and hills beneath. There was anger in the air, and fear. The sheep felt it, cantering past Benet to huddle on the lower terrace, heads inward, in seamless grey phalanxes. A few remained on the height, and chained themselves around the lee of the tor. They had frozen into the rock, and did not so much as turn their heads as Benet crept in behind them. He grazed his scalp on an overhanging cornice, but the pain barely impinged. His head still rang dully with ale; he was thirsty again; and he was sober enough to realise that beneath the single gappy layer of his tunic he was beginning to burn with cold.

For a while, the storm seemed to have trapped itself in the valley below him, where it muttered and slavered like a tethered hound. But it wrenched and writhed, and would not be contained. A slim plume of cloud, dark as a raven's wing, erupted from the pit and cut a long sabre-gash of shadow across the belly of the hill. Then came another tendril to twine with the first; and then another and another, until the sky above Benet's head was fused into a relentless canopy of black. In the valley, barbed fingers of lightning began to claw and drum – ominous and threatening, but not yet issuing any clear hint of the fury to come. The gale spun a last dying throe, then surrendered the air to a clinging, creeping pall which Benet found almost too heavy to breathe. For as far as he could see, nothing stirred; not a leaf.

He was too much a man of the moor to believe that the calm would remain long undisturbed; and yet nothing in all his life had prepared him for the shock of the thunderbolt. It stunned him. He could not move, or utter, or compose any thought beyond a vague premonition that he might already be dead. The idea, for the split second that it lasted, did not dismay him; indeed he surprised himself afterwards when he reflected upon it, for his terror had been a moment of purest serenity. If there had been pain, he was sure he would not have felt it. The first crack, from below him and to his right, was as loud as anything he was capable of imagining; those that followed, galloping in a tumult of echoes and re-echoes around the valley, were of a violence that seemed more physical than aural. As the final, awful thunderburst electrified the sky above his head, the dead grey rock tingled at his back like a living creature. And then, when he opened his eyes, there was nothing but the hard cold splash of rain and the raw new smell of churning earth.

Benet slept again before he arose. He worked his shoulders against the granite until he found a contour that suited him; then clasped his hands between his legs and let his head fall slack. He was awakened by the cold – he did not know how long afterwards – to discover that his lips had traced a pearly snail-track of saliva across his chest and shoulder. The ache in his head had subsided to a faint ticking, deep in the bone behind one eye; but his limbs felt as brittle as sticks, tugging painfully along the grain as he straightened. The sky was still too thickly blanketed to settle his uncertainty about the time; but it was much lighter now, and offered no threat. In his memory the thunder seemed already curiously distant: no more than an imperfectly remembered dream. Only the tumult of rushing water served to persuade him that the storm had been real. The streams and brooks were everywhere in full voice, growling in a passion of scurrying pebbles. Benet noted the fishbone patterns of the new frets, cutting sharp stony chevrons into the banks; and he felt the first small shiver of excitement.

He gave little pause to consideration, but set off at once in a direction which, allowing for the skirting of hills, would bring him eventually to Buckland. Once or twice he swung his arms and stamped, but the cold had ceased to concern him. At each tiny watercourse he would dart forward like a hound at a scent, snuffling over shovelfuls of rainwashed grit. He would peer fixedly into each new slick of mud, and pick out stones to weigh against each other in his hands. Once or twice he broke one against another, and scratched at the fragments with his nails; but if there was disappointment in what he saw, he did not reveal it. In a green valley beyond the Widecombe road, where a number of streamlets had met in a surge, he rested for a moment and looked upward, beatifically smiling. The clouds had sunk like ore into an alluvial band across the horizon. Solemnly he pressed his palms together and bowed his head towards the retreating storm. The revelation, he knew, was there amid the gravel, and before nightfall he would be led to find it.

"*Gloria*," he said aloud. "*Gloria in excelsis Deo.*"

The Orthodox true Minister,   the Seducer and false Prophet.

HUMPHY

Hanniball Corbyn the tailor wrestled with his letters as his conscience wrestled with his soul. The scratches of the quill were broad and deliberate, heavily drawn with a knotted arm that might have been carving granite. His hair, hanging from the scalp in oily grizzled cords, obscured the hand that supported his head. His fingertips, scratching idly among the roots, garnered powdery crescents of grit and dust beneath the nails. He sneezed and muttered to himself as he etched the words, pausing often to tip back his head and stare into the rafters.

The tailor's clothes were of stout dark stuff, homespun and uncompromised by fashion. The only embellishments to their puritan simplicity were ruffles of loose threads that had detached themselves at the cuffs, and a pattern of pale dusty stains that clogged the fibres on his back. His face wore the pallor of uneasy nights, with dark bruises encircling narrow eyes. His expression was fixed and intent, undisturbed by the patter of a moth at the window glass, or by the piping of a bat in shrill duet with his pen. Neither was he persuaded to leave his chair by the scratch and scrape of footsteps outside his door; nor even by the gruffly excited voice of the rector, Robert Dove, and the repeated rapping of a stick.

"Corbyn! I know you're there. Come down, I want to talk."

Corbyn, the tailor and occasional schoolmaster, drew the candle more closely towards him and read his own hurried, sloping script. "To the everlasting praise of God," he had written, "in memory of a most wonderful deliverance. September, 1639."

He closed his eyes and clasped his hands in an attitude of penitence, waiting until the caller downstairs had wearied of his door and had made his unwilling, truculent retreat. "Corbyn! You hear me! Tomorrow we talk."

Tomorrow, then. Tomorrow. A dew of perspiration had broken on Corbyn's brow, cutting white channels in the dirt. But he made himself snap from the trance, dipped his quill with new urgency and resumed his writing. The pen moved more rapidly now, with fewer pauses as the thoughts unlocked themselves and began to flow.

"Over the west gate of the Churchyard in Ilsington there was a room anntiently built, about ten feet from the ground, sixteen feet in length, and twelve feet in height. The east and west side walls were about ten feet in height. The covering was of slate or shingle stone layd uppon fayre timber. Rafters about twelve feet in length. This room was lately converted to a Schoolhouse whither there usually came heere to the number of 30 scholler boyes . . ."

Hanniball Corbyn was not the only one to whom the morning of Tuesday September 17th had been an unwelcome dawning. Humphrey Degon, too, had arisen in fear of being punished. Humphy, as everyone called him, was six, but younger than his years. From his next birthday his age would permit legal betrothal, or hanging for a crime, yet he clung to his infancy as if he would never let go of it.

It was still dark when Humphy emerged from the stone porch of the Smallacombe farmhouse, beating his arms to ward off the first bleak hint of winter. Behind him the long thatched roof sprawled like the flank of an animal, hugging the slants of the ground. At the upper end, to the left of the porch, lived the farmer William Degon and his wife, with their sons Humphy and his step-brother John, who was twelve. To the right were penned fourteen head of cattle. It was from this lower end, the shippon, that Humphy could hear the angry voice of his father.

When he touched his buttocks that morning, Humphy's fingers had found the blood still wet from yesterday's beating. He was in dread of confronting his father again, and scurried about his chores on whispering feet. In the kitchen, where he found his mother setting a crock of cream for scalding in the hearth, he put down the armful of turfs he had brought for the fire and looked to her for a sign of forgiveness. She gave it, as she always did, with a warm sad smile.

"Go to your lessons now," she said, smoothing his hair. "And remember your father in your prayers."

In his way, she knew, Humphy had been trying to help. The straw thatch above the wool chamber, where the fleeces were stored in the space over the porch, had leaked and let the damp run in. The damp had crumbled the plaster. And that had let in the rats, whose greedy yellow teeth had sliced deep into the family's stock. Humphy, child though he was, recognised in his father a man of almost Biblical devotion to duty; and he knew that the time had come for him to take up his own share of the burden. After the spoiling of the fleeces, he had seen the perfect opportunity.

William Degon had been an old man at thirty, broken-winded like a miner's pack horse. Since he had been a child – younger even than Humphy – every minute of daylight, and the dark hours at both ends of the night, had been dedicated to toil. He had pitted himself against the thin moorland soil in a battle for improvement he could not win. His only hope was that through his own defeat he might pass to his sons the means to succeed, and enable them to break their own bondage to the plough. He drove them to their classes with the same passionate energy in which he continued to drive himself to the fields. The elder boy, John, was still sent to Corbyn even at the age of twelve and at a cost of fourpence a week, to extend his knowledge of the testaments and to learn how to write.

Only on Sundays did William Degon set aside his work, in obedience to his faith. Yet even at church his mind had little encouragement to rest. The Reverend Robert Dove was a true follower of Archbishop Laud, with the threat of the Star Chamber essential to the manner of his preaching. Petty offenders were denounced from the pulpit in a way that turned the church itself into a summary court of law, if not of justice. Dove's small pink eyes, masked beneath his brows, would single out the offenders as he spoke, drawing noisy protests from the brave, or tearful admissions from the meek. If the victim was not present, which might in itself be the entire substance of his offence, then Dove would direct his hectorings to the South Door, as if the miscreant might materialise in the porch and repent. This last Sunday he had condemned Charles Gurrell for drunkenness; Hosias Smerdon for infidelity; and, with the charge levelled unerringly at the slammed South Door, the schoolmaster Hanniball Corbyn for sedition.

Never had William Degon himself been the subject of Dove's righteous fulmination. But he lived in perpetual fear of it, and the denunciation of Corbyn had struck him with painful force. To Degon, as much as to Dove, Corbyn's offence had seemed extraordinary. One Sunday afternoon, according to his usual practice, the schoolmaster had brought his pupils into the service to hear the rector give his sermon. And yet as soon as Robert Dove had begun to speak, Corbyn had turned on his heel and marched conspicuously out of the church. Worse: he had not removed his hat, and had bowed his head neither at the speaking of Christ's name, nor as he passed before the altar. Small deeds, but Degon had recognised them for what they were – a private declaration of war. War on Roman mysticism; war on what Corbyn saw as the heresy of a Popish king; war on Robert Dove. It was a self-damaging, futile war which would mean the end of Hanniball Corbyn as a teacher of letters, the end of the school, and the end of William Degon's ambition for his sons. Less than ever, as he had walked the lane back to Smallacombe that afternoon, had his thoughts been capable of rest. His lips had moved in a soundless recital of his fears, so that people had been afraid to greet him; and his eyes had sorted the sheep with the crazed intensity of a tin-streamer sifting ore. In his anxiety he had seen injury or moor-sickness in every droop of an animal's head. The discovery of the spotted fleeces next morning had been almost unsurprising, the fulfilment of a nightmare.

It was on the Monday afternoon that Humphy's plan had come to him. He was lying in the hay loft above the shippon, hiding while his father believed him to be stone-picking in the field, when an old black rat, fat with the harvest, sat up on its tail and looked at him with casual disinterest. The arrogance of its gait as it waddled away, contentedly to digest its stolen meal, aroused in Humphy a sudden passion of hate. It was the rats that had hurt his father; *it was the rats that must pay*. Outside in the yard, with its long nose stretched along its paws and only half an eye attending to the world, an old farm dog dozed in a pale flood of autumn sun. Humphy kicked it hard in the ribs as he passed, in punishment for its failure to keep down the vermin.

At the Narracombe farmstead not far away, the Leere family owned a different kind of dog: smaller, with sharp features and rapid, darting movements. Henry Leere said this dog had once killed seventy rats in one day, though this was more than Hanniball Corbyn had taught either boy to count. Humphy, in whose plan the terrier played a major part, had to wait for his friend at the fork in the lane, for Henry had spent the day in Corbyn's classroom and had not troubled himself to hurry home. The delay, when at last he appeared, was explained by a tiny smear of blood on one of his cheeks.

"Will Soaper," he said, "caught me with a rock." For there had been a fracas. As they had run out from the lychgate schoolroom, the boys had seen a strange man, ragged and dirty with a bundle over his shoulder, slip through the hedge into the lane near the blacksmith's cottage. In the way of country boys with strangers, these sons of yeomen had pelted him with stones – one of which, from Will Soaper, had accidentally flicked Henry's face. Henry had forgiven him, but continued to wear the bloodmark as an ornament – suggestive, he thought, of a cavaliering nature.

"We gave the man a right good bloodying," he said. "Will Surrage caught him properly when he fell, so it poured out thick from his nose."

(Two days later this man – a journeyman stonemason disqualified from work by his enslavement to ale – met with a similar greeting from cottagers at Ashburton. Afterwards, when his body was found robbed of its bundle and stiffened against a boulder by the river, no man could name him, nor cared to inquire. Relief was the most any would admit, that it was no friend or relation.)

Humphy thought wistfully of the sport he had missed for, though he did not care for school, he cared even less for stone-picking. His father's determination to keep him from class that day had surprised him, and he supposed it must follow in some way from the schoolmaster's behaviour in church. Master Corbyn's rebellion had frightened Humphy, too, but then Humphy was always afraid of him, whatever he did. Yet in his child's mind the schoolmaster was as incapable of fault as his father, or the Reverend Robert Dove. It was beyond his understanding that there could be any point of dispute between these three rigid moral guardians, each of whom railed against him for his sin, and who were united in their predictions of fiery doom. He decided, after pondering the matter further, that his father must simply have needed his labour in the field. Whatever the reason, his mother had told him he must return to his lessons tomorrow.

Consideration of his father brought him back to the idea in mind. "Your dog," he said to Henry, "can it really be so hard on the rats?" The hint of challenge was deliberate but unnecessary, for to Henry the mere promise of sport was bait enough. The bloodstain thinned into the crease of a smile as he listened. "What a game!" he said. "You just watch! It will bite off their heads faster than Master Corbyn could keep count!"

True to its character, the dog was found in the corn barn, worrying at shadows in the straw. The boys trapped it in a corner and Henry secured it with a bent hazel halter, cut like the tethering yokes his father used on the cows. The animal's fur had been recently wet, and was drying in short gritty points. Henry said it had been diving for fish, and he displayed a row of small triangular scars on the back of his hand to show the quality of its teeth.

The walk across the valley, with the dog fighting every yard of the way against the hazel, was slower than Humphy had anticipated, and it ate so deeply into the afternoon that by the time they reached Smallacombe the sun seemed already perched on Hay Tor rocks. William and John Degon were still absent in the field, but the heavy slap of a drashel could be heard flailing rhythmically in the corn-barn passageway. This, Humphy knew, would be his mother threshing the week's bread corn, and he hesitated with the idea of explaining his enterprise to her. But no, he thought, let it be a surprise.

In the wool chamber, to which they ascended through the trap-door, the fleeces were stacked around the walls in loose bundles that gave off a sickly, soapy kind of smell that neither boy liked. In one corner was a gap where the wet and damaged fleeces had been removed. A thin white mark, like a chalk line on the floor, showed exactly where they had stood.

"There," said Humphy. A trickle of perfectly clear water still sprang from the mossy thatch above his head and splashed on his arm as he pointed. "That's where the rats came in. There, in the corner."

As the first owl serenaded the evening, Henry let slip the dog. For a moment it stood quite still; then its tail, which had sunk between its legs during the final, strangulating haul up through the trap-door, slowly raised itself and stood out stiffly in a semaphore of arousal. Its ears pricked and swivelled, and its nose twitched excitedly to scan the range of new possibilities. And then, with not so much as a glance to betray its intention, the animal was gone. Humphy and Henry stared bewildered at each other across the open trap. Silence hung in the air like a falling boulder, a fragile instant of peace made awful by the certainty of disaster. They heard the dog's paws strike the ground beneath the trap-door, and the rapid scuffle as it turned the corner into the shippon. Then, uproar.

The dog dashed beneath the bellies of the cows at their mangers, yapping in and out between the hooves and spattering noisily through the slurry in the drainway. The bellowing carried right across the valley to Henry Leere's father at Narracombe, and brought Humphy's mother running across the yard from the corn-barn. The big brown Devonshire cattle, fixed at their heads by hazel yokes sprung around the stall-posts, tugged and swung at their moorings like tide-sucked ships. With anchored necks they could not turn quickly enough to identify the intruder, so that their alarm was intensified by fear of an attacker they could not see. But almost immediately the dog grew weary of random dashes and pinned its attention on one animal in particular – a plainly terrified young heifer with a broken horn. Flattening itself to the floor, darting from left to right and back again, it easily defeated its victim's guileless attempts to meet it head to head.

The stall post gave way at precisely the moment Humphy and Henry appeared in the doorway: Humphy frightened and silent; Henry frightened and yelling. For an instant the terrier was distracted. The stall-post, from the constant soaking in water, damp earth and urine, had rotted inside its granite socket, and now it snapped off close to the kerb, giving the cow a sudden, unexpected release of energy that flung it backwards into the alleyway. Three hooves scrabbled for purchase on the wet stone; the fourth clipped the dog, pinning it and crushing a shoulder. Instinctively Henry took a half step forward; but a more fundamental instinct pulled him smartly back, for he knew enough about cattle to understand the danger he was in. The dog screamed and tried to drag itself away, paddling frantically in a circle like a drowning swimmer. But there could be no hope. The cow caught it once beneath the ribs with a thrust of the head that spun it upwards and over, weightless as a twig. Down it came, belly-first on to the horn, where it impaled itself and hung, to be shaken again and again until it dropped. A flutter of ears and a slither of limbs allowed a brief illusion of life, but none remained.

"Now! Now, be still!" Humphy's mother pushed between the boys and made towards the cow, to calm it. With a final, irritable shake of its head, it tipped her backwards into the mess, then trotted to the field end of the shippon where it turned and stood looking back at them with lowered head.

Humphy heard the running footsteps of his father and step-brother in the yard outside. He did not know what to do then, so he laughed.

In the thorn hedge, spun like lace between spiteful black bobbins, spiders' webs glimmered in the low grey light. The morning was hung about with mist. From his window, where he had sat and suffered his disgrace the night before, Humphy had watched the long wraiths climb up from the valley bottom like breath from a dragon, to steal the countryside from his view. In the morning it sat still and heavy on the moor, so that the whole of Humphy's world, which he shared with his step-brother John, stretched no more than twenty paces from horizon to horizon. They moved to school in a grey cupboard of silence. Humphy had drawn some comfort from his mother's sympathy, but still the flames of guilt were roaring unquenchably inside his head. He knew that he was not too little to go to Hell. If he had learned no other lesson from his father, and from the frightening sermons of Hanniball Corbyn, he well understood that he dwelt in constant hazard from the Devil. He knew that every boy was born into wickedness, with an inheritance of sin that could be expiated only by a profound repentance that was *more than simply feeling sorry,* and by a true inner commitment to Christ. Hell fire was the only alternative. Humphy's torment was that, whereas he felt the full weight of his sin – and never more dolorously than this morning – at the same time he had never felt more distantly removed from his Maker. All night he had prayed that he might be spared the everlasting flames, yet the Almighty had given him no sign; and he had wept bitter tears at the certainty of what must become of him in the afterlife. His catechism, in which he had been schooled at church every Sunday afternoon since his birthday, obstinately eluded his memory. All he could bring to mind were the spiritual morsels his father had fed him at the cradle.

"God alone saveth me," he said aloud, to the great astonishment of his step-brother. "There is no damnation in them that are in Jesus Christ."

And his eyes, made sore by a sleepless night of prayer and grief, welled again in sorrow. It had come to him suddenly that this was the first morning he could remember on which his father had not led them together in family prayers.

Hanniball Corbyn's stomach shifted uncomfortably and stained his breath with a sour remnant of last night's mutton pasty. In the room above the lychgate he sat alone and waited, his long elbows propped carelessly against his Bible. From the yellowed pages sprouted a tangle of knotted threads marking the passages he had been studying. It was the oldest and mustiest of his volumes, but carefully preserved and with every leaf intact. Beneath it was William Lily's *Royal Grammar* (for he still nursed ambitions in Latin); then a primer and a catechism, some ABC books and a torn copy of John Brinsley's advice to schoolmasters, *Ludus Literarius* – torn by Corbyn himself, in a spate of temper. He might be a simple Puritan tailor, obliged by poverty to give petty lessons for money. Yet this obligation to necessity need not imply any lack of conviction, nor any neglect of his duty. On the contrary, he habitually laboured like a zealot. He saw to it that his charges were properly schooled in their religion, and he worked them cruelly hard at their ABC. It had been to expand his knowledge of the schoolmaster's craft that he had bought Brinsley's book, and he had been enraged by what he read. In Brinsley's insistence on recreational interludes for the scholars, he had seen a contemptible encouragement to sloth. And in the suggestion that the school might be, as Brinsley put it, *a place of play*, he had found the most perfidious of blasphemies.

"You can keep your play," he had shouted, alone in his fury while wrenching out the leaves. "Keep your play and go to Hell!"

Corbyn's long furrowed face fell readily into unease, and on this particular Tuesday morning it wore a mask of bleakest malevolence. It was twelve minutes to six o'clock and his pupils had not yet arrived. With nothing to occupy him, he closed his eyes and sat rocking slowly backward and forward on his seat, his whole body clenched in pent up anger. Godly belligerence was woven even into the fabric of his suit. Most Puritans of sober demeanour were content merely to avoid the gaudiest extravagances of the tailors' or dressmakers' arts. Not so Corbyn, who garbed himself all over in coarse, dark grey cloth, with plain white collar and cuffs and a high-crowned hat, shorn of band and feathers. He had once even cropped his hair against the scalp to erase the last trace of popular style, so that it had grown out lank, ugly and uneven. For, despite the strictness of his theology, Corbyn was by nature a romantic. He preached self-denial for its essential cleansing properties, but had embroidered his own notion of it until it was indistinguishable from self-sacrifice – or "martyrdom", as he conceived it, the highest affirmation of his faith. He flaunted his Calvinism like a battle standard, and in his defiance of Robert Dove he believed, with absolute sincerity, that he had struck the flint beneath his own martyr's pyre. He had hoped, as he made his echoingly lonely walk from the church on Sunday, that other men of true Puritan worth would turn also and follow him; but none did. At first, being alone in the churchyard and in a condition of high nervous excitement, he had feared for himself.

"But," he had said aloud, as he recited again now in the ominous dusty quiet of the schoolroom, "how can I be afraid? The soul that is with Christ cannot be lost. To die in Godliness is to live for ever!"

Yet he *was* afraid. Yesterday, he knew, the tongues had been busy. Through Robert Dove himself, word of his misdemeanour had passed at a gallop to the Dean at Totnes; and thence, by now, it would be on its way to the Bishop. At the very least, his licence to teach was certain to be rescinded. This very day, he was sure, Dove would return to confront him: he would have conspired with the Dean and would be secure in his authority to act. Corbyn intended that his reply to the charge should be a plainly phrased speech of unanswerable theological purity; but every time he ran through it in his mind the argument became tangled and he would lose himself in a maze of tangential speculation. Renewed anxiety cut fresh lines into his brow as the emotional heat rose once more to fever point, and he beat his temple achingly hard with the heel of his hand.

Again the mutton pasty disturbed his gut, so that his sphincter was obliged to release the tension in a long low trumpet call against the bench. The note was answered, from close at hand, by the gulp and snort of laughter imperfectly stifled. Corbyn swivelled and sprang fearfully to his feet, trapping his long thigh bones beneath the table and spinning *Ludus Literarius* in several parts to the floor. He stood idiotically fixed in the half crouch at which the table had arrested him, and blinked hard to focus on the figures in the doorway. Then:

"*Master Humphrey Degon and Master John Degon in all their imperfection!*"

Humphy stood half hidden behind his step-brother at the head of the stair, white faced and apprehensive. John's fingers had been clasped to his mouth, but now the hand dropped limply to his side. With the shock of fear translated into a new release of anger, honed to a fury by embarrassment, the ice in the schoolmaster's eye would have frozen a braver soul than John Degon.

"*In all their several imperfections!* And how kind of you to pay me a call! Yesterday you were too busy to join with us? Your souls beyond improvement?"

Corbyn wiped his cuff across his brow, smearing the hair into coiled grey tails that licked downwards in moist little points. The truth was that behind the irritation lurked an almost joyful surge of relief. After Sunday, he had been afraid that no boys would come; but yesterday there had been twenty-three out of the thirty, which was good enough for any Monday. And here to add to their number were the Degons. With a kind of gratitude peculiar to the moment, he resolved to concentrate their education and to make the most energetic use of whatever time remained to them.

"Humphrey Degon!" he ordered. "Come out from behind your brother there. Stand where I can see you."

Humphy's apprehension was well placed. Anticipating the arrival of his accuser, Corbyn's temper was as fitful as a weathercock in a whirlwind.

"Humphrey Degon, I say! Tell me, this morning, how did you pray?"

The boy was too frightened even to go on with his weeping. It was unthinkable that he should betray the substance of his private grief, and yet his family prayers, with their safe generalities, had been left unsaid. He blinked and stared shamefacedly at Hanniball Corbyn's feet, resting his eyes, without noticing it, on a small white hole in the stocking just above the shoe. It fell to John Degon to step forward and speak for him.

"Please, Master Corbyn, Sir. My brother is much vexed today, and unhappy."

"I have no doubt of it, but let him tell me so himself. What afflicts you, Humphrey Degon? Is there, then, no comfort for you in Christ? Tell me how you have prayed!"

Humphy's cheeks were shiny with tears. He lifted his face to the schoolmaster as he might have done to his mother, in mute appeal for comfort. But there was none: the long grey face was leached of all but contempt.

"Master Corbyn, Sir, this morning we did not pray."

Corbyn's face almost touched the boy's, nose to nose. His breath was sour and repulsive, but Humphy dare not turn away. Spots of brown blood were dried into Corbyn's smudgy white collar, and his shoulders carried a pale dusting from his hair. As he bent forward his stomach sang out in a concert of waterfalls, louder than anything Humphy had heard even through the flank of a cow. Yet the absurdity of the man did nothing to lessen his awfulness. His voice savoured the words with a slow and terrible relish, like the pronouncement of a judge.

"They which never pray, Humphrey Degon, God will pour out his wrath upon them! And when they beg and pray in Hell fire, God will not forgive them and there they must lie for ever!"

There was nothing in this speech that was new to Humphy, but the power of the image was in no whit diminished by its familiarity. Behind closed eyes, Humphy saw once again a picture of his own body burning.

"Open your eyes, Humphrey Degon, and look at me! Are you *willing* to go to Hell to be burned with the Devil? How do you know that you will not be the next child to die? And where are you then if you are not God's child?"

Tiny, chicken-like noises were rising from Humphy's throat. His eyes, which had opened briefly at Corbyn's command, were screwed tight again, with a new brimming of tears crushed like crystals between the lashes. His whole body trembled with the force of his sobbing so that Hanniball Corbyn, too, felt the sting of remorse. He wanted to reach out and embrace the boy, to press their cheeks together, to give and to take comfort from their shared vision of Hell. Yet outwardly the sad proud man could offer nothing but rage.

"Fall upon your knees! Weep and mourn and tell Christ you are afraid he does not love you. Beg him to give you his grace and pardon for your sins, and that He will make you His child. Beg as for your life, and do not be contented until you have an answer!"

It was past six o'clock. From the doorway at John and Humphy's back came the din of boys arriving on the stair: Henry Leere with his brothers David, Thomas and John; and Thomas Smerdon with Bartholomew Potter. But the interruption of Corbyn's disquisition brought no relief to Humphy in his torment, and he could not be comforted – not even by Henry Leere, who mistook his friend's grief as ordinary mourning for the terrier and assured him of his forgiveness. Indeed Humphy was driven to burst out all the more tearfully, for every act of friendship added its weight to the burden of his guilt. For more than an hour, as Corbyn settled the boys one by one to their books, the spelling and lettering were disrupted by his moans and sighs. Only seventeen boys had answered to their names which, after the promising start, was not encouraging to Corbyn. As he sat distantly again at the bench, his hands fiddled at some tailoring and his mind fiddled idly at theology. He spoke little, save to command Humphy Degon be silent.

At eleven o'clock, a few moments before the boys were due their lunch, Corbyn and Humphy Degon happened both to be staring from the same window. Both, in their distraction, had fixed their gaze on some uncomprehended object in the middle distance. Both then saw a fair-haired woman in a wide white apron approaching the lychgate from the churchyard. Humphy remarked the sharpness of her features, as if the face had been made of wet clay and drawn forward with a pinch of the fingers. Her skin was heavily pocked from some disease, and Humphy saw that she carried the same marks on the backs of her hands. She was a cottager whose name Humphy could not at once remember, though he knew her face well enough, and her temper. Earlier in the year, at around corn-tilling time, he had been the youngest among a gang of boys, led by his step-brother John, who had burst out from behind a hedge and called names to this woman's strangely puckered face. For twenty paces she had walked on without giving heed, and then she had whirled against them with a shrieking outpour of invective, using forbidden words and cursing them for demons. More shocking still, she had thrown stones at them with stinging power and accuracy, as strong as any man. John said she was a witch who could turn men to stone, and that the pebbles in her apron pocket were the souls of those she had destroyed. Humphy was glad to be out of her way, upstairs in the schoolroom. He watched her head pass out of sight beneath the floor, and heard the slow grate of the iron hinge as she pushed against the heavy wooden gate. The latch snapped like a whipcrack. And then Humphy found himself in Hell.

There were a few screams from the boys, but not many. There was not time. Hanniball Corbyn did not so much hear the slamming of the gate as feel it. The floor shuddered beneath his feet and a splash of wind-driven rain slapped cold against his face. It took a long part of a second for the disaster to find shape in his brain, and then the shock of it stripped him of all coherence. At the south end of the schoolroom the heavy stone wall which held up the roof timbers had buckled outwards and fallen from sight, leaving a jagged hole through which the wind whipped angry eddies of dust. Corbyn's bench overturned as a second, more violent tremor tipped him backwards and spilled him across the boards. One of the boys, more alert and agile than his master, sprang across his body to take shelter in the chimney. Everything was falling. The corner of Corbyn's Bible caught him a cutting blow on the side of the head, and *Ludus Literarius* slipped away to final disintegration in a corner. The boys were thrown against each other in a turmoil of benches and books, jammed tight against the closed classroom door. Corbyn himself was resting on his elbows, half sitting and half lying, with his head thrown back and his mouth and eyes gaping wide. Above him, the roof squealed like a falling elm.

Corbyn watched it settling slowly on top of him, holding quite still, as if he were content to be crushed. For an instant it hung in suspension as the east and west walls, forced outwards by the spreading of the eaves, found one last, impossible moment of equilibrium.

It was oddly quiet. The east end went first, taking four boys with it into the churchyard; and then the whole structure burst out and settled into the road. For some moments a swirling, russet plume of dust stood over the rubble as if it were the schoolroom's own ghost, cloaking the wreckage and shielding it from the public eye. A dozen or more tradesmen and women had run from their cottages to stand and stare in mute confusion. The truth descended on them with the slow certainty of settling dust. Among the litter of broken stones and splintered timbers, there lay the grimed fragments of bodies, mere reminders of boys. Here was a hand, still gripping a book. There a foot, robbed of its shoe. Here a head, there a torso; some of them moving, some of them not. A woman in the crowd screamed. Another voice shouted a name.

"William! Where's my Will?"

Driven by fear, the frail hands of women grew strong as black-smiths'. Blurred in the dust that smoked again where they stirred it, mothers and urchins raised rocks that might have defeated oxen. They worked in a kind of madness, with their minds cut off from the panic like limbs made numb by injury. The mother of Will Soaper, burrowing after the body of her son, thought suddenly of a rabbit stew that stood spoiling in the hearth.

The first small whimper of life came from a tiny boy called Hanniball Satturly. *"Help me!"*

For an instant the diggers paused, believing the cry to have come from one of their own. And then, from all around their feet, came a crescendo of wails and sobs as the other boys, almost in unison, found their breath and emptied their mouths of dust. The catastrophe had become a miracle. The bodies, that had seemed so utterly lifeless, shook and tested their limbs as they were unearthed one by one as grey as effigies, and stood up strong and healthy. Among all of them there was no cut deeper than the skin, no damage more urgent than shock. Not a limb had been broken, not even a finger; and no more blood spilled than might have been drawn by a thorn. Hanniball Corbyn himself had suffered not so much as a rending of his coat, though he had been submerged beneath a great weight of debris. Pride had obliged him to deny all difficulty, so that the diggers had left him to free his own body from the heap while they attended to the boys. It was almost with disappointment that he found himself able to struggle to his feet and examine his wholeness. The possibility of martyrdom had attracted him, and there seemed now almost a measure of disgrace in his total avoidance of hurt. He was the last to rise save only for the boy Stephen Tyler, who lay trapped at the chest by a balk of oak. But still the miracle held good. When the timber was lifted from him, the boy sprang to his feet, thrust aside the arms that offered support, and ran without stopping all the way to his home.

With the boys all fled, one voice alone remained mournful, echoing across the rubble and tolling back from the church wall like a funeral bell. Mistress Soaper had lost hope for her eldest son Will. When she learned that he had escaped the fall by playing truant with his friends Henry Lampseed and John Gurrell, her joy was touched with anger in a burst of wordless chatter that was neither sobbing nor laughter, but something of both. Corbyn felt the pang of relief as a physical sensation in his belly, and the emotion tugged hard at the corners of his mouth.

"Oh thank God for his salvation!" he cried. "Let us *all* now give thanks for our merciful deliverance." But there were few left to share his prayer. Of all the boys, only John Degon and John Michelmore had not run at once to their homes; and these two had raced in search of the three truants, Will Soaper, Henry Lampseed and John Gurrell, to warn them of the singular manner in which their mischief had been discovered. The knot of villagers, too, was unravelling and returning quietly to work. Corbyn opened his mouth to call after them but the rasp of breath in his throat, which was sorely parched with dust, brought a paroxysm of coughing that pinched his stomach and obliged him to grip his knees. A torn leaf from an ABC book, fluttering loosely between his feet, grew indistinct as his eyes misted; then was obliterated as the spasm clawed up from his stomach and he vomited. Yet the purge improved him wonderfully. The breeze clung like cool ointment to his skin, and he soothed his lungs with long clean swallows of air.

Mistress Soaper had gone, and he was alone save only two others: a very old man who had helped among the diggers, and the sharp-faced woman whose passage through the lychgate had provoked its collapse. She was standing at a distance, rolling a single brown pebble in the palm of her hand.

"Will that be all, Master?" said the old man.

Corbyn understood that he was being asked for payment, and spat angrily into the dust.

Alone in his cottage, Corbyn tried not to be idle. He took up some sewing but laid it aside when he found he could not keep his fingers from fumbling error. Outside, the lychgate and schoolroom were reduced to what now appeared an impossibly small and unimportant heap of spoil. He tried to rebuild it in his mind, but already the fine points of the building were obscure in his memory. Guilt attacked him painfully. There was an indefinable, but nonetheless deeply-felt guilt in the fact of the collapse itself, quite unrelieved by the knowledge that he could have done nothing to prevent it. And there was a whole impotent rage of guilt at his present barren inertia. But what could he do? He wondered if the accident had been designed to punish him, by the damage it inflicted on his dignity and his livelihood. What, otherwise, could have been the purpose of it? His death at this time of conflict might have been evidence of God's grace. Was his humiliation, then, to be taken as a sign that the Almighty had abandoned him? Or, in being left to yet greater suffering at the mercy of Robert Dove, was he being prepared for even higher grace? It was a presumptuous, and a careless, pattern of thought for which, even in his condition of bewilderment, he began to despise himself.

For two hours he sat, yawning and shivering on the borders of sleep, before his attention was awakened by a new commotion at the lychgate ruins. William Degon and John Degon, with a group of farmers and cottagers, were tearing at the rubble with their fingers, casting the stones aside in frenzied haste. With chill clarity, Corbyn read the message in their faces. The realisation of it froze his limbs in a river of icy needles, so that his feet sensed no connection with the floor. In the time it took him to run outside to the school – his breath choking in his throat, the hair stinging blindingly in his eyes – the upper part of the body had already been dug free. Humphy's clothes had been torn from him and his skin showed white as pearl through the dirt. Deep blue indentations remained where the stones and rafters had pinioned him. His eyes and his mouth were tight shut, and his head fell back upon his shoulders as if the neck were broken. A single trickle of blood, dried black, cut into the dust beneath his nose. Humphy was dead. Gently, as if they were still afraid of hurting him, William and John cleared his legs and laid him to rest on the churchyard grass. Corbyn, lacking the power to speak, put out a hand to the boy's wrist and found it limp and cold.

William Degon's eyes were red and filled with hate; but Hanniball Corbyn needed neither this rebuke nor any other. He had sat trifling while sweet Humphy Degon lay dying. From that knowledge he might never find rest.

And then, quite slowly, Humphy recovered from his faint and opened his eyes. Above him was a circle of sweat-grimed faces, upside down to his way of looking, that stared with haunted expressions of torment and disbelief. At once he shut his eyes again and resumed his prayer, for he was certain that this was Hell.

"God alone saveth me!" He gabbled in his haste. "There is no damnation that are in Jesus Christ! As my Father lives, *please God keep me from the flames.*"

AN AFFAIR WITH THE REGIMENT

The woman did not look upon herself as a whore; but this was the only respect in which her view of the world was flawed, and it was forgivable. In all other matters her freedom from illusion might have been the envy of kings. She knew the meaning of defeat. She had learned the value of surrender; and she expected nothing of tomorrow. As clearly as if it had been written in a book, she knew that her affair with the cavalry must end as violently as it had begun, and as suddenly. It had been nearly two years ago, during the advance against the Earl of Essex's roundheads at Lostwithiel in August 1644, that the party of cavaliers had ridden into her village. Lord George Goring had been appointed Lieutenant General of the Horse and, in fulsome tribute to the style of their new commander, the men were drunk with the scent of victory. The nearness of the King had excited the Cornish peasantry in its hatred for the rebels, and it had submitted to the Royalists like a bitch on heat. There was little need for plunder: the spoils of the country were laid as gifts at the horsemen's feet.

Those two summers ago the woman had been a girl: awkward as a foal, with a mane of copper hair that fell across a beaky, bird-like face. With sharp nose and tiny hooded eyes, it was a face in which even the simple innocence of childhood could seem barbed and predatory. To the countrywomen, such features bespoke only cruelty and revulsion; but to their husbands the reading was more complex. The cruelty remained, but the revulsion was turned upon its head. There was a suggestion – more than a suggestion, a *promise* – of carnality that made them almost eager to suffer by her hand. No man could explain it. Such a face ought to have repelled; yet, while even a maiden, she was the mistress of their imaginations. All the cruelty, and all the knowingness, were mere accidents of flesh and bone. Yet, for their different reasons, neither man nor woman could speak easily to her face, and she felt it as a rebuff. She had yet to understand the power of her allure, and the glances of the men served only to muddle her.

Through her isolation she was driven to an early awareness of her peculiarity, if not to an understanding of it. On a misty morning in August 1644, it came as small surprise that a young officer of horse should single her out for particular favour. Neither did the nature of the favour itself shock her as much as it might, though it hurt her a great deal and there was much about it that puzzled her. It was administered at the point of a sword in a room of the neighbour's house, which the officer had taken for his quarters.

Afterwards her father had raised a storm of protest, and petitioned the captain in charge to make an adjudication against this Lieutenant Bullhead. But the girl observed, without displeasure, that her father was not so outraged that he had forgotten his peasant's gift of cunning. His speech was not concerned solely with complaints of dishonour: there were, too, the questions of restitution and marriage.

The captain heard him graciously, stroking his long moustaches and turning cold grey eyes on the girl. "This is truly a sombre affair," he said, nodding gravely. "If the lieutenant is guilty, then he must be punished. The matter shall be heard at once!"

A trumpeter was ordered to assemble the men, and all the people were formed in two half circles: soldiers on one side, villagers facing them on the other. The defendant Bullhead was marched at pistol point into the centre of this arena and there he was made to take off his clothes – every stitch, from head to toe. He was a flamboyant young man, evidently of good income, whose wardrobe would not have disgraced a prince. His buff coat was richly laced, with a broad red satin scarf tied in a bow at the hip; and his Flemish beaver hat carried an enormous scarlet plume tucked into a wide silk band of matching colour. Beneath the coat, his fringed breeches reached almost to the tops of his boots, which were extravagantly ruffled with white lawn. Never had the girl seen such stuff. The coat alone must have cost ten pounds or more; and the man who wore it would indeed be a treasure to bring to the altar! She understood little of the legal ritual, though she sensed, in the humour of the captain, a disturbing malevolence of intent that caused her to fear for Bullhead's safety. She hoped he would not be made to suffer too greatly, and anxiously set about examining his condition.

Shorn of his finery, he reminded her of a plucked chicken. His body was smooth and babyish, in high contrast to the weathered skin and dark tufted hair of the face and neck. He had narrow, unmuscular shoulders and a chest from which his ribs stood out like rafters. His limbs, too, were delicate and pale. Only the slight swelling of the belly served to betray the richness of his nobleman's diet. His penis was black with dried blood.

"Guilty beyond question!" said the captain. "Has the girl a grandmother?"

"Sir?"

"I said has the girl a grandmother? You must understand there is a procedure to these things."

The peasant father nodded his recognition of the fact. "No grandmother, Sir, nor grandfather neither. Only her mother and a brother."

"No sister?"

"No, Sir. No sister."

"Very well then. Let the mother step forward."

The woman had the same copper hair as her daughter, but age had not dealt kindly with her. The poverty of her diet had pinched the flesh, so that the lines at the corners of her mouth were etched deep and sharp in a fixture of worry. Under the eyes, the dark blue circles were sunk into hollows that scooped her cheeks even down to the jaw. So reduced was her condition by bad food, hard labour and disease that few who knew her believed she could have many weeks left to live. She made no movement when the captain called out her name, but was revealed, shrinking in her rags, as the crowd opened in front of her. The captain waited for her to be brought forward into the circle, then drew his rapier and pointed it at Bullhead.

"You have behaved like a puppy-dog!" he shouted. "If you value the esteem of your comrades, then you must prove yourself a man."

He pointed to the girl.

"Ravishing a maid, even a hawk-faced witch such as this one, is the work of any unpoxed pup. No business for a man!"

Now he pointed at the mother.

"To pleasure the old woman here, who looks as if she must want for it, now that is the job for a man! Forty strokes of your pizzle,

Lieutenant Bullhead, or you ride without your breeches!"

From the attitude of those surrounding her, the girl knew that the hearing had been resolved unfavourably; but only as hands were laid to her mother did she fully understand. For one act of rape, the penalty was to be another.

"*Forty strokes,* Bullhead, or your best breeches shall be put to the match!"

As she listened to her mother's screams, a slow tear ran from the girl's eye and cut a crooked channel through the dirt. But one tear only, no more. Even afterwards, looking back, she would wonder at her own inability to grieve. In her dark moments she would look hard for remorse, but there was none to find. Her emptiness was her strength. It was what kept her alive.

Her father, too, bowed his head as the officers did their work on the ragged bundle in the dust, and he did not move. Afterwards the captain took Bullhead's purse and tossed two handfuls of coins into the dirt. Eightpence for the girl, and eightpence for her mother.

"Restitution!" he said. "Which leaves us to settle only the question of marriage. Marry, my sweet young witch? Of course you shall. You shall marry the regiment!"

The girl closed her eyes and let her body fall limp as the many hands drew her into the house. Her left hand alone was fastened against their intrusion. Inside it lay the eightpence! A whole penny more than her father could earn by a day in the fields.

Cornwall had proved already too much for the roundheads to swallow, and it was Lostwithiel that finally choked them. On the day that the village girl arrived nearby, with sores on her feet and sixteen pennies in her purse, the King's men had already pounced on Essex's tactical lethargy and wrung the life from his campaign. With their backs turned to the sea, the roundheads had been called upon to summon their courage: to turn like cornered rats and fight. And yet, in neglecting to secure the high ground at Lostwithiel, they had ignored the advantage that might have been theirs. It was a failure of command, a hopeless folly, begging for punishment. If Essex had ordered his pikemen to leave off their corslets, he could not have sold their blood more cheaply. Grateful for the gift, the cavaliers had scaled Beacon Hill beneath a fog-bank and had worked all night to throw up a redoubt. By first light, the die had been cast. Essex was counting the cost of inescapable defeat; Charles was left to plan only the *manner* of his victory; and the village girl was weighing proposals of marriage from both a sergeant of foot and a captain of dragoons. It was the twenty-second day of August, 1644. In her purse were two shillings and a penny.

Never had she known such excitement. There had been no heart-searching. The self-neglecting stink of her mother; the wordless refusal of her father even to turn his face from the wall; the shunning by the village people: all had conspired to make her departure, in her own mind, a matter of course. There were 16,000 men of the Royalist regiments marching on Lostwithiel, an army of nobles to whom gallantry was a kind of birthright. The assault by sound and spectacle was overwhelming; and in an instant, with a thrill of fear, she was in love. She loved their arrogance, the red-blooded, conquesting male-ness that mocked the gelded quiescence of the peasants. She accepted their contempt as a mark of their given superiority; and she despised her village for being the object of it. The cavalry surely were God's own army!

Her first evening, in a cornfield two miles from the town, was divided between the sergeant of foot and the captain of dragoons. She did not fully understand the pleasure they took in her, and she judged from the torture in their faces that the pain they suffered was at least as sharp as her own. With a mustering of will, she stifled her screams in order to seem, in some small way, their equal. Then, when each had been given the promise he demanded, and each had added to the weight of her purse, she huddled herself to rest beneath a thorn hedge against the Liskeard road. In her mind she held a picture of Lieutenant Bullhead; and if she had understood that there was anything she should forgive him for, then she would have forgiven him at once. She regretted only her own unworthiness to keep hold of such a man; and she promised suitably to improve herself as rapidly as fortune would allow. In the cold, she slept only fitfully. It was not the first time she had lain without a bed, nor would it be the last; but she was resolved that such nights would be few.

And so they would. In the morning of the next day she met the lieutenant: not Bullhead, but a stranger who spurred his heavy black horse as if he meant to run her down. He sprang from the saddle while still at the gallop, and astonished her with his agility, holding his balance even under the weight of his armour. There was natural command, too, in the way he brushed aside her hair to more closely examine her face. She cast down her head as far as his grip would permit, but rolled up her eyes with an instinctive coquetry whose force she was at last beginning to suspect. He was indeed a thing to admire: a soldier and a thinker. He had the taut narrow cheeks, pointed jaw and high-bridged nose of the warrior-aristocrat; the earnest brown eyes and deep furrowed brow of the thinker. His hair and beard were curly, and black as December night. There was wisdom in his face; yet she judged, with a stab of surprise, that he was but a few years older than herself.

All the time they were speaking, other men were riding or walking in the road behind him. She noticed that they were all staring at her; and many of them called aloud in strange accents that she did not recognise. One voice in particular impressed her by the musicality of its tone, which reminded her of church-singing.

"Now *there's* worth catching the pox for, eh boys?" It came from a tall sunburned man who carried a pike almost three times his own height.

The lieutenant seemed amused by her bewilderment. "Welsh peasants," he said. "Fighting for the pay."

She did not understand the meaning of Welsh; nor did she recognise any slight to herself in his contempt for the peasantry. And for his own part the lieutenant did not care whether he flattered her or not. He wooed, as was his custom, with his purse. She wooed, for she still thought she must, with her eyes, and with her curiosity. She asked to be shown his sword, which hung from a richly-decorated baldrick across his right shoulder. Then the gun, as long as his arm, which he said was called a harquebus; and the two wheel-lock pistols, so heavy that she could barely steady them in her hands. On a ribbon around his wrist was his pole-axe, part hammer and part axe, with which he broke the heads of infantrymen. He pointed to the marks on the blade where it had done its work; and he showed her the dull metal balls for the guns, and the flask of powder. The girl stroked the barrel of his harquebus, softly with her fingers, until he laughed and drew it away.

"Stay, girl!" he said. "Play a man's weapon like that and it will go off before battle is properly joined." She shared his laughter without understanding the reason for it. "Later," he said, "you may play some more." He explained exactly where his billet lay, and made her repeat the instruction; then he mentioned an hour of the clock and sealed the assignation with a coin.

The spray of thin white mud had barely settled behind his horse before the girl was surrounded by a group of women in brightly-coloured rags, who jostled and stabbed at her with their fingers. She noticed a bad odour, on their breath and about their bodies, which was quite unlike the body smells of the people in the village. They asked rough questions and laughed at her answers, for they were truly astonished by her lack of knowledge. Yet they did not lack kindness. Before they let her go, they stayed their mockery and told her many things she needed to know.

For eight nights the girl slept at the lieutenant's billet in a yeoman's house and was given food from the yeoman's table. Every night she filled the lieutenant's bed. Every day he filled her belly, her purse – and her dreams. Again, despite the strictures of the street-women, she began to foresee a life of plump cushions, silken petticoats and obedient servants; until, on August 30th, the lieutenant did not return to the billet and the yeoman barred his door to her as if she were a common beggar. She called on the other officers in the house to speak for her, but they only laughed. By rejecting their favours and holding fast to her one man she had removed all possibility of their friendship. Only the yeoman's wife would speak to her, and told her that the lieutenant would not come back until morning: he had met two roundhead deserters in the field and had ridden with them to the King. It preserved the dream: she was proud that her man would be brought to the attention of the King, and she wished she had a friend she might tell of it. But other matters were pressing: a cold mist threatened, and she had little appetite for a bed among the quickthorn.

The day was old before its time. A mountain of slate-coloured cloud crumbled across the country and took away the light. Candles began to flicker, and the girl could see the glimmer of the musketeers' match, smouldering like an army of glow-worms in the dusk. Standing by the Liskeard road, she realised that the fields and hedgerows were coming rapidly to life. First a galloper came by; then a sprinkle of soldiers, hasty and disorganised; then a steady procession; and then the swarm. Facing each other across the Liskeard road, as if they were intent on some private battle of their own, were assembled the Royalist armies of Prince Maurice and the King. Along the way between them, the girl was overtaken by many hundreds of hurrying men, too intent upon their duty to impede her. Few even looked, and only one officer turned to call out.

"Get away, girl! If you would live to be a hag, get away. Get off the road!" From the dark of the roadside hedge came the answering voice of a soldier. "Let the harlot be. It's time she felt the prick of a Puritan's lance!" And there was laughter in the shadows.

Across the country, the hubbub died to a seething calm. Everyone except the girl seemed to be moving to a purpose, and she was deeply frightened. Most of the foot soldiers were musketeers, at least two of them to every pike. And the pace of their advance was governed neither by fear of the enemy, nor by stealth. They announced their approach with a glowering of match cord, burning in each man's hand, and with the rattle of the tin powder cases on their bandoliers. Some of them were already in battle order, with bullets clamped between their teeth as if even their lips would frame sentences of death.

The girl hovered uncertainly as the men peeled away on either side of the road. She watched their shadows merge against the hedge and detach themselves on the field side, moving towards the armies. But suddenly it all stopped: a moment of horror. Men and trees flashed lividly out of the dark, and from behind her came a puff of sound like the coughing of a horse. It was, she later learned, a common enough kind of accident. A musketeer had caught his match cord into his bandolier, so that the flame leaped in a chain from one powder-case to the next. The man's face flared, died away, flared. The girl saw that his tongue as he yelled was poking out straight and stiff; and that his eyes, dark as beads, seemed fixed in astonishment, as if he was transfixed by some magic he could not persuade himself to believe. No one dared approach him until the final explosion, the twelfth, had lifted away the last charred rag of his coat. The girl looked at the pale smoke rising from his chest and beard; then, with no thought beyond a simple urge to escape from what she had seen, she turned towards Lostwithiel and ran.

Around a sharp bend, the lane grew immediately dark and deserted. The only sounds were the sibilant falsetto of her own breath and the clapping of her feet in the liquid mud. For an instant, in the space of a single stride, she sensed the presence of another; and then a violent kick on the legs sent her sprawling. The strong hands that fell on her were looking for weapons, but they became no less inquisitive when they discovered her breast. A rough country voice roared in her ear.

"Whoa there! Whoa! What's this now, that heaven's sent?"

She could feel the stale gust of the man's breath, and the scratch of his beard on her neck as he pinioned her like a lover. His weight was painful to her shoulders and chest, and the cold ground-water was biting through her clothing to the skin. But she had no strength left to struggle. She gave herself up and found herself a prisoner of a tall, grey-bearded sergeant of foot. Above his shoulder she could see the dark silhouette and bright window-cracks of a shuttered roadside cottage; and behind that the first pale stroke of a crescent moon. He put one hand over her mouth and lifted her easily to her feet with the other. His fingers smelled sickeningly of iron and excrement. His voice was an excited whisper.

"Best be quiet now!"

He held her steady for a moment, as if he were undecided; and then, almost at a run, pulled her into the cottage porch, where they stood panting together like staghounds. "It's been a long day," he whispered, linking arms to fasten her in a kind of twist-lock that would work against her elbow if she tried to pull away. His lips as he spoke were spread wetly against the back of her neck, while his free hand reached round again to her breast and he thrust himself hard against her buttocks. "The night could be a long one, too." But he did not persist. An oven-blast of heat struck the girl as he eased back the door, and she saw that the cottage was filled with a burning orange glow: fifty match cords reflected in fifty pairs of eyes.

"Here you are, boys," called the sergeant. "Just get yourselves a feel of this! And don't let them Puritans be thinking that God's not on our side!" He took a soldier's hand and pressed it beneath his own, firmly against the girl's bosom. For a moment it seemed that there would be uproar. The men cheered and jostled so savagely that the girl was certain they must blow themselves up with careless misapplications of their match cords. Order was restored – though only with great difficulty – by a string of increasingly furious orders from the captain in charge, a ruddy young man (he looked like a farmer, she thought) with coiled black moustaches who gripped and ungripped his pistol butt as if he were suppressing an ambition to do murder.

"Sergeant! What in Heaven do you mean by it? This is a battle station, not a bordel! Put the girl outside and let her go on her way!"

The sergeant was older: a professional soldier, with a professional's eye for the weaknesses of gentlemen officers. And like a professional he had prepared his ground.

"But, sir," he said. "Begging your pardon, sir, but do we want her running loose upon the road to give us all away, sir? Until the danger's past, sir, wouldn't it be better to keep her here, nice and safe?" He smiled, almost sweetly, and bowed.

Then he took the girl outside, robbed her of her purse and raped her.

The sergeant was right in his prediction: the night was a long one. At the King's headquarters in Boconnoc, the two captured roundheads had paid, in the currency of the deserter, a heavy ransom for their lives. The intelligence they gave up had been startling. It did not surprise the King to learn that this was the night on which the Earl of Essex would begin the withdrawal of his infantry and artillery along the estuary to Fowey, for this much had been expected. What caused him to gasp was the fugitives' insistence (and they were under the heaviest kind of persuasion to be truthful) that the roundhead cavalry would not join the retreat but would break out of Lostwithiel and make a gallop for freedom along the Liskeard road, *right through the Royalist lines*. The impertinence was laughable: not so much a challenge to the King's authority as a gift into his hands.

"Let them come," he said, "and we shall swallow them whole." First to greet them would be a viper's nest of a half-hundred muskets, lying in ambush at a roadside cottage; and then the combined Royal armies, arranged along the tongue of road like the gaping jaws of a wolf.

Yet come they did. In the lowest part of the night, at three o'clock in the morning, two thousand horsemen came out of Lostwithiel, galloped clean through the trap and made safely on to Braddock Down. Along the hedgerows the cavaliers' battle-fever had turned through disbelief into boredom, and from boredom into sleep. At the cottage, the musketeers had extinguished their match and were bidding at auction for the favours of the girl. The sergeant, who had assumed proprietorship, brought down his hammer on a bid of three days' pay. The girl, who had remembered something of what the old prostitutes had told her, let her legs fall dead and waited for the violation with her thoughts as empty as she could make them. But the soldier never came. There was a silence, almost a suspension of breath, as the men dared themselves to believe the sounds of hoof and harness from the road outside; and then pandemonium. The rebel riders, who gained their objective without receiving a single shot, could not know what they owed to the dark-haired girl who passed them in the night.

The sun rose on a fever of accusation that reached even to Lord

Goring at St. Blazey, who was slandered for having failed to lead out his cavalry. Full of wine again, the scandal-mongers said, and playing stallion to a filly of markedly unmilitary pedigree. Yet the King himself had no ear for recrimination, being still eager to formalise his victory. He took Lostwithiel at seven o'clock the same morning, and harried Essex so cruelly that the retreating infantry shed their arms like seed on the field. A cartload of muskets and five heavy cannon were lost in the flight, all sunk so deeply in the Cornish mud that not even a team of thirty drawing-horses could retrieve them. Essex's invasion of Cornwall was stamped into the dirt. On the second day of September he made his escape by fishing boat to Plymouth, leaving his men to surrender as they would.

On the top of a low grassy tump, where the red and yellow meadow flowers lay fading at the end of their season, the girl joined a group of peasants who had gathered there to watch the Royalist advance. With dreadful fascination she realised that the pikes and colours on the facing hillside were those of the enemy's rearguard. She heard the thin crackle of muskets, and joined in the cheering that saluted the fall of each rebel soldier. An icy shiver ran through her as the words of a psalm drifted faintly from the Puritan rear, yet still she kept up her clamour for their blood. Foam-glossed horses were straining to bring the King's artillery to bear on their backs, and she jeered as the men broke ranks and ran to save themselves from it.

It was a picture that would return again and again to scold her the following summer. She was serving the garrison at Exeter when the news came from Langport: her lieutenant had been made up to captain and had led his men in a brave defence of the Royalist line. As he unsheathed his sword to rally them, a six-pound ball from a field cannon had passed clean through a rank of horse and carried away his head.

Around Ilsington in the early days of 1646 the soil lay hard as granite beneath a brittle crust of snow. Birds fluffed themselves forlornly on the bare branches and fought over tiny scraps of nourishment. The ice reached down between the roots into the ground and extinguished the wintering animals in their nests. At Bovey Tracey, two-and-a-half miles distant, the woman was sheltering in the billet of some young Royalist officers. Lostwithiel was remembered now only as a place of baptism and the foundation of her widowhood. In spirit it seemed a whole lifetime apart. Who, on the King's side, could now reach into his heart and pull out even a hundredth part of the same high hope? There was no tomfool Essex in the field against them now. Instead there came, like a plague, the new model army of Lord Thomas Fairfax and Oliver Cromwell. The King and Prince Rupert had succumbed to it at Naseby; Goring at Langport. Bristol, too, had been lost and the country – sickened by their plunderings – had turned against them. Goring himself had made off to France, leaving the Western army to take its chance under the generalship of Lord Wentworth, who was Goring's equal only in his thirst for strong wine.

Time had rounded the woman. The approach of maturity, and a scraps-from-the-table diet of fatty meats, had thickened her at bosom and hip. The precocity was over, yet her attractiveness remained undiminished – enhanced, even, by her knowledge of how to employ it. Her coquetry, once a girlish instinct, had become practised, offering a calculated measure of promise from behind the teasing mask of hair. She had learned that demureness, with just a *suggestion* of corruptibility in the framing of the lips, would inflame men's passions far more readily than the tawdry beckonings of the cheaper women; and the calculation had extended also to her costume. Although seldom penniless, her purse did not permit the elaborate finery of a high-born lady, and she eschewed all imitation of it. There was never a flounce nor a frill, never a stitch of embroidery nor a yellowing flop of lace. If it were not for the low plunge of her dress on the shoulders, the plain colour of the stuff might have persuaded a stranger to accept her for a Puritan housewife. She did possess one full-cut satin skirt and fine embroidered petticoat, looted from a mansion wardrobe by an admirer of easy gallantry, but she had found precious little use for it.

In the months after Lostwithiel she had moved from garrison to garrison in the train of the army, holding close to her lieutenant whenever she could come up with him. At other times, in defiance of sentiment, she had made easy profit from casual lovers. Once a month, at her onset, she swallowed a green poison of herbs which the older women prescribed against fertility. She was warmed by their lack of jealousy and would often pass them scraps of food or clothing which her lovers had provided. With her money, however, she was close. For she saw, in the other women, all that might befall her when the years had taken their revenge; and she knew that money alone could prevent it. The sergeant of foot, at the cottage outside Lostwithiel, was the last common soldier ever to gain knowledge of her. For the rest, she would entertain only men of rank – a particularity of taste which could only hasten the rise of her celebrity. Her magic was deeply potent. Within weeks, the army was bewitched. It was not uncommon for her to reach a garrison to find that the eldest sons of noblemen were already gathered to bid for the right to pay court. It was said even that Goring himself had been amused by her; and more regiments of men boasted of her charms than there were nights in the year.

Only with her lieutenant did she yield to thraldom. In truth he had grown weary of her company, yet it suited his vanity to be adored by a courtesan of such high renown. He spoke little to her, accepting her devotion as a matter of small account. Sometimes he gambled with her virtue at the card table, and watched with languid contempt as the winners took their prize. At other times he would burst out in a cuckold's rage if he entered a garrison unheralded and found she had traded the moment to another officer. Yet always he kept her generously provisioned from his purse and always, when she reminded him, willingly enough told her what she asked to hear.

"When the war is over, you shall be a lady."

In the January of 1646 her prostitution was a question of material need, not something that reached in and touched her soul. With her lover killed she was no whore but a war widow as innocent as any other. And she had made a plan – or been driven to it. With the tide now running so strongly against the King, and with the walls of the city already under siege, it was but a matter of time before Exeter must fall. She could not wait. There could be no hope of sanctuary in changing her allegiance from a beaten army to the victor. She knew how the Puritan zealots had rampaged after Naseby. With the King's army having taken to its heels, they had broken in among the camp followers and ran amuck on a God-crazed orgy of moral redress. Unlike the Irish, whose skulls had been crushed with musket butts, the English harlots had been granted the privilege of life. But their purifiers had seen to it that they would never again look temptation in the face. The persuasion, delivered with sword and dagger, had been unanswerable. Noses had been cleft open like the petals of deep-flowering roses; eyes thumbed out; cheeks slit by blades drawn outward from the corners of the mouth. These had become women whom none but a blind man would pay to lie with; and for some, not even that. For not all the vengeance had been kept to the face. Breasts had been mutilated; and there was one punishment, a single stroke of the sword, which the women at Exeter knew between themselves as "feeling the prick of the Almighty". One might live after such an operation, but not as a woman.

As 1645 drew to an end, it had begun to seem that there could be no escape. Fairfax had set his garrisons all around the city and, though there was plague in the roundhead ranks and men were dying at a dozen a day, the siege had held fast. As winter bared the citizens' larders, there had seemed little hope that the defenders could last until spring. And then news had reached the roundhead commanders that a new Royalist force was coming from the west, brazenly announcing its intention to break the siege. It had been a vain boast which Fairfax had been in no humour to tolerate. Early in January he had set off to intercept and slap down his challengers in the field; and in the confusion that surrounded his departure the woman had managed to slip clear of the city.

Her plan was to return to Cornwall, to make what fortune she could while time remained, and then to find safety in her village. But they were dangerous days. Dangerous for a man travelling alone; doubly dangerous for a woman. For a bedding-wench with money in her purse, the risks were as many as the paces she took. On the first day she made good speed and spent the night at Chudleigh, where she found shelter in a thatched corn barn. But on the second morning, when she had nothing to eat but two raw stolen eggs, her steps were slow and heavy. The snow clung to her soles in thick icy clogs that unbalanced her. Away from the beaten path, where the snow had drifted among the trees, she sank sometimes as deep as her hips, so that by midday she was too tired to move more than a few yards without pausing to recover her strength. As the sky faded towards evening she was near to Bovey Tracey, not three miles from where she had set out in the morning. She was faint with cold and hunger, and so exhausted that she began seriously to fear that she might die. Beyond any doubt she knew that she could not live through another night without food or warmth.

When she saw the Royalist cavalrymen she laughed aloud. They were unsaddling their horses and bullying the country wives with an easy arrogance that rang an echo of Lostwithiel. She made professional adjustments to her hair as she came down the slope towards them, and attended to the contour of her lips. Already her vigour was wondrously restored. In front of a well-patched cob cottage she found an officer she recognised as an admirer, and whispered her name in his ear like a password between conspirators. At first he drew back and would not believe her, for the poverty of her condition was in dire conflict with his memory. But she shook her hair and persuaded him with her eyes.

The kitchen was a cocoon of warmth and scent. Glistening on the spit were the pale bodies of two fowls, both split clean through the breastbone where an impatient lieutenant had drawn his sword and opened them like knapsacks. The spill of entrails had made food for the crows; the twist of the blade, where he had cleaned it on her apron, a sufficient persuasion for the wife to serve them. She attended to her guests reluctantly still, but with haste: coldly courteous towards the men, but directing her spite through narrow glances at the woman. It was a little before six o'clock in the evening, though the sky outside was already blacker than midnight. The six officers, all men of high civilian rank and quality, sat at the table as they waited, and set out their stakes for a hand of cards. The piles of coins, which they exchanged with casual good humour, did nothing to soften the hostess's resentment.

"I wonder," she said, "shall you gentlemen be resting here long?" She spoke from the turnspit, calling over her shoulder, insolently polite. "It's said that Master Cromwell is coming this way."

The oldest man, a major, brayed with laughter and fanned the cards across the table with a heavy slap of his hand. "'Tis true, Master Cromwell has thought to show his face in Crediton!" He pronounced the town mockingly in the local way: *Curton*. "Now if he is planning a visit to Bovey Tracey, then so much the better. He'll spare us the effort of finding him. We are ready for Master Cromwell! We are ready for ten Master Cromwells! We shall make him eat his footsteps all the way home to the Eastern sea!"

A pale-haired young captain giggled and scooped up the stake money which the major had disarranged. "Well, Cromwell or no, here's a fine pot," he said. "The winner tonight shall have plenty with which to bid for a mistress."

"Ah now, stay your hand!" rejoined the elder. "We shall have none of this dicing for the wench. She has already named her price to me and we are agreed on it. You must play instead for the old house-bitch." He rubbed his beard and made a gesture with his forefinger. "Loser takes all!"

It was like a scene from a drama, as if events offstage were taking their cue from the players' mouths. At first, pounded by waves of laughter, the small percussions in the road outside were indistinguishable from the spitting of the chickens. The housewife heard them first, and then the young woman crouching at the hearthside. Together they rose, shaken out of their enmity, each looking to the other for some contradiction of what she feared. But the next volley was close at hand, unmistakable. It cut the laughter like a guillotine and brought the six gentlemen thudding to their feet.

"Some fool with a pistol!"

"*Some fool!*"

No look-outs had been posted, and the enemy's approach had been cushioned by the snow. A full brigade of the Parliamentary horse and foot, led by Lieutenant General Cromwell, was already in among the first billets with sword and pistol. The defenders had been taken cold, with their match dead and their pistols unprimed: a rabble of gentry whose boasts rebounded on them now like musket balls from a wall.

In the cottage, only the housewife was a stranger to the clamours of war: the ringing of blades and the spluttering of muskets; the screams and the sobs; oaths and psalms. All coming towards them now at the speed of a man running. Acting, it appeared, on the oddest of impulses, it was the major who moved first, seizing his hat and sweeping into it the stake money from the card table. This he took in his left hand; in his right, an unloaded flintlock. There was not time for him to buckle his sword.

"Follow me!"

He reached the doorway only a dozen paces ahead of the battle. Five roundhead troopers with bawling mouths were already running at the cottage, swords raised crudely like axes. Not flinching, quite expressionless, he braced himself in the doorframe and levelled the empty pistol.

"Follow me!"

The troopers had no firearms of their own, and were afraid to be shot. The man at the head slithered and tried to turn away, but not quickly enough to prevent the others piling into him from behind and bringing them all down stupidly in a heap. With a gracious flourish of his hat, like a greeting to the King, the major cast the coins across the snow beneath their noses.

"Follow me!"

But only the captain came after him, to step across the quarrelling troopers into the mainstream of the war. The four young lieutenants had run out through the back door, whence they made clear across the frozen River Bovey and away towards the village of Ilsington.

The housewife had no side in the war. She had no deep understanding or opinion; neither on the divine right of kings nor on the meaning of Holy Eucharist. She cared only to live innocently and to cherish her husband. Whomsoever was powerful, then she would be meek. When great powers collided, each calling upon God as its champion, her convictions hovered like a songbird; for to show favour to one, it seemed, was only to invite reprisal from the other. Now she saw the presence of Royalists in her house as a matter of shame, a culpable uncleanliness for which punishment must swiftly follow.

"My husband!" she whispered to the other woman. "My husband is not yet back from the field! Where is he? *What have they done?*"

The courtesan left her and ran to the window. For a moment she was heartened by the approach of the Royalist colours, bearing the arms of King Charles himself, hoisted high above the mob. But all her joy turned to dust when she saw that it was in the hands of the Puritans. A building was on fire, and by its light she saw the young captain, who had followed the major into the fight, come running straight as a deer towards the window: she recognised him by his strange pale hair and perfect boots with their white lawn ruffs. His hands were stretched out in front of him like a beggar's, and he stumbled repeatedly as if he were about to fall. A roundhead officer called him to stand at the point of a pistol, yet held his fire and stood aside to let him pass. Not until he struck the cottage wall, with his face outside the window not an arm's length from the woman's own, was he brought to halt. The face had been divided by two cuts of a sword, downwards and across, in a crucifix. There were no eyes, no mouth, no nose; only a rhythmically pumping bubble, like a storm in a crimson sea.

She turned away without looking at the housewife. There was an officer's buff coat left draped across a bench, and she bundled it up. The chickens on the spit had begun to char, and came away easily in her hand; but they burned her fingers, so that she had to wrap them in the coat. From the back door she followed the broad scatter of footprints to the riverbank, then across the ice to the other side. The tracks vanished in the dense shadow beneath the trees, but she ran on blindly until the sounds of killing had faded to a murmur. Once, as she paused to take breath, she could hear a column of horses passing not far away to her left. It was dangerously cold. The heavy coat hung in empty folds from her shoulders and she was in constant danger of tripping on the hem. One of the chickens had been lost during the flight, but she clasped the other beneath her arm and kept up as fast a walk as she could manage. The brief respite in the cottage had strengthened her; but she knew that, if she was to live through the night, *then she must keep on moving.*

There was no moon; she cast no shadow. For two hours she fought through the snowdrifts, upwards on a hill she thought would never end. When it did end, and she raised her head above the crest, she at once fell back in alarm. On the other side, resting in the valley bottom, was a widely-scattered army of musketeers. She could see the winking red eyes of their match-cords, moving and mingling as they fell into their ranks, and could hear the tin rattle of their bandoliers. At first she thought she might move along behind the ridge and pass them on their flank; but when she looked again she saw that they were advancing across too wide a front and would cut her off. All she could do was conceal herself and hope she might remain undiscovered. For half an hour she pressed herself into the barbed clutch of a holly tree, listening to the rasping of her own breath, scarcely able to believe that no one could hear it. She prayed that at least the soldiers might be the King's men, and would let her pass in safety.

She squatted and kept her face so low in the bush that she heard the animal long before she saw it. Snorting steamily in the frozen air, an army draw-horse was nuzzling the ice in hope of a morsel to eat. Knotted into its harness, and hanging from its mane and tail, were burning match cords and empty bandoliers. The musketeers were horses, every one of them: decoys set by the Royalists to cover their retreat.

With her limbs chilled beyond pain, the woman bit into the chicken and drew raw blood from beneath the blackened skin.

Morning dawned late and cold. The tailor Hanniball Corbyn had brought warning that 120 cavaliers were hiding in Ilsington Church, but the roundhead force had not been in time to catch them. Before first light, the fugitives had made off towards a new rendezvous at Ashburton – an escape which had grated on roundhead tempers. The infantry had been issued new stockings and shoes before they left Tiverton, but this had not saved them from raw feet in their dash behind the horse from Bovey Tracey.

"God damn the tailor!" cried a disaffected sergeant, clapping his frost-bitten hands. "God damn him!"

The captain of horse was one Bartholomew Lucas, as solemn and devout a Calvinist as Corbyn himself. In the days before Fairfax, it had been his habit to seize parish pulpits and scarify local congregations with hellfire sermons of terrifying ferocity. Unorthodoxy of that kind was now prohibited by regulation, but this did not oblige him to tolerate a foul mouth.

"Sergeant! Do you know what is the penalty for blasphemers?"

"Yes, sir." The man stood stiffly, with no cockiness in his manner, for he had seen the operation done. "A red hot iron through the tongue, sir."

"Very well then. Best still your lips before they deliver you to the Devil."

Captain Lucas elbowed his way through the knot of red-coated infantrymen and glared peevishly at their officer. Ill-discipline of this kind would not be tolerated in the cavalry. Inside the church he saw that the floor had been stained by the stabling of horses, and that a tombstone next to the font had been chopped through with the imprint of a hoof. He had to incline his head to read the inscription: In Memory of Elizabeth Ford. Died 1628, wife of Thomas Ford of Bagtor: and the mother, he knew, of the dramatist John Ford, who had written some vile stuff about incest.

He smiled to himself at the irony of it: the defenders of the grand families, breaking into a church and defiling the memory of one of their own. But humour, even of this cruel kind, was a stranger to him, and not welcome. It was anger that fired his soul; that, and a hunger for retribution which no amount of cracked tombstones could satisfy. His next victims in the holy war would be the painted saints on the rood screen panels, which he began to belabour with the tip of his sword. The obliteration was practised and methodical, for he had done the work many times before. Idolatry was a higher blasphemy than any oath: he began, as he always did, by scratching out the eyes.

As he worked, some words of the Second Psalm came to him. "Ask of me, and I shall give thee the heathen for thine inheritance, and the uttermost parts of the earth for thy possession." For every word, a jab of the sword. "Thou shalt break them with a rod of iron; thou shalt dash them in pieces like a potter's vessel."

He was interrupted by a disturbance in the porch: angry mutterings and excited conversation; a deathly fit of coughing. The infantrymen had stood aside to admit a tall stooping figure in black Puritan's garb, who stood hugging his chest and wheezing in obvious pain from his lungs. At his side, a lieutenant of the cavalry was tugging at an elbow to hurry him on his errand.

"Begging your pardon Captain Lucas, sir," the lieutenant said. "This is the tailor Corbyn. He asked to be brought to you."

The newcomer's demeanour was nervously agitated. He was wet to the skin, as much from perspiration as from the melting snow that dripped from his clothing and made sparkling rivulets on the uneven stone floor. There was a fleck of something yellow on his lips, and a thin smear of blood where he had wiped his hand after coughing. His whole body shuddered with fever.

Lucas stood a little away from him, but greeted him courteously. "Ah yes. Good day to you, Master Corbyn. It was you who brought us the alarm, I think? You are to be thanked for a good night's work."

Corbyn's throat rattled so ticklishly that he had to clutch himself to stave off another spasm. Each word came separately, with its own rasping intake of breath. "You speak kindly, sir. Yet I did not come to be thanked. *I bring news.*"

Lucas tapped the heel of his boot, impatient to put himself beyond the reach of the tailor's breath. "So? What news?"

"The church plate, sir. The silver. Some of the village men took it when they heard the soldiers were coming, and buried it for safe-keeping in the Coxisland woods, a quarter of a mile from here in the valley."

With his long experience, Lucas began to read the sense of it. "And this morning the silver is gone? That would not be uncommon!"

"Yes, sir, you have it right. But hear me out, I beg you. The thief has been seen, and is still not more than half a mile along the way."

"And so? Are we in the business of chasing common thieves? What do you care for these trappings of silver anyway?"

"Sir, the thief is a King's officer of high rank. He is without his horse and is headed on foot for the moor!"

The disturbance in the snow where the silver had been buried was clear for any thief to find. Clear, too, was the single set of footprints that diverged from the others and made off towards the high moor. The snow was deep, with a hard shell of ice. For more than an hour, the captain and his sergeant followed the valley bottom, flattening them-selves along their horses' necks to avoid being snared by the curtains of thorn. At each twist in the path they stopped and shaded their eyes. The footprints had begun to wander from side to side, as if the fugitive were becoming unsteady, and twice there were deep impressions in the snow where he had fallen.

It was touching noon when they saw the man ahead of them: a slightly-built, red-haired cavalry officer in a leather buff coat. In his right hand, hanging almost to the ground, was the grey canvas bag containing the silver. Captain Lucas dismounted, leaving the sergeant to hold the horses, and followed from tree to tree on foot. The wood was thinning out now, and he could see open country ahead of him, rising towards some black, snow-capped rocks. His finger on the trigger of the harquebus was numb with cold, so that he could not feel the light pressure of the metal. In his mind the anger churned. The war had divided towns and villages inwardly against themselves: families had been broken by it, and cousin set against cousin. He saw a picture of his own home, defenceless in the path of a Royalist advance; and a worse picture, of his daughter, who had paid a terrible price for her burgeoning womanhood. In his hands the harquebus seemed to have no weight.

"Thou shalt break them with a rod of iron; thou shalt dash them in pieces like a potter's vessel."

The woman heard nothing. In her mind was an immeasurable distance, and an elusive vision of a young man with a handsome black beard.

THE CHAMPION

When she awoke she found herself in heaven. There was a balmy warmth making a faint stir in the leaves, and a fluffy coverlet of steam lying deep across her blanket. And honeysuckle in the air, like a sweet aching in the head. Her tongue felt big in her mouth, and dry, so that it was only with effort that she could push forward and unstick the lips from her gums.

"Oh bless me, Lord. Bless thy daughter Mary Woollacott and keep her."

Beyond the dark wooden cross that hung over her, the sky spilled a lake of pale heavenly light. Mary flinched with her eyes and raised her arms to be taken. From behind and above her, a spotted woodpecker hammered feverishly at a birch. Like a carpenter: nails into her coffin.

"Oh bless me, Lord, and keep me."

Bees hummed in the parlour glade, recalling other insects that nagged at her legs. Painfully Mary shifted her body in the straw and felt the sharp edge of the box, hard beneath her elbows. The cross of the Lord disarranged itself and became a random junction of timbers: two nailed roof spars, propped against a ruined wall. She took the corner of her blanket, warm with its faint reek of vomit, and began contentedly to suck. She was still at home after all.

Her box was exactly the right size for her to lie down in, with her body bunched at one end and her legs pushed out in front of her. The cottage within which it lay was barely recognisable: only two stump-ends of cob, where the gable walls still stood, and a powdery pink rubble from which sprang bright yellow clusters of charlock and wild radish. At one time there had been an upstairs bedroom, where she had slept on a proper mattress. But even in those days the thatch had been so badly preserved that, to retain the illusion of shelter, she had found it necessary to block the chimney with a sack of chaff and to sleep with her head in the fireplace. Fat brown fungi had hung from her chamber walls like dish-covers on a rack; and the boards of the floor had become as cold and spongy as mutton. Inch by inch the rain and the ice had bitten deeper, until the staircase had been entirely consumed by rot. Confined thereafter to the ground floor, her comfort had, if anything, been enhanced, for the thatch had almost immediately fallen inward and made a deep warm blanket across the floor above. But the rot had been too far into the beam ends, and it had not been long before the floor, too, had spilled into the parlour. The box, which now had been her home for more than two years, was her last refuge. She had pulled it into a corner, where the gable wall still supported a remnant of the flank, and had surrounded it with a gappy stockade of spars. For all the shelter it gave, she might as well have been a vixen on the moor.

This closeness to the earth was not the only respect in which Mary's hovel copied the rudeness of a lair. Old grey bones and animal skins were strewn across the floor, and whole carcasses – rabbits, hares, and rumpled birds with thin speckled breasts – dangled their heads from the timbers among a drapery of nets. Her brown blanket showed black and rusty blots where the bodies had dripped, and there was a sour tang in the air, of life-smells and death-smells together.

Yet Mary did not believe herself unhappy. Until the knot in her chest had prevented it, she had walked every Sunday to worship at Ilsington church and even afterwards, with her breath reduced to a thin and laboured rasp, she had accepted the ill-fortune with simple grace.

"Well . . . per'aps 'tis for the best."

This had been the guiding principle of her life. It had served as an answer when George Woollacott had made his coarse proposal of marriage; and it had served her forty years later when he had died in his cell, a poacher and stealer of sheep. She had been comforted by it each time the gamekeepers had given up a son of hers, or a grandson, to the law; just as she had recited it each time they had escaped. For her conception of rightness depended on a higher authority than the English criminal law. Among her meagre store she kept only one item which she admitted to herself was truly the product of theft. It was a ragged square of paper which her husband had given her, torn from the Bible at Chudleigh Church. Psalm 50, verses ten and eleven.

For every beast of the forest is mine, and the cattle upon a thousand hills.

I know all the fowls of the mountains: and the wild beasts of
the field are mine.

She dug down into the box beneath her hips, sifting through the
straw with her fingers until she touched the thin canvas envelope that
contained the treasure. She did not need to withdraw it; only to feel the
texture of the canvas to reassure herself that all was well. The verses
were as indelibly a part of her as the names of her family. She could
recite them unfalteringly by rote – though, if called upon to do so, she
could recognise the printed words by their shape; and she delighted to
startle visitors with her apparent ability to read. But visitors, in these
declining days, were few. The rector came sometimes, to pat her hand
and offer such reassurances as he thought he must; and her grandson
came often, bearing the still-warm corpses from his traps. It had
occurred to Mary to wonder how much his attention was due to his
affection for her as his grandmother, and how much to his need for a
safe place of concealment. But, if there was suspicion in her mind, she
had never put it to the test.
   Yet, in truth, it was no small service that he required of her, and no
small risk. Less than a week earlier, to illuminate the danger, an entire
shooting party had walked through her parlour with their gamekeeper.
Newly woken and desperately afraid, she had pressed a hand to her
breastbone, as if forcefully to suspend her own breathing, and had
peered out through the twigs like a squirrel from her drey. There had
been six gentlemen standing there, all of whom, by their clothes and
manner, she had taken to be visitors from the city. Mostly they had been
so nervous of their flintlocks that they would neither prime nor load
them without both a suck at the brandy flask (in one case, even, a nip of
laudanum) and a steadying hand from Ambrose Beare the keeper. Beare
alone had known that Mary was there in her box. He knew both her
condition and the reason for it but, being a churchman of at least ordinary conscience, he knew also that he owed her no further embarrass-
ments. He had set himself in the middle of the grassy parlour, diverting
each gentleman in turn across the low clitter of wall. And when his
dogs had begun to frisk at the ripeness of scent from Mary's corner, he
had called them gruffly to heel and driven them into the trees.
   Above Mary's head, a rabbit swayed gently from the twine. She
followed it with her eyes, almost in a trance, with a curious feeling of
distance that seemed to flatten the perspectives like a painting on a wall.
She blinked urgently, in an effort to restore her focus, and tried to push
up out of the box. But the iron band was closing about her chest again,

dragging her down. A cold grey dew sprang to her face, and her shoulders shook with the pain as the cold air cut through the spasm into her lungs. Afterwards she lay calmly floating with the rabbit. There was no urgency to the day: she could afford to lie a moment longer.

But then, wafting from a distance, came the first faint prickle of memory. No urgency . . . *but there was!* The rabbit continued to circle gravely, with its paws outstretched like a wrestler searching for a hold. A wrestler with a broken neck . . . . And at once she remembered. Her grandson Thomas! It was today that he would return from Devonport after his match with the Aveton Gifford maltster. If he had won, then the ripples of his celebrity would spread far beyond his native county – across the Tamar into Cornwall; perhaps even to London. There would be new challengers for him to meet; new championships; big-money wagers; an escape from poverty. Mary saw it from her half-slumber as a victory already won, though the images – even the real ones of the wakening day – remained flat and distant, like the surface of a dream. There was in this vision a degree of presumption which, to those who did not know Mary well, might have seemed foreign to her character. But it was not so. Her modest self-opinion was unaffected by her admiration for her grandson; and she held out no hope, nor even a wish, for personal advance.

The ox-blood still made black crescents under her fingernails. Together they had used a great bowl of it to soak his shoes, which afterwards she had baked for him over the peat until the toes had been as hard as flint. It had been the first move in their campaign against the maltster – for success in Devonshire wrestling had little to do with the sinuous shoulder-throws of the Cornish: it was a matter of tripping and hacking at the shins. Thomas was not unusually tall – only five feet eight inches in his stockings; and neither, for a wrestler, was he heavy – less than twelve-and-a-half stones. And yet he had the toughness of a pony and the agility of a cat. Against wrestlers of his own size he could win by strength; against bigger men he had the advantages of speed and skill. He was a master of the feint, able to snatch his legs to safety at the very last instant, while simultaneously seizing his opponent's kicking foot to spring him on to his back. On one famous occasion he had broken the thigh of a Tiverton innkeeper by bringing up his knee to guard against a kick – a feat which had contributed much to his reputation, and which had the extra benefit of encouraging the local gamekeepers to regard him with uncommon respect. They spoke bravely enough, but there was none among them who would approach him single-handed.

But the maltster was no gamekeeper. He was bigger by far than any man Thomas had met before: a wrestler who had fought in many counties and had beaten the Cornish champion – a wheelwright of eighteen stones – by throwing him over his back and dislocating his shoulder. Mary's confidence in Thomas's victory was the latest in a lifelong history of simple eccentricities that had made her locally unique. She had backed her grandson with her prayers; though in the inns and taverns all the clever money was on the maltster.

But Mary had never been where the clever money was. Her ambitions had never extended to – or perhaps, rather, had transcended – simple greed; and if there was a grieving in her (for she knew for certain that she was dying), then it was not for anything she had failed to gain but was entirely for what had been lost. She did not crave any simple turning back of the years, for the re-opening of missed opportunities; what she mourned, without crystallising the thought in words, was her own innocence. She longed for a fresh eye; for the forgotten quality of surprise. Out beyond the olive-drab cliff of her knees, a young rabbit was stirring in the ocean depths. She saw nothing – only a swirl among the seedy wavelets of grasses – but she *knew*. The bleached sea of fruiting heads hung nearly grey from their overload of grain, and their crests parted to reveal a brilliant flotsam of colour. Mary tried to notice it: low ripples of purple betony and waxy yellow vetch; drifts of purple knapweed; foaming white breakērs of meadow-sweet and angelica, with the clustered heads of the ragwort making bright reflected suns. Towering above them all were the huge mauve thistles, like harbour lights commanding the horizon; while down below, amid the wreckage of seasons past, lay the spiky green hulks of old marsh orchids. The air, too, was alive. Bees cruised fatly: tub-shaped honey-barges laden almost to sinking. Butterflies rode the swells in a busy flotilla of dusky browns and oranges; and long, black-and-yellow dragonflies patrolled with the menace of frigates. Mary had never before looked *inward* at the meadow in this way, like a picture; and although she did acknowledge a small pang of disappointment, she was not surprised by its lack of mystery. She might as well have demanded wonderment from the water in the spring.

Drifting again. Invisibly behind the oaks, a buzzard soared mewing into the indigo; and Mary drew new warmth from her oneness, her inseparable twinship with the green. She *was* the rabbit; was the bee; was the sun.

It was a matter of the blood. Her own father and her uncles; her husband and his father; her son and, now, her grandson Thomas – all had been men of the same cushioned tread. All labourers of little skill save in the schooling of a lurcher and the setting of a snare. In the woods and meadows, and along riverbanks, three generations of keepers had been tormented by the family of Woollacott. But, as each of them had understood, nature has its symmetry, and the price had been settled in full. A higgler one day had been caught with a coatful of hares, who to spare himself had turned informer; and among those at whom the finger had pointed was Mary's husband. George Woollacott had been a master of the open field who knew every sinew of the breeze; but he had been so quickly broken by confinement that he had died in his cell while awaiting transportation. The magistrates who sentenced him had been among the most voracious of his own illegal customers; but Mary had not long concerned herself with feelings of injustice. When a man needed fifty times more property to be allowed to shoot a partridge than he did to send a man to the gallows from the jury-bench, it did not seem any more a mystery of nature than the reckless winter cold or the mortality of infants.

So it followed that Mary had been driven from her husband's cottage. She had packed her blanket on top of the psalm in a sooty iron crock and moved beyond the parish to live with her son. His cottage stood on the higher ground in a perpetual curtain of mist, where the seasons seemed to have merged into a kind of eternal twilight. Even in the summer, when the bare rock baked in the sun, the distance seemed loth to yield up its secrets, concealing its moods behind a veil of shimmering opalescence. Mary's sense of imprisonment had been heightened by the dark resentments of her son. He had gathered around himself a nameless corps of shadows – sleepless men who darkened their faces and swam through the night as stealthily as carp. They carried guns, and used them; for there was no mercy in their war. The price of conviction was a whipping, or worse. There was no remission for those who allowed themselves to be caught, and a man would as well be hanged for a keeper as for a hare. Sam Woollacott might have spared his family the miseries of hunger, but he had locked them in a cell of impermeable dread.

To Mary he had been the shade of her husband: alike in form and skill, but drained of tone and degree. He had the same vulpine judgment of a rabbit's hop, so that his twists of horsehair would rarely miss their aim. He had his father's way with a dog: his lurcher was half greyhound – long haired and fawn – as elusive to the eye as it was to the foot. But there had been no mercy in him. He had been herding sheep when the mantrap took him – not to steal them, though he would have been no stranger to the offence, but to overprint their scent on his own. The jaws had caught him an inch below the knee, and had bitten through to the bone. At court he had been made to pay a fine, which Mary herself had raised by means of blackmail among the dealers. His release, she had said, was the price of her silence – a common enough transaction at the time. Yet any sentence of imprisonment would have been squanderous of his guardians' time; for Sam Woollacott already was as good as dead. He had retired, black-browed, to his hearth, where he had sat with the black-and-purple limb propped high on a milking stool. He had eaten little and would receive no one, not even the rector. By rapid degrees his body had taken flame; then, just as quickly, had numbed. The maggots came, and the stench from the flesh had grown such that, in his rare moments of wakefulness, his own stomach would rack with nausea. Within days, the wakeful periods had ceased altogether.

Afterwards Mary had gathered her things and taken the path back down into the valley. She had no wish to be a burden; and if she herself was to die, then she would prefer to do it among ghosts of her own. No new tenant had been appointed to the old cottage, and like a grub she had wormed her way back in among the decay.

Above her head again, the rabbit spun gently on the twine. The boy Thomas at least had recaptured his grandfather's manhood; had recognised the corrosive force of his father's rancour and had kept his own eye clear. If he stole, it was for the love of his family and not through any wish to harm the keeper. Just as he wrestled in the ring: to do what he had to do, but without hatred for the man who must be overcome.

Mary went on watching the drowsy antics of the rabbit, continuing its life-in-death spiral on the warm faint stir of breeze. The motion lulled her so that the focus of her vision contracted again, to a kind of gauzy wafer, as if she were peering through window-glass. The stiff-limp head; the dangling limbs; the eyes. Immediately, burned like pokerwork into the wafer, she saw the face of Campion. It had been two years since she had seen him at the Bovey heathfield – in the year of 1795, the last time she had walked outside the parish. William Campion had been a young blacksmith from Ilsington village, the son and grandson of blacksmiths from Bickington, across the Plymouth road. From the steps of St. Michael's he had preached against the price of corn and had joined with others in blackening the name of Mr. Pitt; and afterwards he had made himself the leader of a mob, drinking and raising a column from farm to farm until they had taken a mill-house by force and robbed the miller of his corn.

To some among the rural poor he remained a champion still; but to others, who had heard the story of his French banner, he was a traitor and a blasphemer before God. Felony, riot and sedition had been his crimes at law, for which Mr. Justice Heath had sentenced him to hang. There had been some mutterings concerning a rescue, but the great throng at the heathfield had been cowed by the thousand-strong force of dragoons, artillerymen and volunteers which had brought him on the thirteen-mile march over Haldon from Exeter. At this moment of abasement, the mutiny had died. What had happened then was not like anything Mary had heard of hangings in London, where the mobs would hiss or cheer as their allegiances directed them. Within sight of the twin moorland peaks, Campion had dropped through silence and left in Mary's ear the slow dry creaking of the rope.

She slept, and did not stir again until late in the afternoon. The knot in her chest seemed to have loosened a little, though there were delicate needles playing on her limbs. She felt relaxed; but it was a blissful, floating kind of relaxation that would lead to a renewal of sleep, not the vigorous refreshment of the newly awakened. She felt no sensation of her own weight; none of the usual tensions in her hips and legs. With open eyes, through the frosted panel of her dreams, she saw her husband spilling the entrails from a dangling rabbit; saw Campion spinning; saw her grandson Thomas pinning his man on the dark green sward. She fumbled for the envelope, but it did not matter that her fingers closed on empty straw: she knew the verses by heart, and perhaps it was for the best. The sky seemed lower – dove grey, opening through a cloudless arch to a peach-coloured distance. Mary looked, and it seemed to her like a window through which she might be lifted into heaven. From its pale melting pediment, thin shafts of buttery light flooded out from the hub of the arch, slicing the grey like rays from a painted halo.

Her shoulders settled more deeply into the box and she folded her hands across her chest. Into her mind came a sudden picture of flowers, white and purple. At this time in late summer, the damp scented lanes were divided like vestments into the white flowers and the purple. Her own lane, she saw, was purple; and she was no longer without a companion. Thomas stood beside her in the long river of shadow: solemn as a rabbit, softly staring. He lifted a strand from her face and offered a kiss: his mouth and eyes pleading with the fullness of wells.

But why was he not rejoicing in his victory? She smiled for him, to show that this was not a day for tears.

TOO MUCH CIDER

If George Templer had been king, he could not have prayed for a more open demonstration of his subjects' loyalty. They had respected his father, James. But they loved George and cried hosannas to his name. It was like a coronation.

George himself drove in an open carriage, flanked by his courtiers and ambassadors – the Lord Clifford of Ugbrooke, Sir Thomas Carew, Sir Lawrence Palk, Sir Thomas Dycke Acland and many others to whom the festival congregation could not fit names. With their ladies all dazzlingly elegant in ribboned bonnets and floating white dresses, they could have spilled through the frame of some romantic court painting. Thronging the road ahead of them, and jostling in their wake, came armies of musicians, high-stepping horses, and workmen with their families, all in a gay fever of flags and laurels. Along the way from Bovey Heathfield, the flood had grown steadily more turbulent as one tributary after another had swelled the current uphill towards Haytor. In all the history of the two parishes, there had been no other day to rival it.

On the rock itself was a flag, and on the sward beneath it a seething horde of people. Every boulder and tussock was contested for the fractional advantage it might afford, and the scene from above was like the view from a palace balcony, an ecstatic ocean of heads. When the bands joined together for "God Save the King", the great hymn rolled across the down in colliding waves, some voices following the musicians and some their echo, so that the effect was of a tumultuous singing in the round. George Templer, as he passed among them to his platform on the rock, shone out like a greyhound among terriers. Not for him the stockings and breeches of the Dartmoor squire. His London tailor had adorned him in cream-coloured trousers, strapped beneath the instep, that stretched without a wrinkle. His cutaway hunting coat was of midnight blue; his cravat silken black, with the points of his collar like scimitars against his cheekbones; and the glossy top hat of the garden-party fashion, wider at the crown than at the brim. From a ledge halfway up the southern face of the rock he accepted the cheers with unembarrassed grace, then cut them silent with a flourish of his cane. Snatched by the wind, his speech was audible only to the central segment of the crowd; yet those on the flanks were happy to take their cue from neighbours, and to applaud the mere movement of his lips.

"It is," he was saying, "the proudest moment. The flowering of a dream." And so it was.

For what his father had done for china clay, now George himself had done for the granite. James Templer's Stover Canal bore clay from Ventiford, near the family's home at Stover House, down a staircase of five locks to the River Teign. Now his son's new railway had made a link with the Haytor quarries – a life-bringing artery to the world beyond. Already there were whispers of rich new contracts: vast shipments of Haytor stone, it was being said, would sail to London for assembly into palaces and bridges and banks. It fed the people's pride; and best of all it held the promise of work. They were no engineers, and no theologians either; but the Devon people knew a miracle when they saw one. What set George's railway apart from all others was its singular mode of construction, for his rails were shaped not of cast iron, as the gossips had anticipated, but of *dressed granite blocks*. At first the people had laughed; then they had come to look, and then they had marvelled. It was all true. For a length of seven miles, dropping 1,300 feet towards the sea, loaded granite trains would pass over a flanged track that was made entirely of stone. It would not rust; it would not crack; it would last for ever. The cars would roll down gentle gradients under the control of brakemen; and would be hauled back up by teams of horses. It was, Sir Thomas remarked to Lady Carew as George poured the last of his speech into the wind, the Golden Pavement of the moor.

"And above all things," George was bellowing, "on this historic day, my grateful thanks to you all for your encouragements." He had reached his climax. "I hope you will find pleasure in the dancing and the sports, and take full savour, I do beg you, of the cider and the pies."

Behind him, his beautiful young wife basked shyly in the glow. It was said that he had married her for the enchantment of her voice.

When walking his horse through her father's farmyard after a foxhunt one day, he had overheard her in the kitchen singing a love song from *The Duenna.*

Humphrey Copplestone threw an arm around his friend's shoulder and beat him playfully on the biceps. "What, you'm not wrestlin' today, Sam? Surely you'm not 'vraid of ol' Homer Shute?"

Sam Woodbury shrugged off the arm and glared angrily at the grass. "Ban't 'vraid o' that ol' lanky-bones! Nor Elias Honeyball, nor Ed Sheldon, nor none of 'em. I shid a-whop they gurt toads one by one an' still 'ave the legs to smite thee, Humphrey Copplestone!"

"Nay, man, doan' be nettled! What ails thee, then? Why d'ye not wrestle?"

"Darney, if I woan' whop thee now! Sam Woodbury an't no cawbaby!"

"Man, I know that. There mus' be zummat, though, to hold 'e back? An't like ol' Sam t'carry on so! I be axin', like a frien', what ails thee?"

Sam considered the question fretfully. "Ye'll not tell? . . . Ye'd best not, else I make squab pie o' thee!"

"I'll not tell, Sam! 'E knows I'd not tell. Why d'ye vex yoursel' so? Humphrey Copplestone's your frien'."

Around a level green square, far below them next to the Widecombe road, the focus of the revellers had switched from George Templer's picnic feast to the serious business of a Railway Day Championship. The prize was a smoked ham, given on the day by Templer himself: that, and the admiration of the dancing girls, who had been holding their own contest for a bonnet. Once or twice from out of the babble Sam had picked out the syllables of his own name, but mainly now it was *Homer,* or *Elias,* that he heard. He could see the two heads bobbing in the ring beyond the crowd, and turned away to gaze miserably into the clouds.

"I think I be ruptured."

"What! Not . . .?" Humphrey pointed down at himself and grimaced. "Are ye sure?"

"There's a lump." Sam shuffled a hand in his pocket, as if to

164

confirm the fact, then rounded on his friend with a direct, accusatory stare. *"Remember Thomas Woollacott?"*

As if either of them could forget. In his declining years, the old champion had lived strangely. He had taken to sleeping in a wooden hut which he had built of rough timbers within the ruins of an old cottage among the trees, and here Sam and Humphrey had been admitted for occasional visits. Everything about him had been extraordinary, exaggerated and unforgettable: his great strength, his eccentric good humour, his poverty. He had continued to set his snares, and had prowled occasionally with a dog, but had made himself virtually a prisoner of the valley, seldom accepting work, or any invitation, that would take him beyond the sight of his wood. His garments had been as rude as his dwelling. For a coat he had worn only a kind of blanket bag, with holes torn out for his arms and neck, which he had pulled on over his head. Its single refinement had been a deep pocket in which he had carried a pipe and tobacco, with flint and steel, and a rag which he had kept soaked in saltpetre for tinder. He had never been known to change his clothes. If he had ever removed his slouch hat, it could only have been to fight or to sleep; and he had possessed only a single pair of breeches. Never, for as long as Sam and Humphrey had been his friends, had he wrestled; but he had remained fond of testing his arm – chiefly by raising huge granite boulders over his head – and by this means had earned a modest profit in wagers.

He would seldom speak of his earlier triumphs, but other tongues had been less constrained. By common consent he had been one of the finest wrestlers in all Devon, and Sam had met no greater hero. On the day that Thomas had accepted his final challenge, they had been sitting together with Humphrey on the long oaken bench outside the quarrymen's inn. Thomas had announced his rupture to them with rueful good-humour, as if he were reporting a wasp sting, or a blackened thumbnail; but they could see at once that he had been taken badly. His cheeks were clammy white, like cold sheep-fat, and he had only an imperfect command of his limbs. After his one, futile attempt to move a rock, Sam and Humphrey had struggled between them to raise him from his knees; for he had been too weak even to rise to the taunts of the shepherds, who had felt suddenly safe to mock. His chest had been troubling him, and Sam noticed that he would clench his jaws and clutch a hand between his legs each time he coughed. To Sam alone, he had confessed that the pain from the swelling there had become almost too hot for him to bear. His abdomen burned inside, and nothing had passed through his bowels for more than two days.

The manner of Woollacott's death had been described to them afterwards by the apothecary. The greatest of champions had spent his last hours with his knees drawn to his chest, howling like a baby. From his wrenched-open jaws had been forced the stoppered contents of his bowel, squeezed by the contractions upward into his stomach, whence they had been vomited. In Sam's brain the picture had fused indelibly into a nightmare.

Humphrey knew it, and chose his words with caution. *"I remember,"* he said. "'Course I do, but 'tisn't the same. 'E knows 'tisn't! Tom Woollacott was an ol' man, an' 'e didn't know 'ow to 'elp 'isself. You'm young, Sam. Why doan' ye get zummat from th' traveller?"

"Got zummat!" said Sam. "Pills. Taste like soap." He wiped an imaginary drip from his nose and grinned.

"Pills? What d'they do for 'e?"

Sam clucked and bunched his arms like wings, pushing down on the muscles of his abdomen until the wind broke. He laughed.

"Thass what they do."

But the laughter, like the wind itself, cost him a long, low-down growl of unease.

George Templer was a skilful rider, but too inclined to be reckless. His appetite for adventure could still lead him into prankish behaviour (hurdling the toll-gates at Shaldon Bridge, for example), but in the main these days his ruder energies were burned off with the hunt. The Dartmoor fox hereabouts was a smaller, redder fellow than its more northerly relation – its constitution supposedly reinforced by infusions of foreign blood. A certain Mr. John Bulteel was remembered for having brought French foxes to the commons, unleashing a plague which had driven the Widecombe farmers almost to despair. In an unprecedented surge of corporate resolve, they had engaged a professional huntsman, Tom French, to pursue a campaign of extermination; but the cause had been entirely without hope. The Haytor fox was fast and tireless, with more miles in its legs than all but the most determined of hounds; and its terrain would deter all but the most accomplished of horses and riders. To a huntsman of George Templer's stamp, it was pure delight.

His pack was second in the public imagination only to the spectral Wish Hounds themselves. It had all the intuitive, shared intelligence of a swarm of bees, with each hound following not so much a leader as a common impulse. It could read the meaning in every shade of its master's voice, and although Templer's groom was an uncompromising disciplinarian, with an arm like a ship's hawser, he seldom had call for his whip. In the week that followed the grand opening of the railway, the pack had been scouring the brakes for cubs; and, in the long river valley immediately beneath the tor, George Templer had committed an indiscretion. In a rush of excitement, of the kind he would not have forgiven in his hounds, he had galloped into a thicket and overturned his horse. Fortune, as usual, had favoured him, and neither he nor the animal had suffered mortal damage; yet the young mare was too lame to ride further and George was facing a long walk home to Stover.

He started up the valley side from a point immediately beneath the quarry terrace where, beyond the skyline, his workmen were already swarming in tight eager groups. But their business that day had nothing to do with London Bridge, or with any other fabled metropolitan contract. What engaged them was the dressing of stone for their own cottages. George Templer's reasons for allowing them to live by the quarry were in part practical, and in equal part humanitarian. Practical, because of the obvious benefit of maintaining a captive force within a hammer-throw of the work-face. Humanitarian, because he understood the hardship of long winter marches across the moor. Two Widecombe men the previous year had lain undiscovered until the shepherds had come up after the snows to count the bodies of their sheep.

Sam and Humphrey had been toiling hard all morning, and Sam thought it typical of his luck that, the moment he straightened his back to rest, Mr. Templer should appear. He dived guiltily for his hammer, but arrested himself with a small cry of pain. Templer watched him with amusement.

"Your back?" he said.

Sam scratched his hip, in a nervous way that he had, and tried to understand what was expected of him. It was not usual for the owner to speak to a quarryman directly, as an individual; or for anyone in authority to require more of Sam than a simple acknowledgement of assent.

"Mr. Templer, *zur*?"

"*Your back*. I said have you hurt your back? You're holding yourself."

"Oh no, zur." He hastily removed his hand; then, just as quickly, replaced it. "Well . . . yes, zur. Mebbe jus' a little. But nothin' t'vex me, zur! I can still lift more stone than . . . than . . ." He stared about him in a panic, not wanting to boast at the expense of Humphrey and his friends, who had done nothing to deserve a slander. There was no silence that anyone else noticed, but to Sam it seemed to echo for an age.

"I'm sure you can," said Templer, saving him. "You're the wrestler, aren't you? We missed you the other day. It was too easy for the others, but I've no doubt you had your reasons. Your back, perhaps? But no matter. Look now, I want you to do me a service. Would you oblige? See here, my horse is lame and I need a reliable man to walk her home to Stover. I have it in mind to remain here for a while, and then to ride down to Ventiford on the train."

He could not restrain a smile in anticipation of the pleasure he had promised himself, and Sam responded in kind. He felt easier now that he could revert to his customary language of nods. Only as Sam took the leading rein from his hand did Templer's brow become clouded. Behind him as he turned to begin the seven-mile descent, Sam could see the chief clerk scuttling worriedly across the grass with a dog-eared scroll of papers in his hands.

The way downhill was made unexpectedly easy by the line of the railway. Sam walked the horse between the setts, thankful for the gentle curves and shallow gradients, and he calculated that they had covered a full four miles before he felt the need to stop. He tethered the animal loosely to a quickthorn, and sat to rest on a granite milestone. He felt unusually tired, and prickly-hot, though the level of exertion by his customary standard had been mild. The lump in his scrotum moved back up into his body when he prodded it with a forefinger. It did not exactly hurt, but the experience was far from pleasant and he had to brace himself to touch. He had found that when he lay down, or leaned back on his hands, he would suffer a particularly uncomfortable gurgling sensation, like an unreleased fart. He closed his eyes and felt the disturbance intensify into a deep shiver which seemed to course all through his legs to his feet, and then up again into his head where it set up a tremendous rumbling in his ears. More astonishing still, it seemed to have communicated itself to the horse, which had begun to paw and fret at the rein. And then Sam realised: the greater part of the vibration was external, coming upward from out of the earth. It was the train.

It came past at a walking pace: two flat waggons coupled together, their wooden wheels booming like millstones on the flanged granite rails. The first one, at which a brakeman sweated busily at his lever, carried a light load of dressed stone blocks; the second was empty save for the recumbent form of the huntsman. Templer raised himself on an elbow as he passed, and waved his hunting horn.

"Everything in order, young man? Don't delay too long, now. I'll meet you at the bottom."

Sam bowed and grinned, inwardly cursing. Twice in a day he had been surprised by his master, and twice he had been found idle. He shook the mare into a trot, and made sure to keep the train in sight for the last three miles of the journey.

At the Ventiford basin, Templer's greeting was disconcertingly familiar. "Remarkable," he said, indicating the railway. "Quite remarkable! Just look! It is everything I had hoped for, and more, much more besides. Here is the way to our lasting prosperity. This is the finest granite stone in all England, and now we can serve it to the world! What d'ye say to that, young man?"

Sam pondered earnestly. "A fine thing, zur," he said. "I think 'tis a fine thing. We'm all proud of 'un."

"Proud, eh? That's good. Very good! With spirit like that we should want for nothing." Templer sighed and petted the mare lovingly on the cheek. "If only our partners in London would serve us half as well! But they keep us wanting for investment. Starving us with their unbelief. Obliging me to plead for money like some common pauper! Mark my words, in commerce you can depend upon no man but yourself. Yourself, and your horse . . . . Did you know, young man, what a miracle is a horse? In every leg it has nine bones. Is that not a wondrous thing?"

"Yes, zur." Templer had become suddenly vague, and Sam was less than ever certain what kind of response was required of him. Yet he could not leave until he was dismissed, and he had recognised – if only he had the courage to grasp it – that here was a rare opportunity. George Templer was a rich employer, but he had revealed himself to be a man like any other – as generous, and as vulnerable.

"I was wonderin', zur, if I might ask 'e a question?"

"A question?" Templer seemed more than ever distracted, even mildly impatient, but Sam had left himself no option but to continue.

"It was by way o' wantin' your counsel, zur . . . if 'e didn' mind?"

"My counsel? On what subject?"

"'Tis a frien', zur, that works wi' us in th' quarry. A good worker, 'e is, an' wi' an 'andsome wench t'marry! 'E's problem . . . . 'E's problem is, zur, 'e reckons 'e'm ruptured, an' 'e doan' know what t'do . . ."

"Well surely he should speak to a physician. They can make a kind of belt."

"Beggin' pardon, zur, but th' money . . ."

"Ah yes, I see." Templer fidgeted with the horse's head, plainly anxious to be on his way. "Then perhaps some pills from the traveller."

"Yes, zur."

"Is the man in pain? Can he continue with his work?"

"Oh yes, zur. No pain, zur. No pain at all! Jus' a gushy kind o' feelin' in 'is belly."

Templer stared at him thoughtfully for a moment, and then began to walk. "No pain? Then I'll be bound it's no rupture at all. Too much cider I'll wager!"

"Yes zur, thank 'e zur. Thass what I tol' 'un, zur."

Date: 1880

THE HOUSEMAID AND THE DANCER

The boys were baiting the Bear, leaning over and tapping softly against his basement window with a bun on a string. The Bear roared through his beard and showed his teeth; but he was too busy to give chase. He was a mould-maker by trade: a grizzly giant of a man, with thick sloping shoulders and a belly for the cider. The boys liked to make him chase them for a game, and he would readily join in their laughter as they dodged around the yard. But he was not ill-named. From time to time, when the alcohol fired his colic, the bun would properly enrage him; and on such days a raking from his paws was too painful to be funny.

What tied the Bear to his bench today was not any late reawakening of professional conscience: the fact was simply that the pottery foreman was dancing too closely – and too officiously – in attendance. But the disappointment was the same. To the Bovey boys it allowed the cruel pleasure of goading a captive, but it lacked the longed-for spice of danger and would not assuage their boredom for long. The danger, when it came, was from a different quarter altogether. If they had been thinking of it, they could have read the warning in the budding of the hedgerow, for it was inextricably bound up with the coming of spring. It arrived by train at Heathfield station.

The men were baiting Ralph. With obscene gestures of their thumbs, and with shovel-stems thrust between their legs, they schooled him in the art of courtship.

171

"Look 'e here, m'lover, an' I'll learn 'e. 'E juss rips up 'er flapper an' gives un to 'er thissaway. Pitch un in an' work un till 'er quails!"

Ralph's head was too large for his body: too large and, it seemed, too heavy, for he would often settle it sideways on his shoulder and heft it like a log. The scalp was roped around with knotted seams of filthy brown hair, but the face underneath was pink as a baby's, smooth and beardless. Its features were tightly bunched at the apex of a rubbery swell that piled up from his chest, without interruption from jawbone or chin. The whole of his body was plump and yielding: soft and boneless, flesh hulking against flesh like swaddling. When he was young they had called him the *diddlecumb chield*; the silly boy, soft in the belly and soft in the head. They still called him the same, for no one had ever noticed that he had grown up. Ralph was the village idiot.

"I tell 'e zummit!" said the carpenter, showing him a penny. "Vor a pair o' these, that missie Jane wud hitch up 'er clothes an' show 'e the 'airs on 'er belly." He raised his apron and mimed the treat, wagging his hips and jabbing his trouser-front with a finger. "Vor six, 'er wud flop down an' give 'e the blessin' o' moisty combe!" He thrust his shovel-stem in and out between the buttocks of a young labourer, then linked arms with the man and stood close to him side by side. "Vor ten, 'er wud wed 'e!"

The carpenter held out the penny again. "'Tis vor 'e, if 'e'll climb a top o' the cob an' tread! Vor 'e to keep vur missie Jane if 'e wants 'er to love 'e. This penny, an' a bib at the zider!"

The cottage they were building had begun to take shape five months earlier, in September, when a pair of ponies had been brought up to dump wet yellow clay, pannier after pannier, in a corner of the field. Into the clay the men had forked a gritty porridge of seeds, husks, straws and weeds swept out from the granary floors. Into the middle of the mound, as winter began to bite, they had set a rustic wooden cradle, nailed to four heavy stakes which they had driven deep through the clay into the earth. Into the cradle had gone hay and straw for the young South Devon bullocks, which had repaid the kindness with dung and water, stirred into the mixture with their hooves. In January the cob had been shovelled into a tidy rectangular cake in the wind-shadow of a quickthorn hedge, and sealed with a topping of wheat-reed thatch. It had bulked large: twenty-five feet from end to end, fifteen feet from front to back, sloping from ten feet down to five. What the carpenter wanted Ralph to do now was to tread it, layer by layer, with his naked feet.

The construction had been started with a foundation of fieldstone, to which the mason had added a granite fireplace and an encircling half-wall rising five-and-a-half feet to the height of the doorway. Enclosing this wall, inside and out, was a gappy shuttering of bleached oaken boards which reached up to form a trough three feet deep on top of the stone. Into this, balanced on a scaffold lashed together from poles wedged in earth-filled beer kegs, the men had ladled the first layer of cob.

"Up with 'e now," said the carpenter. "Doan't be afeared to bescummer yer legs. Vor missie Jane, now! Vor this penny! Tread un hard, an' do thy bettermost!"

"*Vor mizzie Jane! Vor mizzie Jane!*"

Ralph wore a pair of old black boots which had been given him by a gentleman guest at the rectory. They were a size too small, so that his toes were curled and empurpled, but his purpose in removing them was only to preserve the leather from damage. To the height of mid-calf, his feet and legs showed triangular white pits through the grime where the straws had cut him on earlier treadings.

Miss Jane was a housemaid at the farm, a yellow-haired young woman who had been born in the village in the same year as himself. He had neither spoken to her nor heard the sound of her voice.

The six Lancashire clog-makers swung their axes on to their shoulders and made off in Indian file from the station towards Bovey Tracey. At this same time every year they came to cut fresh alder from the Ilsington stream banks – seldom more in number than these six, but always with the impact of an army. Their nailed boots beat the road with the particular pride of conquerors in a foreign land. Among the local men, the miners and the claycutters, they were celebrated for their sporting qualities, for their willingness to enjoy trouble wherever they could make it. Everything about them was boastfully foreign: their speech, all dark and bullfroggy from the throat; their smell, of dead firepits; and their uniforms – soft felt hats, thick shirts and double knotted mufflers tucked into their braces. And on their feet the hard leather boots, heavily nailed and greased, with which they had upset the symmetry of many a challenger's nose. Eyes were worn purple, lips split, and hair dried to a cock's comb of bloodstained points.

As they moved on through Bovey the file grew suddenly longer as the boys, lured from their game with the Bear, fell in behind and mimicked their planting of feet. Several old wives, who had been reviewing the world at their gates, hearing the swell of noise, remembered urgent business in their parlours; and a fine lady clipping towards them in a dog cart, herself all got up in sealskin and satin, wheeled about and trotted away, clutching hastily at her ostrich feather hat. The man at the head of the column struck sparks with his boots, and shouted into the doorways.

"Girt owd futtocks! Gang t'yer wark. We'st not be roun' ter snuddle wi' thee till tamarra!"

Downstairs in the finer houses the curtains flicked, squinted and flicked shut again; and the men obliged with raucous calls that meant nothing to the housemaids' ears beyond Danger. But the shouting quietened as the houses grew more infrequent, and ceased altogether when the procession reached the further fringe of Bovey Tracey and was faced with the long climb of Ilsington hill. The men had brought no private belongings, but their axes and wedges lay bruisingly across their shoulders and they were travel-weary beyond any appetite for banter. The heavy southern air, moulded like a warm ingot in the deep cleft of lane, added its own clinging weight to the load. On a moist afternoon, coddled in their thick woollen clothes and with a gallon of ale in each man's belly, even the flat stretches could loom like mountains.

The boys carried on their mimicking until blank sky showed behind the trees. Then the man at the rear of the column, who had laughed good-humouredly at their antics, at last grew weary of their cheek. "Wot th' ferrups arto doin' wi' yer gawpin'? Aw'st prod yer chitty faces in a cow-clap, see if aw dunnot!"

They could neither separate the noises into words, nor divine the exact nature of the threat. But the bellicosity of tone and posture were part of a common language. They answered with their heels.

At the foot of the hill on the Ilsington side, the men stayed to rest at a narrow stone bridge. Fussed from its race down a granite staircase from the moor, the stream paused here to settle its temper before gliding silkily onward through an emerald pan of meadow. The men threw themselves down to drink, and noted with satisfaction the swift dark shimmer of a trout. They did not palm the water to their lips but sank their faces deep into the iron-coloured swirls, to suck and feel each swallow as a long winding chill, gathering to a heavy weight like cold steel in the belly. They arose wet to their chests and cast

174

around them warily with their eyes. Two meadows away, beyond a lane that followed the valley bottom and cut at a right angle across their own, they became slowly aware of other movement; of other eyes watching.

They could see the huge heap of yellow clay next to the thorn hedge, and the new pile growing neatly against the bank beneath the wood. Three men stood looking back at them across the lane, while a fourth figure, hunched and lost to everything but the intricacy of his steps, was following the pattern of a dance, round and around the muddy ramparts. The eldest among the clog-men, the one in the moleskin waistcoat who had marched at the head of the file, cupped his hands around a stump of clay pipe and blew out a long slow cloud of storm-coloured smoke.

"E'en this aback-a-beheend place is improved for a reech o' bacco. Naw . . . *whor's them girt ninnyhammers gawpin' at?*" He spread his feet and thrust out his neck, settling into an aggressive parody of the builders' stare. Alongside him, the other men did the same.

"What's 'm geet in that girt heap o' muck! Cow-sharn? Aw'm reckonin' yon dancer considers hissel' cock o' th' midden!" Tiredness forgotten, he flexed his fingers in happy anticipation of a fight.

Jane was in poor humour. She had compressed the day into little more than half its length, skipping from task to task like a hedge-bird at its nest. She had heaved and slapped at the beds until her back ached; then had scalded her fingers in the kitchen, wringing glass cloths and antimacassars in a crock taken straight from the fire. There had been no time to fetch cold water. Under the direction of her mistress she had churned the butter – now faster, now slower as she was directed, but never pausing to rest. At first she had tried to tally the number of turns on the handle, to take her mind from the racking of her arms and back, but she had soon lost count: the butter was slow, so slow, she had thought it would never come. Afterwards there had been the windows to wash – a day early, but the panes were marbled with raindrops in the dust, and her mistress would not let them wait. In her haste to be rid of the job, Jane had scooped great clothfuls of stony brook-water that had run back down her arms and soaked her dress and apron; but she had been too busy to admit the discomfort. Her soft pale hair had begun to cling, creeping in tails from beneath her cap. Yet, for all her exhaustion, her lips had been drawn up in a smile which refused to fade. This afternoon Roland was coming, Roland the shoe-maker, to speak on some matter he said was close to his heart. He had asked her to be sure to be alone.

But the moment had come and gone, and all her ambition now lay in ruins. The blow had been stunningly cruel, for the afternoon had begun unusually kindly when her mistress, lured by the promise of sunshine, had gone out earlier than usual for her drive in the dog-cart, giving Jane the unexpected advantage of time to recover her strength and to prepare herself. The cook had gone to market, leaving her to sit alone in the great farmhouse kitchen with a dinner of cold mutton and pudding. It was a dry meal which on most days she would have moistened with a cup of beer. But today, mindful of her breath, she drank only tea. She carried it to her mistress's bedroom where she could look at herself in the long mirror, in the way she thought a man would look, swivelling her eyes to catch herself half from the side. The inspection began at the blonde hair (so unusual in the village, and quite unlike her pony-brown mother), which made a little golden cloud where it flew away from her cap; then the open, countrywoman's face with its simple honesty of feature. It was above all a *capable* face, the face of a girl who was already wise in the ways of the dairy and the hearth. Yet she was woman enough to understand the special value to such a face of her clear blue eyes and pink darting tongue. She turned all the way round and regarded herself from behind. The body was not too thin, but well-fleshed and firm; it showed health and strength, a capacity for work, with neither flabbiness nor frailty. She stuck out a hip and raised her hem to her knee. But yes, there was something else, too, beyond the simple virtues: barely hinted at, and half hidden even from herself, yet a promise that no man would overlook – a promise which owed nothing to her work-roughened hands or efficiency at the laundry tub.

Long before the hour was due, she stood in the flagged granite porch at the back of the house and looked up the mud slope towards the boundary behind the byre. She held back against the door jamb, where she would be out of sight of anyone walking against the hedge. It was a matter of womanly insight: not wanting to show her eagerness, yet happily anticipating the disappointment that would pass across his face when at first he failed to see her. A cloud melted from the sun and fired the cob walls with a warm buttery glow, as rich as pie-crust. To Jane's left, midway up the steep ramp to the byre, a sparrow fought to loosen a stump of corn straw from a cob wall where the plaster had flaked at a corner. In the end it was animal intuition rather than the obvious futility of the struggle which persuaded the bird to desist. It suddenly darted beneath the eaves of the house, stirring the whole yard into a whirl of alarm, birds rushing everywhere for sanctuary in treetops and roofs. Jane, too, had caught the sudden movement of a man behind the hazel, and pressed even deeper into the shadow; then, just as quickly, she sprang forward again into the light, every bit as disturbed as the birds. From behind her, on the other side of the house, had come the slow grind of a vehicle turning into the drive. She listened hard, disbelieving at first, but there could be no mistaking the light wheels and sharp clipping hooves of the dog-cart. The mistress had returned, more than an hour ahead of her time. Jane abandoned all thought of coquetry and ran into the yard, making furious signals with her arms as if she were shooing sheep. Roland saw her at once, stared for a moment, then walked quickly back the way he had come. Neither by expression nor by gesture did he show any sign that he had understood.

In the kitchen Jane set the water for her mistress's tea, then went resentfully to take the ostrich-plume hat and sealskin coat. She moved loudly, with careless haste, and kept her eyes fixed down at the floor. Her lower jaw was shot out in a clench of irritation.

"There is something the matter, Jane?"

"Ma'am?"

"You seem vexed. I asked you what is the matter."

Jane's eyes came up for a moment, accusingly, then went down again. She loosened her fists, and let her arms hang drably from the shoulders, so that the picture of tension was replaced by one of sullen resignation.

"Nothin's the matter, ma'am. Everything's as e'wud wish it."

"That is by the way. It is plain that everything is not as *you* would wish it. Have the men been teasing you again? You must tell me, and I shall speak to my husband."

"*No man* has spoken to me, ma'am. 'Tis nowt."

The woman gave her a look of lingering suspicion, then half dismissed her with a wave of the hand. "Very well. It you do not wish to speak of it, then I shall say no more."

But she smiled cunningly and held up a finger to keep the housemaid from finally leaving the room. "I am sorry. My own afternoon has been spoiled, too. The lane beyond Brimley was quite

177

blocked by a rabble of drunken men. Not village men. Strangers. They put up a great shout as soon as they saw me, so that I had to give up my drive and turn about.

"I know who they are. They are the woodcutters who come from Lancashire to cut the alder. I don't know what my husband can be thinking of! Why must he invite them? As if the miners were not already a sore enough trial, he would inflict these heathen brutes on us, too. No woman can be safe to venture out alone!"

She bent forward and rolled up her eyes to peer at Jane from beneath lowered brows – an expression designed to emphasise the seriousness of the warning. For the first time that afternoon the servant found it necessary to suppress a giggle rather than a scowl. The idea of her mistress, whose age could not be a day under thirty, being pestered in that way by men!

The woman turned up her palms in an exaggeration of bewilderment. "For two months! They steal the trout and the rabbits, and the hens from our own farmyard. And still my husband says they serve us by clearing a weed! He even lends them our wagons and our horses. I sometimes think the world would be a more sensible place if there were no men in it at all!"

"Yes, ma'am."

After she had served tea, Jane spent a few stolen moments at the front of the house, standing at the iron railings and gazing out beyond the meadows across the floor of the valley. Here and there among the trees, faint columns of woodsmoke stood up vertically in the limp afternoon air. She traced one such wisp downwards in her imagination, and saw a plump little cob cottage with a bright new bonnet of thatch. Inside: a busy warm kitchen with cushioned chairs, and a tall dresser full of blue china and brightly polished dish covers. On the wall a portrait of the Queen; on the floor a brightly-coloured home-made rug. The ambition was plain in her mind, but simple.

Behind her a young farmworker had finished stabling the dog-cart and stood idly looking at her, nursing a billhook in his hands. He tilted his head, first one way and then the other, as if he were trying to determine which angle afforded the better view; then he shouldered the hook and stepped up close to her shoulder.

"*Are yer ready fer y'rub-down?*" he said. "I've a-done wi' the 'oss."

Silently at the window, the mistress watched as Jane gathered her skirts and flounced in through the porch. She smiled thinly, as if to congratulate herself for her acuity, and went out to look for her husband.

As soon as they realised the newcomers' identity, the builders converted their curiosity into a display of welcome. The carpenter himself was not shy of fistic exercise, and he was a gambler; but he knew how to count the odds and had never yet accepted a wager he knew he must lose. He held out the small wooden barrel of cider that he had carried with him to the field. Better, he thought, to surrender with dignity that which would otherwise be beaten from him in defeat.

"Halloa, m'lovers! Darney! Can it be ten months since us've zeen thee? Bide wi' us a hile an' guddle a drop of us zider. You'm welcome to un."

The moleskinned clog-maker twisted out the bung and tossed it into the hedge. He took a long, satisfying draught and did not speak until he had wiped his lips fastidiously on his muffler and passed the barrel to his neighbour. "Thank 'e, Thomas," he said. "Aw'm fain 'at we two are met." He patted his belly and belched. "Ah, aw'st pickle m'haggus! 'Tis a gradely drop tha's geet, Thomas. Tha name *is* Thomas, am aw reet?"

"M' name's Will."

"There 'tis then! Aw knew aw couldn' b'wrang. Thomas is thi' name!"

"Will!"

"Thi name's Thomas."

And so, for the moment, it had to be. The carpenter swallowed the slight, but no further than the gullet; there it stuck, ready to be brought out again when the challenge could be taken up on more favourable ground. The Lancastrian looked up to where Ralph was still plodding his solitary course around the mud-sill.

"Thi' brother?"

"He'm mazed," said Will, screwing a finger to his temple, though he had not failed to store this second insult alongside the first. "Zimple in eez 'ead."

The clog-makers came to live, as they always did, a gypsy life among the trees. Their shelters were as much like the dens of animals as they were the homes of men. Each among them made his own: a frame of rough-hewn poles, so crudely formed that it might have been taken

179

for a random heap, and sealed against the worst of the weather with a thick dressing of bracken. Into these dank and earthy nests they crawled and burrowed like badgers. They were the coarsest of men, for such a life could have sustained no other kind. In their two months each year they felled eighty tons of timber, shaving the bark and hacking the raw wood into rough foot shapes for the craftsmen clog-finishers of their native county. Each wagon load, lolling dangerously down the steep narrow lanes to the station at Heathfield, was truly an errand of mercy. A well-fitted pair of alder clogs – some plain, some banded with steel – might bring comfort to their wearer, even in the wet, for a full two years, and offer a small measure of relief from the daily hell of coalpit or mill. Alder was a common tree, but it colonised the Devonshire brooksides with uncommon vigour. Not for nothing had the Lancastrians travelled such a distance: few places in the whole of England could rival Ilsington for the quantity and quality of its timber.

Throughout the parish, the characteristic smell of springtime was the musky sharpness of green alder brush, snapping and spitting on the clog-makers' bonfires. The smell crept into every furthest corner, leaving its taint on clothing, curtains and hair. The villagers, too, crept out among the trees and gleaned armfuls of waste for their kitchen fires and bake-ovens, so that the clog-makers were not the only men whose suppers were eaten to the song of boiling sap. But it was always in the woods that the heat was fiercest. Children lingered in a torment of excitement, half in hope and half in dread that they would be asked to help tend the fires and to share, for a dangerous, forbidden moment, the disreputable romance of the travellers. In the evening, when the flames had died to ashes, the trickles of smoke would grow rich with the scents of meat. Whole hedgehogs and chickens were baked in envelopes of clay; tiny brown trout steamed and dulled on glowing irons; rabbits and hares glistened on greenwood spits; and sudden fingers of flame shot danger signals through the trees as the body fats turned to grease and dripped into the embers. On luckier nights there were woodcock, or bits of fat bacon bought from farmers; on plainer days a simple repetition of their midday staple – dry bread and cheese floated on a torrent of beer, and whole raw onions bitten and swallowed like apples. It was the stolen poultry and game which held the favourite spice of danger; but it was the bread and cheese which would give Will the carpenter his revenge.

The growth of the new cob cottage was unavoidably slow, for each layer of cob, packed solid by the dance, had to be biscuit-dry before the next one could be spread on top. It would not be until late May or June that Will would see the copse-oak roof timbers solidly nailed into place and the thatcher could take his station among the thunderflies and the warm summer odour of wheaten reed; not until September that the walls and ceilings would be plastered and the floors cobbled, ready for the young gamekeeper and his family to make it their home. But although the timespan overall was long, there was no leisure in it. As the sparrows filched the straw for their nests and the magpies flapped into the air with impossible beakfuls of wet clay, so did the men match them sinew for sinew. Will was necessarily jealous of every minute. An hour frittered when the air was dry could grow into a week lost through rain, for the moor was seldom without its cap of cloud. He was a strict master: hard, verging on the tyrannical. Had fate dealt him the proper birthright he would have been a formidable farmer, clinging to each grain of corn with a tenacity that would have made him rich. Instead he was master only by proxy, though he cherished each moment as if it were his own. The zeal of his preaching (hard work, he said, was the only road to moral good health) might have suggested the stirring influence of robust rural Christianity. But his philosophy, and the method by which he served it, lay well beyond the boundaries of religious orthodoxy.

On a bright blossomy morning, when the second course of cob was being levelled ready for Ralph to tread, the clog-makers came again, all six of them together. This time they took Will's cider-barrel without waiting to be asked, and took with it the builders' dinners of bread and cheese. They offered no greeting but spoke only between themselves, lounging with their backs to Will and his men, and ate and drank as carelessly as if they were in their own back kitchens. Will noticed that the chief antagonist had one eye shrunk in a tiny purple bruise, and that there were dark elliptical scabs on the backs of his hands. For a moment he felt angry enough to rise to the provocation, for their disdain could be taken as a denial of his manhood. But he knew also that his manhood would gain nothing from a thrashing. He decided to be cunning.

"I knew us'd learn 'e t'zup good zider! An' good bread an' good cheese, too. Dith it all meet with yore 'proval?" He stood empty handed, and at a distance sufficient to give no appearance of a threat. "If us'd known t'expect 'e, us'd've brung a cake."

The moleskin waistcoat turned slowly and raised a finger to hold him silent while he swallowed the last of the cider, straining the liquid through a mouth that was still roundly pouched with bread. He spun the keg upside down and beat the base to show that no more remained. "Aw'm afeard," he said, "thut th' steyme's run outta wayter." But the apology was meant for the man sitting next to him, who had missed his turn at the drink, and not for Will.

The carpenter spoke again. "Us be zich vules! Thar y'all zits, an' us've brung scarce enough zider t'fill a tay-dish. But pray doan't you voaks think to 'ard on us. Thar's more at 'ome. Us'll bring un out to 'e."

"*Well, g'day t'thee, Thomas!*" cried the clog-maker, starting up in mock surprise. "We didn' spy thee theer. But why so deep i' th' dumps, mun? Come, no fiddle-faddle now! Ye'll fetch us a drap o' drink an' we'st thank 'e forrit. 'Tis fair kind o' ye t'think on't."

Will drew nearer and pressed his advantage. "Zider, an' bread too, an' cheese! 'Tis only proper. Us'll bring un t'the wood an' drop un down for 'e, a' back o' yore butty."

"Egodsnam! Thee's proper quality, Thomas, an' no mistake! Ye'll no' forget, mind!"

"Us'll no' forget." Will changed the subject quickly, as if a new thought had suddenly occurred. "You'm sportin' men?"

The clog-maker grinned toothlessly, and laced his fingers to make the knuckles crack. "Happen we are. What're ye thinkin' of?"

"Badgers in yore wood?"

"Brocks? Aye, we seen their muck. For what raison d'ye ask?"

"Us've got a good ol' terrier back 'ome, wi' a gob like a mantrap."

The man clapped his hands and let the smile break into a long open laugh. He understood. "Our brock agin' thi dog? In a butt a' th' jerry-shop?"

"T'morrah, then? Zinday morn?"

It was agreed. The clog-makers' badger would meet the builders' terrier in a half-barrel in the yard at the New Inn, whose low yellow lamp they had seen beckoning nightly from the Ashburton road. Bets would be taken.

"An' afterwards," said the moleskin waiscoat, "we could bait thi bear!" He nodded at Ralph, who stood barefoot waiting to begin his plod.

Will laughed and winked. "Oh, no," he said, "not that one. Us needs 'e ter finish eez steppin'. 'E's collectin' eez pennies ter wed the 'ousemaid up ter the big 'ouse. Ban't I right, Ralph?"

"*Vor mizzie Jane! Vor mizzie Jane!*"

Jane herself was at the kitchen window when the Lancastrians arrived a little later in the yard. They loped down the hill like a hunting pack on cushioned pads, their nailed boots muffled by thick platforms of straw-bristled mud. She saw how they prowled with their eyes, lingeringly into doorways and lofts; intruding without furtiveness, and with a purpose that seemed far beyond innocent curiosity. They neither crept nor yet swaggered, but quite naturally *possessed*. The village men if they called for work at harvest time would gather in a diffident huddle, to elect the one whose duty it would be to go to the door and state their business. Not so these Lancastrians: they spread across the yard in a cordon and called aloud to be attended to.

For a moment Jane shrank from the window, afraid that they would see her; or that they would grow impatient and come to the house so that she would have to open the door to them. She slipped behind a settle, to kneel on the horsehair cushion and peek timidly over the back. From this distance, with the length of the kitchen table intervening, the window gave only a narrow sight across one corner of the yard. Only two of the men were in her view, and their attention seemed fixed on something far beyond them, behind the byre. She saw them pick up stones and throw, and turn to each other laughing at some invisible eruption of wings; she guessed that their object had been one of the master's white doves and she felt a sharp stab of anger at their presumption. Then all the calling ceased and the two men moved away beyond her line of vision; from somewhere close in front of the porch came another, milder, outbreak of laughter which died to a quiet hubble of conversation. With relief she recognised the voice of her master.

Beside the window again she had to press her cheek against the wall to make an angle from which she could see. Even so, the master remained invisible to her, though she could read from the attitudes and gestures of the clog-makers that a matter of business was being discussed. Only one of the men did not seem completely absorbed in the negotiation, but hung back to follow the antics of a tabby cat that stalked in the damp ferny shadows along the flank wall. Like so many men in the anonymous, string-tied bundles of their working clothes, this clog-maker had seemed almost ageless. It surprised, almost shocked, her now to realise that he was no older than herself. His clothes were as tattered and as tangled as the others', timelessly unfashionable and deeply encrusted with filth, but from the colourless remnant of his shirt – incongruously, it seemed to Jane – emerged the neck and face of a boy. She moved half a pace across the window to improve her view of him, shutting the majority of the party from her sight. Looking more closely, she found other incongruities: the lumpen coarseness of his posture and the massive ugliness of his hands and feet; and then the faint smile, almost wistful, on his face. Inclining her head, she dressed him in one of her master's good cloth suits. What a handsome gentleman he would make with his fine strong profile and straight white teeth . . . and his unblinking ash-grey eyes.

She had realised the colour in the same instant that told her she was discovered. And the illusion burst. He was no gentleman. The clamour of taunting voices, and the sound of her own name being called, burned in her ears as she ran.

No one encountering the clog-makers, or even watching circumspectly from a distance, could have remained long in doubt about which among them was the leader. Reuben, the man in the moleskin waistcoat, had a natural authority that transcended all limitations of education and class. To the gentlemen whose land he cropped, and to the God-fearing mill-owners whose work people he shod, he extended all the elaborate courtesies that "The Quality" demanded for themselves. But his manner was more sardonic than deferential. Few landowners of his acquaintance had not from time to time felt the icy lance of Reuben's politeness, within whose strange conventions the word "Sir" was seldom heard without a suggestion of mockery. And there were few among them who had not now learned to send an emissary to treat with him rather than risk further humiliations of their own. It was not so much an *asset* in Reuben's character that made him so fearsome, but rather a shortcoming. He had no particular intelligence beyond a certain ordinary cunning; but it was this very simplicity upon which his reputation for terror finally rested. Among the several qualities of which his incapacity deprived him, the most crucial was fear.

He was a powerfully built man: not tall, but square in the shoulder like a wrestler, and broad in hip and thigh. Physically his distinguishing features were twofold: a pair of unnaturally pale blue eyes that caught the light like polished glass; and enormous sidewhiskers, as densely curled and knotted as sheep's wool, which hung from his temples to the middle of his waistcoat. In colour they recorded the ages of his life: baby-brown around the ears, ash-streaked at the jaw, and purest silver at their pendulous tips. Between them the chin had been shaved, but now showed a thick mat of mottled grey stubble. Another peculiarity hung from a thong around his neck – a pair of long-handled, peeled-wood tweezers with which he would suddenly dive into the underbrush to nip and seize a viper. (The reptiles accounted for a useful supplement to his income, clarified snake-fat being an efficacious remedy for sprains and rheumatism.) In sum, it was a picture not lightly to be forgotten; and one from which bolder men than Will the carpenter had been known to recoil in honest dread.

Reuben did not trust Will to provide the bread, cheese and cider he had promised, and exulted in anticipation of the quarrel he would provoke. His aggression towards the carpenter was like that, say, of a robin towards a territorial rival; not founded on any particular dislike of the man, but springing only from a reactive desire to command and to control. For as long as Reuben was in the valley, then the valley must be Reuben's. But once the point had been accepted, once Will had acknowledged that he had met his better, then the two of them might be comrades. For a moment, however, there was disappointment as Reuben stooped beneath the wagon and found the two cloth-covered bundles and the barrel, exactly where Will had said they would be. He began actually to despise the carpenter for his spinelessness, for the watery meekness with which he had succumbed to the assaults on his dignity. But then he lifted the cloth and sampled the bread. It was flat, hardly risen; and when he broke the crust it yielded a sickly-sweet ooze of glutinous, half-baked dough that stuck fast to his fingers. He knew at once what it was. After the wet harvest, the flour had been milled from sprouted grain; no bread made from it would rise or even bake before it burned. To offer it as a gift was an insult.

"Aw'st quock[1] on't," he said, holding his throat and poking out his tongue to make the meaning plain. "Aw'st quock upon Maister Carpenter!"

The cheese, too, was an insolence. Wrapped in a dry rag of sacking, a dank compress of wet straw and apple cores.[2] Reuben moulded it between his fists and burst it high among the branches of an ash tree, dashing forward to flail at the drifting fragments with his boots. But when it came to the cask of cider, he was more circumspect. Having recognised at last that the carpenter was an adversary worthy of his attention, it did not tax his imagination to guess what the vessel might contain. He knocked out the bung and spilled a little of the pale golden nastiness away from him on to the forest floor.

[1] Vomit. [2] The pommage from a cider press, known as "cheese".

"Lant! 'Tis nowt but owd lant!" And his face hung open in a grin of almost childlike pleasure.

In the morning it did not take the men long to unearth the solitary, irate badger from its sett, batting its rump with their shovels to bring it within reach of the tongs. They noted with pleasure the wicked, razoring power of its claws and teeth, and took care to hamshackle it, roping its head to a foreleg before hefting it by boot and shovel into a sack. They did not trouble to burrow into its fur to determine its sex, but it was of formidable size, measuring nearly three feet from snout to tail and weighing, they thought, no less than forty pounds. It would be a rare kind of terrier that could face a beast like that and escape with its belly intact. Only the youngest among them, the smooth-faced youth who had caught Jane's attention in the yard, showed any sign of apprehension at the turbulent entertainments that lay ahead.

In the matter of drinking, the local men needed no instruction from the Lancastrians. The room inside the New Inn was not the stooping heavily-beamed cavern of most village alehouses: in its more sober moments – at first light on a Monday morning, for instance – it could seem spacious and airy, though never quite without the brewhouse tang of puddled beer and tobacco ash. At half-past-noon on a Sunday, however, the high ceiling was yellowing above an almost tangible screen of smoke, which clung to the plaster and pressed down upon the drinkers' heads with the glooming weight of the 'tweendecks. To churchwomen, and to the more scholarly of the small children who were sent sometimes to fetch their fathers to their dinners, it resembled nothing so much as an anteroom to Hell – a waiting-chamber of condemned souls, herding to the furnace door. Its clients answered a particular definition of manliness, in which intellectual prowess did not rank high among the virtues. Accomplishment lay in the capacity of belly and bladder for the drink. Wisdom was in the knuckle.

They were, for the most part, an unsurprising mix: farm labourers and shepherds; miners, quarrymen and claycutters. There were the usual individualists – thatchers, wheelwrights, smiths and the like – and a sprinkling of more thoroughgoing eccentrics. Best beloved among the latter, and a familiar sight along the whole eight miles of his route, was a red-bearded haberdasher who rode from Newton Abbot every Sunday morning, giddily atop a black-painted penny-farthing bicycle. He was never without a nosewarmer – a clay pipe snapped down to a stump – and he would never swallow less than a gallon of strong cider before calling for a helping hand to set himself back on the saddle. He was endearing for the indefatigable stoicism with which he resumed the machine after each of his frequent mishaps, and, more especially, for his habit of breaking the homeward journey to snore himself sober in a ditch. It set him apart: other, more snappish, tradesmen who had attempted to cross the social divide had been driven out like ducks from a hen coop.

A small amount of business was transacted at the New Inn itself, but mainly in fur and feather. After alcohol, the most important subject of exchange was gambling. They would bet on pitch-and-toss, shove-halfpenny, crib, euchre, dominoes, rings, skittles – even marbles – and would settle their debts in drink, rabbits or bits of bacon. Most of the drinking – though not all of it – was done within permitted hours, and they suffered few intrusions from the law. One unusually zealous constable had made a couple of arrests during the winter, but since his prisoners declined to come voluntarily and had to be escorted on foot all the way to Ashburton, his enthusiasm for the Licensing Acts had not survived the turn of the year.

This, then, was the den to which pride-driven Reuben and his men had come to leave their imprint. It did not take Reuben long to seek out the carpenter, for the throng divided readily enough to match them face to face; and each found a quick understanding in the other's eye – an acknowledgement that the carpenter's standing had changed, that there lay between them now a matter of honour to be settled, from which there must emerge a victor and a vanquished. Reuben jerked his head towards the door.

"Yo got thi tyke?"

"A good un." Will indicated a bright-eyed smudge of shadow beneath a bench. "'E've a-brung thy brock?"

"Aye. What's thi bet?"

Will grinned with ill-concealed pleasure, but his reply was cut short by a sudden pandemonium at his back and a pressure of bodies shoving towards the door. The culprit was the Bear, the pottery mould-maker, who had declared himself too occupied to walk outside and had urinated where he sat at the dominoes. The other players had overturned the table in their haste to escape as the hot flood gushed towards them along the bench-top. Reuben looked down at the pool on the floor, then back again at Will.

"Aw'm fair vexed wi' ye, Thomas. God'struth! Why d'ye not stoop under th' girt lobcock an' gather 'is leavin's fer thi cider? We've ready golloped all as ye lef' us yesserdy . . ."

Will raised a finger in comic reproach. "Doan' 'e take on so! Us'll bring thee all 'e wants. Thar's plenty more whar that lot a-come from. 'E'll not go thirsty, us'll zee to that."

They might have fought where they stood had not the Bear interrupted them further. "I dunnaw what's makin' 'e all so fretsome," he roared, taking pained offence at his companions' disapproval. *"I'm the one that's got t'zit in un!"*

In the yard, a fat sawn-off barrel had been rolled out for a badger-pit. Deep scratch marks and dark brown blots on the staves showed that this was not the first Sunday on which it had performed its function as an arena. The badger was still snorting and scolding inside its sack, but a claw had ripped through the hessian and was knifing the air in crazy hunger for revenge. The angle of the claw, and the tattoo of punches from within the bag, showed that the animal had rolled on to its back and was well placed to savage any attacker that would come upon it from above. Across the yard the terrier stiffened its tail and ears, and mewed loudly in excitement. Reuben viewed it with contempt: a small, smooth-haired bitch, white with a streaked head and a reddish-brown patch on its back like a saddle. He nodded to his men to tip out the badger, whose grey and white cascade so nearly filled the barrel that there seemed hardly room left to add the terrier. Reuben himself cut the hamshackle, then turned to face Will.

"Well now, Thomas. What's thi bet?"

"The wager's this. If our dog should kill thy brock, then our prize shall be the badger to eat[1]." Will smiled viciously at the thought. "An' then, t'be fair like, if thy brock should kill the dog, *then the dog is thy dinner*. Us'll roast un for 'e!"

The circle of faces, within which Reuben could pick out all the men he had seen at the building site (even Ralph, resting his blubbery lip on the rim of a cider mug), broke out in a wild sea of laughter. Reuben, too, made himself grin. He had planned that the reckoning should be a closed affair between the carpenter and himself, but he saw now that this had been a miscalculation; that the carpenter had chosen his ground with the cunning of a wolf and that the real odds would be of a different kind altogether.

"We accept thi terms! When our girt brock 'as skinned thi scraggy tyke, we'st not only eat th' tyke. We'st eat thee for afters!"

The badger had wind of the dog now and was becoming noisy, quavering and squalling as it fought to climb the steepening curve from the bottom of the cask. It screamed like a baby as it fell back, then rose again, clumsily on its hind feet, to renew the assault.

---

[1] There is nothing unusual in this. Badger hams were commonly eaten.

"Shall us feed un the dog now?"

"Aye. We're waitin'."

Will held off until the badger was standing almost upright against the staves, then dropped the terrier neatly on to its back. The long pale nape stiffened in revulsion as the sharp little jaws scissored through the pelt – once, and then again to tighten their grip – grinding forward tooth by tooth towards the vital cord. The teeth reddened instantly, and blood began to seep into the fine grey coat – at first a pinkish smear, then a darkly soaking stain. The cask became a maelstrom of fur. Bucking and whirling, the badger shook its great bulk again and again until the terrier's claws were made to relinquish their hold; but even then the dog refused to be shaken free, and clung on cruelly with its teeth.

"Thass the way, Emmy! Hold hard there! Bite un through!"

And then the badger did the only thing it could to save itself. It rolled. The terrier sprang and twisted in a desperate attempt to hold its advantage as the huge body came crashing backward – and for a moment it seemed that it might succeed. With salmon-like agility it evaded the first great sweep of the claws; but by gravity it was doomed to the second. They locked: tooth against claw, the terrier's elastic energy smothered beneath the badger's immovable weight. The maelstrom subsided and became limp in the slow, inevitable ebbing of life.

Death for the dog came lingeringly, whimperingly, for the badger was not a tidy killer. Afterwards, Will tipped the barrel and stirred the tiny twist of rag with the cap of his boot. He closed his eyes in languid pleasure, and made a great show of licking his lips.

"Yer 'tis then. Dinner's ready!"

Behind him the badger burst through the circle of drinkers and dropped out of sight into the lane. Reuben watched it go, then rubbed his hands in a rough parody of the carpenter's glee. "Thi dog's a boneless morsel like thisel. There's nowt for a man on either o' ye!"

There was a heavy shuffling of feet as the crowd declared itself. A few stood against the wall to watch, but the great body of farmworkers assembled behind the carpenter, laying aside their mugs and disporting themselves in positions of jocular bellicosity. Some favoured the hand on hip; others thought folded arms would show their brawn to better advantage. Only Ralph, to the amusement of all sides, fell immediately into the posture of a prize-fighter, pudgy fists bunching from baby-smooth arms. Behind Reuben the five Lancastrians stood shoulder to shoulder; only the youth continued to wear a smile on his lips that was not reflected in his eyes.

"Thee's geet thisel a flaysome rabblement, Thomas. A pretty band o' sap-heads an' hackslavers. 'Tis small wonder thee's lookin' so uppish."

"M'name's Will!"

"Thi name's Thomas, th' timmersome muck-stamper! An' what name d'ye give thi clam-stave-an'-daub, Thomas, that builds thi dwellin'-midden?"

"Dinderhead! 'Tis no daub. 'Tis cob, thou runty shammock!"

"Tha kens cob, then? 'Tis thy gradely good luck, for be sure aw'st cob[1] thee well!"

The fight, like all such affairs, was an untidy business, a formless mêlée of arms and legs. Punches and kicks were directed more or less at random, with most of the blows constrained by the pressure of the throng and reduced to harmless buffets. Nevertheless, the weight of numbers stood against Reuben by a factor of some twenty to six. Even if the farmworkers had been gentlemen, or half-grown callow boys – which emphatically they were not – then the clog-makers' task would have been hardly less improbable. In the end Reuben found himself pinned to the earth by four heavy men, each taking him one to a limb, and with Will's nailed boot held insolently above his face. It was the Lancastrian, from his position of enforced submission, who spoke.

"I've but one thing more to say to thee, Thomas."

"An' what might that be, then?"

"Thi name's Will."

The concern which Jane's mistress felt for the safety of women walking alone in the parish was not sufficient to deter her from sending the housemaid with a message to a neighbour.

"I would ask my husband to send one of the men, but you know what it is with him. Always too busy to be concerned about the tiny affairs of us poor ladies. Sometimes I think the world . . ."

Jane took the dainty white envelope and hurried away with it, glad for a reason to be out of the house. She was a simple girl with little book-learning and no pretensions beyond the strict limitations of her class, yet she could see through her mistress at a glance, and seldom

[1] In Lancashire, "cob" meant to strike or to thrash.

troubled to envy her. The woman could pick her way through a tune at the piano, and could paint a recognisable watercolour of Haytor rocks, but nothing could disguise the suffocating boredom, the high-buttoned, tight-trussed emptiness of parlour life. She had been a spoilt child, the daughter of a wealthy shipper, who had married – so she now believed – more than a little beneath herself. With no children of her own to extend her perspectives, she still viewed the world with the innocent selfishness of youth, and still complained like a spoilt child if any of her demands should go unheeded. She was, in her childlike way, a generous mistress, and eager to be regarded as such; but Jane often found her company tiresome and was never reluctant to be rid of it for an hour.

The girl's errand took her along the bottom lane through Liverton, past the field where Will and his men were still busy at the cottage. She noticed that all work stopped as she passed, and that a low remark by one of the men drew a gale of laughter that far exceeded the usual coarse ribaldry that followed her about the farm. But it did not disturb her. The afternoon was perfect for walking: pleasantly warm, with just enough breeze to flutter the leaves and cool the face. A quarter-of-a-mile on the home side of Liverton, the lane twisted sharply left at a junction and became an airless gutter between two towering hedge-banks, stone-faced and crowned with thick ramparts of hazel and holly. This narrow cleft curved away gently to the right, hugging the side of the combe, then plunged steeply downhill to open on to the valley bottom where the hamlet lay. Jane had not reached far beyond the junction at the top of the cut when she heard the sharp *clack* of a nailed boot on the road not far behind her. She looked, and quickened her step at once, for her companion was not, as she had innocently supposed, a hedge-tacker or a stockman fetching his herd. Even from a distance, the soft-brimmed hat, the particular slope of the shoulders, the easy rhythm of his step – all were unmistakably those of the young clog-maker.

He carried no tools and did not appear to be walking with any purpose save, perhaps, to follow her. Such was her alarm (for she did not ignore all that her mistress said to her) that she picked up her skirts ready to run; but then, from ahead of her, came a new sound, of hooves easing into their stride after the hill, and the rattle of wheels. At first, when she saw the number of the party rounding the bend towards her, she thought it was a charabanc; but she quickly realised, to her considerable surprise, that it was only a wagonette. It seemed dangerously overloaded with passengers – men in high domed hats and ladies in fine feathered bonnets – and was being drawn by what seemed to be two impossibly tiny ponies. If she had not seen the evidence of it, Jane would not have believed them capable of climbing the short hill out of Liverton; and she was certain that they would be unable in such a fashion to complete the long ascent to Ilsington village. Behind her the young man was drawing closer, but there was no possibility of escape. She would have to stand against the hedge-bank and wait until the vehicle had passed. At the reins – a further surprise – was not a local driver but a stranger who was evidently a gentleman, all done up in a thick dark suit with a waistcoat and bowler. To her horror, he leaned back on the reins and stopped.

"Pardon me, ma'am," he said, raising his hat and bowing from the seat. "We are bound for Lustleigh Cleave. How should we proceed at this fork ahead of us here?"

She followed the line of his arm and saw, with dull dismay, that the clog-maker had approached to within a dozen paces of where she stood. He came right up then and waited, nodding solemnly while she directed the travellers over the high terraced lane across the open moor to Manaton. When she had finished, and the driver had thanked her and flicked the ponies forward again, she saw that there were two other gentlemen in the wagonette, and three ladies with a large picnic hamper and a small wire-haired dog. One of the men said something as he raised his hat, provoking his wife to lean across and slap him sharply on the knee.

"Th' clot-head. Yon ponies be done in. Aw'm afeard 'at they'll no' make the 'ill wi'out 'e gi'es 'em a gradely good leatherin'." To Jane's astonishment there was a tinge of honest regret in the Lancastrian's voice. He did not look at her but watched the wagonette until it was out of sight, shaking his head mournfully at the misuse of the animals. Jane felt more than a little foolish. With his attention diverted, she could have walked on and left him standing there; and yet she waited, out of some absurd dedication to good manners, composing a reply.

"'Tis so," she said at last. "Wi' that load on, they'll not make it so far as Silverbrook. Least, not 'less they fine folks climbs out an' walks. An' then they won't be to Lustleigh Cleave afore tomorrow nightfall. 'Tis 'oliday visitors."

"'oliday visitors!" he said, copying her scorn. But still he did not turn to face her, even though the wagonette had already disappeared around the corner; and still, though she might now easily have excused herself, Jane held fast and did not continue her walk. She did not dare to think why this was so; and neither did she realise – not now, nor ever – that his failure to look at her when he spoke had little to do with his simple peasant's rudeness, nor with any real absorption in the picnickers, and still less with any nonchalant disregard of her presence, but was a matter of ordinary boyish unease. Of a shy young man in a strange lane, confronted by a pretty young woman.

It was a sudden movement of birds, high in a holly tree on the hedge-bank, which at last gave him a reason to turn; and once again Jane was impressed by the clean straight profile. On any other man she would have considered it handsome. On this man – for the moment – she could think of it only as a surprise, as if it had in some confusing way been wasted on a body that was unworthy of it. The ash-grey eyes flicked to their left, found her staring, and flicked back again. Jane looked down at her feet, and the silence stretched into the heavy, uncomfortable kind that would become harder to break the longer it continued. Together, for fear of seeming purposeless, they began to walk.

At the brink of the hill, with the Liverton rooftops showing below them to their left, the young man managed to collect himself. *"Aw seen yo in th' winder, Miss Jane."*

"How did 'e know my name, then?"

"Aw've heard it spoke."

"What's yours, then?"

"Benjamin."

They walked until they came to the foot of the hill and paused at the bridge across the stream. There, sharing some inexplicable common impulse which neither could have explained to the other, they sat on the stone parapet and talked to each other about their lives.

It was Sunday again. There had been rain, but the sun had made a late appearance around midday and the hedgerows shimmered with tiny swirls of steam. Ralph stood at a gate, leaning across and nuzzling the soft velvet lips of a chestnut mare. In his hands were two thick bunches of long-bladed grass, sharp as scythes, with damp red crumbs still showering from the roots. He solicited a lick from the horse, then passed over the reward, one bunch – and one lick – at a time. Ralph approached all living things in the same spirit of innocent inquiry, offering unconditional friendship in the manner of the child he still was. Among the human population of the parish he was used and abused with tolerant good humour: only a few of the women, perhaps through some immutable fear of the unexplained, would rebuff him entirely and use their tongues with intent to wound. The men, even the miners in their rough-hewn way, were for the most part not unkind to him. Like Will, they would tease and give him small money for hard filthy work; but few would be willing to see him harmed. Nevertheless, for all his inarticulateness and dullness of mind, Ralph was intelligent enough to grasp the fact of his own unintelligence. He knew himself to be a man apart, excluded from the normal commerce of adult human life, and felt a genuine community of spirit only with young children of his own intellectual age (whose company, not surprisingly, he was seldom granted) and with animals. His Sunday walks took him from paddock to paddock, from one end of the parish to the other, so that he would arrive home to his mother with hair and collar plastered with the saliva of pampered horses. In the autumn he carried apples, and his attempt to prolong this kindness deeper into the year had caused the only incident in his life which had earned general displeasure and put him at risk of the asylum. One day in a moment of charitable resourcefulness he had taken fermented cores from the cider pommage and fed them in handfuls to the animals. The rumours of equine madness and epidemic thereafter had taken the farmers many weeks to refute.

Reuben, on this same Sunday afternoon, was returning with four of his men from Kingsteignton, where they had spent Saturday night and Sunday morning in riotous amusements with the claypit workers. The absentee was Benjamin, who had elected to remain at Ilsington. His company would have made small difference to their pleasure, so they had wasted little effort in trying to dissuade him; but it was not until late in the afternoon, when they came upon him by chance in the Brimley lane, that they properly understood his reason. Jane withdrew her hand from his, as violently as if it had been stung, the instant she saw the file of hat-brims nodding up the hill towards them, and stepped away from him shamefacedly. Again she felt the same absurd impulse to run; again, even more absurdly, she felt herself unable to move. The five pairs of eyes worked across her in pointed examination, as if they were farmers at market who might at any moment reach out and take a pinch of flesh. One of the men began a ridiculous stamping dance, thumping his knees to his chest and crying out her name in a peculiar voice, with his tongue stuck out between his lips.

"Mizzie Jane! Oh Mizzie Jane!"

Reuben silenced him with a clenched fist gesture, and greeted her with a wide flourish of his hat. "Gudday t'ye, ma'am. 'Tis a viewsome picture ye make together. Will th' pair o' ye no' join us for a drap o' tay? Ye could do wi' a drap, aw'm sure, arter all thi gallivantin'." And he sealed the compact with a wink, as if he shared with her some dark and conspiratorial secret.

Jane looked to Benjamin to make an excuse, to decline the invitation and let her be on her way, but he said nothing. His face showed neither pleasure nor alarm, only an abject submissiveness before the will of the elder. To Benjamin, Reuben's words were not an invitation at all, but a summons. In part, Jane could understand this: an invitation to take tea with her own mistress was not, after all, a thing she would feel able to refuse. But she saw, too, that if she were to avoid the folly of entering a darkening wood with five violent strangers and another too weak to defend her, then she would have to discover some way of taking her leave. Not the least of her concerns was the scandal that would arise if anyone should see her, and the consequence of such a tale reaching the ears of her mistress. (In walking out alone with Benjamin she knew she had already taken a chance which bordered on the reckless.) Yet at the same time, even more than if she were a guest in some gracious parlour, she dare not give offence.

"Thank 'e, sir," she said at length. "But my mistress . . ."

"'Tis only a dish o 'tay!" he said, and there was the end of the matter. The little procession continued on its way, and Benjamin and Jane walked with them.

At the top of the hill the lane swung sharply to the right and emerged on to a narrow terrace looking out over the distant sea. A huge stone barn stood on the outside corner of the bend, perched above a giddily-sloping pasture and commanding the valley like a fortress. Beyond it on the right, where the lane held straight and level for a hundred yards or more, stood a row of tiny cottages: pretty rose-covered bonnets trailing neat ribbons of vegetable green. From somewhere at the back, Jane could hear the clack of a hoe among the stones. A pair of clogs lay kicked off in front of an open door, and a rambling wet ribbon in the dust showed that a cottager had only recently brought his pails up the long cruel hill from Woodhouse Brook. It was not clear in Jane's mind which concerned her more: to be 'saved' by an encounter with a neighbour, or to pass by with her shame unobserved. In the event she was not called upon to make a choice. No one came out to challenge or to greet them, despite (or

195

perhaps because of) the unmistakable clatter of the Lancastrians' boots.

Immediately beyond the cottages the lane resumed its earlier course, cutting away to the left and locking itself beneath hedge-banks that reached across and meshed their branches overhead. Jane paused at the threshold of this dark underworld, almost as if she felt a need to make some kind of farewell. Fleetingly in her imagination she saw once again the cottage of her dreams, as yellow and rounded as a cheese, and (she would have been surprised, had there been time to reflect on it) the sturdy figure of faint-hearted Roland, busy in the garden.

The lane was cold, a dripping arcade of ferns and moss where white oyster mushrooms and the eerie clusters of honey-fungus gave stumps and branches the appearance of some disfiguring human disease. The tunnel burrowed ahead of them like a mole-run, only briefly inter-rupted, in the far distance, by a single stripe of pale yellow light from a gateway. It seemed to Jane that this narrow embrasure offered the one last possibility of escape, for the field behind the hedge belonged to her own farm. Late on a Sunday afternoon it was a fragile hope that the master might come by, but she embraced it now with the devoutness of a prayer. (There could no longer be any doubt, in this Stygian cloister, that discovery – even with dishonour – was the smaller terror.) It is possible that the supplication did not go unheard; yet the answer it received was brutal. There was indeed a figure waiting in the gateway, but it was not the figure of salvation. It was Ralph.

This time when a man began the foot-slapping dance and called out Jane's name in that oddly insulting voice, Reuben joined the boot-stamping and threw back his head in merriment.

"Hail to thee, Maister Ralph," he cried, when at last he was fit to speak. "Never yo heed these girt ninnyhammers! Rough-spun as they be, they mean yo no 'arm. See, thi mistress Jane is come along for thi pleasure! She axes yo t'gang wi' us an' join us at our tay. Doan' be feart! Be a gent an' tak 'er by th'arm. Look 'e now! Baint she a viewsome doxy?"

He drew the pair of them forward and made them join their arms

196

like a couple at the altar. More than ever Jane was revolted by the sour mix of body smells and the sickly, rotten-fruit odour of drink on their breath. She was confusedly aware that, at best, she was being made to take part in some degrading prank of which she, as much as Ralph, was the victim. Never before had she stood so close to this alarming young man. Like every other woman in the village she knew him both by sight and by repute, but she had never thought it proper to speak with him. It was clear from the very look of him (though she did not know *why* it was clear, for she had never seen anyone who resembled him in any way) that he was mad. And madness to Jane meant violence, especially since her mistress had delighted so often to frighten her with tales of atrocity – murderings and disembowellings which she said had befallen innocent victims at the hands of lunatics. It was a notion which lent its full weight now to a surprise, and to a shock. The surprise was in the subtlety – gentle, full of tenderness – of Ralph's touch on her arm. The shock was in his eyes, which, wet with emotion, poured out their gratitude with an intensity so adoringly pitiful that she could not bear to look at them. Instantly, in one glance, she had seen the full cruelty of Reuben's game.

The wood was darker, colder and damper even than the lane, and alive with hidden flutterings and rustlings which mounted to a furious clamour as they approached the clearing. The ground looked hard and safe beneath its dry-crackling of leaves, but the mould was surprisingly wet and black, muddying Jane's legs and making a damp gritty mess of her hem. She ploughed on carelessly, as if she, too, had been infected by the slovenliness of the clog-makers' ways. But still she was not fully prepared for the squalor of their camp. As a girl she had slipped through the trees and watched – with amazement at their functional ingenuity – how the gypsies had managed the daily affairs of their travelling households. But she had seen nothing to compare with the sight which met her now. The six low hovels had all but fallen in upon themselves and it was only with an effort that she could make herself believe that they were intended for habitation. Everywhere, in watery mud that looked as if it had been churned by animals, lay the discarded relics of the forest existence: feathers and skins; bones and heads and claws; unburied human waste. Only the massive wooden tripod over the fire pit had the appearance of stability.

It was to this shallow pit, thinly flooded with a filmy skein of pale grey water, that Benjamin was sent to brew the tea. Jane did her best to absorb herself in watching him, grateful for any reason to withhold her attention from Ralph, and to keep her eyes from the insolent, oppressively silent inspections of the older Lancastrians. Benjamin huddled foolishly in the mud, seemingly careless of the chill, cupping a tiny pyramid of bark shavings and blowing up small stinging spirals of yellow-grey smoke. One by one, as the flames burst and sent long, curiously pale shadows dancing across the gloom, the men fired their clay pipes and sat parlourishly at their logs, stretching out their feet and making little grunts of satisfaction. Jane felt their eyes. Bitterly she cursed the timidity, the refusal to risk offence, which had led her into such a folly, and tried almost frantically to loosen the tension with her tongue. She realised the stupidity of the thought almost before she had uttered it. "It mus' be awful cowd," she said. "Out 'ere at night, wi' all the damp creepin' up from the stream!"

Reuben eyed her again, chilly as a hawk, and took a deep swallow of his pipe. He formed his words slowly, with delicious care, smugly pleased with the quality of his wit. "Aye, yo're reet. Yo're no' wrang theer. 'Tis cowd 'nuff some naights t'chill y'lugs off. Mind, though, we doan' reckon oursel's ill-done-to. We've ways o' keepin' oursel's warm . . ."

In the thickening dark, the five pipes arose and made a glowing red constellation that closed in about her like moons to their sun. Jane shivered and felt the sudden renewed pressure of Ralph's courtship at her side. Her own want of innocence contributed its full mite to the agony of her anticipation. She knew enough of men to be able to picture the limp and helpless nakedness of the village idiot; and wondered if they would force him upon her before taking their own brute reprisal for her foolish lack of caution.

Reuben stretched out a hand. "Thi tay," he said. "Doan' yo want thi tay?"

THE MEMORIAL

Sunday School had finished early and it was not quite time for tea. Bill hovered at the top of Fore Street, opposite the Town Hall on the shady side, uncertain whether to walk on and be early or to wait and risk the attention of the Gang. The Gang did not go to Sunday School: if they saw him they would steal his Prayer Book and make a football of his cap. He had characterised them neatly in one of Miss Manley's readings from Isaiah: "Their feet run to evil, and they make haste to shed innocent blood." He had shouted it in their faces once as they closed around him in the meadow below the mill but, unlike a Cross held up to the Devil, this rag of scripture seemed to hold little power to protect. For his own guidance now he pondered another of his teacher's favourites, from the First Book of Kings: "How long halt ye between two opinions?" He decided: no time at all.

It was Bill's turn this Sunday to take tea with Miss Nosworthy, in her brown and lacy room at the lower end of the Mary Street yards, where the members of the Gang lived with their parents. Miss Nosworthy exhibited most of the symptoms of acute poverty, but her fine white china and fastidious habits lent weight to the rumour – a *certainty* in Bill's mind – that she had not completed her descent from gentility empty-handed. Every Sunday, by arrangement with the Sunday School teacher Miss Manley, she would give tea to one of a small circle of favoured pupils. Thin slices of stale bread and butter, and bittersweet cups of warm strong tea. Always the milk was poured into the cups first, from a tall fluted jug which was protected from flies, even in winter, by a damp muslin cloth weighted at the corners with tiny black beads. It reminded Bill of a widow's veil.

The bread was stale because Miss Nosworthy refused to buy fresh from the Mary Street bakery: she would fetch in a loaf only on the days when she felt strong enough to bring it up from lower Fore Street. Mr. Frank Roe was the baker in Mary Street, and it was the least among his several peculiarities that he had not the smallest understanding of his own craft. He simply did not know how to bake bread. For more than ten years, both before and during the war, he had worked as a journalist for *The Times* – in London and, so it was said, in other European capitals too. But, unlike other men who had avoided the army, he had entirely escaped public opprobrium. Locally he had gained for himself the reputation of a man who had broken the constraints of his upbringing and had made a success of himself in the harder, faster, richer world outside. To Bill's older brothers, indeed, he had been held up as an example to be admired, if not literally to be emulated (for ambition in the wartime years was as severely rationed as everything else). But his father had died, his own brother had not been seen again after the order to advance at Vimy, and Frank Roe had had to return to Bovey Tracey to shoulder the responsibilities of his inheritance. His conscientiously-made efforts to curb his naturally more adventurous disposition, and to trim his ambition to the size of a small country bakery, had earned him the fond affections of the Mary Street residents – even, for a while, the sympathetic regard of Miss Nosworthy herself. But then Frank Roe had disgraced himself. The truly dreadful quality of his bread had not contributed in any way to Miss Nosworthy's decision to buy elsewhere. It was wholly a question of morals.

For Frank Roe's pleasure was to walk the wilder slopes of Dartmoor, passing from hamlet to hamlet on an habitual circuit, pausing for tea and talk – and fathering bastards. Accounts were at variance as to their actual number, but a grievously – almost tragically – damaging fight between two women at Ilsington had established beyond question that there could not be fewer than three.

Bill himself retained an obstinate, though consciously guilty, fondness for Mr. Roe that no contempt for his sinfulness could entirely erase. On several occasions before the scandal he had accompanied him on walks and, on one quite unforgettable afternoon, they had crouched together at the very tip of Haytor rock. Seemingly immune to the bitter cold, the baker had brought the landscape glowingly to life with sharply-etched tales of mystery and adventure. Through the colour of Frank Roe's language, Bill had seen the hunched red figures of the cave people, butchering their horses in the crimson swirls of the Teign; the awesome torchlit ceremonies of the earliest – and last – moor-dwellers, whose stone avenues still stood as monuments to their crazy fortitude;

the puffed square sails and sun-dipped oars of the Vikings; the rust-pimpled armour of fleeing Royalist horse. Immediately below them, Roe had picked out the line of the granite tramway and fed the boy's imagination with pictures from its prime. Bill listened, and drained the story-teller's brew to the last intoxicating dreg. He had spent many hours, amounting almost to days, in balancing along those granite setts, exploring the haunted chambers of the quarries and awakening whole choruses of echoes with his voice. But there had been a kind of churchiness about the place which had hushed him and taken possession of his mood. For as long as he was there he had felt himself profoundly altered, with a strong but indefinable sense of belonging to something larger than he could grasp: it made him less of an individual, he felt, but less of a child, too. Up there on the rock he had needed little encouragement from Frank Roe to visualise the small daily heroisms of the quarrymen's lives – the sweltering summers and lethal winters, when each day of life was a brave defiance of death.

The cheating of death on the moor was one of the most powerful elements in Roe's own aura. During one of the cruellest winters that anyone could remember, when the surface of the snow had been unbroken even by the tops of the hedges, he had burrowed his way through to Manaton and back, just for the pleasure, he said, of seeing Becky Falls as a silent crystal staircase. Between Ilsington and Liverton on the same day, a cousin of Miss Nosworthy's had died within sight of his own cottage roof; and out on the moor the sheep had frozen in their hundreds. But Frank Roe had taken the chance *for pleasure,* and had suffered no injury too harmful to be remedied by a tumbler of rum and hot water.

Sunday School society, however, had been less forgiving than the snow, and had put a higher price on his trespasses. There were a number of women who enjoyed the easy notoriety that came from being seen in his shop; a few others who continued to buy his lumpy grey loaves either through laziness or as a gesture of nonconformity; and an increasing number who came to him because they had exhausted their credit elsewhere. They were not the kinds of people with whom Roe felt instinctively at ease, though he continued to oblige them with favours – baking their home-made tarts and pasties in his bread oven – and uncomplainingly to accept whatever excuses they offered for the non-payment of their bills. The depressed condition of his business was held out as further, conclusive, evidence of moral decay.

Among the several consequences of his new reputation was the peculiar embarrassment it brought to his former friends like Bill –

who, as he passed along Mary Street on the way to his Sunday tea, was hardly less afraid of meeting the baker than he was of the Gang itself. He did not want to offend the undeniably correct moral code of the Misses Manley and Nosworthy, but neither could he comfortably offer a snub to a man he had once been encouraged to revere. There was a brief fright as he saw a tall male figure in the road outside the baker's shop; but half-an-eye reassured him that it was only the oddly-named Mr. Runner, who spent his day stumping about the streets on a wooden leg – a rough ex-soldier, alternately wheedling and abusive as occasion demanded, but not someone of whom it was necessary to feel afraid. He was standing back from Frank Roe's window in the attitude of a man who had a favour to ask.

Bill increased his speed to escape into the yards before the bakery door could open. It was like passing into a nightworld – a covered passageway so profoundly gloomy that visitors would grope with their feet and put out their hands like blind men. The ground sloped sharply down from Mary Street and guarded its privacy with an obstacle course of shallow pits and wet broken cobbles, so precarious that it frequently – and at least once fatally – trapped even its own denizens. It echoed splashy and hollow like a sea-cave, and was alive with unseen scuttlings. Bill plumped his jacket against the cold, and counted his way along the doorways. He kept his eyes ahead of him and down, only occasionally glancing half sideward to keep his bearings. The people here were no respecters of youth or virtue, and could not be relied upon to restrain their sons from mischief. With the one exception of Miss Nosworthy, they lived no fewer than seven to each tiny cottage, and in some instances as many as ten. In one family, Bill had heard, a girl aged fourteen had been made to share a bedroom with her three older brothers. He sympathised, and could see that sleep in such crowded conditions must be almost impossibly difficult; yet he could not fully understand the outrage that it caused among his own parents and aunts.

Today he was lucky. There was one muffled call from out of the depths, strangely low down in a deep black corner to his right, but no one challenged him seriously, not even a dog or a child. The Gang were abroad, and their parents still dozy from their lunch. In front of Miss Nosworthy's door he combed his fingers through his hair and breathed deeply to calm himself; then knocked and waited.

"Bill? You're early! I wasn't expecting you so soon."

"I'm sorry, Miss Nosworthy. Miss Manley sent us out early. Should I go away and come back later?"

He did not expect the offer to be accepted, and it wasn't; but still Miss Nosworthy seemed unwilling to let him enter. She stood squarely at the threshold, staring at him, apparently deep in thought. From the dim yellow lamp behind her, he could see that she wore a stiff white apron streaked with parallel orange stains (she really had been taken by surprise) over her usual heavy dress – a repeatedly patched, voluminously folded garment which looked to Bill as if it had been stitched together from some kind of matting. It had the colour of rotting meat, alternately black or green depending on the strength and direction of the light. Behind her, Bill could see the soapy gleam of plates on a dresser; among them a large crazed meat dish which held the outline of her head like a blue-rimmed halo; and the two cups and muslin-draped milk jug standing ready. There was a faint, edgy smell which might have been fish. For a moment Bill believed, with amazement, that she was sucking a boiled sweet; then realised that the bulging and hollowing of her jaw was due to the tension of a muscle.

"I'm sorry, Miss Nosworthy," he said again. "I could go . . ."

She made a slight movement backwards into the room, as if at last to let him pass; then waved a hand to make him stand back again. The fish smell gusted strongly, and it was only with an effort that Bill stifled an urge to cover his mouth.

"There is something I want to show you."

Bill had always thought of Miss Nosworthy as a particularly bulky woman; it had something to do with the squareness of her head, the cornerstone jaw and hard, mannish mouth. Even beneath a straw bonnet or, as now, a downy cap of stark white hair, her broad features could not easily grasp the trick of femininity. It was a patriarchal, forbiddingly powerful head – the kind that belonged with a powerful frame. But Bill was surprised, when she came down the step, to find that she was half-a-head shorter than himself, and needed his arm to steady herself on the cobbles.

"Something to show me, Miss Nosworthy?"

"In the orchard."

She narrowed her eyes to focus on a memory. Within a few yards of where they stood, she said, there had once been a very grand house with a terraced garden, so bright with colour that it had seemed to glow in the night. There had been flowers from many countries, and torrents of cool green foliage cascading from level to level over dry granite walls. There had been huge iron crocks with flowering shrubs in them; broad clean flights of balustraded stairs, and a *sundial*. Now all that remained, on a scrap of enclosed land down the hill from the yards, was the orchard. Bill let himself be led into the open again, screwing his eyes against the sudden stab of sun. At the top of the orchard, nearest the yards, the soil was strewn with rubbish and mixed to a red-grey paste with the rivulet from the gutter. Some pages from a book fluttered like a butterfly trapped in the mud, and there were some scraps of blue-grey material that might once have been a man's shirt. But Bill noticed them only peripherally, for his attention was riveted to the orchard itself: he could not believe that the old lady really meant them both to enter it. The wasted wrecks of the trees, bearded with lichen and knotted with tiny knobs of fruit that would rot before they ripened, thrust out their spindly arms from a fathomless wash of nettles. Miss Nosworthy paused as if she, too, had apprehended the unlikelihood of what she had proposed.

"Something to show me?" said Bill. "In there?"

She pointed, indicating a faint parting in the nettles that sketched the direction of a path. "Something you must see."

The path would have been barely wide enough for a cat. With the old lady on his arm, Bill was obliged to push through waist-high nettles, feeling uncertainly ahead of him as the ground shelved unevenly beneath his feet. The stings struck painfully through his stockings, yet Miss Nosworthy would pay no attention to his discomfort and only urged him deeper and deeper into the drift. Beneath the soles of his boots he could feel the solid outlines of tree roots and old stumps; and some rust-softened metal objects he could not identify. Around his head, and around Miss Nosworthy's too, a gauzy helmet of insects teased into the hair and made him scratch. He felt that his blood must be swarming with venom. His legs were aflame, and the backs of his hands clumped with smooth white platelets from the nettles.

"We always had to be careful where we put our feet down here," Miss Nosworthy said. "There's vipers."

She paused where a fallen trunk had made a clearing. Directly in front of them stood a single tree which was very obviously larger than any of its companions. It was dead on one side, as if it had suffered a stroke, and the living portion was at risk of being throttled by dense curtains of ivy and honeysuckle like hempen rope. Halfway up, just above the division of the main boughs, a branch had been sawn off many years earlier to leave a thick stump like a pot-hook. Miss Nosworthy raised a finger.

"*This* is what you wanted me to see?" said Bill, incredulous. "An old apple tree?" He knew he might earn himself a rebuke, but he could not conceal his scorn.

"It is what you *had* to see. Tell me, Bill, do you remember your grandfather Elias?"

"Only what he looked like. He died when I was five. Why do you ask? Was he your friend?"

"Did they tell you how he died?" She pulled in her lip distastefully, as if she were sucking on a lemon, and braced the finger that was still pointing into the tree.

"Of an illness, my father said . . ."

"No," she said, with sudden firmness. "No! *This is the tree from which your grandfather hanged himself.*"

Pictures flooded into his mind of the small silent house, and of his father brooding darkly with buried face. Of himself staring into the coal scuttle. Of his mother, whose breath smelled of raw onions, soothing him gently to bed, and of the uncles who gathered beyond his hearing to mutter. Of the single word *shame* that had come up to him through the floorboards from beneath. He shrank back, as if this terrible tree might be ready to strike again.

"Oh, Miss Nosworthy . . ." His head seethed, but it was all pictures and no words. "Oh *bugger*!"

Most of the apples came down not long afterwards in an unseasonable storm of truly awful violence. From the plantation behind the family garden on the Liverton road, the splitting of branches kept up a desultory exchange of sniper-fire that lasted almost exactly twelve hours from midnight. There was no cooked lunch that day, for Bill's mother knelt all morning at the hearth with bucket and sackcloth, mopping up the oily deluge from the chimney. Upstairs in the dark, Bill had feared for the safety of the chimney itself but, by dint of his earnest prayers, they had not lost so much as a slate. By noon, the downpour had slackened to a soaking, wind-driven smoke that hissed around the trees and shut off the garden behind a wall of grey flannel. The ground gargled and spewed its overload of water. Even the pump, which normally would claim the skin of Bill's palm before it would yield a cupful of water, was so eager to disgorge that it barely needed priming. At Bovey Tracey, he later discovered, the river had risen with a sudden surge which had carried away the mill-wheel and sent the Fore Street hoteliers running for their sandbags.

Out in the road the air was heavy with the wet-weather smell of fox; and crescent-shaped washings of grit wrote half-completed messages across the mud. Pot-holes shimmered like miniature seas, brimming to an ocean at the bend by the bridge, where a group of men had gathered with a rope and some poles. The honey-brown haunches of a drowned cow were making gentle ripples in the ditch. As the mist lifted, the countryside emerged slicked and spiky like a dog from a swim. Swampy hedgerows partitioned a distance in which the trees were half-washed ink-blots, and the cattle congealed in low tabby clumps. The stillness was a confusion to the senses: spongy to the eye but sharp as a bell-clapper to the ear. Even the crystal droplets, slapping fatly from the leaves, had the taut resonance of a musical box.

By the time Bill reached Bovey Tracey, it was clear to him that his own home could have suffered only a fraction of the storm's full force. At the lower end of Fore Street, which had lately been a tributary of the river, every hallway and porch was washing to the sibilance of brooms. Coming towards him, across the junction of the Manaton road, two heavy horses stirred a wake that provoked one or two of the less fortunate householders to curse and wave their fists. Astride the first animal, and leading the second on a rope, sat "young" carter Harrison ("young" because there were old folk still alive in the parish who remembered his father), who responded to the oaths with polite waves and a cidery grin. Bill saw that the horses were sweated and muddy from recent work, but that there was no sign of the cart.

"What's up?" he called. "Wagon broke?"

"Wheel fell off," said the carter, and jerked his thumb backward up the street.

On the lower bank of the river, Bill saw what he meant. The broken waterwheel had been hauled out of the current and lay on its side opposite the mill; dark gravelly gashes in the earth showed where Harrison's team had done its work. As Bill approached, three men were bouncing on the wheel as if it were a seesaw, laughing and pointing to the scars in the stone where it had been hurled against the bridge pier. One he knew was Amos Pinsent, the millwright; another, unmistakably, was one-legged Alf Runner; and the third was Frank Roe the baker.

"Bill?"

The boy faltered, but there was no possibility of escape. It was a moment for which long weeks of preparation had armed him with nothing more useful than confusion and dread. He did not know, even as he stood, which way he should declare himself. The question had haunted him for many restless hours when he should have been sleeping. He knew from Miss Manley that it was fully in the Christian spirit to forgive the sinner who had repented. But how could he know whether Frank Roe had repented or not? Jumping up and down on the waterwheel, evidently enjoying the company of two notorious wasters, he had not looked obviously penitent. Yet there was no time left for the niceties of debate. He had either ostentatiously to turn his back; or he had to stand his ground and face the man.

"Bill? Is that you?"

"Mr. Roe?"

They stared awkwardly across the chasm while their minds continued to circle like cats. Bill stretched his arms stiffly at his sides, locking the elbows, and tried not to flinch; for he understood that he was being challenged. What he did *not* understand was his own sudden stirring of guilt, as if it were himself, and not the man, who wanted for absolution. Yet he saw the welcome in Frank Roe's eyes, and caught himself feeling grateful for it. He glanced at the outsiders Pinsent and Runner, and resented their intrusion. Roe, too, turned away and looked at the river while he spoke.

"You catch the storm over Liverton way?"

"Yes, but not so bad as here. The house didn't flood."

"Been hellish in Bovey. Look at the wheel, smashed to bits. Lucky there was no one on the bridge." He loosened his collar, releasing a sudden swell of Adam's apple. "It was bad, very bad. I wonder how the shepherds could have fared, up there on the moor. And the quarrymen . . ."

"Quarrymen?"

"At Haytor. You remember . . ." The baker had a habit, when he was embarrassed, of vigorously scratching his neck.

"I know, but who . . ."

"Some masons, didn't you know? From Exeter. They've come to cut stone for a monument. You must have heard . . . They're putting up huge memorial stones with the names of all the people who were killed in the war. My brother Jack. Your uncle Sam . . ."

"Masons in the quarries? But where?"

Roe stepped down from the waterwheel and began to scan the ground. Along the riverbank, for as far as Bill could see, stretched a thick tideline of flood-borne detritus, like an endless rook's nest of sticks and straw. Roe plucked out a twig and began to scratch with it in the grit.

"Look. Here's the road up from Bovey. Here's the Manaton road. This is the granite tramway and these are Haytor rocks. You see?"

It was a slyly-wrought invitation, which Bill recognised, for him to cross the divide and stand by his shoulder. "They're in this part here." The stick sketched a diagonal cross. "You ought to go and see. It may never happen again in our lifetime."

Bill nodded mechanically, determined not to betray his fascination. "It's like you said. Like history happening all over again."

"That's right!" Roe's neck reddened angrily where he scrubbed it. "That's it exactly! You really should see it for yourself, make a point of it. Look, on Saturday afternoon, after I've shut up shop, I'll be passing that way myself." He nodded his head in the vague direction of the moor. "Maybe . . .?"

Bill scuffed through the diagram with his toe. "I don't know," he said. "Maybe."

It was a whim, prompted by a late change in the weather. Bill followed the Becka Brook upstream along the narrowing valley from the Falls until he knew he was directly beneath the pinnacled slabs of Greator rocks. This was one of his favourite places. The brook in the valley bottom had been dammed to make a pair of thorn-fringed lagoons which looked from above like a pair of blue rabbit's ears. Here on hotter days he had stripped off his things and plunged naked into the reedy deeps to bask as contentedly – and as uninvitedly – as an otter. Today, however, he turned his back on the water and made his way diagonally up the steep valley slope to the west. There were a few yards of rock-littered scrub, then the sharp rise of open moorland to the tor. The soil here had been leached from the hillside in a curiously regular staircase of moon-shaped bites, perfectly measured for Bill to run up one step at a time. He did not pause when he reached the rock itself, but swarmed up past the solitary rowan tree, taking tight handfuls of the precariously rooted grass to pull himself from shelf to shelf. On a tilted slab above the last few strands of green, he stood firmly upright and made the dizzying leap across the crevice to the tower-stack.

It was here that he had built his throne – a laboriously assembled pile of stones and small boulders, wedged into the shape of a backrest and two arms – from which he could survey what he liked to think of as his kingdom. Beneath his feet the valley ran roughly south to north (right to left as he looked), from the huge bare stump of Rippon Tor to the sylvan glades that opened on to Manaton village, with the great wall of Lustleigh Cleave shutting off the horizon behind it. Widecombe, to the south-west, was hidden by the massive blue saddle of Chinkwell Tor and Honeybag; while, directly in front of him, the opposing valley slope was capped with the twin steeples of Haytor itself. He shaded his eyes straight across at the heathery bluff, where the course of the quarrymen's tramway pencilled a thin green line around the terrace above the scree. Almost at the extreme of the line, and just below it, he could make out another of his favourite eyries – a large grassy ledge, so trim and so level that, from a distance, it looked like a perfect gardener's lawn, which had in one corner of it a ruined stoned hut where, he supposed, the Victorian workmen had kept their tools. Slow white shapes were moving; but sheep, not masons. Bill scanned back along the terrace, pausing to adjust to the muted lights and darks of the deeper cuts, but could see no other human form: no one to challenge his right to the throne, or to disturb the feeling of timelessness which water and rock always aroused in him.

Somewhere below him to his right, drowned in the bracken beneath the boundary wall of the valley estate, lay the relics of a bygone age – the fallen skeletons of dwellings and enclosures, traced in mossy grids of stone. There were more of them, easier to find in the sheep-cropped grass, on the rise towards Hound Tor behind him. The old walls had provided stones for the newer field boundaries; and Bill had stolen some of the smaller rocks himself, to haul up for his throne. He reassembled them in his imagination, and topped them with ragged domes of thatch. From a distance they would have looked like giant rough-coated dogs, pegged to the sky on twisted thongs of smoke. And the people . . . He saw sooty-faced men in mud-coloured cloaks, gritting their way up the hillside with bulging animal skins seeping water. Naked children, younger than himself, with whip-like wands of green wood, driving sheep. And on the high pinnacle where he now arose and stretched out his hands, a holy man in a gleaming white robe . . .

He slipped, and sat back heavily on to the throne; but his mind still carried the echo of the suddenly remembered voice. A holy man in a plain white garment, holding up a stave of peeled white wood. It was

209

not a picture of his own making. It was Frank Roe's. The throne, the kingship of the valley, the vision and the communion: for all its seeming inevitability, the awakening of his relationship with the moor was, he discovered, the sum of his relationship with Frank Roe. It was the baker who had opened his eyes; who now, ridiculously, was separated from him by the very substance of his own vision. The valley yawned steep and wide. Bill looked at the sun and calculated: no more than an hour after midday. If Frank Roe were really going to the quarry today, then there was still time.

On the lip of the Becka Brook he crouched to take a drink, cupping his hands to his mouth like a squirrel with a nut. He sipped slowly, with exaggerated appreciativeness, dabbing his lips with the tip of his tongue to enjoy the full mineral richness of the water. Far away to his left, somewhere along the valley towards the Falls, a branch cracked. He stood and craned his eyes into the deepening bands of shadow. Next to him on the ground lay a careless heap of fence palings, betraying their newness by the cheesy texture of the white sharpened tips. Bill picked one up and ran with it, away from the source of the sound, doubling from the waist to keep his head and shoulders below the height of the thorn scrub. He had no idea who was coming: it could have been Frank Roe, or a gamekeeper, or an innocent intruder like himself. In his mind it was a foreign horde; the fence paling was a rifle, and the musty valley pathway a trench. With pounding heart he went over the top into another of Frank Roe's pictures.

Through the barbed coils of thorn he struck directly upwards through a no-man's-land of bracken. The fronds loomed so high above his head that it was only by stretching on his toes that he could peep back through the living thatch at landmarks on the far slope and make even a rough estimate of his position. Ahead of him he could see nothing. His clothes had begun to cling, and the rifle had become a stick again, to help him beat a path. After half an hour, he thought, he broke through on to the granite tramway; half an hour more would see him to the top. A blue lake of cloud shadow was flooding up the hill towards him, and for a moment he conjured a picture of advancing gas. But his thighs and calves were still too numb from the climb to run, and his skin was prickling with the heat; the cloud remained just a cloud, shuddering him deliciously in its pall.

At the summit he exchanged greetings with a stranger in a dark cloth suit, who was hurrying on his way to meet the only other human figure in the whole circle of landscape – a pale-frocked woman waiting by the Widecombe road. Bill stood for a while on the apex of the tor, watching the couple disappear towards Ilsington, then climbed quickly down and stamped out a nest for himself in the bracken beneath the rock. From here he could command the approaches from both the Manaton and Widecombe roads: to see and not be seen. He did not know what impulse made him hide. He was still occasionally troubled by the thin-lipped denunciations of Frank Roe which he had heard from his moral guardians. But insofar as they touched him at all, it was merely as a caution. The misgivings were sufficient for him to eschew intimate contacts with the man in public, but he owed himself no such duty of discretion in the private wilderness of the moor.

It was not until the sun had slipped round towards three o'clock that the baker came up through the sheep on Haytor Down, crossing the Manaton road by the old granite siding and following the tramway up the gentle slope towards the quarry. Bill recognised him at once by the characteristic unevenness of his stride and the raffish suit of orange tweeds − a costume which had made a rich contribution to local folklore and which Roe himself, with the studied self-mockery in which he specialised, had called "my ratting outfit". He now disappeared into the upper chamber of the quarry, where the gibbet-like wooden winch stood gauntly reflected in a weed-choked lake, and reappeared a few moments later on the grassy crest of the old spoil-heap. Bill watched him lay down his thumbstick and small khaki haversack (more of those disgusting cheese sandwiches, he thought), and shade his eyes away down towards the lower working. He stood for several minutes on the skyline, then descended back out of sight towards the tramway, where the boy could hear him calling faintly in the distance.

Bill was torn. He wanted to reveal himself, and yet he was stiff with reserve. He listened to Roe's voice quavering hopefully into each of the chambers in turn, fading into silence as he circled behind the hill, then rising again as he came the steep way back towards the summit. There was a brief, terrifying crescendo as the baker surmounted the tor immediately at his back; and then only the sound of his boot-nails chiming across the rock. It was too late. If Bill were to emerge from his nook now, it could only be to admit that he had been hiding there all along. It was too stupid: he could not pass it off as a joke.

Frank Roe walked away down the long green slope towards Ilsington, and Bill chopped a slit through the bracken to watch him go. He suffered the loss calmly, in a kind of emotional lull, as if a relative had died. But he knew that something irreplaceable had passed away from inside him. At his shoulder the rock loomed and glowered immovably, and he remembered how Roe had once described it: like an insatiable sponge, soaking up history. Time, in Roe's language, was the most elusive of all life's mysteries. Each moment of it – each pulse of a heart, or beat of an insect's wing – was the sum of all that had passed, and the seed of all that was to come. In the clap of a hand, Bill could hear the sound of history becoming the future. A minute passed: and then the moment came, as he had realised it would, when Roe stalled his descent and gazed back lingeringly – *mortally* – at the tor.

There was a small sadness in the carriage of the man's shoulders, and no joy in his stride as he struck out again for home. From the eyrie by the rock, he seemed suddenly smaller than an ant.

Afterwards Bill searched the quarries, chamber after chamber, until he found the place where the masons had been working. It was exactly as Roe had said it would be. An impossibly large, rough-dressed monolith lay on a bed of fresh chippings, its tiny crystals winking like a forest of eyes. A red-painted notice, designed to restrain the over-curious, warned of some unspecified danger. A falling stone, maybe? It seemed oddly over-protective – almost ironic – in the light of what the monolith itself would come to represent. Bill imagined the engraved columns that would make up the litany of the war dead: beginning, he supposed, with the Abbots and ending with – what? White? Young-husband? He wondered how he would have been remembered if his own name had been on the roll. Or his grandfather Elias, who had fallen victim in a different kind of war. Or . . . Frank Roe?

He tried to bring the picture alive again by shouting the name into the great cathedral of rock. "FRANK ROE. FRANK ROE. HOW SHALL I REMEMBER YOU?"

He waited, but there was nothing: only a distant sheep and the sound of his own voice echoing.

Wild Horses

Kent's Cavern, at Torquay, was a refuge for hunters of the Palaeolithic period (Old Stone Age) intermittently between 100,000 and 8,000 BC. Their hunting grounds might reasonably be expected to have included what is now the Teign estuary, from which they would have seen a distant aspect of Hay Tor rocks. For a thorough academic study of finds at Kent's Cavern, see J.B. Campbell and C.G. Sampson, 1971, "A new analysis of finds at Kent's Cavern, Devonshire, England", University of Oregon Anthropological Papers 3, 17–23. A show-cave is open to the public, and a number of finds are displayed at Torquay Museum.

Circle of Light

The standing stones, circles and stone rows with which Dartmoor is littered date from the Bronze Age. No certain evidence exists to explain their purpose (some authorities have even speculated that they might have been running-tracks), but the strongest likelihood is that they were used in connection with religious observance. Numerous guides exist to the prehistoric sites of Dartmoor, but the best general study is probably still Aileen Fox, *South West England*.

Julius Sabinus

There is no evidence that the country beyond the River Exe was ever colonised by the Romans, their westernmost garrison being *Isca Dumoniorum* (Exeter). It is likely that the initial advance of the Legion II Augusta, under Vespasian, from *Rutupiae* (Richborough, Kent) carried them as far as *Isca*; and it is possible to imagine their having penetrated a few more miles into the wilderness before deciding to turn back. For a general account of the legions' campaign, see Peter Hunter Blair, *Roman Britain and Early England*; J. Lindsay, *The Romans Were Here*.

The Prophet

Many early Christians from western England and Wales, feeling themselves threatened by the Saxon advance, fled across the Channel to *Armorica* (Brittany). The character of Dewi Sant in the story represents St. David. Menevia is his monastery on the site of what is now the town of St. David's. It seems not unreasonable to speculate that a Celtic-Christian settlement would have existed at Ilsington. See C. J. Godfrey, *The Church in Anglo-Saxon England*.

Ielfstan's Place

The Domesday name for Ilsington was *Ilestintona*, which it is thought may have derived from the Old English personal name Ielfstan. The Danish plundering of the Devon coast was sporadic, but extended over a long period of years – and it seems to have been aided in many cases by native treachery. The village of Kingsteignton was sacked and burned in 1001, shortly before the battle for Exeter. See Peter Hunter Blair, *An Introduction to Anglo-Saxon England*; W.G. Hoskins, *Devon*.

Chivalry

The medieval tournament, nothing like the stylised jousting of subsequent periods, was hardly distinguishable from a battle. It took place in open country between opposing forces of knights and barons, many of whom were attracted by the opportunity to enrich themselves through the taking of ransoms. See F.H. Cripps-Day, *The History of the Tournament in England and France*.

The Apple Tree

The Black Death made a cruel impact on the Devon parishes and was at its height there around December-January 1348–49. (In the neighbouring deanery of Kenn, 86 parish priests died in a deanery with only 17 parish churches.) See Philip Ziegler, *The Black Death*; H.S. Bennett, *Life on the English Manor*.

The Prayer

St Michael's Church, Ilsington, as it now stands is principally the product of two building periods. Nave, chancel and transepts date from around 1290; tower, aisles and chancel chapels from around 1480 (see Pevsner, *Buildings of England, S. Devon*). For a general account of English church building and architecture, see Hugh Braun, *Parish Churches*.

Manna

Ilsington parish is richly endowed with tin, iron and other mining remains of various periods. The two main periods of activity were in the sixteenth and nineteenth centuries. See Helen Harris, *The Industrial Archaeology of Dartmoor*; G.R. Lewis, *The Stannaries*.

Humphy

The schoolroom over the church lychgate collapsed during a lesson on 17 September 1639. An account in the church registers is believed to have been the work of the schoolmaster Hanniball Corbyn:

"To the everlasting praise of God in memory of a most wonderful deliverance. September, 1639.

"Over the west gate of the Churchyard in Ilsington there was a room anntiently built, about ten feet from the ground, sixteen feet in length, and twelve feet in height. The east and west side walls were about ten feet in height. The covering was of slate or shingle stone layd uppon fayre timber. Rafters about twelve feet in length. This room was lately converted to a Schoolhouse whither there usually came heere to the number of 30 scholler boyes. But September 17 being tuesday AD 1639, the morning was wett, w'ch w'th other . . . orations kept some at Home. Others to the number of seventeene were together at schoole w'th their Schoolmaster neere upon eleven of the clocke, at w'ch time the schollers ready to dep't for dinner: a woman passed under-neath and lett the gate being heavy fall too as formerly it had done. Before she was gone to a house about six yards from the place Part of the south stone wall w'ch bare up the Timber worke of the Roofe slidd away soe that the whole Roofe spread abroad drove out both side walls east and west and fell downe uppon the flouer of the Roome, not one stick, stone or pinn of the whole structure remayning where it was formerly placed.

"The Schools doore w'h opened to the inside was shutt when the house began to fall.

"Fower of the scholar boyes fell downe into the churchyard with the east side wall and escaped with little hurt. One ran into the chymny, where he continued safe. Some were stricken down with Timber and stones w'h fell from over their heads.

"The Timber locked one boy fast in the middle of the Roome and when it was lifted he Rose up and Ran away.

"And w'h was yet more wonderfull another sweet child (called Humphy Degon) fell out w'th the east side wall into the street, where he was close weged and buried under the Rubbish so that no p't of his body or cloths appeared. There he lay for a quarter of an howrs 2 spare or more. At length perceiving that child to be wanting, a stricter search was made among the Rubbish w'h fell into the Roome, then seeking among the Rubbish w'h fell into the street. He was there happily found and taken up for dead in the judgment of all that beheld him. But he was not utterly gone. The child recovered life, is healthy and well and free from any grief.

"In the Accident and speciall demonstration of God's Providence and Goodnesse in delivering from imminent danger twelve had their heads cut and broken soe that they bledd, for it to mind them all of the Danger they were in. But God with their guard of Angells surrounded them soe that not a bone was broken nor a joynt displaced, their wounds are all healed and there is not any member of them any wayes enfeebled from doing its proper office as in former times. At the wrighting hereof they are all in health and soe living to Praise God for their deliverance . . ."

For religious and educational background to the period, see H.O. Wakeman, *The Church and the Puritans*; Ivy Pinchbeck and Margaret Hewitt, *Children in English Society*.

An Affair with the Regiment

There are many general histories of the Civil War which include accounts of the battle of Lostwithiel, the siege of Exeter and the engagement at Bovey Tracey. See S.R. Gardiner, *The History of the Great Civil War*; Burne and Young, *The Great Civil War*. The damage to Elizabeth Ford's memorial stone, reputedly caused by a blow from a hoof during the occupation by Royalist horsemen, can still be seen near the font in Ilsington Church. It is also a traditional local belief that, at the approach of armed soldiers, the church plate was buried for safekeeping in Coxisland Wood – never to be seen again.

The Champion

For an account of the Devonshire wrestling style, see S. Baring Gould, *Devonshire Characters and Strange Events*. For an excellent general history of the game laws and their social consequences, see Charles Chenevix Trench, *The Poacher and the Squire*.

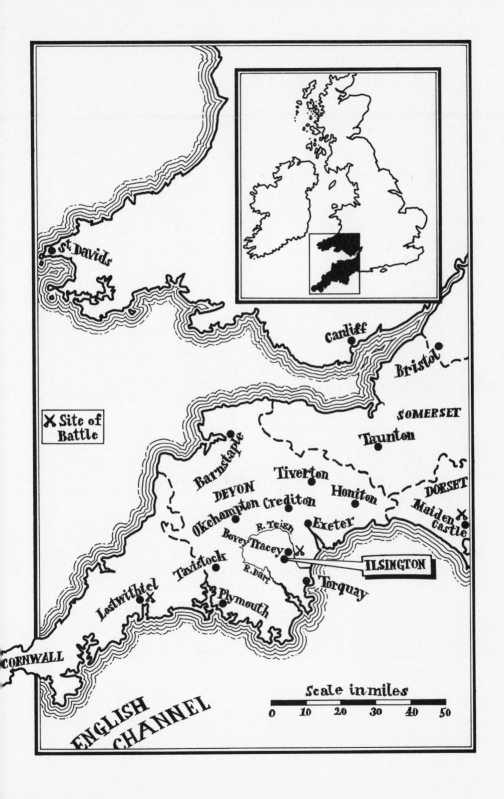

St Davids

Cardiff

Bristol

SOMERSET

Taunton

☒ Site of
Battle

Barnstaple

Tiverton

Honiton

DORSET

DEVON

Okehampton Crediton

Maiden
Castle ☒

R. Teign

Exeter

Bovey Tracey ☒

ILSINGTON

Tavistock

R. Dart

Torquay

Lostwithiel ☒

Plymouth

CORNWALL

ENGLISH CHANNEL

Scale in miles

0   10   20   30   40   50

Too Much Cider

The Haytor tramway opened on September 16, 1820. For a full account of the Templers' engineering and commercial enterprises, see M.C. Ewans, *The Haytor Granite Tramway and Stover Canal*. For period background see William Crossing, *One Hundred Years on Dartmoor*.

The Housemaid and the Dancer

It is a fact that during the latter part of the nineteenth century Lancashire clog-makers would come annually to cut green alder from the Ilsington stream-banks. For social background – particularly the role of women – see G.E. and K.R. Fussell, *The English Countrywoman*.

The Memorial

The Hay Tor quarry was briefly reopened in 1919 for the cutting of war memorials. There was a baker's shop in Mary Street, Bovey Tracey, during the war years, but the character of Frank Roe is entirely fictional and is not intended to represent any living or historical individual.

The books mentioned above do not of course amount to a complete bibliography of the region, still less of the individual subjects. That would require a separate volume in its own right. The best general introductions to the history of Dartmoor are probably W.G. Hoskins, *Devon*, and Crispin Gill (ed.), *Dartmoor: a New Study*.